The
Heart's
Awakening

"Leave you here alone with *him*?" Mr. Hession exclaimed. "I most certainly will not!"

But Georgina paid no heed to him. She was looking only at Shannon. She had the oddest feeling, as those hard grey eyes, strangely softening now, met hers, that her heart was trying to jump into her throat.

Now, for a moment, she quite forgot her surroundings—the Oriental splendour of the room, Lady Eliza's ball, even the indignant Mr. Hession. If she had been questioned on the matter, she might have answered, rather dazedly, that she was standing in a wide empty space, far removed from any place she knew, and that she was quite alone—with Shannon.

Georgina

By

Clare Darcy

A DELL BOOK

Published by
DELL PUBLISHING CO., INC.
1 Dag Hammarskjold Plaza
New York, N.Y. 10017

Dell ® TM 681510, Dell Publishing Co., Inc.

ISBN: 0-440-12837-4

Reprinted by arrangement with
Walker and Company
Printed in the United States of America
Previous Dell edition #2837
New Dell edition
First printing—September 1977

Georgina

CHAPTER 1

A hush of expectancy lay over Lady Mercer's house in Great Pulteney Street on this brightest of March mornings in Bath. The entire household, from Finch, Lady Mercer's sedate, elderly butler, to the youngest housemaid, knew that behind the closed door of the Long Drawing-room Miss Georgina was receiving an offer of marriage from Mr. Burford Smallwoods, only son and heir of Sir Anthony Smallwoods, Bart.; and a number of plausible excuses were made by various members of the staff to enable them to linger within sight of that intriguing door.

In what way the news had gotten about it would have been hard to say. Certainly neither Lady Mercer nor her daughter, Mrs. Power, had been heard to mention the possibility of an alliance between Mr. Smallwoods and Miss Georgina, nor had Miss Georgina herself shown any of the signs of a young lady in love. On the other hand, Mr. Smallwoods was known to have been assiduous in his visits to Great Pulteney Street, and his mama, Lady Smallwoods, while drawing on her pelisse preparatory to leaving the house after a call made on Lady Mercer on Wednesday last, had been overheard to say that Miss Georgina was "a pretty creature."

Finch, who was experienced in such matters, gave it as his opinion that it would be a match, which led Mrs. Nudge, the housekeeper, to remark with great feeling that, if Sir John were still alive, there would be no thought of Miss Georgina's being married off to such a pompous little toad.

Their vigilance, on this afternoon, was soon rewarded. Scarcely a quarter of an hour after Mr. Smallwoods had been shown into the Long Drawing-room, the door was abruptly opened and that young gentleman, wearing an exceedingly crestfallen air, came out, ran downstairs, received his curly-brimmed beaver and gloves from Finch, and left the house without a word. Some five seconds later, Miss Georgina herself, looking very fetching in a chintz morning-dress of palest lilac, but with a rather high flush on her face, emerged and marched down the hall to the morning-room, where Lady Mercer and Mrs. Power were sitting over their tambour-frames.

As she closed the door of this apartment with considerable emphasis behind her, what conversation she held there with her mama and her grandmother was to remain unknown. Speculation had it, however, that there would be a rare turn-up when Lady Mercer discovered that Miss Georgina had whistled Mr. Smallwoods, his prospective title, and his comfortable fortune down the wind.

Speculation in this case was quite correct. Lady Mercer, on receiving the news from her granddaughter that she had refused Mr. Smallwoods, sat bolt upright, declared that of all defects of character ingratitude was the one she most greatly abhorred, and favoured her granddaughter with a glance of such concentrated disapproval that a weaker young lady must have quailed beneath it.

Georgina, however, whose charmingly coiffed head, with its wheat-gold curls cropped in the current mode and clustering in natural ringlets about her face, concealed a buoyant spirit and an excellent understanding, merely remarked, her colour still rather high, "I do not *quite* see how it would be showing gratitude to *you* for me to accept Mr. Smallwoods' offer, Grandmama. To *him*, perhaps—but then what has he done for me but bring me prosy books out of Meyler's Library and escort us all to the Pump Room or Bath Abbey?"

Lady Mercer was a small woman, of a sallow complexion and a general dun-coloured appearance; but any tendency of a person meeting her for the first time to dismiss her as having a character as unimpressive as her appearance was soon dispelled. She said now, with acid emphasis, "I daresay if Mr. Smallwoods were a gentleman of less delicate principles, and had disregarded the fact that, until a fortnight ago, you were in mourning and had escorted you about to frivolous entertainments, you would be more inclined to favour his suit?"

"Not at all," Georgina said decidedly. "I should not like him one whit better if I had stood up at balls with him every day in the week. Do stop crying, Mama!" she said to Mrs. Power, a faded, rather pretty woman who, as usual, had dissolved into tears at the first threat of trouble between her mother and her daughter. "I am persuaded that, whatever Grandmama thinks, *you* cannot have wished me to accept Mr. Smallwoods' offer. He is exactly what Sir John would have called an odious little bounce!"

"Oh, no, my dear!" Mrs. Power faltered, with a terrified glance at Lady Mercer. "A gentleman of the *first* respectability—such an acceptable fortune—everything about him of the most genteel—"

"Mama, that cannot signify when I tell you that I cannot love him!"

Lady Mercer set her tambour-frame carefully aside. "You will oblige me, Georgina," she said quellingly, "by omitting such vulgar expressions from your conversation in future. A young lady of your breeding should indeed *esteem* the gentleman to whom she is betrothed. Any stronger expression of emotion, however, leaves her open to the suspicion of harbouring an unbecoming violence of feeling which is not at all suited to her condition in life."

Georgina looked somewhat inclined to dispute this dictum, but a glance at her mother's agitated face decided her against it. Mrs. Power, she knew, was particularly sensitive on this point, because she herself, at the age of seventeen, had made a runaway match with Owen Power, the improvident younger son of an Irish family of considerable consequence. This was a fact that her mother had never allowed her in the ten years of her impecunious widowhood, to forget. Indeed, Lady Mercer had declared her intention of leaving her own fortune, a very comfortable one, directly to Georgina, as she still, at this late date, found herself quite unable to condone the shocking want of good conduct that her daughter had shown at that crucial period in her life.

It seemed, however, that Georgina, at a similar period in her life, intended to be almost equally disobliging in the matter of fulfilling Lady Mercer's expectations, for she said now, with an obstinate air, "At any rate, I do not at all wish to marry Mr. Smallwoods. And I do not see why I must, for I am only eighteen—not *quite* old-cattish yet, you will admit, Grandmama!"

"Yes, indeed," Mrs. Power said, finding the courage to come, albeit with some timidity, to her daughter's aid. "Recollect, Mama, that she has not had even one Season in London! Perhaps when she has had the opportunity to meet more young gentlemen than she yet has—so retired as we have been living here in Bath since Papa died—and before that, in Herefordshire, she was only a child—"

Lady Mercer cut short this rather disjointed appeal by a single glance cast in her daughter's direction.

"I wonder," she pronounced, "that you should be so ill-advised as to bring up the subject of London, Maria! You must be aware that Lady Smallwoods has been so kind as to offer to allow Georgina to visit her when she and Sir Anthony open their house in Hill Street in May, and to take her about and even present her at Court. Nothing could have been more amiable, or better suited to our own situation, for Dr. Porton does not in the least agree to my exposing myself to the excitements of a London Season. But if the match with Mr. Smallwoods is to go off, of course there the matter must end."

"I do not care about that in the least," Georgina said, unregenerately. "Sir John always said I should find it a dead bore, going about to balls and fashionable squeezes every night, and being obliged to do the civil to a parcel of people I scarcely knew."

"Sir John," Lady Mercer began, with marked asperity, and then, recollecting that her spouse was dead and that it was therefore scarcely proper for her to cast any of the bitter animadversions on his conduct that had enlivened their married life, checked herself. "Your grandfather's influence on your opinions, my dear Georgina," she said, with austere moderation, "can scarcely be thought to have been a happy one. I blame myself for having allowed your education to have fallen so entirely in his hands."

"Well, you could not help it, of course," Georgina said reasonably, "for once Sir John had made up his mind to something, there was very little even *you* could do to alter it, you know." She gave a tiny sigh. "I miss him very much," she said. "I am sure he would not have liked Mr. Smallwoods any better than I do."

Lady Mercer, though she had shown the strictest nicety in mourning her husband over an entire year, did not appear to share these sentiments. She merely observed her granddaughter with a darkly thoughtful air, and after a few moments said abruptly, "You had best be sent to Ireland, I expect."

"To Ireland?" Georgina looked inquiring, and her mother repeated faintly, "To Ireland, Mama! But how?—where—?"

"To visit your husband's cousin, Arabella Quinlevan," Lady Mercer said, referring to the widowed lady who had been invited by Declan Power, Owen Power's elder brother, following the death of his wife some dozen years before, to make her home, with her son Brandon, on his estate in Kerry so that she might preside over his household and take charge of the rearing of his daughter Nuala. "I had, of course, intended to reply to her letter of invitation, which arrived this morning, with a civil refusal, but under the circumstances it appears to me that it had best be accepted. That, at least, will remove Georgina from the gossip that is certain to arise when it becomes known that she is not to marry Mr. Smallwoods, and relieve Lady Smallwoods of the embarrassment of withdrawing her own very generous invitation to take her to London."

"But—Ireland! The Quinlevans!" Georgina's surprise had begun to merge into interest and pleasurable excitement. "Do you really mean it, Grandmama? Cousin Bella has asked me? But we have scarcely heard from her since she and Brandon visited us in Herefordshire four years ago!"

"On the contrary," Lady Mercer said exactly, "we received, if you will remember, a very proper letter from her on the occasion of the death of your uncle, Declan Power, two years ago, and a second on the equally unexpected demise of his daughter Nuala in Brussels in the following year. I am not, on the whole, an admirer of your cousin Arabella's style, my dear Georgina, but I am obliged to admit that in such matters she is most punctilious. I could wish, however, that in other respects she were less shatterbrained. How, for example, she could have been so careless as to allow your cousin Nuala to have contracted such a dreadful marriage, I have *never* understood."

"But *she* had nothing to say to that, Grandmama," Georgina reminded her. "Do you not remember that she wrote us that Nuala was visiting in Scotland with friends when she ran off with Mr. Shannon?"

"I should not, I think," Lady Mercer said dampingly, "be likely to forget any of the circumstances of that most regrettable affair—nor do I believe, Georgina, that it is a matter on which a delicately bred young female should allow herself to converse."

"Well, there is no use in my pretending that I know nothing about it," Georgina said candidly, "for Sir John and I discussed the whole matter at the time, and he told me everything—I mean, that Mr. Shannon was a—"

"Georgie!" her mother exclaimed faintly.

"A natural son of the present Lord Cartan's father," Georgina said mildly. "Am I not to admit I know of such things, Mama? Sir John said it was missish for young ladies to pretend they do not."

"If you had the least sense of delicacy, Georgina," Lady Mercer said, with awful emphasis, "it would not be necessary for me to warn you that such sentiments are most improper ones to come from a young lady's lips. It is this sort of behaviour on your part that gives me the gravest misgivings about placing you in Arabella Quinlevan's care, for she has shown herself quite incapable, in your cousin's case, of curbing such reprehensible tendencies. Indeed, I have often reflected on how unfortunate it was that Mrs. Declan Power's early demise obliged your uncle to entrust Nuala's rearing to her. However, I believe she is well served for her carelessness now. She writes me that, as Nuala's fortune has gone entirely to Mr. Shannon, she and her son are now under the necessity of removing from The Place of the Oaks and retiring to her own property at Craythorne—a sad come-down, but one for which I am obliged to confess she has no one to thank but herself."

Georgina considered this. "Well, for my part, I should not think it was at all her fault that Nuala fell in love with Mr. Shannon," she said. "I expect she would much rather that she had not, for it must be dreadfully disagreeable to her now to have to give up living in a great house that she has been used, for years, to thinking of as her home and see it go to a horrid fortune-hunter. Not," she added thoughtfully, "that he is probably *entirely* horrid, or my cousin Nuala would not have fallen so desperately in love with him. In fact, I daresay he may be quite attractive!"

"Georgie!" Mrs. Power again protested, in a failing voice. "*Not* a man of *such* a character!"

Lady Mercer looked grim. "If," she said, "I believed there was the slightest possibility that you would be brought into Mr. Shannon's company in Kerry, Georgina, I should not dream of allowing you to accept Mrs. Quinlevan's invitation. I understand from her letter, however, that he is still travelling abroad and has not yet set foot in Ireland to take up his inheritance. There will therefore be no occasion whatever for you to meet him."

She signified at this point that the interview was at an end by rising, shaking out her skirts, and departing from the room—a circumstance that brought the apprehensive look back into her daughter's eyes.

"Oh, dear!" she said. "She is so very much displeased with you, I daresay, that she cannot trust herself to remain any longer in the room with you!" She looked timidly at her daughter. "You do not think, my dearest love—that is, you would not perhaps care to reconsider—?"

"Marry Mr. Smallwoods? Mama, I could not—even for *your* sake," Georgina said, shaking her curls. "I *know* how agreeable it would be for you if I had an establishment of my own, so that you could live with me, instead of being *immured* here with Grandmama, but indeed I cannot accept Mr. Smallwoods' offer!"

"No, my dear. If you have taken him in dislike, no more must be said of it, of course," Mrs. Power agreed, wistfully. "And perhaps you will meet a young man in Ireland— It would be very pleasant to live in Ireland, I think."

"Miles and *miles* from Grandmama," Georgina said irrepressibly, bringing a faint, but not entirely convincing, sound of reproach from her mother. She jumped up and dropped a kiss on Mrs. Power's head. "Never mind, Mama," she said. "If I am to be sent to Ireland in disgrace, I shall certainly make the most of my opportunities. Perhaps my cousin Brandon will have the house full of young men, and some of them *must* be well-breeched enough to suit even Grandmama's notions!"

"But—he is lame, and very bookish, you recollect, my love," Mrs. Power said, looking up at her doubtfully.

"Oh yes, I know! But still *not* a dead bore—like Mr. Smallwoods!"

She left her mama on this cheerful note, running upstairs to her own bedchamber to begin an inventory of her wardrobe against her departure. Her untroubled demeanour led Mrs. Nudge to spread the opinion belowstairs that it would require more than a rakedown from the old lady to take the curl out of Miss Georgina; but Finch, when he learned of the projected visit to Ireland, made his own gloomy pronouncement to the effect that Miss Georgina, made a Victim of the Gorgon's spite by being sent off into Exile, was merely putting on a brave front to hide a Bruised Heart.

This, however, the youngest housemaid found hard to believe. She was not at all certain what a Gorgon was, but it appeared to her that any young lady who was to have the felicity of escaping, even for a time, from Lady Mercer's iron rule could certainly not be called a Victim. Indeed, she rather thought that, as usual, Miss Georgina had come off the Victor in this encounter.

CHAPTER 2

On an April morning some few weeks after these events had occurred, Mrs. Quinlevan was in the estate-room at The Place of the Oaks, going through a jumble of accounts, and having recourse frequently to her vinaigrette to soothe the agitation into which this task always cast her, when her brother, Mr. Jeremy Barnwall, was announced.

"Show him into the book-room, Higgins," she directed the butler, who, as did most of the other servants at The Place since the death of her cousin, Declan Power, seemed to be new, or incompetent, or both. "I'm sure it's the only room in the house that's not in a huggermugger with the moving."

Higgins departed, and she sat gazing disconsolately for a moment at the undulating lawn outside the windows, at the end of which a row of the ancient oaks that gave the estate its name showed the beginning of the Home Wood. Then she sighed and took her round, soft, foolish face, with its French lace cap tied under the chin, and her stout, bustling figure in its dove-coloured morning-dress into the book-room, where she found Jeremy Barnwall's even more ample figure already disposed in the room's most comfortable chair.

"What the deuce are you about, Bella?" he demanded, as soon as she had set foot inside the door. "Never saw such a devilish uproar in my life as you have here! I expected you'd have removed to Craythorne by this time. Drove over there—nobody about—servants raising such a deuced dust it was as much as your life was worth to walk into the place."

Mrs. Quinlevan sank into a chair, requesting Higgins to see if the Madeira had been crated up yet, and, if not, to fetch a bottle for Mr. Barnwall.

"Though I am not sure," she said, "that it will be fit to drink, for you know Papa always warned us that good wine will not bear rough handling, and what they have been doing with it I have *no* way of knowing."

Mr. Barnwall reflected for a moment on this speech. He was a largish gentleman, with a glistening bald head encircled by a crown of stiff black hair. The son of a highly improvident Irish gentleman, cast on the world with neither fortune nor profession, he had early discovered that an excellent baritone voice and a lucky ability at piquet and faro could procure him a very satisfactory existence in London society with the expenditure of scarcely any of the revenues from his modest estate in Kerry. This estate lay within five miles of The Place of the Oaks, and he usually made it a point to drive over and call on his widowed sister on his occasional visits to Ireland.

"The Madeira, eh?" he remarked now, with a slight frown. "Well, I tell you what, Bella, it seems to me you're taking something on yourself there. Doesn't belong to *you*, you know. Declan left everything to Nuala. Shannon would have the right to it now."

Mrs. Quinlevan shook her head, the ribbons on her cap quivering with her exasperation. "Shannon, again!" she said. "I am sure I have learned to detest that name! How it can be lawful—or Christian—or anything at all proper, for him to have *everything,* merely because that foolish girl was weak enough to let him carry her off and marry her—"

"Know how you feel, m'dear," Mr. Barnwall said. "Devilish rum business, having to see it all go out of the family. But the fellow has his rights, you see. Married the girl. Not his fault she died within the year. Might have lived together for forty years, had a dozen children—wouldn't have seemed so queer to you then."

"I daresay it wouldn't, for I shouldn't have been alive to see it," Mrs. Quinlevan said, still with great asperity. "But it puts me out of all patience when I think of a wretch like that coming in and turning us out without a by-your-leave. And now he will be here tomorrow, he writes—tomorrow! It is the most fortunate thing in the world that you have turned up, Jeremy, for I am at my wits' end over what to do! There is Georgina Power arriving this afternoon, and the Huddlestons not being able to remove from Craythorne until two days ago, so that Brandon and I have been obliged to remain here—oh, I am in such a whirl, I have not the least notion where to turn! And then there is that dreadful bailiff, who seems to have made the *worst* possible muddle of the accounts—"

Mr. Barnwall, his jaw dropping slightly at this catalogue of misfortunes, raised his hand at this juncture and said, "Hold up a minute! What's all this? Owen's daughter? Deuce take it, Bella, you don't mean to tell me you invited her here in the midst of *this* rowdy-do!"

Mrs. Quinlevan found her handkerchief, applied it to her eyes, and said defiantly, "Yes, I did!"

"But why, in the name of heaven?"

"Because she is to marry Brandon!"

The arrival of Higgins with the Madeira silenced the startled response that this statement seemed about to elicit from Mr. Barnwall. By the time the butler had departed, however, he had recovered his equanimity sufficiently to be able to say, with some satisfaction, "Well, if that is so, you are a lucky woman, Bella! Never thought you'd be able to make a catch like that for the boy—damme, I mean to say, that affliction of his and all! Not but what he ain't well-looking enough, but I'd never have said you could have settled him so easy, with a tight little fortune like this chit of Owen's will have if her grandmother comes up to scratch."

Mrs. Quinlevan, who had several times endeavoured to interrupt this speech, broke in at this point to desire her brother to stop being such a ninnyhammer.

"Of course it is not settled yet," she said. "Why, she has not seen him since he was fifteen years old! But I think it must be very likely that, if the two of them are together every day, something will come of it—"

This time it was Mr. Barnwall's turn to interrupt. "Tell me the truth, Bella," he said severely. "Is this all a scheme of yours, and nothing more?"

"Naturally it is a scheme *now*, as you put it," Mrs. Quinlevan said, defensively. "But there is no reason in the world why it should not work out. I am sure she and Brandon dealt extremely well together when we were in Herefordshire—"

"They were children then," Mr. Barnwall said ruthlessly.

"Yes, that is true, but what has that to say to anything?"

Mr. Barnwall shook his head. "Best face facts, Bella. The boy's a cripple, or next to it. Dashed ugly way of putting it, but the truth."

"So," Mrs. Quinlevan retorted, "is Lord Byron! But that doesn't stop half the silly women in England from running after *him*. And Brandon may turn out to be a famous poet, or something of the sort, one day, too, for Mr. Peabody has always said he never had a pupil with more aptitude."

"Come down off your high ropes, Bella," Mr. Barnwall said, with brotherly candour. "*I'm* not saying the boy's not a bright 'un. But if you're bringing that girl over here with the expectation that she'll fall in like a lamb with your idea of her marrying him, you must have windmills in your head. Deuce take it, you know as well as I do that he won't have more than a couple of thousand a year, and you needn't think he'll come into anything handsome from *me* when I die, for I don't mind telling you I'm badly dipped." He added, returning to a consideration of problems more pressingly at hand, "Didn't you tell me you're expecting that husband of Nuala's, too?" He glanced around at the disordered room. "He ain't thinking of taking up residence here *now*, I hope?"

Mrs. Quinlevan gave a distracted shake of the head. "Well, to speak the truth, Jeremy," she said, "I haven't the least idea! You know—or perhaps you *don't* know, for I am sure you paid not the slightest attention to the letters I sent you asking for your advice—that I had heard nothing from that wretched man for months, ever since he wrote me to say that he would continue to travel abroad for a time, as he has done since Nuala's death, and that I could remove from The Place quite at my leisure. And I am sure I had every intention of leaving before now, only, as bad luck would have it, the Huddlestons were unable to vacate Craythorne at Lady Day—" She saw her brother shaking his head disapprovingly, and said with renewed asperity, "Naturally I would have done if I had had the slightest idea this odious Mr. Shannon was to turn up just now. But how could I know that, when I hadn't had a word from him for months, and was almost thinking that he might have caught the fever, too, like poor Nuala?" She looked hopefully at Mr. Barnwall. "I suppose it is too much to expect that he is of a sickly constitution, and won't last long?" she inquired.

Mr. Barnwall fetched his snuffbox from his pocket, took a delicate pinch from it, and advised his sister not to place her hopes in that basket.

"From what I hear, he's the image of Cartan—the old earl, of course, not the present one," he said. "Regular out-and-outer old Cartan was in his grasstime, you know—a prime goer after hounds, a top-sawyer with a four-in-hand, devil of a fellow with his fives. *And* lived to be seventy-nine."

"Well, there is no hope in that, certainly," Mrs. Quinlevan said despondently. "I daresay the tiresome creature will be here tomorrow, just as he wrote he would—and what I am to do I have not the least idea, for I cannot possibly go to Craythorne for at least a week."

"Tell him to rack up at the Cock and Stars," Mr. Barnwall suggested. "He may not like it, but you can't have him here. As a matter of fact," he added, "if I was you, I wouldn't have anything to do with the fellow. Give him the keys when you're ready to leave and let him have the place. It's what he was after, and now he's got it, but I'm damned if I'd help him to set himself up in the neighbourhood."

"Indeed I shall not," Mrs. Quinlevan assured him. "I expect he will be excessively uncomfortable here, for nobody intends to take the least notice of him, not even the Malladons, though they have been putting it about that he is not so far beneath one's touch, after all. But that is only because it is *their* doing that Nuala was able to slip off and marry him. I have always believed that Lady Eliza was a widgeon, but, if it had ever remotely crossed my mind that she would be so henwitted as not to see that man was making up to Nuala, I should *never* have allowed Nuala to travel with her and Colonel Malladon to Scotland!"

Mr. Barnwall said, a trifle uncomfortably, "Well, the way I hear the story, Bella, it didn't exactly happen like that, you know. I mean, about his making up to *her*. Matter of fact, I've had a strong hint or two thrown out to me that it was just the other way round."

"Do you mean to say that Nuala was on the catch for *him?* That I will never believe, Jeremy—never!"

"You can believe what you like, but that don't change matters," Mr. Barnwall said obstinately. "Good Lord, Bella, you knew Nuala as well as I did—better! She never in her life saw something she wanted that she didn't set straight out to get it."

"And you wish to tell me that she wanted this—this Shannon?" Mrs. Quinlevan said, in high dudgeon. "You must be all about in your head, Jeremy!"

Mr. Barnwall pursed his lips. "Fine figure of a man, I understand," he suggested tentatively, after a moment.

"And thirty years old, at least! She would have thought him quite antiquated, I am sure." She added hopefully, as a new thought struck her, "Perhaps he is a very persuadable man? I mean someone that one might easily manage—?"

"No, no!" Mr. Barnwall said. "He's a surly brute, by all accounts—never in his life got on with anyone but Cartan. Not too surprising, for there's wild blood there. The mother, it seems, was some Irish tinker's wench Cartan picked up in Tothill Fields, on one of his roaring nights. She had the brass to take the brat to him when he was eight or nine and set him before him—bid him tell her whether he wasn't his own spit and image. Kind of joke Cartan would have enjoyed. He gave the woman a few guineas, enough to drink herself to death on, I should think, and had the lad scrubbed up and sent to school—"

"I wish you will stop raking up such dreadful stories, Jeremy," Mrs. Quinlevan said fretfully. "After all, Nuala *did* marry him, and though I intend to have no connexion with him it can do our credit no good to have it known that the matter is really as bad as you have been saying. What a pity that Sir John Mercer's estate was entailed on a male heir, for he had the most delightful property in Herefordshire, and I am persuaded that when Brandon and Georgina are married it would be far better for them to set up somewhere quite removed from this odious scandal—"

"Moonshine, Bella!" Mr. Barnwall interrupted her. "You had much better put the whole thing out of your head. By the way, where is Brandon?"

"I sent him this morning to Craythorne, to stir them up there—for there is no depending on the servants in that house since Mrs. Heaton left, you know, and yet she *would* go with the Huddlestons, though I told her I should be very glad to pay her the same wages."

Mr. Barnwall listened for a while longer to her strictures on the servants one was obliged to put up with these days, and presently announced his intention of taking his leave. He was an indolent man, and the prospect of becoming involved in the set of crises his sister was facing now was most disagreeable to him. He accordingly declined an invitation to stay to dinner, pleading pressing business at his own house, and went off, leaving Mrs. Quinlevan in full possession of the problems deriving from the arrival of her two prospective visitors.

The first of these visitors arrived at The Place of the Oaks at dusk. Mrs. Quinlevan had sent Nora Quill, Brandon's old nurse and her own trusted right arm in all affairs of domestic management, to meet Georgina in Kenmare, where the friends with whom she had travelled to Ireland were to part company with her; and the two had made the remainder of the journey to The Place in Mrs. Quinlevan's own travelling chaise. Although Georgina was surprised to learn that she was being taken to The Place instead of to Craythorne—for Mrs. Quinlevan had prudently decided not to jeopardize the plans for her visit by communicating to Lady Mercer the unsettled state of her domestic affairs —she was not in the least disconcerted by the discovery. In fact, when the chaise drove up the carriage sweep before the rambling stone Tudor mansion, she was even able to feel a certain satisfaction in the idea that it was the home of her ancestors that was to receive her, instead of Mrs. Quinlevan's own smaller house at Craythorne.

The front door opened as the steps of the chaise were let down, and Georgina saw a slender youth about a year older than herself, with wheat-gold hair of the same colour as her own, come out to greet her, walking as quickly as an obvious limp would permit.

"Hallo!" he called. "I've been on the watch for you. I must say you made poor time—but then that's to be expected, with these lazy nags my mother keeps."

Georgina gave him her hand with great pleasure.

"Brandon! How you've grown!" she said, looking up at him. "You're a head taller than I am, I am sure—and do you remember, in Herefordshire I was the taller by at least an inch!"

"And *you've* turned into a young lady," Brandon retorted, eyeing her fashionable almond-green redingote and shallow-crowned bonnet of the same colour. "Who would have imagined it? For a greater madcap I never saw in those days."

He shepherded her into the great hall, where his mother was waiting to receive their guest.

"My dear love," Mrs. Quinlevan said to Georgina, as she embraced her warmly, "I don't know *what* you will think of us! The house is in such a state! Everything at sixes and sevens! But it is all that horrid Shannon's fault, for if he had not taken it into his head to come down on us so suddenly it would not have signified about the Huddlestons' being unable to remove— But I am sure you are tired. Will you go upstairs at once, or shall I send for tea? We keep country hours here, you know, so we usually dine by six, but I have had dinner put back today, knowing you would be late."

Georgina broke in to say that she was not tired at all, but would enjoy a cup of tea. She was thereupon led into the book-room, and her redingote and bonnet having been borne off by Higgins, while Grady, the coachman, and a stout footman carried her portmanteaux and bandboxes upstairs, she settled down to a cosy chat with Brandon and Mrs. Quinlevan. This was soon interrupted, however, by the appearance of Nora Quill, who came in bearing a tea-tray and giving it as her opinion that no dinner worth the eating would be forthcoming from *that* kitchen unless she returned at once to take charge of it herself.

When Mrs. Quinlevan inquired doubtfully what the matter was, Nora said ominously that the cook, who had not been consulted in the packing up of the kitchen utensils, was unable or unwilling to prepare a meal in the makeshift collection of vessels that had been left to her, and was dropping strong hints of giving her notice on the spot.

Mrs. Quinlevan's response to this news was to demand her vinaigrette immediately. "I do not believe, my love," she said to Georgina, "that I can endure one more such shock today, in the unsettled state of my nerves! You can have no idea what this day has been!"

Georgina could not help but reflect that her own arrival seemed to be lumped in with the other disasters that had overtaken her cousin during the past twenty-four hours. But she was fast coming to the conclusion that Cousin Bella on her home grounds was going to turn out to be an even greater pea-goose than she had seemed four years before in Herefordshire, so she did not allow the reflection to depress her.

When the tea had been drunk, she was shown upstairs to the bedchamber she was to occupy while the family remained at The Place. As did every other room she had seen in the house, it bore signs of having been rifled of all but its heavier furnishings, but there was an ancient-appearing, carved-oak, four-poster bed, a chair that looked as if it, too, had survived from Elizabethan days, and a more modern three-drawer dressing table with a mirror, which she was told had been purchased especially for her cousin Nuala.

Nuala's name again appeared in the conversation when Georgina came downstairs to dinner, having changed her travelling dress to one of French muslin. As she entered the dining-room, the first thing that caught her eye was a magnificent full-length portrait of a young woman on the wall opposite the head of the table. From the recent cut of the high-waisted, sea-green gown, she realized at once that the girl in the portrait must be Nuala, and she scrutinised it with a great deal of interest.

"My cousin Nuala, of course?" she said to Mrs. Quinlevan, as she sat down at the table. "She was *very* beautiful, wasn't she?"

"The belle of the county," Mrs. Quinlevan said with pride. "The young men called her 'The Dark Lily,' for she had black hair, you know, and such a lovely complexion, and great dark-blue eyes with the longest black lashes! Indeed, if she had had a Season in London, there is no telling how high she might not have looked to bestow her hand."

"Well, then," Brandon said, "it is a pity you didn't see she had one, Mama, for I am sure she teased you enough to let her visit the Martin-Burnes in Brook Street two years ago, when she might have made her come-out in style."

"Oh, but she was a mere child then!" Mrs. Quinlevan protested. "And you know how fortunate it was that I did not listen to her, for she would have been out of the country then when her poor father died. I believe, in fact, that I must have had a premonition that that very thing might occur."

"You had a premonition that she'd meet some Bond Street beau who'd offer for her and knock all your hopes that she'd marry *me* into a cocked hat, m'dear," Brandon said, with cheerful frankness. "As if she and I didn't always get on like cats and dogs! She wouldn't have had me if I'd been plated with diamonds—nor I her, for that matter. Curst bad temper, for one thing, that girl had."

Mrs. Quinlevan, ruffling up, said it was no such thing, and he was a wicked boy to speak so. But her indignation faded to distress at the sight of the decidedly unappetising-looking plate of Hessian soup that was being placed before her. It appeared that Nora Quill had been correct in her assessment of the state of the kitchen, and that even her best efforts had been insufficient to inspire the cook to set on the table anything better than what Mrs. Quinlevan despairingly characterised as "a nasty mess."

"I am sure I don't know *what* Lady Mercer and your dear mama would say to my sitting you down to such a dinner!" she said tearfully to Georgina. "I assure you, I should be quite *sunk* in their esteem, and it is no wonder—but how I am to contrive to make anything go right in such a house I do not know! I vow I have never been so plagued in my life as I am with that dreadful man—for we should be quite comfortable if it was not for this moving, and that, as you can see, is all his fault!"

Georgina scarcely thought it could properly be laid at Mr. Shannon's door that Mrs. Quinlevan had engaged what seemed to be a houseful of very unaccommodating servants, or that he could even be considered unreasonable in wishing to take possession of property that had legally been his for the past twelve months, but not wishing to offend her cousin, she kept these thoughts to herself.

It did occur to her, however, that she had placed herself in an oddly uncomfortable situation in coming to Ireland, and if she had not been blessed with an optimistic nature, which required more than a shatterbrained hostess, a muddled household, and a bad dinner to cast her down, she might have been somewhat unhappy at the prospect before her by the time she retired to her bed that night.

CHAPTER 3

The next morning, however, she found a fine April day awaiting her, and when she had jumped out of bed and flung open a window she was so pleased with what lay before her that her doubts of the evening before quite vanished. She saw a sky flecked with white clouds over a quiet, lovely park, with hills covered with new boggy grass rising in the distance, and determined to dress quickly and persuade Brandon to take her on a tour of the estate, which, she told herself, she would certainly have no opportunity to see again, once the encroaching Mr. Shannon had settled himself there.

To her satisfaction, she found when she came downstairs that this idea had already occurred to Brandon, and that he was at that very moment in the breakfast-parlour, instructing Nora to see if she could have something more than cheese and ham put together in the kitchen for the luncheon that they would take with them.

"I didn't expect you'd care to stay here and run the chance of meeting Shannon," he explained to Georgina, "though perhaps you're not like other girls, and wouldn't make a kick-up if you were obliged to say half a dozen words to a ramshackle fellow who ain't to be received in respectable society. I must say I'm a bit curious about him myself."

"So am I," confessed Georgina, "but I daresay I shouldn't own it. I expect, though, it *will* be better if we are out of the way when he comes."

"That is what Mama says," Brandon agreed regretfully. "By the way, you are to excuse her this morning; she has Mulqueen, the bailiff, with her in the estate-room, and they are having a tremendous row over the accounts. I expect he has muddled them again, as he always does. And Mama is *not* the one to set him straight."

"No," Georgina said cautiously, as she removed the cover from a dish of decidedly burnt bacon on the side-table and resigned herself to breakfasting on hot chocolate and cold toast, "I can see that she might *not* have a turn for management. Good gracious, Brandon, I hope you will not take it amiss if I say I should think she would be glad to be rid of the responsibility of this place, even if it must go to someone like that wretched Shannon."

"Well, I expect she is, really," Brandon said, "only she has always been fond of the consequence it gives her to be Mrs. Quinlevan of The Place of the Oaks, you know. She had some queer idea for years that Nuala and I would marry one day, and then she'd never have to leave it. I ought to warn you," he added, with an engaging grin, "that she has you set down for her next victim. If she begins on the advantages of *your* marrying me, I wish you will tell her that I personally gave you to understand that I haven't the least notion of marrying anyone."

Georgina laughed. "Well, that is a great relief!" she said. "Not," she added affably, as she sat down at the table, "that I don't believe we should rub on very well, for you are exactly as I remember you, and we dealt wonderfully together in Herefordshire, I recollect. But I have no notion of marrying only to be comfortable."

"And I have no notion of marrying at all," Brandon said cheerfully. "Or not for years and years, at any rate. Why, Dr. Culreavy is of the opinion that, if I continue as I am, I may go up to Oxford later in the year—and I had a good deal rather do that than marry anyone, you know. Though if I *did* have it in mind to marry, I should not at all care if you were the one," he admitted handsomely. "I expect you know you've turned into a devilish pretty girl? And then you're a prime goer on a horse, besides having no nonsense at all about you—"

"Yes, but you had much better not tell that to your mama," she objected. "Say you think well enough of me, but that—that I'm too tall for your taste, perhaps—and a bit obstinate—and fond of my own way—"

"Oh, she wouldn't care a button for that!" Brandon declared. "If I wanted to put her off, I'd be obliged to say

Lady Mercer has taken such a dislike to you that she has decided to cut you out of her will."

"Well, you can't tell her that," Georgina said, "for it would be sure to get back to Grandmama and she would not like it at all. Besides, I can't think that Cousin Bella is as mercenary as *that!*"

"Well, our pockets *are* pretty well to let, you know," Brandon said apologetically. "It doesn't bother *me*, for I think it will be much jollier living at Craythorne than in this great, rambling house, but Mama is different. And this is her way of being practical, I expect, inviting you here and then hoping the two of us will make a match of it."

It was somewhat lowering to Georgina's self-esteem to reflect that the welcome that had been extended to her at The Place rested on nothing more personal than the expectation that she would one day inherit a snug fortune, but on the whole she was glad to have had this explanation with Brandon. She had sensed something of what he had just disclosed to her in the complacent manner in which Mrs. Quinlevan had regarded the two of them as they had sat together on the previous evening, and it made her much more comfortable with her cousin when they drove out a little later to tour the estate to know that the same idea was not also in *his* head. Indeed, they were soon on the same brother-and-sister terms with each other that had prevailed during his earlier visit to Herefordshire.

She was enchanted with the beauty of the Kerry landscape as they drove—the leafy woods, the particoloured fields and tiny whitewashed cottages roofed with brownish-grey thatch, and the blue hills from which came the tinkle of bells as sheep and goats browsed in placid flocks. But her eyes, accustomed to the rigorous standards set by her grandfather in the farming of his estate, soon discovered a great deal to find fault with in the management of the land.

"I can't think why you have allowed everything to fall into such neglect!" she said, looking accusingly at Brandon. "I am sure I know nothing at all about farming, except from hearing Sir John's comments when we rode out together, but even I can see that you have let things slide into a shocking state here."

Brandon shrugged. "Well, that is Mulqueen," he said frankly. "Mama *would* hire him as bailiff, though he is known all over the neighbourhood as a great lover of the bottle. She is perfectly bird-witted when it comes to such matters, and is persuaded that because his sister, who was once our housekeeper at The Place, was a very respectable woman, he is cut from the same cloth." He added, "Of course things were not in this state when my cousin Declan was alive. But he has been dead for two years, and since then Mama and Mulqueen have held full sway."

"But surely Cousin Bella was not left in sole charge of The Place!" Georgina said. "Was there no other relative to interest himself—?"

"Yes, there is my Uncle Barnwall," Brandon said, "but he is as bad as Mama, besides spending almost all his time in England, so that he has no idea of what is going on." He said ruefully, "I expect you will be saying now that I ought to have looked around myself and prevailed on Mama to use more sense. But to tell the truth, I am not at all interested in farming!"

"Nor I," she said, "but Sir John always said that if one had land, it was one's obligation to see to it that neither it nor the people who lived on it were abused. And he was right, you know!"

Her disapproval shortly vanished in her enjoyment of the excursion, however, and she was obliged to admit, when they stopped at one of the cottages for a draught of new milk to accompany the game pie and Queen cakes that had been packed up in a hamper for their luncheon, that this "houseen," at least, was in apple-pie order. The broad flagged steps leading to the door were swept and clean, and when they entered, on the invitation of the plain little woman who came to greet them, there was a turf fire on the hearth, with the kettle steaming on the hob, and a great, crusty, new-baked soda-cake on the spotless table.

This was the cottage of Dansel Lynch, who soon appeared himself—a red-faced, good-humoured countryman, whose heavy woollen trousers and hobnailed boots showed the signs of his morning's work in the fields. He made his manners to Miss Power, but it was plain that his chief interest was not in her, but in the second newcomer who was expected at The Place—the new owner.

"I expect there'll be a rare bit of change when he comes," he said unhappily. "Wasn't I saying only this morning now, I've yet to lay eyes on the Scotsman that wasn't clutchfisted? And this one a *claen istock,* to boot. There's never luck in the land when it goes to one of *them.*"

"What is a *claen istock?*" Georgina asked curiously.

"Why, miss," Daniel said, " 'tis the man who comes in when there's no son to take up the land—the husband, ye see, of the woman that has the inheritance. And now, with Miss Nuala dead, what should he care about The Place except to wring money out of it?"

"Oh, it may not be as bad as you expect," Brandon said. "After all, you'll be rid of old Mulqueen, and this fellow had the management of Lord Cartan's estates, you know, so at least he's not a greenhead."

But Dansel shook his head forebodingly. "Better a greenhead than a meddler," he said. "No, it's a sad day for us, Master Brandon, seeing the last of the Power blood leave The Place." He looked at Georgina. "Wouldn't it be this young lady's, now, if Miss Nuala had never gone off and married? The old woman and me was saying that only this morning—her being Mr. Owen's one child—"

Brandon grinned and said, "Well, I hadn't thought of it, but you're quite right, of course. It should have gone to her."

Later, as they were driving back to the house, he remarked to Georgina, "So *you* are really the one Shannon is cutting out, and not Mama and me! Do you know, I'm sure that has never occurred to her; she has been too full of *our* wrongs to think of anyone else's. But it's true that you are Nuala's first cousin—her closest relation. Mama and I are more distant cousins."

Georgina looked at the grey, ancient bulk of the house before them.

"Well, I *should* have liked living here," she admitted, "and being quite rich and independent—and then you and Cousin Bella could have lived with me, too, just as you did when Nuala was alive. But there is no use in thinking about that now, is there? For I cannot suppose, after all, that Mr. Shannon should care anything about what my claims might have been if he had never married my cousin."

It was past two o'clock in the afternoon when she and Brandon walked in the front door at The Place, and both were admitting to a certain curiosity as to whether the new owner had yet arrived and perhaps gone off again. He was forgotten the next instant, however, when Nora Quill came hurrying downstairs, her normally ruddy face pale and her manner suggesting that a catastrophe of nature had occurred.

"Oh, Master Brandon, it's only you!" she cried. "I made sure it was the doctor."

"The doctor!" Brandon exclaimed. "Why, what is the matter, Nurse? Why is the doctor needed? Is my mother—?"

"Yes, indeed, it's the mistress," Nora said distressfully. "Oh, Master Brandon, indeed and indeed, you've no idea what a morning this has been! First there was that wicked Mulqueen, taking it into his head to quarrel with the mistress and fling out of here like a lord—"

"Good God, Nurse, you can't have sent for Dr. Culreavy merely because my mother has had words with Mulqueen!" Brandon exclaimed impatiently. "What is the matter with her? Is she really ill?"

"Ill!" Nora said wrathfully. "Why, indeed, she *is* ill, if you'd but give me leave to tell my tale. Fallen down these very stairs she's done—and her so upset with Mulqueen's impudence and that Shannon coming down on us that she didn't rightly know whether she was on her head or her feet. I misdoubt very much that she's broken her leg."

She whipped up the corner of her apron to her eyes, while Brandon and Georgina stood looking at her in alarm. Georgina was the first to recover herself.

"I'll go up to her," she said, but Nora barred her way as she started up the stairs.

"No, indeed, you won't, miss," she said decidedly, "for I've just calmed her down out of a fit of strong hysterics, and there's no saying you might not set her off again. If you please, you and Master Brandon will do much better to stay below and see Mr. Shannon when he comes. Bad cess to him, the divil, to have to turn up on this day of all the ones in the year!"

The arrival of the doctor at that moment put an end to any further conversation, for he hurried upstairs at once to his patient, accompanied by Nora. Brandon and Georgina were left standing in the hall, staring blankly at each other.

"Well, of all the rum starts!" Brandon said unhappily,

after a moment. "Fallen downstairs! If she really *has* broken her leg—"

"There's no use in thinking of that until we know it's so," Georgina said firmly. "More than likely it's only a bad sprain. But in the meantime, what are we to do about Mr. Shannon? Of course Cousin Bella can't see him today. Perhaps he could talk to your bailiff?"

Brandon shook his head. "I shouldn't think that was at all likely," he said. "You heard what Nurse said. If he hasn't thrown up the job entirely, he'll be so badly foxed by this time that he won't know his right hand from his left. I can send one of the grooms to fetch my Uncle Barnwall, if they haven't done so already, but if he doesn't arrive in time I expect we shall just have to see the fellow ourselves."

"We?" Georgina exclaimed.

"Well, you can't expect me to manage the whole business myself," Brandon said, with an asperity that seemed to his cousin to conceal a certain degree of perturbation. "Dash it, Georgie, I should think you'd *want* to stand by me."

"Well, so I do," Georgina said somewhat mendaciously, for she was actually thinking that it was one thing to be an interested onlooker at an affair of this kind, but quite another to be thrust into the position of carrying it off against such a formidable unknown as Mr. Shannon.

She was about to suggest that she should go upstairs and repair her toilette, for she was conscious that the morning's excursion had left her hair in some disarray and that the plain round gown she wore was hardly a dress in which to receive visitors. But at that moment there came a peremptory rap on the knocker. She and Brandon started, and looked at each other.

"It's Shannon, of course!" Brandon said, in a hasty undertone. "We had better not be standing here! Come into the book-room."

He seized her hand and drew her across the hall, and they stood waiting for Higgins to open the door to the caller.

But no Higgins appeared, and the rapping sounded again, this time even more insistently than before.

"Deuce take it!" Brandon muttered, under his breath. "This is really the outside of enough! The whole house at sixes and sevens, my mother laid up, and now there is not even a servant to answer the door! Ten to one they have all been sent off to the garret or the cellar to help in the packing." He tugged furiously at the bell-rope beside the mantel, but there was no response. "I suppose I shall have to go myself," he said despairingly.

"I'll come with you," Georgina said, with dignity. "We shall simply tell him that there has been an accident, and that he must return another time."

"No, good God, we can't do that!" Brandon said. "He owns the curst place, you know. Let me handle it."

He limped across the hall to the door, and Georgina, restraining the curiosity that prompted her to forget her eighteen years and peep from the doorway like a schoolgirl, hastily selected a book at random from the shelves and sat down with it in a chair beside the fireplace. She did not feel called on to carry her pretence of occupation so far as actually to read the page that she opened before her, but instead kept a sharp ear on what was going forward in the hall.

CHAPTER 4

The first thing she heard, on the opening of the front door, was a masculine voice inquiring for Mrs. Quinlevan, followed at once by Brandon's rather confused and headlong explanation of the state of affairs in the house that had brought him to the door in place of a servant, and that made it impossible for the visitor to see his mother. Georgina could not overhear a great deal of the colloquy that followed, because the newcomer spoke in a low, calm voice, but she gained the distinct impression that Mr. Shannon was not at all ill at ease in the embarrassing situation into which he had walked. For some reason this raised her hackles. She was quite conscious of being in something of a flurry herself, and of the fact that Brandon was in even a worse one, and their visitor's contrasting self-composure rapidly assumed in her mind the proportions of an intolerable arrogance.

She had no time to form any further impression of him before he walked into the book-room with Brandon. Her concept of arrogance was immediately strengthened by the sight of a tall figure, carried with distinction and set off to careless advantage in a well-fitting drab coat, buckskins, and top boots, and a harsh-featured face with cool grey eyes.

"This is Mr. Shannon, Georgie," Brandon said, his lack of composure showing in the angry punctiliousness of his tone. "My cousin, Miss Power."

Shannon bowed slightly, glancing about the room immediately afterward in a manner that indicated plainly that he considered Miss Power to be hardly his first consideration at the moment.

"I see that I must apologize for coming at such a time, Mr. Quinlevan," he went on at once, rather coolly, to Brandon. "But naturally I had no reason to believe, after a twelvemonth, that my arrival would be entirely unexpected. Nor could I have foreseen your mother's unfortunate accident—which, however, would appear to have nothing to do with the fact that she has not yet removed from this house."

"If you think it is all a hum, to put you off, you are quite mistaken!" Brandon said, reacting hotly to his words. "She really had a fall, you know, not two hours ago! The doctor is with her now."

"Yes, of course," Shannon said, in the same reserved tone. "I assure you, I do not in the least doubt your word. At any rate, there is no need for us to come to cuffs over the matter. Perhaps if I might speak to some older relative of yours— You have an uncle, I believe?"

"He will be sent for, but he is not in the house."

"Then your bailiff—?"

"He—is not available just now, either," Brandon was obliged to admit.

"Indeed? Then perhaps *he* could be sent for?"

"He is—dismissed or drunk, sir!" Brandon replied, flushing up more and more hotly as he was driven into making the confession. "I believe he and my mother had words this morning."

Shannon's brows went up. "In that case," he suggested, "perhaps I might sit down with *you* and have a brief conversation—that is, if you have no more pressing matters to attend to."

"No—of course not," Brandon stammered, suddenly becoming conscious of his woeful deficiencies as a host. "Please sit down, sir! I'll ring for some refreshment."

He pulled the bell-rope, looking imploringly at Georgina as he did so. She came to his assistance and said to Shannon, with an assumption of dignified ease, "You must forgive the disorder in the house, sir. It should hardly surprise you; you can no doubt see that my cousins were almost on the point of removing to Craythorne when Mrs. Quinlevan's accident occurred this morning. Perhaps you might allow me to suggest that, when you have had some refreshment, you would go to the local inn, where I am sure you will be quite comfortable until arrangements are made to receive you here."

She had spoken in her best imitation of her grandmother's most quelling tones, but it infuriated her further that the maddeningly self-composed visitor seemed less than impressed with her dignity.

His reply was even less satisfactory to her. "I beg your pardon," he said, with his rather harsh air of civility, "but that is exactly what I do *not* intend to do, Miss Power, at least until I have satisfied myself that there is someone in this house who is capable of managing its affairs and those of this estate. I had ample opportunity, as I was driving here, to see the shocking state into which the land has been allowed to fall; now it seems that even the house is to be given over to chaos."

Brandon burst out angrily, "That is none of *your* affair" —but caught himself up at once. "Dash it all, yes, it is, of course," he said, flushing up red, "but—but—my uncle—"

He was interrupted by the appearance of Higgins at the door.

"You rang, sir?" he asked helpfully, as Brandon stood staring at him.

And well he might stare, Georgina thought. Higgins, in the helterskelter state of the house that day, and perhaps in sympathy with the wrongs of his friend Mulqueen, had allowed himself to sample some of the Madeira that he had been charged with making ready for conveyance to Craythorne. His gingery hair looked as if he had just come in out of a high wind, and his manner, far from the modest civility required even of a passable butler, was confidingly forward.

"Thought you might care to know, Master Brandon," he volunteered, as Brandon, stunned by his appearance, sought for words. "Mr. Barnwall's gone back to London. Left this morning. Sent a message to the mistress—messenger crossed ours on the way."

"That will do, Higgins," Brandon said, in a strangled tone.

Higgins bowed and walked out of the room, adding amiably, as he departed, "Thought you might care to know, Master Brandon."

"This is the outside of enough!" Brandon exploded. "I've told my mother time and again to get rid of that fellow!"

"An excellent piece of advice, I should say," Shannon remarked dryly. He rose and said, "If you will allow me, Mr. Quinlevan—I drove my own horses here, and I scarcely care to leave them standing any longer in this wind. Would you object if I order my groom to take them around to the stables?"

"Not at all, sir—if you—if you mean to stay!" Brandon stammered.

"Very well. If you will excuse me, Miss Power—I shan't be a moment."

He strode out of the room, leaving the two cousins almost speechless behind him. It was Georgina who recovered herself first.

"Of all the—the arrogant presumption!" she said furiously. "He *does* mean to stay, Brandon; there is no other explanation for it. Oh! No one but a rag-mannered basket-scrambler would think of forcing his company on a household at such a time! How *could* my cousin have married him!"

"Hush! He'll hear you," Brandon said uncomfortably. He added, "I daresay you're right—but all the same, with Mulqueen gone and my uncle off to London and Mama laid up—well, you know, there really ought to be someone here to look after The Place."

"We might manage very well ourselves, with Nora and the servants," Georgina fumed. "Good God, Brandon, you are not going to be cowhearted enough to tell me that you *wish* him to stay? He is an impertinent coxcomb, and it is no affair of *his* if your butler is a trifle bosky. If I were standing in your shoes, I should tell him straight to his face to go!"

"Then it is a very good thing that you are not standing in them," Shannon's calm voice remarked from the doorway, "since I should certainly pay no attention to such a piece of impertinence from him." He came into the room, leisurely stripping off his driving gloves, and went on in the same matter-of-fact way, to Brandon, "I wonder if it would be possible for you to find *some* servant in this confusion who would have the presence of mind to be able to fetch a bottle of the excellent Madeira my late wife assured me her father had laid down here? I have had rather a long drive, and you were kind enough to speak of offering me some refreshment."

Brandon looked unhappily at Georgina. Apparently he felt that it was his duty to rebuke Shannon for the deliberate rudeness of his remark, but he was far from used to having such responsibilities thrust on him, and finally settled the matter by throwing the idea up and saying, "Oh, Lord, very well, then! There must be *someone*—"

He limped out of the room, while Georgina remained standing by the mantelpiece, regarding Shannon in a decidedly unfriendly manner. Shannon returned the gaze without noticeable expression on his face, and finally remarked, in the tone of quite obviously careless civility that had so offended her previously, "Will you sit down, Miss Power? I can hardly do so myself until you do, and I really believe we might both be more comfortable seated than standing here facing each other as if we were about to engage in a sparring match."

She flushed angrily, conscious of the justness of what he had said even though she disliked intensely the way in which he had said it, and sat down abruptly in the nearest chair. Shannon then deliberately sat down himself and, stretching his long legs out before him in what appeared to her remarkably like the comfortable way of a man making himself at ease in his own house, said to her, "I gather from your name, Miss Power, that we are relations by marriage. Perhaps you will be good enough to tell me in what degree?"

"I am Owen Power's daughter—Nuala's first cousin," she said, with a coldness that matched his own.

He looked thoughtful, as if he were trying to recollect something. "I see," he said. "Then this is not your home? I seem to recollect my wife's speaking of having relations in Shropshire—"

"Herefordshire," Georgina corrected him. "That is, our residence is in Bath now, since Sir John—since my grandfather's death. But I cannot see what possible concern all this is of yours, Mr. Shannon. Your wife is dead, so it may be as well for you to consider that any connexion there has been between us is now at an end."

He bowed slightly, but she had the distinct notion that again he was not impressed by her pretentions of formality and was regarding her with only the rather negligent attention he might have bestowed on a forward schoolgirl.

"In that I shall be happy to oblige you," he said in a level voice. "The fact remains, however, that you are apparently residing in my house, and I have a natural curiosity to know who my guests may be."

She was confounded as to how to reply to this speech, and felt a certain relief when Brandon walked into the room again, carrying a decanter and a single glass.

"Here is your wine, sir," he said stiffly, setting the glass down on a table and filling it.

"You won't join me?" Shannon asked him, with lazy— and, Georgina thought, rather mocking—civility.

"No, thank you" Brandon said curtly. "Sir, I have been thinking—"

But at that moment there was a slight cough from the direction of the hall, and the eyes of all three of the occupants of the room lifted to behold a small, thin, soberly dressed elderly gentleman standing in the doorway.

"Dr. Culreavy!" Brandon exclaimed. "Come in, sir— pray! How is my mother? Are there any bones broken?"

The doctor looked in some surprise at Shannon's tall figure comfortably reposing in the easy-chair across the room.

"I beg your pardon, Brandon," he said, "I had no idea you had a caller."

"This is Mr. Shannon, the—my cousin Nuala's husband," Brandon stammered. "Dr. Culreavy."

"Your servant, sir," Shannon said, rising with an easy movement. "Will you share a glass of this excellent Madeira with me?"

Georgina gave an indignant gasp on hearing him so coolly assuming the role of host, and Dr. Culreavy, too, looked at him with a certain suspicion and disapproval.

"No, I thank you, sir," he said, with testy formality. "I want only a word with young Quinlevan." He paused, seeming to expect that Shannon would excuse himself and take himself out of the room, but Shannon showed no inclination to do so.

"You have not met my cousin, Miss Power, Dr. Culreavy," Brandon said, turning his back on Shannon with an angry flush.

Dr. Culreavy bowed. "May I say that it is indeed fortunate that you are here, Miss Power?" he said. "Mrs. Quinlevan has had a very nasty shock—very nasty, indeed. There are no bones broken, I believe, but she is experiencing a considerable degree of discomfort from a very bad sprain. I should much dislike leaving her to the care of servants alone, though I have no doubt that Nora Quill will cosset her beyond all need. But *your* presence here must be of the greatest reassurance to her."

Georgina was not certain how much of this speech was to be set down to the doctor's old-fashioned civility and how much to his genuine belief in what her being in the house must mean to her cousin, but she murmured some proper response. Her concern for her cousin Bella was almost swallowed up, however, by her indignation over Shannon's continuing to force his presence on such a conversation.

The next moment that indignation rose even higher when he interrupted Brandon's colloquy with Dr. Culreavy to inquire of the latter, "Am I to understand, then, that it will be some time before Mrs. Quinlevan is able either to remove to Craythorne or to resume any supervision of this house and estate?"

Dr. Culreavy looked at him disapprovingly. "Oh dear, yes!" he said positively. "I won't hear of her leaving her bed for at least a week, and then she must proceed with the greatest of care. A strong irritation of the nerves, you see, my dear sir, coupled with the physical shock and contusions of a nasty fall— And Mrs. Quinlevan is a lady whose nerves are very easily disordered."

Shannon said no more, but as soon as the doctor had departed he set down his glass and remarked to Brandon in a matter-of-fact voice, "That settles it, of course. I shall stay. If one of your admirable servants can be found to fetch my portmanteau upstairs to a bedchamber, I shall employ the time between now and dinner in trying to discover the whereabouts of your bailiff and putting him into a state of sufficient sobriety to be able to give me some sort of account of his stewardship."

He then strode out of the room, as if he had said everything that was necessary to be said. Georgina looked at Brandon, her eyes beginning to sparkle dangerously.

"Cousin," she said, "am I to understand that you are

going to allow that *abominable* man to walk into his house and behave in such a way?—as if we were children, as if *we* could have nothing to say—?"

"Well, I don't care for it myself, of course," Brandon said uncomfortably. "But what am I to do? I can't turn him out if he chooses to stay; you must see that."

"I don't see anything of the kind," Georgina retorted. "You might at least show him that you resent his conduct!"

Brandon smiled a little, ruefully. "Lord, you sound as if you would like me to call him out," he said.

"So I would!" Georgina said ruthlessly.

"But he wouldn't pay the slightest heed, if I *were* such a nodcock as to do it," Brandon protested. "He'd only think I was queer in my attic. Dash it, Georgie, *we* are the ones who ought not to be here, if you come right down to it. Mama has had a twelvemonth to vacate and she hasn't done it, and I know for a fact that she has given him promises by the yard, and not lived up to a single one. You can hardly blame him for growing tired of it at last."

The logic of this argument had little effect on Georgina, however, and she incautiously taxed her cousin with being afraid of Shannon, concluding by vowing that if she were a man she would have him out of the house in the space of five minutes. This accusation succeeded in firing Brandon up a great deal more than Shannon's rudeness had done. He declared vehemently that she was making a cake of herself and that for his part he was sorry that she had ever come to Ireland, as they would have got on a great deal better without her, concluding this speech by limping out of the room to go upstairs and see how his mother did.

Georgina swallowed her wrath as best she might, and sat down to consider what she was to do next. After five minutes, however, as no answer presented itself to this problem, she followed Brandon upstairs to inquire after Mrs. Quinlevan. Nora Quill was sitting with her; on seeing Georgina, she rose at once, with her finger to her lips, and went into the hall to meet her, closing the door behind her.

"The doctor's given her a draught and she's gone off at last," she said in a low, rather belligerent voice, "so you needn't be thinking of disturbing her, miss. A sad time she's had of it today, you know, and I'm sure it's a miracle that there's no bones broken."

Georgina expressed her sympathy and inquired if there was anything she could do to aid the sufferer.

Nora, somewhat mollified, shook her head. "Not for the mistress, for I'll see to her myself, miss; I wouldn't have it any other way. But if you could take things in hand a bit belowstairs—for I'm sure Master Brandon is of no more use than a babe-in-arms when it comes to anything that isn't in those wearisome books of his. And now he says that that divil of a Shannon is determined to stop here in the house this very night—as if we weren't in enough of a lather as it is!"

"Yes," Georgina said, "he desires a bedchamber prepared for him." She did not wish to gossip with a servant about the future master of The Place, no matter how angry he had made her, but she had no doubt that Nora could read her feelings from her looks. "If you could tell me which will be most suitable—" she suggested.

"Suitable!" Nora fired off. "If ye're asking me what's suitable for *him*, I'd tell you the coal-hole!" She shrugged her shoulders at Georgina's disapproving unresponsiveness and said rather sulkily, "Well, then, you might ask Mrs. Hopkins to put him in the green bedchamber at the front of the house. It was Mr. Declan's, and as he's to be master here—"

She returned to her patient, while Georgina went in search of the housekeeper, whom she eventually ran to earth in the kitchen, having words with the cook. The constant turmoil in the house made her wonder how anyone had ever contrived to live comfortably in it, but when she had given directions to Mrs. Hopkins about the green bedchamber and had gone back to the book-room to find Brandon closeted there with a volume of Latin poetry, he enlightened her on the matter by saying that when Declan Power had been alive he had kept all the reins in his own hands.

"Mama has never been worth a button as far as managing *anything* is concerned," he said frankly. "I daresay Cousin Declan never hoped she would be, when he brought her to live here. All he wanted was a respectable female relation to stand behind Nuala; everything else he took care of himself. I mean to say, we had a bang-up housekeeper all those years, Mrs. Curran—but when Cousin Declan died

Mama felt it to be her duty to take an interest in household matters, and—well, the fact of the matter is that Mrs. Curran got up on her high ropes at her interfering, and before we knew it she had packed up and gone back to Cork."

He seemed to have forgotten the note of animosity on which they had parted, and Georgina, glad to find him so forgiving, sat down and asked him what they were to do about dinner. "I suppose Shannon intends to take his meals here," she said.

"I expect he does," Brandon conceded. "I stopped round at the stables just now, and his groom was settling the horses in as if *he* had no idea, at any rate, of going anywhere else today. Pair of match-greys they are, by the way —sixteen-mile-an-hour tits if I ever saw any. Hanger—the groom—says Shannon bought 'em in Cork. Has an eye for good horseflesh: I'll give him that."

"Well, I should not go about it to become familiar with his groom, if I were you," Georgina said severely. "We are obliged to live in the same house with Shannon as long as your mother cannot remove from here, but I, for one, intend to have nothing at all to do with him personally."

Brandon shrugged. "Well, that is your affair," he said. "But there's no use making a kick-up about it, Coz. You said yourself you wanted someone to take hold here, you know. Well, it seems that someone is about to do so, and I must say I am glad of it. It will make it a deuced bit more comfortable while Mama is laid up."

"You are not going to defend him!" Georgina said. "I am sure he is laughing at us, behind that odious civility." She added darkly, "I may be obliged to sit down to dinner with him, but I assure you I shall not give him any more consequence in this house than he has already taken, by addressing so much as a word to him."

This resolution proved singularly easy to carry out, as, when they sat down to the table a little later, Shannon appeared to have no interest whatever in speaking to her. Instead, he carried on a very practical conversation with Brandon on the subject of the estate, endeavouring to learn from him, it seemed, anything that might be of value in his future conduct of affairs there.

Nor did Brandon, who was a little miffed, in spite of his good nature, at the strong words she had spoken to him earlier in the day, make any attempt to draw her into the conversation. As a matter of fact, when the Savoy cake with which the meal ended had been eaten, he seemed quite inclined to remain in the dining-room to sit with Shannon as the latter sampled a glass of Declan Power's excellent brandy, instead of accompanying his cousin from the room. This was too much for Georgina. Finding herself quite provoked by this uncousinly behaviour, she withdrew to her own bedchamber, where she occupied herself for some time in pacing it from end to end, throwing out various indignant and unflattering ejaculations from time to time.

It would have made her even unhappier if she had known that Brandon continued to sit with Shannon for the better part of the hour that followed, and that the conversation flowed amicably all the while. It was, in fact, Shannon, and not her cousin, who put an end to it by declaring his purpose of closeting himself in the estate-room for the remainder of the evening over the accounts.

Brandon then went to seek his cousin, and, on being informed by one of the maids that she had retired to her chamber, went quite contentedly into the book-room to continue his reading.

CHAPTER 5

On the following morning Georgina was relieved to find that she was to breakfast, at least, without the benefit of Shannon's company, for she was told, on coming downstairs, that he had already gone out, accompanied by Brandon and the bailiff, Mulqueen. She ate her meal in solitary state, and then went upstairs to inquire of Nora Quill whether her cousin Bella was awake. She was admitted at once to the sick room and found Mrs. Quinlevan sitting up in bed with a breakfast tray, looking much more robust than she had been prepared to see her by Nora's gloomy observations.

When she congratulated her cousin on this, however, she was treated to a long catalogue of the distressing symptoms with which Mrs. Quinlevan had been plagued during the night, so that any hope she might have had of soon being able to leave The Place and Shannon's unwelcome company was immediately laid to rest.

"Of course," Mrs. Quinlevan said, presently making reference herself to the obnoxious presence of the new owner, "*that* has added immeasurably to my anxieties, my love. You have only to imagine my feelings when Nora told me this morning that he had actually spent the night here! So improper! So dreadfully pushing!"

"Yes, indeed, ma'am. So it seems to me, too," Georgina said, "but I beg you won't make yourself uncomfortable over it on *my* account."

"Well, I will not do so, if you are sure it does not trouble you," Mrs. Quinlevan said doubtfully, "but I am not at all certain that Lady Mercer would approve of your even *meeting* Mr. Shannon—far less of your sitting down to dinner with him yesterday, which Brandon tells me you were obliged to do."

Georgina would have been glad to express her own feelings on that subject, but she did not wish to upset her cousin further, and thus merely said that it did not signify.

She left the room soon afterward, on a hint from Nora Quill that her mistress required more repose, and, after returning downstairs, was beginning a letter to her mother in the book-room when Higgins came in to inform her that Lady Mott and her daughter had arrived to inquire after Mrs. Quinlevan. Georgina had no idea who Lady Mott might be, but in Brandon's absence she thought it incumbent on her to act the part of hostess, and she accordingly asked Higgins to show the callers into the book-room.

A few moments later a homely middle-aged lady of imposing bulk, in a pomona-green gown and a high-crowned bonnet decorated with a cluster of curled ostrich plumes, sailed into the room, accompanied by a young girl of about Georgina's own age in a quiet frock of dove-coloured silk.

"My dear child," the elder lady exclaimed, as Georgina rose to greet her, "I came the moment I heard! Now I shan't stand on points with you, for I must tell you that I knew your father when he was still in short coats. Do pray tell me—how is poor Bella?"

"I believe she is much improved this morning," Georgina said. "But you have the advantage of me, I am afraid, ma'am."

"Of course—of course!" the lady interrupted, in her reassuringly frank voice. "Naturally you will not know us. I am Lady Mott, and this is my daughter Betsy. Our land marches with the Powers', you see—or it did, until Nuala Power was wet-goose enough to marry this man Shannon. Pho! I must say it will not suit either me or Sir Humphrey to have him as a neighbour, but then I expect Nuala was not considering that when she ran off with the fellow."

Georgina broke in on this flow of conversation long enough to beg the visitors to be seated and to ask Higgins if he would bring some refreshment for them, and then sat down herself to attend further to Lady Mott. She could not help being somewhat amused by her appearance, for indeed the fashionable clothes and bright colours she wore did not at all suit her plain face and stout figure, but at the same time she felt in Lady Mott a kindred spirit—a frankness and a commonsense approach to life that accorded with her own.

Her daughter, who sat silently in her mama's exuberant presence, did not resemble her in the least. She had a rather pretty, good-humoured face, the greatest attraction of which was a pair of blue eyes the colour of cornflowers. As her conversation consisted chiefly of "No, Mama," and "Yes, Mama," Georgina was unable to form much of an opinion of her character or intelligence.

When they had all sat down, Lady Mott had first to hear a full account of Mrs. Quinlevan's accident and Shannon's arrival, and then took matters into her own hands by declaring that in her opinion it would not do at all for Georgina to remain at The Place as Shannon's guest.

"Which is what it comes to, my dear, however one may talk round it," she said. "And with Bella confined to her room, there is no one to chaperon you but Brandon, and that is as good as saying no one at all. No, it won't do. I think it will be much better if you come home with me until Bella is ready to remove to Craythorne. You will be very welcome, you know, and as you and Betsy are of an age, you won't be bored with only the company of old people like Sir Humphrey and myself."

She seemed to believe that the matter was already settled, but Georgina discovered, to her own surprise, that, far from being pleased by this, she was in reality rather put out. Under cover of the pause in the conversation that occurred as Higgins appeared to hand around glasses of ratafia, she made a hasty attempt to examine her own feelings. Certainly it was not because she had taken an instant dislike to Lady Mott that she was disinclined to accept her invitation; on the contrary, she thought she would get on with her very well. Nor was it because she felt that her presence in the house would be of any particular comfort to Mrs. Quinlevan; more probably, she thought, her cousin would be relieved to be rid of the problems of entertaining a guest under such peculiar circumstances.

No, the truth was, she was obliged to confess, that it was Shannon who was making her desire to stay. She had flung down the gauntlet to him, and to run away tamely before the battle between them had fairly been joined was a poor-spirited course of conduct against which all her instincts rebelled. It would be one thing if she were to remove to Craythorne with her cousins in the natural course of events; it was quite another to give him the satisfaction of knowing that his highhanded rudeness had driven her from the house.

Lady Mott, when Higgins had left the room, fortunately gave her added time to formulate some excuse for declining her invitation by charging off into certain rather startling reminiscences of Georgina's father, who had been, it appeared, a childhood playmate of hers, and then by rising and saying that she must go upstairs and look in on poor Bella.

"Not," she added, "that I expect I shall do her a particle of good, for I am never out of frame myself and Sir Humphrey assures me I have no tact whatever with those who are. But of course it won't do for me to go off without looking in on her. And I must see to it that she receives the pork jelly that I brought. Her own cook—as I suppose you have found by this time—is a positive monster of inefficiency, and I doubt can concoct *anything* in the least restorative to an invalid."

She swept out of the room on these words, instructing her daughter to remain behind with Georgina. Georgina then discovered that Miss Mott, relieved of her mama's overpowering presence, could indeed chatter with the best of her sex, for she was treated, in the space of a quarter hour, to a complete description of the amusements the neighbourhood afforded, from assemblies and private balls to picnics and riding excursions, with side glances at the young gentlemen whom she might be expected to meet while attending these events.

"I shall be very jealous of you, I am sure, for you are much prettier than I am," Betsy said candidly, "or that is, I should be, except that I do not believe Robert will be deflected from his devotion to me, no matter to how much disadvantage I appear beside you."

Georgina shook herself out of her own private reflections to a semblance of attention.

"Robert?" she said politely. "Oh—you are betrothed, then?"

Betsy sighed. "Not—betrothed, actually," she said. "Papa believes I am too young."

Georgina stared. "Too young? How old are you? You must be as old as I am!"

"I am turned eighteen."

"So am I," said Georgina, satisfied. "But my problem is exactly the opposite of yours. I have been *plagued* to marry."

"Someone you—could not love?" Betsy inquired, her eyes lighting up at the hint of a romantic story.

"Exactly!" Georgina said curtly. "Someone no one could love—except his mother, who dotes on him."

She caught herself up, feeling that this was no time for exchanging confidences, even if Betsy Mott were the sort of confidante she would have chosen. But Betsy, once on the subject of romance, was not so easily to be led off it.

"How sad!" she said eagerly. "Do you know, I had been trying to picture you, since Mrs. Quinlevan told us you were to visit here, and as you are Nuala's cousin, I always imagined you like her—but I see now that you are much, much different. I mean—how very brave of you to stand out against your family, when they were *determined* that you should marry this—this *man!*"

"Well, as to that," Georgina objected, "one can hardly call him a *man,* for he is only twenty and looks eighteen, and is a perfect looby! And as for my being braver than Nuala, that is nonsense. *I* didn't run off and marry someone like Shannon!"

"Yes, but I expect he married *her,* you know," Betsy said reasonably. "Mama always said she would meet someone some day who would take her at her word—for you must know she was a desperate flirt, and was never satisfied unless she had every man in sight dangling after her. But then everyone here knew she didn't *mean* anything by it—and I expect Mr. Shannon didn't, or if he did, it didn't signify to him." She leaned a little closer to Georgina, lowering her voice. "What is he *really* like?" she asked urgently. "Is he —fatally attractive?"

"He is the rudest, most abominable creature I have ever seen in my life," Georgina said unequivocally. "*That's* what he's like." She paused at the sight of Higgins again in the doorway.

"Lady Eliza Malladon," he announced, and, with the words, a lady of some thirty years, dressed in the first stare of fashion, in a cherry gown and spencer set off with a pink neck scarf with cherry stripes, swept into the room. At first sight Georgina scarcely considered that the face, beneath the tall straight hat trimmed with a tuft of feathers hanging to one side, was a pretty one, for the nose was a decided pug, the lips were overly full, and the brown eyes rather prominent. But Lady Eliza had not been in the room more than five minutes before she had established, by her manner, that she was accustomed to being the belle of any occasion to which she lent her presence. She had an exceedingly vivacious manner, which quite bore down Georgina's attempts to act the hostess, and made the point at once that, as she was so well acquainted at The Place, she considered *she* might rather do the honours.

She greeted Miss Mott with condescending amiability, and, after inquiring rather perfunctorily after Mrs. Quinlevan, said to Georgina, "Higgins tells me that you actually have Shannon in the house! What a coil you must be in! But that is exactly like the creature, you know. He will never be bound to do as anyone else would." She accepted a glass of ratafia and sat down comfortably on the sofa. "Tell me, what do you think of him, my dear? Of course one must admit he is handsome, in his own abominable way."

"I should not call him so, ma'am," Georgina said bluntly.

Lady Eliza raised her brows. "No? Then I take it he has been behaving *un*handsomely to you already—for, my dear child, disregarding the face, which I grant you may be somewhat harsh, that magnificent figure! Cartan—the old earl—was considered quite an Adonis in his day, I believe —though 'Adonis' may not *quite* convey all that masculinity. And Shannon is said to be his image. Not that you are not perfectly correct in refusing to admire such a rogue, my dear. Of course it was your poor cousin's undoing!"

Georgina did not at all care for the direction the conversation was taking, considering that Lady Eliza's freedom in abusing the man under whose roof she was sitting was in at least as bad taste as Shannon's own rudeness; and she was relieved when Lady Mott again entered the room, having completed her visit to the invalid upstairs.

"Well, Eliza! You here!" she said, regarding Lady Eliza

with a glance of some disfavour. "I must say you surprise me, I thought you never rose before noon."

"Nonsense," Lady Eliza said briskly. "Of course I came at once when I heard of poor Bella's accident."

"More than likely you have come to have a look for yourself at what is going on here," Lady Mott said, bluntly demolishing Lady Eliza's charitable pretensions. "I declare I never saw such a muddle as Bella has got herself into now! There she lies, put down on her bed with a sprain and her nerves, while this turkey-cock comes in to rule the roast! If I were in her place, give me leave to tell you, not another night would I spend under this roof, if they carried me out of it to my grave!"

Lady Eliza laughed. "Oh, Lucinda, indeed, you are too severe," she said. "Shannon won't *eat* her, you know! And if you are thinking of Miss Power—I doubt exceedingly that he will try the same game twice in the same family."

"No, indeed he won't," Lady Mott said roundly, "for I intend to carry her home directly with me."

This was too much for Georgina, who did not at all care to be made an object of discussion between the two ladies, as if she were no more than a child.

"As to *that*, Lady Mott," she said with dignity, "as deeply as I appreciate your kind invitation, I really believe I ought not to leave Cousin Bella. I shall remain here as long as she does."

"The deuce you say!" Lady Mott said, in her forthright manner. "Why, I have spoken to Bella and she quite agrees with me that you should be got out of the way."

"I am not a child, Lady Mott!"

Lady Eliza gave her tinkle of laughter again. "No, indeed you are not!" she said. "Which is precisely, my dear, why Lucinda is so anxious to have you out of this." She was seated facing the door, and at this moment her face suddenly lit up with a sparkle of mischief. "But here is Shannon himself!" she said. "Do let us have him in! Shannon! Shannon! Do you not mean to say good morning to your guests?"

Georgina, her eyes snapping across to the door at Lady Eliza's first intimation that Shannon had come into the house, saw him pause in the hall and then come deliberately forward toward the door of the book-room. He was accompanied by Brandon, who came limping in behind him with a frown that seemed to show that neither Lady Mott nor Lady Eliza was a particular favorite of his.

"Good morning, Lady Eliza," Shannon said, with the same rather indifferent composure that had so nettled Georgina the day before.

She fancied that Lady Eliza did not care a great deal for it, either, for there was a note of resentment in her voice as she said, giving him her hand in a negligent gesture, "I see that you are still the same odious creature, Shannon! Have you *no* sympathy for poor Mrs. Quinlevan? Laid down on her bed, and *you* taking over her house—"

"On the contrary, Lady Eliza, it is *my* house." Shannon ignored the slight pat on the sofa beside her with which Lady Eliza had indicated that he was to take his place there, and instead strolled over to the mantelpiece and leaned his shoulders against it, driving his hands into his pockets. "And I have every sympathy for Mrs. Quinlevan," he continued, "which is precisely why I have taken up residence here, rather than see the entire place fall into a state of chaos."

Lady Eliza and Lady Mott, each in her own way, received this speech with an air of complete scepticism, and Lady Mott was moved to utter the comment, "Stuff!"

But Brandon, unexpectedly, came to his host's defense.

"He's right, you know!" he said warmly. "He has spent the entire morning taking things in hand here, and I mean to tell you he has them running more smoothly already!" He grinned appreciatively. "He even has Cook eating out of his hand, if you'll believe it, and as a result I daresay we may have a tolerable sort of dinner here today, instead of the messes we are used to."

At this point Georgina, feeling obliged once more, in this muddled situation, to act as hostess, made Mr. Shannon known to Lady Mott and her daughter in a cool voice which indicated that only a stern sense of the proprieties impelled her to recognise his presence at all. Lady Mott at once added to the effect by rising and saying to him forthrightly, "We are not come to call upon *you*, Mr. Shannon, but to visit Mrs. Quinlevan and Miss Power. Georgina, my dear, if you will direct the servants to send your portmanteaux to Mott House this afternoon, I see no reason why you should not leave with us at once."

Shannon's brows went up, and he looked at Georgina.

"You are leaving us, then, Miss Power?" he asked, without—as far as she could determine—the slightest interest in whether she was or was not.

"No!" she said quickly. "That is—Lady Mott, *indeed* I appreciate your kindness, but I cannot feel it is right for me to leave my cousin under these circumstances." She saw Shannon's brows rise again, which infuriated her further. "Not," she said, "but that I should be *most* happy to leave this house—"

"Then do so, by all means," Shannon said. "I imagine that you can be of little real use to Mrs. Quinlevan, and as I understand it may be some time before she may be expected to leave here, I should advise you not to turn down such an excellent offer."

Georgina coloured warmly. "Nonetheless, I shall remain here, Mr. Shannon," she said, adding pointedly, "I cannot see that it concerns *you*. I assure you, my cousin will bear any expense that is incurred."

He laughed unexpectedly, interrupting her. "No, no, I am not so clutchfisted as that!" he said. "You may suit yourself, Miss Power." He pushed his shoulders away from the mantelpiece. "Lady Eliza, my compliments to Colonel Malladon. Lady Mott—Miss Mott—your servant. Brandon, if you are coming with me, come along."

He strode out of the room without further ado, leaving Georgina seething. Lady Eliza looking piqued, and Lady Mott bristling.

"You are right for once, Eliza," the latter declared. "He really is an insufferable man, and has wound Brandon around his little finger already, I see. *And* I expect you, too, miss!" she rounded on Georgina.

Georgina choked. "I! I assure you, ma'am—"

Lady Eliza laughed. "Why, they are at daggers' points, Lucinda; you must be quite paperskulled if you haven't seen that!" she said. She went on, to Georgina, "I believe you intend to stay only to plague him, you wicked girl. But take care! He really can be quite a brute, you know. In fact, I shouldn't scruple to call him dangerous."

A suddenly meaningful note in her bantering voice made Lady Mott look at her sharply, but the next moment she had risen and was saying in a quite different tone, "But do let us go now, Lucinda. I am sure we have stayed quite long enough; I believe I must not inflict another visitor on Bella this morning. Georgina, my love, I have made up my mind that we are to be great friends. As soon as Bella is up and about again and you are removed to Craythorne, I expect you to be constantly at Stokings. I shall be giving a ball in May, you know, and there will be a great deal of company in the house."

Georgina murmured some polite response, feeling that she might indeed find a ball at Stokings enjoyable, but hoping at the same time that she would be fortunate enough to find somewhat more congenial friends in Ireland than Lady Eliza. She did not at all care for her manners, which might do very well in a certain fashionable London set of which she had heard, though she had never met anyone who belonged to it, and she felt, besides, that there was a certain animosity toward herself on Lady Eliza's part, which she was discerning enough to realise came from her dislike of being outshone by a younger, prettier woman.

If Lady Eliza were indeed to have "a great friend" of the female sex, Georgina was quite certain she would be plain and dull and certainly at least as old as the lady herself.

CHAPTER 6

As the days went by Georgina found that even Lady Eliza's company would have been a welcome relief to her.

Quite unthinkingly, by her refusal of Lady Mott's invitation, she had placed herself in a highly unenviable situation. Shannon's presence in the house, when it became known in the neighbourhood, was an effective preventive of any further calls, though messages and gifts for the invalid arrived in an almost constant flow. At the same time, her own professed devotion to the task of attending Mrs. Quinlevan's sick bed kept her from receiving any of the invitations that would have been forthcoming had it been known that, in fact, she could be of little use to her cousin.

Nora Quill would not consider leaving her post as nurse to anyone as inexperienced as Miss Power—a decision that was reinforced by her patient's own preference. Indeed, Georgina soon found that her presence in the sick room only agitated her cousin, by putting her in mind of the disagreeable situation in which she had placed her young guest by inviting her to her home at such a time, and thus she fell into the habit of limiting her visits to a brief quarter hour twice a day.

This left her with a great deal of time on her hands. There was Brandon, of course, but his afternoons were occupied with sessions with the elderly clergyman who acted as his tutor, and as he, too, had taken her at her word, that she cared to have nothing to do with Shannon, it seemingly never occurred to him to invite her to accompany them on their morning rides or drives around the estate. Georgina thought rather vengefully that Shannon was properly served by having Brandon tagging about everywhere after him like a friendly puppy, for certainly any use that he might have made of him initially in seeking acquaintance with The Place had soon been exhausted. Brandon knew nothing about either farming or money management, and it was apparent to any unbiassed onlooker that his sole interest in attending Shannon so faithfully was in Shannon's company itself.

It did not occur to her that the boy, who since Declan Power's death had been thrown almost exclusively in the company of women, except for servants and his elderly tutor, was starved for male companionship, particularly that of an older man who might act as a mentor. All she saw in Brandon's predilection for Shannon's company was a direct flouting of her own pronounced dislike of the new owner of The Place, and, as a consequence, the relationship between the two cousins was so lacking in cordiality at this period that it seemed almost to have reached the state of mutual dislike.

She might have been more content to see her cousin ride out with Shannon every day if she could have had the pleasure of a daily ride herself, with no better company than that of a groom, but unfortunately the reduced stables that Mrs. Quinlevan had kept since Declan Power's death could not provide her with a proper mount. There was no horse suitable for a lady, except the elderly cob that Brandon, to his bitter disappointment, was condemned by his invalid state to ride and a single dawdling, frustrating excursion on this animal had convinced Georgina that she would rather walk.

So she went for long rambles to pass the time, thinking longingly, on the days when Shannon was driving the gig, of the handsome blood-mare he had bought for himself that was standing idle in the stable. But she would have bitten her tongue off before she would have asked his permission to ride any of his horses.

Soon, as one empty day followed another, she began first to wish that she had never come to Ireland and then to cast about for something to lighten the tedium of her present existence. She found it, about a week after Mrs. Quinlevan's accident, in an escapade she was quite certain her cousin would have disapproved of, had she known of it—but then she had no idea of telling Cousin Bella what she was about.

The idea had come to her when she had broken one of

her solitary rambles at the Lynch cottage and had been persuaded by Cilly Lynch, Dansel's eldest daughter, to stop
for a cup of tea and a slice of fresh-baked raisin-cake. Cilly
was full of the wedding that was to take place the following
day at one of the neighbouring cottages on the estate, and
in speaking of it to Georgina she described the Kerry custom of "strawing" the newly married pair. A group of
boys, she said, were already preparing the straw caps, hats,
and skirts in which they would disguise themselves to visit
the wedding house. The "strawboys," as they were called,
would march in order to the house, where they would join
the festivities while still maintaining their disguise, dance
and sing with the guests, and then march off again.

What the significance of the straw costumes was Cilly
could not say. She knew only that "strawing" was an ancient
Kerry custom, and that it was usually impossible, owing
to the nature of the costumes, which made their wearers
look like walking haystacks, for the disguise of the strawboys to be penetrated.

Georgina, seated in the neat cottage drinking her tea,
first thought regretfully of the jollity that would occur so
close to The Place, and yet so far removed from her; from
this it was only a step, in her bored and restless state of
mind, to the idea that it would be perfectly possible for her
to disguise herself, with Cilly's connivance, as one of the
strawboys, and thus have at least a taste of the excitement
of the wedding festivities. It was the sort of prank that Sir
John, with his lack of appreciation of the conventions and
niceties with which well-brought-up young girls were hob-
bled, would have had no objection to her planning when
she had been half a dozen years younger.

It did not occur to her—or if it did, she put the thought
wilfully from her mind—that she was no longer a twelve-
year-old schoolgirl engaging in a lark, but a young lady
whose dignity would be sadly compromised if she were to
be discovered in such a masquerade.

Cilly was by no means an obstacle to her plans. Indeed,
she fell in with them with the greatest enthusiasm, promising to procure the proper "strawboy" attire for her and to
ensure her acceptance in the company by taking into her
confidence her youngest brother, who was to be one of the
strawing party.

"He can give out ye're a cousin of ours from Kilgarvan," she said. "He's a shy lad, that niver has two words to say for himself, and sure ye needn't open your mouth at all if ye've no mind to, miss: Oh, it'll be rare fun! I doubt I'll be able to keep from laughing when you walk in with the others!"

"Well, you must not laugh," Georgina warned her sternly, "for if you do everyone will wonder why, and I wouldn't for the world have anyone know of it but you and Tim."

She found that she was growing a little uncomfortable over the escapade already, as Cilly's inventiveness cleared away all the obstacles to it that had seemed to her to exist when she had first broached the matter. But she was too proud to admit this to Cilly, and when she returned to the house she was fully committed to the masquerade.

She had no difficulty, on the following evening, in finding her straw disguise in the spinney where Cilly had promised to leave it, but donning the stiffly pleated cape and skirt so that they perfectly covered her own clothing took some time, and she had only just completed the task to her satisfaction when she heard footsteps in the little wood. It was Cilly's brother Tim, a boy of fifteen, come to fetch her along to the others. He showed her how to pull the tall, pointed straw cap down over her head so that her golden curls and even her face were quite concealed, using a bare minimum of words to convey his instructions, for he seemed to be quite tonguetied at the idea of a young lady's joining in their merrymaking. Georgina was obliged to repeat each question at least twice before she could elicit a response from him, and almost found herself in a fit of giggles at the contrast between the tall, ungainly figure before her, in its stiff straw costume, and the choked adolescent utterances that proceeded from it.

But at last all was arranged to her satisfaction, and the two set off together toward the lane where they were to join the other strawboys.

They soon came in view of them, some fifteen strong. Georgina felt her resolution failing a little as she was confronted with all this exuberant youthful masculinity, even concealed as she was in her straw disguise, but she suffered herself to be introduced as young Master Lynch's cousin and then marched off beside him at the tail of the ranks that were immediately formed. Fortunately the wedding house was around the next turn in the lane. As the whole company was occupied, in the interval before their arrival, in receiving their captain's instructions as to what they were to do when they arrived there, no severe strain was placed on Georgina's anonymity.

The sounds of music and laughter came to her ears as they approached the cottage, and through the open half-door she could see a fiddler leaning against the wall in the kitchen, his bow flying as he played a gay reel for a throng of dancers. The set was broken up, however, as the straw-boys entered, and the guests all came crowding up to see the grotesque visitors. Georgina found herself forgetting her apprehensions as she saw that her disguise indeed seemed to be impenetrable, and for the first time began to be glad that she had come. The cheerful cottage, with its newly whitewashed walls, its jovial company, all dressed in their best, and its welcoming aroma of raisin-cakes and succulent roast pig, appeared especially inviting to her after the jumbled disorder and severe isolation she had been enduring at The Place, and she made up her mind to enjoy the evening.

She stood in the ranks of the strawboys as they sang for the entertainment of the company, not venturing to join in herself, but very well pleased to be where she was. She had been relieved, as they had approached the cottage, to learn that only four of the strawing company had been singled out to take part in the dancing, and that her role would be only that of mingling silently with the guests, nodding her head in grave response to their most outrageous guesses as to her identity, and eluding their attempts to make her betray herself by an incautious word. She saw Cilly standing beside the bride, hiding her giggles behind her hand and looking from one to another of the strawboys as she attempted to decide which one of them was Georgina.

Suddenly, however, in the midst of the cheers and the hubbub as the reel came to an end, her heart gave a jump of apprehension. A new guest had entered the house, someone whose presence caused an immediate hum of interest among the company and an abrupt fall in the merriment. From her position beside the dresser she herself had an ex-

cellent view of the door, and her first impulse, on seeing
Shannon's tall figure entering it, was to flee—but, of
course, this was quite impossible. She must remain where
she was and only hope with the greatest fervour that the
disguise which had thus far protected her from discovery
would see her through this further test.

Shrinking back against the wall, she watched with trepidation as Shannon offered his felicitations to the bride and
groom. He seemed quite at ease among his new tenants, she
noted, and they, too, after their first surprise at his appearing among them, soon overcame their shyness and crowded
around him, full of pleasure, it seemed, at the compliment
he was paying them. In her own severe disapproval of him,
she would not have been astonished to find that he had already been taken in dislike by his tenants, but it appeared
that exactly the opposite was the case. He knew almost
every one of them by name, and though she found much to
reinforce her own opinion of his arrogance in the calm,
rather aloof manner with which he dealt with them, apparently they considered this as only proper to his position.

How he had wrought all this approval for himself she
was puzzled to know. She did recall, however, Sir John's
having remarked to her once that no landlord who knew to
a T what he was about and who made it his business to see
that his tenants were given every opportunity to make the
best of their land would ever run into difficulties with them.
She was loth to admit it, but it did seem to her, from the
tone of the conversation she heard about her now, that
these were the tactics Shannon had used to cause himself to
be accepted so promptly by his tenants. No doubt most of
them, like Dansel Lynch, had been sorry to see the land go
from the Powers, and apprehensive as to the intentions of
the new master—but it seemed equally probable that, once
they had seen that those intentions were meant for their
benefit as well as his own, they were quite willing to be rid
of the inexpert regime under which they had laboured ever
since Declan Power's death.

Georgina's reflections to this purpose were both hurried
and distracted, however, as she was in mortal fear of discovery and occupied in casting about desperately in her
mind for some way to escape from Shannon's presence.
She thought once, as he accepted the foaming glass of

porter that was offered to him in which to drink the newly married pair's health, that his quick grey eyes had singled her out from the strawboy company for a moment's hard inspection, but the next instant he had turned away and she could thankfully breathe again.

All this while she had been keeping her eye on the door, and when the host escorted Shannon into "the room," where the wedding supper had been set out, she saw her opportunity and, under cover of the general move of the company to follow Shannon, edged toward the half-door and slipped through it. Once outside, she breathed a sigh of relief and set off as rapidly as she was able, in her clumsy costume, down the lane. She did not dare remove the straw disguise so close to the cottage, and intended to wait to do so until she had reached the spinney where she had donned it.

She was still some yards short of it, however, when she became aware of the sound of a horse's hooves behind her. The next moment, before she had had time to do more than glance hastily about and see that it was a gig that was bearing down on her, she heard Shannon's voice imperatively calling her name.

"Wait just a moment, Miss Power," he said, drawing up beside her, as she halted in the lane in complete confusion, and speaking in a perfectly matter-of-fact way, as if she had been standing before him clad in the ordinary costume of a well-bred young lady, instead of in her grotesque straw attire. "You have some distance to go to reach the house, and I believe it is coming on to rain. If you will mount up beside me, I shall be happy to drive you home."

His calm certainty that he was correct in his assumption that it was really Miss Power he was addressing for some reason infuriated her to the point that her wrath overcame even her mortification at having been discovered.

"How did you know who I was?" she demanded. "No one else did!"

"I shouldn't be too certain of that, if I were you," he said dryly. "These people have a great deal of tact, Miss Power, and if they were to observe a strawboy wearing footwear of a sort that assuredly is not common among country lads, they would not necessarily take it on themselves to embarrass him—or her—by calling attention to the fact."

She instinctively looked down at the tips of the soft blue slippers peeping from beneath her straw skirt and hastily drew them back into hiding.

"I am afraid it is rather late for that now," Shannon remarked, observing the movement. "As a matter of fact, if I may suggest it, it may be as well for you to remove your entire disguise now, before you attempt to mount up here beside me. My horse, as you can see, seems to have taken it into considerable aversion."

She could only admire the way in which he was controlling, with a seeming lack of effort, the spirited attempts of the young grey he was driving to escape from the vicinity of the startling object she presented. But the admiration did not mollify her wrath, and she replied mulishly, "I have no intention of mounting up beside you, Mr. Shannon, I shall walk home."

"I beg to differ with you, Miss Power. You will do nothing of the kind," he said incisively. "If you have so little sense of the impropriety of a young lady's wandering about alone at night, in or out of disguise, let me assure you that I do not share your lack of concern over the picture you present."

She could not see his face well in the darkness, but she could quite fancy she knew the sort of indifferently arrogant expression it wore. She felt that she was losing her temper completely, in the unfortunate way she had when she had been backed into a corner and knew she was entirely in the wrong, and only with the greatest effort managed to say with reasonable quietness, "How I conduct myself is not in the least your affair, Mr. Shannon. I consider your remarks very intrusive."

"Yes, they are—damned intrusive," he said bluntly. "But there would be no need for me to have made them if you weren't displaying a want of conduct that would make a hoyden blush! As for making it my affair—you are living beneath my roof, Miss Power, and while you are doing so I must demand that you refrain from making yourself the subject of gossip! Once you have removed to Craythorne you may go your length in any folly that pleases you, but while you are in my house you will behave like a lady.

Now remove that ridiculous costume and get up here beside me. I have no mind to enter into any more arguments."

She had the satisfaction of gathering, from a sterner note in these last words, that she had succeeded in making him angry as well, but at the same time she also discovered, somewhat to her surprise, that she had no wish to test that anger further. Hastily, with mutinous fingers, she divested herself of her straw costume and, grasping the hand he reached down to her, mounted into the gig.

Once seated beside him, it had been her intention to maintain a frigid silence until they reached The Place, but the urge to justify herself was too strong, and before the gig had proceeded a dozen yards down the lane she found herself saying warmly, "There is no need for you to say such things to me! I had as much right as you to go to the wedding."

"You had a right to go as Miss Power, if you went properly escorted and for the proper reason, not to make a May-game of yourself," he said brusquely. "But you don't need me to teach you manners, my girl."

"No, I don't! And I'll thank you not to try!"

She stifled a sob of pure vexation at having been caught out by Shannon, of all people. Of course she could not defend herself against his merciless logic; she knew as well as he did that she had been entirely in the wrong. She sat rigidly beside him, feeling every moment that passed to be as long as an hour, and wishing fervently that he would put his horse to a faster pace so that they would reach the house sooner.

The only palliative possible for her miserable state was the suspicion that at least she had made him as angry as she was—but even this consolation was snatched from her when he remarked abruptly, after a silence of several minutes, "I expect the trouble is that you've been devilish bored. Young Quinlevan says you ride well. Why don't you work out some of your energy in that way, instead of haring off into a childish prank like this?"

She did not know whether to be more astonished at this revelation that he understood her predicament or offended by his continuing to make her conduct his own affair. Between the two emotions, she managed to say quellingly, "No, thank you! If you had ever had the misfortune to try one of my cousins' horses—!"

"I am not speaking of them. I mean my own. I don't consider Juno suitable for a lady, but there is a very good-looking chestnut hack Hanger brought in this morning from Kenmare that should carry you to perfection."

Her colour rose; taken aback, she could only say, "But I can't—! I couldn't—!"

"Why not?" he asked. "Don't you think you could handle him?"

"Of course that is not it! It is only—I don't care to accept favours from you, Mr. Shannon!"

He laughed shortly. "I'm aware that a few hours' loan of a horse is a very small recompence for having pushed you out of the way of inheriting a fortune, Miss Power," he said. "But still I don't believe you should reject the offer, if it will keep you from entering into any more such crackbrained starts as you have indulged in tonight."

She stared at him in astonishment. It had never crossed her mind that he believed that the incivility with which she had treated him since his arrival at The Place had been the result of her resentment at his having stepped between her and her cousin Nuala's fortune, and the mere idea that he suspected her of such a motive was enough to cause her to flush up hotly with indignation and confusion.

"But that's not—! I never thought—!" she stammered.

"Never thought what, Miss Power?"

"That I— That you— I never expected to inherit The Place; I never gave such an idea a thought!"

She could see him turn his head to look at her incredulously through the darkness.

"Do you expect me to believe that," his caustic voice demanded, "when you've been cutting me up ever since I stepped into the house?"

"But that was only because—" She halted abruptly, feeling quite unable to explain to him that it was his own arrogance, rather than any monetary considerations, that had caused her to take him in such instant dislike. She sent him a quick sidelong glance, almost an appeal to him to smooth the situation over with some innocuous remark, but he showed no disposition to make matters easier for her.

"Because—?" he repeated ruthlessly. "Yes, Miss Power? I am waiting."

Her temper flared again. "Because you were rude, and overbearing, and inclined to consider no one but yourself!" she finished her sentence baldly. "And that is the plain truth, Mr. Shannon! You may believe it or not, but I never had an idea of inheriting The Place, and if you think I am such an odious creature as to take someone in dislike merely because I am covetous of his good fortune—"

Shannon inclined his head rather ironically. "I accept your condemnation of my manners, Miss Power," he said, "but don't you think you are taking something too much for granted when you speak of my wife's death as my 'good fortune'? That is a subject on which I believe you are hardly qualified to speak with authority."

"I didn't mean— That was not what I meant to imply," she began defensively. "I *don't* know about that—and if you are grieved for her death it was very uncharitable of me—" He said nothing to help her out, and she went on finally, rather hotly, "You have put me in the wrong, but that doesn't alter matters. You *have* been detestably rude, and I won't take that back."

"I see no need for you to do so," he said, with his usual maddening composure. "On the other hand, I also see no need for you to decline my offer of the use of one of my horses for a few hours a day merely because you find my manners leave a great deal to be desired. If it will make you more inclined to do so, I will inform you that my motives in making the offer are purely selfish. As I have told you, it doesn't suit me to have you careering about the countryside like a rag-mannered brat while you are living under my roof."

She was silent from sheer vexation. The worst part of the situation was that she was longing to accept his offer, and that he seemed quite aware of this, for after a moment he went on, in an amused tone, "Pride has its drawbacks, has it not, Miss Power? Brandon tells me that you are as clipping a rider as any girl he has ever seen, so I can't think you prefer to go rambling about on foot to being mounted on a prime hack. However, if you really wish to carry your disapproval of me so far as to object to being indebted to me for the smallest favour—"

"I *don't* wish to carry it so far, but I shall," she said darkly. "No doubt it will be good for me, at any rate. Grandmama says one always derives a great deal of moral advantage from putting one's duty before one's inclinations."

"The question is," Shannon said, still with a note of amusement in his voice, "would she consider it your duty to snub me?"

"Yes, she would!" Georgina declared instantly. "Good gracious, if she could see me now—!" She broke off, daunted again by the road into which her imprudent tongue was leading her. "Not that I at all agree with her ideas on *that* point," she said hastily, in a severely judicious tone. "What I mean is—*she* does not know you, or anything about you except that you married Nuala, so she had no grounds on which to judge you."

"You, on the other hand," he said, with perfect gravity, "had the advantage of at least thirty seconds of observation before you made up *your* mind."

"I didn't!" she objected hotly. "It was a great deal longer!"

"On the contrary, I have probably overestimated the time. The expression on your face when I walked into the book-room—"

"I was upset over my cousin's accident! Of course I did not appear cordial!" She broke off, shrugging her shoulders. "Besides, I am sure it did not signify to you how I looked. You had already made up your mind to be disagreeable; you had not been *five* seconds in the room before I knew that."

"We may cry quits, then," he said. "But I still do not see why you refuse to try the horse. *That* is mere obstinacy."

As obstinacy was one fault for which not only Lady Mercer, but also Sir John, had frequently rebuked her, she was unable to defend herself with conviction against this charge. At any rate, she found that she did not particularly wish to do so; the more she considered the sacrifice to which her pride was committing her, the more strongly it occurred to her that, in rejecting Shannon's offer, she was, in the old nursery phrase, cutting off her nose to spite her face.

She said cautiously, as the windows of The Place came in sight, "Well, as to that—perhaps you are right. And I daresay the horse *will* want exercising."

"Not a doubt of it," he agreed, in a matter-of-fact voice that won her approbation, as it contained no hint whatever of triumph in it. He brought the gig up the carriage-sweep and halted it before the front door, looking down at her then with a glint of rather sardonic amusement, she thought, again in his eyes. "I won't see you inside," he said. "After all, it would never do to let the servants know that you have been driving with me."

"I was *not* driving with you!" she said, with dignity. "You merely insisted on taking me up, when I would much rather have walked. That is another matter altogether."

"So it is," he said. The amusement disappeared and he said indifferently, "At any rate, it will do your credit no good to be seen in my company, so I shall bid you good night, Miss Power. I'll give instructions to Hanger to have the new chestnut ready for you in the morning."

She thought with still-smouldering indignation, as she mounted the steps to the front door, that he was taking a good deal on himself, as she had not actually agreed to accept the loan of his horse. But she was too much occupied during the next few minutes in coping with the obvious astonishment of Higgins, who opened the door to her, and of Brandon, who came walking out of the book-room, at seeing her come in alone at that hour of the night to have the leisure to think of such matters. Higgins' astonishment was modestly confined to an expression of lively curiosity, but Brandon was not so reticent, and he demanded directly to know where she had been.

"Nowhere! That is—for a walk. It is not your business, Brandon!" she said with some asperity.

She walked directly up the stairs, meaning to go to her bedchamber, but she found that Brandon was following her, and at the head of the stairs she stopped and turned around. He said at once, as he climbed the remaining steps. "Not my business! Well, I should think it was *somebody's* then, if you mean to go wandering about alone at this hour! What is the *matter* with you, Georgie? You've been out of reason cross ever since Shannon arrived here, and now you take to slipping out at night—"

"I didn't *slip!*" Georgina said indignantly. "I walked. And I'm tired now, and I'm going to bed. Much you care what I do, at any rate! As far as you are concerned, I might as well not have existed this past week!"

She walked into her bedchamber and closed the door in his face, feeling some satisfaction at having given him, at least, a heavy set-down. The next instant she had grace enough to regret her action, as she was sufficiently honest to admit to herself that what he had been obliged to receive from her should properly have been Shannon's portion. She was not enough in charity with her cousin either, however, to feel much compunction over what she had done, only promising herself to make matters right with him on the morrow.

CHAPTER 7

She rose early in the morning, hoping to see her cousin before he should have gone out with Shannon, but, on inquiring for him when she went downstairs, she was told that both he and Shannon had already gone round to the stables. She felt both disappointed and relieved, as making apologies was not one of her strong suits, and sat down to eat her breakfast with only one pressing matter on her mind—whether or not she would take Shannon at his word and try his new horse that morning.

The view from the breakfast-parlour windows eventually decided that question for her by presenting her with the sight of a perfect spring morning, dew-drenched after a night's gentle rain. The idea of sitting in the house on such a day weighted the scales so decisively in favour of a morning ride that, after a dutiful visit to Mrs. Quinlevan's bedchamber, she went immediately to her own room and donned her riding-habit. She had prudently failed to mention her intentions to her cousin, not so much from the fear that she would disapprove of her accepting Shannon's offer —for it had long been a maxim of Mrs. Quinlevan's never to look either a figurative or a literal gift horse in the mouth—but because of her own embarrassment over being required to explain how he had come to make it.

When she repaired to the stables Shannon's groom, Hanger, at once led out a good-looking chestnut and proceeded to put a lady's saddle on it. This was cool enough, Georgina thought, with mild indignation—as if Shannon had quite taken it for granted that she would wish to ride that morning—but when Hanger brought out one of the greys and saddled it as well before helping her up on her own mount, the indignation turned to resolution.

"You are not thinking of coming with me, surely?" she said. "Where is Grady?"

"Begging your pardon, miss, he's off on an errand for the mistress."

Hanger was a rather slightly built Scotsman, of an age that might have been nearer fifty than forty, as wiry as a whip, and with a dark, pockmarked face which one of the maids had declared in Georgina's hearing to be "enough to fright a babe out of its cradle." He said nothing further now, as if he believed sufficient explanation had been given of his intention to accompany her, but Georgina, when he came round to help her up on her mount, stood looking at him obstinately.

"There is no need for you to go with me," she said. "I am quite accustomed to riding without a groom."

Hanger's dark face remained impassive. "Master's orders, miss," he said briefly.

"Well, he may be *your* master, but he is certainly not *mine*," Georgina said, firing up. "I shall *not* need you, Hanger."

He said nothing, but merely tossed her up on the chestnut. The next moment, however, as she gathered the reins and set the horse into a walk, she heard telltale sounds behind her, and turned to see that Hanger had already swung himself up into his own saddle in preparation to follow her.

There was nothing else for it, she could not engage in a dispute with him under the eyes of gaping stable-boys. With an inward vow to say not a word to him or to indicate by so much as a turn of her head that she was aware of his presence, she set the chestnut into a smart trot and then, as she left the house behind, loosened the reins and cantered off briskly.

She had not been on a horse since she had come to Ireland, with the exception of her single doleful excursion on Brandon's cob, and soon the combination of a high-bred mount and a fine morning did much to improve her humour. Spring was in full blossom now; everywhere she looked great bushes of English furze, the branches of which were much used as firewood by the country people, were showing their rich yellow bloom, and purple violets and bluebells sprang in the coverts beside every hedge. She let the chestnut go into a long, intoxicating gallop, which apparently suited his idea of the proper use of such a morning as well as it did her own, and when she reined him in at last was so much in charity with the world that she could even look around with a smile for Hanger, to see if he was still following her.

He was close behind and, pulling up his grey to walk sedately beside her, said with dour approval, "You handle him to perfection, miss. I told the master he'd make a sweet goer, but I wasn't thinking at the time of him carrying a lady."

"He is a darling," Georgina agreed enthusiastically, reaching out to stroke the chestnut's mane.

"A bit more horse than you need, miss, but that never daunted you."

She laughed at his respectful tone and said, "I expect Mr. Shannon thought I might be 'daunted,' and that was why he insisted you go with me?"

He grinned briefly, but did not deny the charge.

She let her curiosity get the better of her and inquired, "Have you been with him long, Hanger? You're not from these parts, evidently?"

"Oh, no, miss. I was in Lord Cartan's service for twenty years, and I've known the master for that long, too. I set him on his first pony, if you'll know the truth."

He spoke with some pride and she realized, with the same surprise she had felt when she had witnessed Shannon's reception by his tenants the night before, that this man, too, held his employer in respect, if not in downright affection. It made her still more uncertain of her own judgment of him, for she had been taught by Sir John to realize that a man who could make himself respected by those who must serve him could not be without valuable qualities of character.

It would have suited her far better to learn that Hanger considered his employer as arrogant and disagreeable as he appeared to her; but she was fair-minded enough to consider it probable that her own judgment of Shannon was biassed, rather than that of someone who had been as intimately acquainted with him as Hanger had been. She rode back to the house in a rather thoughtful mood.

Shannon, as usual, did not appear at luncheon, but Brandon was there, apparently already acquainted with the fact that she had ridden Shannon's horse that morning.

"You were a gudgeon not to have asked him to mount you sooner," he said frankly. "I told him you were quite up even to handling Juno."

"I did *not* ask him for the loan of his horse!" Georgina exclaimed, her cheeks flying scarlet in a moment. "How can you suppose me to have so much brass?—when I sit there evening after evening at the dinner table, never saying a word to him—"

"Oh—that!" Brandon said kindly. "I daresay he only thinks you are rather shy."

"He knows quite well I am not!" Georgina said darkly, attacking the galantine accompanying the game pie and fruit that had been set before them, and acknowledging for the twentieth time how much the meals in the house had improved since Shannon had come into it. "*He* made me the offer."

"Well, it is handsome of him to let a girl handle his cattle; you'll admit that, at any rate," Brandon said. "Not that I hadn't told him you were up to anything, for I don't expect he'd have cared to chance it if I hadn't." He helped himself to the game pie and went on, "He has his eye out for a couple of hunters now, and I told him I'd bring him over to Hauld Hall tomorrow; Sir Landers has a slapping five-year-old there that ain't quite up to his weight. Do you know Sir Landers Hession? I daresay you don't—nor Lady Hession, neither, for she and Mama don't deal above half. Devilish high sticklers, both she and Sir Landers, but you can't deny that he knows good horseflesh."

Georgina did not attend very closely to this speech; she was too much occupied with the vexing problem, which had suddenly arisen in her mind, of how she was to behave toward Shannon at dinner that evening. She could not very well snub him as she was used to, after she had accepted the loan of his horse, but the idea of presenting him with an appearance of complaisant gratitude, in the circumstances under which she had accepted his offer, was hardly to be thought of, either.

She carried the problem around with her all afternoon and the result was that by the time the dinner hour had arrived she had fretted herself into a state of indecision which

for some reason required her to don one of her most becoming dresses—a primrose muslin with a narrow skirt and
a bodice trimmed with rows of ruching—before she came
downstairs.

She found Shannon and her cousin awaiting her appearance to enter the dining-room, and as she passed before the
former through the doorway she gave him a tentative,
"Good evening." He replied at once in kind, but something
in the look in his eyes as he did so gave her an uncomfortable remembrance of the rather sardonic gleam she had
caught there the night before, and instantly her hackles
went up.

She sat down at the table with an uncompromising gravity of manner, the formal words of thanks that she had been
rehearsing all afternoon dying on her lips. She consoled
herself with the consideration that it would be more natural
to wait until some turn in the conversation afforded her a
logical opening before she uttered them, and determined to
sink into the background for the time being—a resolution
that was immediately thwarted, however, by Brandon's remarking in surprise on her elegant appearance.

"Lord, you are fine enough for a ball!" he said frankly.
"I will say it becomes you, but you had better not waste all
that on Shannon and me. Wait until we are fixed at Craythorne, and then you'll have plenty of opportunity to parade
your duds."

"I am not *parading* anything!" Georgina said, giving him
a look of wrathful reproach. "And—I am extremely sorry
if you feel my frock is inappropriate."

"Not inappropriate. It's just that we ain't used to seeing
you look all the crack like that," Brandon explained, attacking the raised mutton pie which the cook had provided
along with a baked carp and a dish of French beans.

Georgina gave him a damping look, which he quite
disregarded. She then glanced up to find Shannon's eyes regarding her across the table with a faint, rather disconcert-
ing smile, and her composure deserted her entirely.

"I expect you are waiting for me to thank you for the
loan of your horse this morning," she said, blurting the
words out, to her own vexation, in the most graceless manner possible.

The look of amusement deepened for a moment on

Shannon's face, and then disappeared as he remarked in his usual manner that he trusted she had had an agreeable ride.

"It would have been more agreeable if you had not instructed Hanger that he must come with me," she said. "I wish you will tell him that he needn't do so tomorrow."

"If you will take Grady with you, or one of Mrs. Quinlevan's grooms, he will need no telling," Shannon said.

"Yes, but even if I do not," Georgina persisted, "there is no need for him to go."

"There I beg to differ with you," Shannon said calmly. "Do young ladies in Herefordshire make it a habit to ride about the countryside unattended?"

She was about to say that whether they did or did not was hardly his affair, but, remembering her escapade of the night before and the set-down he had given her then, she swallowed down the retort.

"I expect the thing of it is that you are afraid I cannot manage the chestnut," she said instead, mutinously.

He raised his eyes to her face. "Not at all," he said. "Hanger tells me he has the greatest admiration for your skill. That, however, has nothing to do with the matter of your riding alone."

Brandon intervened at this point to say innocently that, if she found it a bore to ride with only a groom, she might accompany him and Shannon to Hauld Hall in the morning to look at Sir Landers' five-year-old—a remark that elicited only a firm, "No, thank you!" from her. If Brandon was such a nodcock as to believe that her jauntering about the countryside with Shannon, with only himself as chaperon, would not do more to rouse the neighbourhood gabblemongers than her riding alone, she was not.

The subject fell there, but the next morning, when she watched her cousin and Shannon ride off together while she set out alone under Grady's sedate charge, she could not help rather regretting her severe adherence to the proprieties, for it would have suited her much better to go along with them to Hauld Hall to see Sir Landers' horse. The invitation had not been repeated, however, so she cantered off with Grady, and soon recovered her good humour in her pleasure in her favorite exercise.

She returned to The Place some time before the luncheon hour, and was surprised to see Brandon's cob already back in the stables. When she walked into the house Brandon himself came out to meet her, and she saw that he looked flushed and angry, quite unlike himself.

"Oh! I thought it might have been Shannon," he said abruptly, as his eyes fell on her, and without further ado he turned on his heel and limped back into the book-room.

Georgina followed him. "Whatever is the matter?" she demanded. "Have you quarrelled with him? Is that it?"

"No, of course not!" Brandon said. He turned about to face her, his eyes resting on her face with a look almost of animosity in them. "The truth is—and I expect you will be deuced glad to hear it!—that the Hessions were thundering rude to him," he said. "I mean to say—well, there was no bearing it, Georgie! Sir Landers had put it all about the neighbourhood that he was looking for a buyer for that horse, and why he should set himself up now with the idea that dealing with Shannon is beneath his touch—!"

Georgina stared at him, frowning slightly. "Do you mean he wouldn't even let him see the horse?" she asked.

"Oh, he let him see it, right enough!" Brandon replied, the angry colour still high in his face. "He could hardly do otherwise, when *I* had brought him. But he made it as plain as a pikestaff that he wanted no part of any acquaintance with him—and then, to make it worse, as we were leaving we were obliged to pass that wretched woman's landaulet—"

"*What* wretched woman?"

"Lady Hession, of course! She was driving out with her two eldest girls, and I did not know *what* to do, after the snubbing Sir Landers had given Shannon—whether to introduce him or not, I mean. But I thought it might look as if *I* was ashamed of being seen with him if I did not, so I did. And that harpy cast her chin up in the air, and gave a glance at her daughters as if she dared them so much as to *look* at Shannon, and ordered her coachman to drive on! I could have run her through!" he concluded, his eyes blazing with reminiscent fury.

Georgina sank down into a chair. She was astonished to find that, far from feeling satisfaction at the set-down Shannon had received, something of Brandon's sharply expressed anger was stirring as well in her own breast. It was one thing, it seemed, for her to cross swords with their host, and quite another for her to hear that some odious female had cut him so rudely.

She awakened from her surprise to find Brandon repeating, "I expect *you* will say it was just what he deserved" —and broke in to contradict him warmly.

"I don't say anything of the sort! It was intolerably unkind of her! After all, he has done nothing to offend *her*."

"Well, I don't know that he had done anything to offend *you*, either, before you took to ripping up at him," Brandon said bluntly, so you needn't give yourself any points over Lady Hession. I don't understand women, I must say— making such a kick-up before they have time to know *what* a fellow is like. Not that Sir Landers wasn't almost as bad."

Georgina said uncomfortably, "I suppose I may have been unjust to him, but you will admit that he has been at least as rude to me as I have been to him! But *this* is another matter altogether. He will have to live among these people, you know, and if this is a sample of the treatment he may expect, it will certainly be excessively uncomfortable for him."

Brandon stared at her. "You are not going to tell me *you* intend to stand on his side now!" he said disbelievingly. "After the things you have said of him—!"

Georgina shrugged, colouring up slightly in her turn. "It is no such thing," she said, with asperity. "Only I can quite see that that stupid woman was shockingly at fault; she might at least have been civil to him. After all, he is not going to eat her precious daughters!"

Brandon, finding his indignation shared, relaxed enough to emit a slight chuckle at this, and owned that Lady Hession might indeed have been thinking of Nuala.

"Yes, that is all very well," Georgina said severely, "but she cannot be so idiotish as to expect that he will be going about the countryside throwing out lures to every stray young woman who happens to come under his eye. If he *did* marry Nuala only for her fortune—which is the worst thing that one can say of him—it is quite clear that he has got it in his hands now and needn't be looking about him for a *second* heiress."

"Deuced little he'd get from any of the Hession girls, at any rate," Brandon said. "There are five of 'em, and, although Peter will come into a very pretty property when he succeeds, Sir Landers is much too fond of good living and good horses to be able to come down handsomely for all those girls when they marry."

"How did Shannon take it?" Georgina demanded. "I expect he did not look cast-down before those people?"

"Oh, Lord, no!" Brandon said. "You know his style—as cool as ice water. If Sir Landers thought *he* was giving the snubbing, he caught one, too, I can tell you! All the same, it's a plaguey awkward business. I don't mean just the Hessions, for they always have been devilish high in the instep, but if people like the Motts and the Malladons mean to act in the same way, I can't think Shannon will have at all a comfortable time of it here. And I *like* him, Georgie; he's a great gun, you know, and it must be a dead bore to him to have me trailing around after him all the time, but he never makes me feel I'm in the way."

Georgina, looking into her cousin's flushed, unhappy face, had a rather guilty realization of the fact that she had scarcely spent a moment's reflection on Brandon's point of view in all this. It could not be often, she told herself, that he found someone willing to overlook his handicap and give him the time and patience necessary to allow him to participate in the normal activities she herself took so much for granted. Whatever Shannon's motives had been, it had to be admitted that he had done so, and Brandon's distress at the thought that the hostility of the neighbourhood might cause him to lose the company of his new friend became quite understandable to her when viewed in such a light.

She carried her thoughtfulness over the matter upstairs with her later that day, when she went to pay her usual afternoon visit to Mrs. Quinlevan's bedchamber. She found her cousin sitting up in bed in high good humour, inspecting the new French lace cap she was wearing in her glass and making plans for an immediate removal to Craythorne.

"Only think, my love," she said, when Georgina entered the room, "Mrs. Hopkins says the house is quite settled now and ready to receive us! And Dr. Culreavy assured me this afternoon that I shall take no harm at all from the journey if the weather holds fine and Grady is careful to walk the horses. I vow I have never been so pleased at anything in my life, for I have quite fretted myself into the vapours time and again over the idea of our remaining here in this house with that dreadful man."

"Well, as to that, I cannot see that it should have distressed you so very greatly, as you were never obliged yourself so much as to set eyes on him," Georgina said, with more candour than diplomacy. "And I must tell you, Cousin, that he has been excessively kind to Brandon."

"To Brandon!" Mrs. Quinlevan turned a startled glance on her. "Why, my love, whatever can you mean? I am sure, if Brandon has been civil to him, it is more than he deserves, but I cannot see that, except for his being properly grateful for any attention Brandon may have shown him, there is any recompence he can have made the boy."

She went back to a further critical consideration of her cap, but Georgina, finding to her own surprise that she was a trifle indignant over this summary dismissal of Shannon's claims to consideration, went on, "Surely, ma'am, you are aware that we all, to an extent, owe Mr. Shannon our gratitude, for it is only because of his management that the household has not fallen into chaos while you have been laid up. As for Brandon, he has been kindness itself to him, I do assure you."

She broke off, finding her cousin staring at her with perturbation and incredulity written large on her face.

" 'Our gratitude'—'kindness itself'!" Mrs. Quinlevan gasped. "My dear child, what *can* you be talking of? Here is this odious creature come to make us all miserable, and you speak as if he had done us a favour by settling himself here! I cannot understand what has come over you, unless"—and at this idea the perturbation on her face deepened to positive horror—"unless he has succeeded in coming round you as he did poor Nuala! But that would be *too* dreadful, indeed! You really cannot mean *that*, my love!"

"Nonsense!" Georgina said, smiling in spite of herself. "Of course he has done no such thing. It is only that I am coming to realize that we may have been overhasty in judging him. Naturally it was quite wrong of him to have married my cousin in that shabby fashion—but people do fall in love, you know, ma'am."

"But he was quite thirty years old at the time, my dear!" Mrs. Quinlevan protested, still in high agitation. "People have no right to fall in love at that age, and in my experience they very seldom do. Oh, dear! Where is my hartshorn? I made sure Nurse had left it on the table!"

"There is no need for you to fly into a taking, ma'am, only because I have said a word in Shannon's favour," Georgina said, beginning a search for the hartshorn while not knowing whether to feel more amused or astonished at the idea of her being cast in the role of Shannon's defender.

She found the bottle and handed it to her cousin, who, after fortifying herself with a teaspoon of its contents in a glass of water, declared that it was all very well for her to speak lightly of it, but indeed she could not know, at her age, the wiles with which unscrupulous rakes were accustomed to seduce their young victims. This picture of Shannon as an artful beau was too much for Georgina's gravity, especially when she recalled the rough exchanges that had taken place between them, and she was unable to prevent herself from laughing as she assured her cousin that she was quite certain Shannon had no designs upon her.

"Yes, but you cannot be *sure,* my love," Mrs. Quinlevan protested doubtfully.

On which Georgina remarked, with still greater amusement, "Good God, ma'am, I assure you he has no such thing in mind! If he bothers to waste a thought on me, it is only to consider me as a rag-mannered schoolgirl who wants *all* sense of proper conduct."

"Well, I am sure he has no need to think *that* of you," Mrs. Quinlevan said disapprovingly, "for you are as pretty-behaved a girl as I have ever set eyes on, and *that* I shall not scruple to tell your dear mama when next we meet."

Georgina, relieved to see that she appeared to be satisfied with her explanation, went off presently to her own chamber to change her dress for dinner. She came downstairs a little before the hour, and was just going into the book-room to see if Brandon might be there when the front door opened and Shannon walked into the hall. Looking into his face, she saw that it bore an expression of more than ordinary grimness upon it, which she at once attributed to his encounter with Sir Landers and Lady Hession that morning.

But she was surprised to read something else there as well, in the unguarded moment before he glanced up and saw her standing at the book-room door—a weariness that seemed quite out of keeping with the picture of total self-sufficiency his powerful figure always presented. With something of a shock she realised what the past few weeks must have been for him—the whole burden of a neglected estate suddenly thrust on him, days spent in the saddle or striding over rough fields, long conciliatory hours with obstinate or hostile tenants, with additional long hours spent at work over muddled accounts when the rest of the household was in bed. And all this without benefit of a comfortable house, or even a pleasant hour of relaxation with friends or family to look forward to.

She was conscious of feeling somewhat ashamed of herself: however disagreeable her own relations with him had been, she was fair enough to admit that the blame for this could be laid as much at her door as at his. A moment's uncomfortable realisation of what Sir John would have said of her behaviour came to her: the prudish scruples she had heard Lady Mercer express over the misfortune of Shannon's birth would have carried no weight whatever with him, and he would have considered her eagerness to take offence at her host's blunt manners intolerably missish.

All in all, it was in a chastened mood that she walked into the dining-room a little later. She even went so far as to attempt to begin a civil conversation on the good points of the new chestnut hack, but she was rewarded by no equally civil response from Shannon. He answered her curtly and went back to his dinner. The snub did nothing to increase Georgina's budding feelings of charity toward him, and she subsided into silence.

Brandon overbore the awkwardness of the moment by bringing up the subject of their removal to Craythorne.

"I expect that will be the last of my riding out with you," he said to Shannon, unhappily, "unless"—he went on, as inspiration struck him—"I were to give instructions to be roused early enough each morning so I could ride over here before you are ready to leave—"

Shannon glanced up at him briefly. "I shouldn't think that would serve," he said discouragingly. "In the first place, a five-mile ride back and forth, added to what you'd do with me, might be rather too much for you. To say nothing of the fact," he added, with the hint of a contemptuous downcurve of his lips, "that I doubt your mother will care to have you pursue my acquaintance, now that she is able to remove to her own house."

"My mother has nothing to say to it!" Brandon declared hotly.

The rather ugly look vanished from Shannon's face. "Oh, yes, she has," he said more mildly. "You are under age, you know, and she is your guardian. She does quite right to be concerned over the company you keep."

"I shan't come to any harm in *your* company," Brandon said mutinously, "and so I shall tell her."

Shannon shrugged. Georgina found herself growing angry with him once more for his cavalier dismissal of Brandon's suggestions, and then reflected that she might again be doing him an injustice. It was quite possible that, having been made to realise that morning the depth of the animosity in which he was held in the neighbourhood, he was taking this means of disengaging Brandon from the onus of his friendship.

At any rate, she thought, as she retired that night to her chamber, it would soon be no concern of hers. She would be at Craythorne on the morrow, and her forced association with Shannon at an end. It was odd, she thought, that this event, to which she had looked forward so eagerly, did not inspire her with any particular feeling of joy, now that it had actually come upon her.

CHAPTER 8

Craythorne was a rather small, rosy-brick house built in the Wren style, with a hipped roof and dormer windows and a charming fanlighted doorway. Mrs. Quinlevan, Georgina knew, considered it a sad come-down from The Place, but for her own part she found its comfortable, low-pitched, chintz-hung rooms a great deal more cheerful than the grander but half-empty apartments in The Place, and was well pleased with the change.

Her approval extended as well to the alteration in their mode of living that set in immediately on their arrival at Craythorne. She had scarcely time to see her portmanteaux and bandboxes unpacked before a steady flow of company began to arrive at the house, and she had had half a dozen invitations tendered to her before twenty-four hours had gone by.

The first of these was from Lady Mott, who insisted on her joining a party of young people that had been got up for the assembly ball the very next evening. Georgina, though her upbringing had been of a sort to make her fonder of riding to hounds than of dancing, had no aversion to attiring herself in the lilac jaconet muslin, with its row on row of frills round the ankles, which her cousin Bella assured her would be suitable for the occasion. With the assistance of her cousin's maid, her wheat-gold hair was dressed high, with a single curl escaping to fall negligently over one shoulder; she wore blue sandals and long French kid gloves, and when Mrs. Quinlevan had seen her complete at all points, with a shawl of Albany gauze caught up over her elbows, she declared with pride that she was sure she would be quite the belle of the evening.

Georgina's expectations, tempered by the far more modest success she had had at Bath under the quelling aegis of one of Lady Mercer's friends, did not run so high, and she was agreeably surprised, on arriving at the assembly rooms, to find her hand solicited eagerly by the succession of gentlemen whom Lady Mott introduced to her. She made the acquaintance as well of several young ladies living in the neighbourhood—among them two of the five daughters of Sir Landers Hession, who were being chaperoned by their mama, a tall, Roman-nosed matron, in puce satin and a turban, who seemed so much aware of her condescension in gracing a provincial ball with her presence, when she was accustomed to spending the Season each year in London, that Georgina could well believe in the veracity of the scene Brandon had described of her meeting with Shannon at Hauld Hall.

In Lady Mott's barouche, on the way to the assembly rooms, Betsy Mott had begged her assistance, in a hasty whisper, in a matter of vital importance, so that Georgina was not surprised when Betsy drew her into a corner in an interval between dances and breathlessly requested her to accept the invitation of one Mr. Robert Darlington to lead her in to supper.

"He does not dare ask *me*, you see," she explained, "because Mama would be sure to disapprove, but if he is with *you* she will have nothing to say, and we can all be together quite comfortably."

Georgina was somewhat surprised to hear this, as she had already met Mr. Darlington—a rather large, cherub-faced young gentleman who was the heir, as Lady Mott had let fall to her, of a considerable property in the neighbourhood. As a matter of fact, Lady Mott had even begged her, with a chuckle, not to set her cap at him, of all the young men in the room, as he had quite a *tendre* for her Betsy and she rather thought the two of them would make a match of it in the end.

"Of course she is young still," she said comfortably, "and Sir Humphrey doubts she knows her own mind well enough to fix her affections yet. But if the two of them continue to rub on together until the New Year, I believe we may well see a wedding at Mott House next spring."

Georgina had assured her, with a smile, that she would make every effort not to disturb so promising an arrangement, even if—which she greatly doubted—it were in her power to do so. The situation standing thus, she could not help being astonished by the earnest application for her assistance that Betsy made to her later, until she reflected that Miss Mott, having received her notions of romance from lending-library novels, was probably merely attempting to invest her own placid love affair with the tribulations always encountered by their heroines.

At any rate, she herself had as yet seen no young man that evening to make her regret the necessity of going to supper with Mr. Darlington, and she accordingly accepted his rather blushing application to her with great complaisance.

"*I* expect Betsy—Miss Mott—has been talking to you," he confided to her, as he escorted her into the supper-room. "*I* think it's gammon, but she's persuaded that Lady Mott don't like it above half if I act any way particular toward her. It won't do for her saying the same about Sir Humphrey, though, for he told me himself, the last time we hunted together, that I was well up to anything, and I don't think he would have said that if he didn't like me—do you?"

Georgina said gravely that she was sure he would not, and contrived with no difficulty to hand him over to Betsy as soon as they had sat down, contenting herself with the conversation of the handsome young man, a few years older than herself, who had led Betsy into the supper-room. She found him agreeable enough company at first, until she learned that he was none other than Peter Hession, Sir Landers' son and heir. *Then* she suddenly discovered that his manner, which seemed to show a great deal more of town-bronze than that of most of his contemporaries at the ball, was self-consequential rather than easy, and that his very long-tailed blue coat, amazingly striped waistcoat of watered silk, and neckcloth arranged in all the intricacies of the *Trône d' Amour,* betrayed not the gentleman of fashion, but the dandy.

It was therefore a relief to her when Lady Eliza Malladon, coming into the supper-room presently, sat down beside her and engaged her in conversation, after sending the young man who had escorted her into the room off to fill a plate for her from the array of creams and Chantillies that had been set out for the guests. Lady Eliza was very smart for a country ball in a gown of celestial blue crape cut low over the bosom, and a headdress supporting a plume of curled feathers. After inquiring for Mrs. Quinlevan, she at once declared that Georgina must come to drink tea with her at Stokings before the week was out.

"We shall have a comfortable coze and get to know each other much, much better," she said, her bold eyes roving over the room with a lack of attention to the person she was addressing that made the rather excessive cordiality of her manner seem somewhat less than convincing. "That is, we shall if I am able to take you away from the gentlemen," she said, "for you should know that Giles has an eye still for a well-favoured female, and tomorrow we are expecting a pair of his friends who, I am afraid, have the same sad failing. But you need not be discomposed by them, my love, for they are all far beyond the age of attracting a child of your years. Major Rothe and Sir Manning Hartily are bachelors, indeed, but I believe they are both past praying for."

Colonel Giles Malladon came up at this point and was presented to Georgina. She was astonished, in view of the character his wife had just given him, to find him a tall, ruddy gentleman who, she immediately guessed, would be a clipping rider to hounds and a man with a few interests beyond his horses and his profession. She had met many such under her grandfather's roof, and could scarcely conceive how he and Lady Eliza went on together, Lady Eliza's interests appearing to lie exclusively in the world of fashion.

She soon discovered, however, that on Lady Eliza's side this difficulty was overcome by her completely ignoring her husband's wishes and pursuing her own way to the farthest extent possible without creating an absolute scandal, while Colonel Malladon, for his part, gave her her head for the sake of a peaceful life and built his own existence around quite different friends and occupations.

When he had gone off, Lady Eliza resumed her conversation with Georgina.

"So you are at last free of that abominable Shannon," she said to her. "Poor Bella! I declare I was never so sorry for anyone in my life as I was for her when I heard he had settled himself at The Place. I expect she is excessively glad to be at Craythorne now?"

Georgina said in an unencouraging voice that she believed she was, but the brevity of her reply did not lay the subject to rest, for Lady Eliza seemed determined to pursue it.

"I must say it surprised even *me*—and I know the creature's audacity," she said, with a tinkling laugh, "to learn that he had actually determined to stay at The Place while Bella was still occupying it. I wonder what his purpose was? Perhaps he thought if he forced the acquaintance Bella would be obliged to recognise him, which she had told me beforehand she had no intention whatever of doing."

Lady Mott gave it as her opinion, uncompromisingly, that the man was an adventurer, whose queer starts no person of breeding could be expected to predict. This brought an appreciative smile from Mr. Hession.

"Oh, indeed, ma'am, very well spoken!" he said. "But you have not heard his latest, perhaps? He had the audacity to present himself at Hauld Hall a few days ago, on the pretext of wishing to buy a horse from my father. You may believe that Sir Landers gave him a thundering set-down! It's my regret that I wasn't there to see it!"

Georgina said steadily, feeling the colour rise slightly in her face, "I fear you have the matter somewhat amiss, Mr. Hession. My cousin Brandon persuaded Mr. Shannon to accompany him to Hauld Hall in the belief that your father wished to sell a horse that Mr. Shannon might be interested in buying."

She checked, conscious that the entire company was staring at her, and that Mr. Hession, in particular, was regarding her with a rather superior smile.

"Oh, my dear Miss Power," he said, "I must say I think you are fair and far out there! I mean to say—it seems to me, a fellow with no acquaintance in the neighborhood, and likely to have none, would be ready enough to pick up any pretext to fob himself off on people of substance."

"I am sorry to disagree with you," Georgina said, her flush mounting still higher under Lady Mott's disapproving frown, "but I believe I am in more of a position to know the true facts than you, Mr. Hession, and I am *quite* persuaded that Mr. Shannon would have visited a farmer's barn as readily as he went to Hauld Hall if he had believed he might find a horse suitable for his stables there."

Lady Mott said, "Really, my dear!" and Lady Eliza laughed and said it was quite apparent that Shannon had found a champion. This had the effect of taking the conversational ball away from Mr. Hession, which was as well, for the shock of hearing Hauld Hall compared to a barn seemed to have quite deprived him of speech for the moment.

"So he has come round you, too, you silly girl!" Lady Eliza said, shaking a finger smilingly at Georgina. "I always wondered how he managed it with Nuala, for we scarcely saw him save by the merest accident, and then he was *quite* uncivil to the lot of us, as if he considered us in the way of his precious sheep, or rye, or whatever it is they raise in Scotland. Lord Cartan was used to apologise for his manners whenever he showed his face—and then one fine evening there the girl was off with him! How does he manage these conquests? Indeed, I am most curious to learn!"

Georgina said in vexation, "He has made no conquest of me, ma'am. I beg you will not say such a thing, even in jest."

Lady Eliza laughed indulgently. "Well, it is likely to be no jest to you if you take him seriously," she said. "Giles and I saw a good deal of Nuala in Brussels before her death, you know, and I must tell you that a more sadly unhappy girl I never clapped eyes on. Indeed, I have seldom seen anyone so altered. She was soon disillusioned of her romantic folly, it seems!"

Lady Mott said firmly that she did not doubt this, but that she was sure Georgina was not so giddy a miss as her cousin had been, so they might as well give over the subject. Georgina, grateful for her intervention, yet felt her thankfulness slightly diminished when Mr. Hession took advantage of the turn in the conversation to request her hand for the set of country dances that was about to form. She was obliged to stand up with him, but her air, as she did so, was not such as to encourage him to believe that she was doing so from any reason other than that of the merest civility.

She could not help modifying her distant air to some degree, however, when he confessed to her, with more ingenuousness than her original opinion of him would have allowed, that he had consented to lead Betsy Mott into the supper-room only when he had learned of the scheme she had been hatching with young Darlington.

"Fact of the matter is, I had it in my head to ask *you*," he said, "as soon as I could find the chance to be properly introduced to you. Spotted you straight off as the prettiest girl in the room. Are you staying long at Craythorne, Miss Power, or will you be going to London for the Season?"

Even their previous crossing of swords over Shannon could not entirely remove the pleasure of receiving so outright a tender of admiration—and from a young man who, as she could see from the envious glances being cast in her direction, was Top-of-the-Trees in the minds of most of the other young ladies in the room.

She only replied, however, in the most demure fashion, "Oh, I believe it may be some time before I return to England. Do *you* go to London, Mr. Hession?"

"Yes, dooce take it—much too soon for me, if you are staying here!" he said frankly. "My father has a house in Portland Place, you see, and one of my sisters is making her come-out this year, so I'm expected to put in an appearance. Not that I'll feel called on to fix myself there for the entire Season, you know! I daresay, if you are still in Kerry then, I might find myself back here by the middle of May."

Georgina laughed, and said she was sure he would not allow such a consideration to govern his movements—a statement that was immediately and vigorously contradicted by Mr. Hession. It was evident that she had made a conquest, and it was also evident that he was not averse to advertising this to the company by soliciting her to stand up with him again later in the evening.

On her part, she could not like the cavalier fashion in which he had dismissed Shannon as quite beneath the touch of anyone of consequence in the neighbourhood, but she found him lively and amusing company, and his attentions flattering, in view of his obvious attractions for the other young ladies in the room. She concluded by accepting his invitation—an incautious action which, during the homeward drive, exposed her to certain congratulatory comments from Lady Mott and Betsy that seemed to her to be taking entirely too much for granted.

"I wish you will not refine so much on my having stood up with him twice!" she felt obliged to say at last. "You will not tell me, I am sure, that every time a girl does such a thing in Kerry she must be suspected of falling in love with the young man!"

"Oh, no! But how could you help it, with Peter?" Betsy said naïvely. "I imagine you cannot have met many young men, even in Bath, to equal him in appearance and address. Of course he has had the advantage of being much in London, which Robert—Mr. Darlington—says is responsible for his always knowing what is the latest crack in fashion."

"Oh, I am sure he is a very Pink of the Ton," Georgina said, with some irony. "But I can assure you that, in spite of his being knowing enough to have his coats made by Weston and his boots by Hoby, I should not have stood up with him the second time if I had known I should be suspected of losing my heart to him on that account!"

To this Lady Mott responded bluntly, "Well, my dear, that is all very well, but you will admit he is a handsome young man, in spite of his being a bit too dandified for *my* taste, and I assure you he is quite the beau ideal of most of the girls in the neighbourhood. And, as it is always a spur to other young men when they see one of their number endeavouring to fix his interest with a young lady, I can't think you should be quite so niffy-naffy about being obliged to dance with him twice."

Georgina shrugged. Miss Mott, however, with her romantic turn of mind, continued to find the situation of great interest, and confided to Georgina in an undertone, as she saw Lady Mott nodding under the influence of the late hour and the soporific motion of her well-sprung carriage, that if it were not for her eternal devotion to Mr. Darlington she would be much in danger of losing her own heart to Mr. Hession, in spite of the fact that she had been acquainted with him since he had worn nankeens and a frilled shirt.

"He was used to tease me half to death when I went to Hauld Hall to play with his sisters," she said reminiscently, adding in a more soulful tone that the Darlingtons were comparative newcomers in the neighbourhood, so that she had never had the pleasure of seeing her dear Robert so attired.

She then inquired thoughtfully whether Georgina had considered how Mr. Shannon would have appeared at that era in *his* life—an idea which made her more literal-minded companion choke as she attempted to stifle a spirt of laughter.

"No, really I have not," she said.

"Nor I," Betsy said. "But it is very affecting to think of it. I mean—Mama, of course, has not told me all the details," she went on, sinking her voice to a whisper as she kept a wary eye on her dozing parent, "but I do believe his history to be a very sad one, don't you? And I consider it quite *noble* of you to have taken his part tonight against the others."

"Goodness! Don't be such a goosecap!" Georgina interrupted her downrightly. "There was nothing 'noble' about it. It was merely that I could not sit by and listen to that ridiculous boy putting a face on the matter that it did not at all deserve."

"All the same," Miss Mott persisted, "I think it was exceedingly romantic, your being obliged to live in the same house with him all the while, with Mrs. Quinlevan confined to her bed and no one but Brandon to chaperon you. Even Papa said it was highly improper. Did he—were you —was it at all—?"

"No, it was not," Georgina said rather crossly, catching the drift of the question Betsy was trying to get out. "And I wish you will stop putting such ideas into anyone's head! It is bad enough to have Lady Eliza dropping her odious hints, without your behaving as if there was anything havey-cavey about Shannon's staying at The Place. We scarcely exchanged two words with each other the whole time, if you must know."

Miss Mott seemed somewhat disappointed at having this damper put on her romantic imaginings, but did not pursue the subject further, in view of Georgina's obvious displeasure.

By what means Mrs. Quinlevan learned the details of what had occurred at the assembly ball Georgina did not know, as she herself gave her cousin only a brief account of the proceedings the next morning, which included no mention of Mr. Hession's name. As early as that afternoon, however, when Georgina returned from a country ride with Betsy Mott and some of the other young people in the neighbourhood, in which she had had the pleasure of being mounted on a fine roan hack from Sir Humphrey's stables, she found her cousin Bella awaiting her return with every indication of a pressing anxiety in her manner. She was reclining on a sofa in her dressing-room, but exerted herself to sit up when Georgina, obeying the summons that had been delivered to her by Higgins, walked into the room, still wearing her riding-habit.

"I hope you are no worse, ma'am?" Georgina inquired solicitously. "I would not have left you if I had believed—"

"No, no, it is nothing of the sort!" Mrs. Quinlevan replied. "In fact, Dr. Culreavy has only just gone, and he finds me so much improved that he says he has no objection whatever to my driving out— But that is not at all the thing I wished to speak to you about!" she exclaimed, catching herself up in vexation. "Sit down, my love. I *do* feel I should have a serious conversation with you."

"About what, ma'am?" Georgina asked, seating herself obediently in a chair, but showing her puzzlement in her manner.

"About—about gentlemen, my dear! And about Peter Hession in particular!"

Georgina's brows came together in a sudden frown. "Why, what of him, ma'am?" she asked, not very encouragingly.

Mrs. Quinlevan clasped her hands together imploringly. "Oh, indeed, if you take that tone, my dear, it must have gone farther than I had imagined!" she said. "But you must believe me—you must *credit* me with having only your best interests at heart, when I tell you that it will not do! You cannot know him yet—you cannot know *any* of those odious Hessions—"

"Indeed, I am quite at a loss!" Georgina said, rising and looking sternly down at her cousin. "What have the Hessions to do with me, pray?"

Mrs. Quinlevan looked somewhat struck by her young cousin's uncompromising and wholly unself-conscious attitude. She faltered: "You are not—not particularly *taken* with him, then?"

"Taken with him!" Georgina repeated. "Good gracious, I met him for the first time only last evening!"

"But did you not stand up with him twice, then? And ride out with him today?"

"He was of the party today, certainly," Georgina said, "but I assure you that there was nothing at all particular between us." She felt a slight qualm of conscience as she made this statement, for Mr. Peter Hession had, in fact, distinguished her by granting her his almost undivided attention during the entire course of the ride. She then continued, on firmer ground now, "I cannot think who may have been putting such ideas in your head, but you have my word for it that they are quite mistaken if they believe I regard Mr. Hession as anything more than the merest acquaintance."

Mrs. Quinlevan showed her a countenance of doubtful relief. "You are quite sure?" she persisted. Then, as Georgina opened her lips for a more vigorous affirmation, she went on, without waiting for her words, "I know I ought not to have thought it of you, my dear, and indeed, as for old Mrs. Scanlan, who told me of it, she has not been near an assembly ball for years, and only repeats whatever her grandnieces bring home to her, which she often does not have *quite* right, so I should have known better from the start. I am sure it was only the wretched state of my nerves that made me give credit even for a single moment to what she said. But you know, my love, that I am to stand in your dear mama's place, now that you are with me, and in Lady Mercer's as well, which I feel to be an even more solemn obligation—as strict as *her* notions are!—so you must not be vexed with me if I wish to know these things."

"I assure you, ma'am, if I feel I am in danger of losing my heart, I shall tell you," Georgina said. "But as for Peter Hession, our acquaintance is so slight that I am sure you may safely disregard any gossip you may hear about my having a partiality for *him*."

Mrs. Quinlevan's face had brightened as this speech progressed, and she now said, with a confiding smile, "Well, I am happy to hear it, my love, for *indeed* that young man is quite unsuitable for you, to say nothing of the misery any girl must look forward to who has the misfortune to find herself daughter-in-law to Miranda Hession. I do not say that Peter is *fast,* but the Hessions spend much of their time in London, you know, and it seems, by what my brother Jeremy tells me, that he has got into some very strange company this past year—*most* unsuitable for a young man of his age. I wonder at Lucinda Mott, that she did not tell you of this before you were obliged to stand up with him twice! I daresay it is something of a trial to you to be dragged about to country balls, at any rate, for I am sure you are the kind of girl who does not care to be flaunting herself before young men in the very *daring*—I shall always say!—gowns young ladies are obliged to wear these days to be all the crack, and would much prefer to spend a quiet hour strolling with your cousin in the shrubbery, or sitting in agreeable conversation with him. We have a very pretty shrubbery here at Craythorne, you know! I am sure the Huddlestons saw that it received the most constant attention, for it was always in the neatest order when we visited here while we were living at The Place."

At this point Georgina, perceiving that her cousin was craftily steering the conversation toward a subject which she herself did not at all care to discuss—her relationship with her cousin Brandon—with an eye to discovering how well her matrimonial plans in that direction were progressing, made an excuse and fled the room. It occurred to her, as she walked down the stairs, that she had seen little of Brandon since they had removed to Craythorne, and she wondered whether he was carrying out the plan he had formed of riding over to The Place in the morning to join Shannon on his rounds of the estate. If he was, he was being very sly about it, but that was not surprising, for his mother, if she heard of it, would be certain to do her best to put an end to it.

She found him now in the small yellow morning-room at the back of the house which he and the Reverend Mr. Peabody used when they were reading together; he was alone, and looked up in slight surprise as she put her head round the corner of the door and asked if she might come in.

"I thought you were gone for the afternoon with your inamorato," he said.

"My *what!*" She saw the grin on his face and went on threateningly, as she walked into the room, "If you ever say such a thing to me again——! I've just come from your mother, so I must suppose you are speaking of Peter Hession?"

He closed his book. "Who else?" he asked, serenely disregarding her minatory air. "She has been in such a taking this afternoon that I made sure I was to wish you joy the very next time I clapped eyes on you."

She gasped, dropping into a chair. "Oh, dear!" she said ruefully. "Was there ever such a piece of work made over nothing! I stood up with him twice last evening—that was all there was in it, and now some busyhead, it seems, has been spreading insinuations——"

"Oh, no! There you are fair and far out," Brandon assured her. "There were no insinuations, only a plain fact or two dropped; from that time on Mama took the bit in her teeth and was off and running. She has been so busy with her own matters, you see, that she had been taking it comfortably for granted that you and I were going on according to her wishes. But the news of your flirtation with Peter has now caused her to see the error of her ways."

"Brandon, I warn you!" Georgina said irefully. "I am *not* setting my cap at him—which your mother all but accused me of doing just now. He is too full of his own consequence, and far too much of a dandy for me."

"Oh, you mustn't be taken in by the neckcloths and waistcoats," Brandon persisted, grinning again. "A very hard goer, Peter—you should see him after hounds." He held up a hand as she opened her mouth to speak again. "Very well! Don't eat me! I cry quits! I take it you've smoothed Mama's feathers, then?"

"Yes, I *think* so. But Heaven forfend I meet a man I really could hope to like while I am here!" She went on, accusingly. "I thought you were going to tell her you would not marry me on any account."

"So I have, m'dear—at least half a dozen times. It won't do. She says I'm too young to know my own mind."

"And so I should think you were! Nineteen is entirely too soon for a man to think of marrying."

"I agree with you entirely. Still, we could be betrothed, you know," Brandon said, a look of unholy innocence appearing on his face.

"Brandon!"

"Save you a good deal of trouble," he suggested. "Save us both a good deal of trouble, when you come right down to it. Then when you leave we could break it off."

"It wouldn't save *me* a good deal of trouble," Georgina declared. "Why, at the merest hint of such a thing, Grandmama would have me back in Bath before the cat could lick her ear! You aren't by any means rich enough for her, and you haven't a title—not even a baronetcy—"

"I expect she *would* be better satisfied with Peter Hession," Brandon said helpfully. "*He* will be Sir Peter some day, and then you might be Lady Hession."

His cousin peremptorily desired him to stop making a cake of himself, and turned the subject by asking him what he had been doing since they had removed to Craythorne.

"I've been so busy racketing about that I've scarcely laid eyes on you," she said. "Have you been to The Place?"

"I went yesterday." A rueful look came over Brandon's face. "It wouldn't do, though," he said. "Shannon sent me home. Said he wasn't going to see me making trouble for myself by being known as a friend of his. He can be dashed autocratic when he wants to be, you know!"

"Yes, I *do* know," Georgina said, in feeling remembrance. She frowned thoughtfully. "It is those odious Hessions," she went on, after a moment. "I expect they brought it home to him that he isn't to hope to be received in the neighbourhood. It puts me out of all patience to see people setting themselves up in that way! I wish there were something we could do about it."

"*We?*" Brandon said sceptically. "You don't even like him. Why should *you* want to do anything for him?"

"I do not at all see what that has to do with it," Georgina said, with some heat. "If it is unjust, it is unjust, regardless of what my personal feelings may be."

Brandon shrugged. "At any rate, it will do you no good to think of interfering," he said. "If he won't hear of *my* even coming to The Place, he certainly won't take kindly to the idea of *your* poking into his affairs."

This aspersion brought a somewhat spirited rejoinder

from Georgina, and a discussion ensued in which Brandon assured her that Shannon was *his* friend and therefore *his* affair, while Georgina maintained that, as she had been the more uncharitable toward him, she had the greater amends to make, and therefore ought to take it on herself to see to it that the entire neighbourhood did not repeat her mistake.

What either of them was to do about the matter, however, was something that for the moment quite eluded their ingenuity, as Shannon himself had forbidden Brandon to come to The Place, and Georgina felt that her own situation, especially in view of Lady Eliza's hint and Miss Mott's eager curiosity, was one of such delicacy that even a word spoken by her in his defence might be misconstrued.

Both young people, however, concluded hopefully that something would eventually turn up that would enable them to set Shannon on a secure basis in the neighbourhood, and on this amicable agreement they came to terms with each other, and, indeed, appeared in such charity with each other at dinner that evening that Mrs. Quinlevan quite took heart, and made sure that her own plans for the two of them were in a prosperous way to be fulfilled.

CHAPTER 9

Lady Eliza was true to her word: two days after the assembly ball she came to Craythorne to carry Georgina back to Stokings with her for the afternoon. She was driving a smart sporting phaeton, drawn by a pair of showy match-bays, with a groom riding behind her on a neat bay hack, and made such a dashing appearance in a severely cut bronze-green cloth habit and a tall-crowned hat of the same colour, with a peak over the eyes, like a shako, that Georgina was at once filled with the desire to emulate her. Sir John had never raised objections to her mounting any horse in his stables, or to her riding neck-or-nothing to hounds in a way that had made her the envy of many a young gentleman in Herefordshire; but a lady handling the reins of a sporting vehicle drawn by a pair of sweet-goers was "fast," in his opinion, and he had never permitted his granddaughter to do more than tool a sedate one-horse gig down country lanes.

She noted now, as they set off, that Lady Eliza handled the ribbons with careless ease; and the manner in which she brought her pair up to a brisk trot with a flick of the whip, and then caught the thong with a dexterous turn of the wrist, at once showed that she was expert in the use of that article. She seemed aware of her passenger's interest, for they had gone only a short distance when she pulled up the bays and invited Georgina to take the reins herself for a time.

"I can see that you are quite longing to," she said, "and am sure I shall be taking no risk in entrusting them to you. Your fame as a horsewoman has already reached us, you see."

Georgina rather ruefully shook her head. "Oh, I should dearly love to," she said, "but I am afraid you are mistaken about my skill. I have never driven a pair, you see, and I am the rankest amateur at handling the ribbons."

"Nonsense!" Lady Eliza said, laughing. "I am sure you are being far too modest."

She would not hear of a refusal, in spite of Georgina's continued protestations, which she evidently set down to a missish reluctance to put herself forward, and Georgina soon found herself, the reins in her hands, driving down the road at as sedate a pace as her inexperience and the rather restive spirit of the bays allowed.

"There! You see how simple it is," Lady Eliza said. "I knew you would be very well up to it."

Georgina herself was not so satisfied with her performance, for the bays, in spite of their showy appearance, seemed hard-mouthed and of uneven temper. But Lady Eliza, quite unaware of this unflattering opinion, sat comfortably looking out over the green spring countryside, leaving Georgina to go her own way without the least thought of attending to any problems she might encounter.

"Giles, you know, was quite cross when I insisted on his buying this pair for me," she rattled on, blithely. "He would have it that they were not at all suited to a lady's management, which is perfect nonsense, as you can see for yourself. I have not had the least trouble with them in the fortnight that I have had them. He and Major Rothe were unkind enough to say last night that I should not be so fortunate in the long run, and that I should end by being overturned, but they are both such slow-tops that they are sure to look on the gloomy side of any matter. I vow they would quite send me into a fit of the vapours if it were not for Sir Manning Hartily's being in the house as well. I positively insisted that Giles ask him, for there is no one so agreeable to have about in a country house—always so obliging and full of spirits! You will meet both him and Rothe today, my love, but I daresay you will not find that a very exciting matter, for of course your interest will lie with the younger beaux—though there is a sad lack of *them* in these parts. Still you need not be in despair, for I shall have the house quite full of company for my ball next month, and then I think I can promise you gentlemen of the first stare of fashion."

Georgina gave only a limited amount of her attention to

Lady Eliza as she chattered on, finding that she had more than enough to do in handling the pair of restive young horses. If she had been obliged to give her opinion of them, she would have stated without hesitation that Colonel Malladon had been correct in his appraisal, and she was on the point of saying frankly to Lady Eliza that she did not at all believe they were a pair to be given into the hands of an amateur when a sudden combination of circumstances put an end to every thought in her mind but that of holding the bays under control.

The first of these was the abrupt appearance on the road of an urchin of five or six years, who bolted out of a hedgerow, with two or three of his peers in hot pursuit. The second was the violent objection taken by the bays to this eruption of small boys in their path, the visible signs of which were their vigorous attempts to rear up simultaneously in the shafts. The third was the approach, around a bend in the road, of a curricle and pair, which came bearing down on the scene of confusion at such a rapid pace that Lady Eliza shrieked and the groom behind her tumbled off his horse into the road in his zeal to get to the horses' heads.

For a moment it seemed to Georgina that either the phaeton or one of the children in the road must certainly be run down, as she grimly fought to hold her team. All her strength and skill would not be sufficient, she feared, and she was conscious of a surge of relief that was almost painful when she became aware that the driver of the curricle, who had wrenched his own greys to a halt, at the same time turning them dexterously across the road, had flung his reins to the groom beside him and leapt down to go to the bays' heads. The whole thing was over in a matter of seconds, and she found herself, pale and shaken, looking down into Shannon's face as he quieted the plunging horses, while simultaneously bestowing some choice epithets on the frightened urchins who were now huddling together at the side of the road.

"None of you scratched? That's more than you deserve!" he said sharply. "You've been taught better than to run into a road under carriage wheels. Now be off with you, you idiotic brats, and don't let me see such manners from you again!"

They scampered off in dismay, while Lady Eliza, who had been clinging to the seat with her eyes tightly shut, popped them open at the sound of a familiar voice and exclaimed, "Shannon! Oh, it is you! I might have known—sweeping down on us like the devil around that turn in the road!"

Georgina rounded on her indignantly. "Indeed, Lady Eliza, that is very unjust of you!" she said. "If it had not been for Mr. Shannon we must certainly have been overturned, for I am sure I could not have held this pair of yours. Colonel Malladon was quite right; they are not fit to be driven by a woman."

"Then I wonder you should have attempted it, Miss Power, if you were already acquainted with Colonel Malladon's opinion of them," Shannon said ungratefully. Abandoning the bays to Lady Eliza's groom, who had by this time picked himself up from the road, he jumped up into the driving-seat of the phaeton, rudely crowding Georgina against Lady Eliza. "Unless you prefer to walk to your destination," he said, in cool explanation, "I believe you will have to make shift with my driving you there; your cattle are in no frame to be handled by a woman, Lady Eliza, and your groom seems almost as shatterbrained as yourself."

Without waiting for her assent, he called to Hanger to take the curricle on and complete the errand on which he himself had been engaged, and immediately set the bays at a safe trot down the road.

"You were going to Stokings, I take it?" he inquired with ironic civility, of Lady Eliza.

She, recovering quickly from her fright, had already set straight the bronze-green hat that had been flung askew during the near-accident, and now peeped at him across Georgina with a laughing and—Georgina thought—rather self-conscious countenance.

"Yes, but—what an abominable autocrat you are, Shannon! As if I should not be able to handle my own horses!"

"If I were genuinely abominable, I'd let you try," Shannon retorted. "It is lucky for you that I have sufficient charity not to care to see you and Miss Power overturned in the nearest ditch."

"I am sure he is right," Georgina said, with conviction.

Then, seeing Shannon glance momentarily down at her with the glint of sardonic amusement on his face that always set her back up, she went on, addressing him in some asperity, "You need not look at me like that! I have no pretensions to be a nonpareil; I told Lady Eliza before I took the reins that I had never driven a pair before in my life."

"The more fool you were, then, to try it for the first time with a pair like this," Shannon said, with unfeeling candour.

Georgina relapsed into mortified silence. She was quite aware that she had come off the worse in this exchange, but she would not excuse herself by laying the blame on Lady Eliza's insistence that she drive the phaeton.

Lady Eliza, however, at once stepped into the conversational breach and, after requesting Shannon not to make such a to-do over nothing, inquired of him in a careless way how he was going on at The Place.

"Very well," he answered, briefly and unencouragingly.

Lady Eliza allowed herself a small pertinacious giggle. "Oh, indeed? That is not at all the tale we hear!" she said. "I understand that you are quite in Coventry out there. Lady Hession has been running all about the neighbourhood telling everyone what a famous set-down she and Sir Landers gave you when you tried to foist yourself upon their acquaintance. Indeed, Shannon, I fear you have not a friend in the county!"

Georgina gasped. Inexperienced as she was in the ways of flirtation in the fashionable world, she was yet dimly aware that this audacious sally of Lady Eliza's had some significance beyond mere rudeness; it might have been an attempt, she thought, to gain and fix Shannon's attention by the very outrageousness of the remarks she had made.

If so, however, the attempt appeared to be a signal failure. Georgina, looking into Shannon's face, saw it harden slightly, but he did not turn his eyes from the road and only remarked, in an even voice, "That is a state to which I am not unaccustomed, Lady Eliza." He then dismissed the subject by addressing Georgina and inquiring how Brandon was getting on at Craythorne.

"Very well," she replied, thankful to be able to do her part in dispelling the effect of Lady Eliza's remarks. "But you have disappointed him, I fear, by telling him that he must not come to The Place."

He shrugged, indifferently, it seemed, and remarked that such disappointments were soon got over.

"I do not think so," Georgina said warmly. "My cousin is not like other boys of his age, you know. He has few diversions, and when he makes a friend it is a matter of importance to him."

Lady Eliza, who was not easily snubbed, broke in at this point to say with a slight laugh that it appeared she had been mistaken. "You have at least *two* friends in the neighbourhood, it seems," she said, "young Quinlevan and Miss Power. Is there some fatal quality in that family, Shannon, that makes you able to captivate its members so easily?"

At this Georgina lost her temper entirely and, speaking with a frankness of which Sir John would have approved, but which would have sent Lady Mercer into an access of horror, requested Lady Eliza to refrain from making a goose of herself.

"I can't think what is the matter with you, to be twisting the merest civility so," she said.

To which Shannon added dryly, "You are certainly on a false scent there, Lady Eliza. Miss Power holds me in even greater dislike than Lady Hession appears to do, though apparently she has the good manners not to run about the neighbourhood boasting of it."

This was a speech that set Georgina between mortification and pleasure—mortification at the idea that her own previous conduct had fully warranted the implication of the same sort of prejudice of which Lady Hession was guilty, and pleasure at the left-handed compliment to her that had ended Shannon's speech. Indeed, the pleasure seemed quite inordinate for the very cool quality of the compliment she had received, and for a startled moment, as the phaeton proceeded steadily along the road, she asked herself what the meaning of this might be. She was not so foolish, surely, as to be developing an interest in a man like Shannon, a gazetted fortune-hunter, more than a dozen years older than herself, who certainly considered her as little more than a tiresome school girl!

She could feel the scarlet colour beginning to rise in her

face, and she was grateful that Lady Eliza only said to Shannon, "Oh, very well, if you will have it so! But have you never thought of applying to Giles and me to stand your friends? We might do so, you know, if properly approached. Giles is the best-natured creature alive, and can never be made to think ill of anyone, and I—well, I am of a forgiving nature, I must own! I might even be prevailed on to send you a card for my ball, if I were certain you would conduct yourself properly."

Shannon cut her short. "I am looking for no invitations, Lady Eliza," he said curtly. "I find my time well occupied."

"With horses and sheep, and crops, and stupid tenants!" she said. "That was all very well when you were Cartan's agent, but you are Shannon of The Place of the Oaks now, and if you had the slightest ambition you would make a push to be accepted in that position! I vow I had no notion you could be so meek-spirited as to let people like the Hessions make you look nohow and then do nothing about it!"

This time she had not even the satisfaction of seeing the slightest appearance of resentment in his manner, for he only said indifferently, with a glance at Georgina, "This is a subject that can hardly interest Miss Power. Since I am here only in the capacity of your driver, may I suggest that you turn your attention to entertaining *her*?"

Lady Eliza laughed, but Georgina caught the annoyance in the sound. "You really are an ungrateful creature, Shannon!" she said. "I shall be surprised, though, if the day does not come when you will be glad enough to accept my assistance—undeserving of it as you may be."

She then directed herself to pointing out to Georgina the objects of interest along the way, opening a conversation that Georgina was glad to let fall when the gates of Stokings came into sight. Lady Eliza then turned again to Shannon.

"You will come in and take some refreshment with us, as a reward for your *galant* gesture in rescuing us?" she asked him, in a teasing voice.

"No, I have business to attend to."

She sighed. "Not even, 'No, I thank you,'" she said. "Really, Shannon, you will never get on if you insist on behaving so ferociously!" she added, "But if you are in such a great hurry to be gone you must certainly take the phaeton for your own use when you have set us down at the front door. Your groom can return it later—or perhaps you had rather do so yourself, when you are less pressed for time."

"I shall do neither, thank you," Shannon said. "I prefer to walk."

"To walk! Oh, you are funning now! It is five miles to The Place, at least!"

"Nevertheless, I prefer to walk."

She shrugged her shoulders with a petulant look, and, when he had halted the phaeton before the door, alighted in haste and swept into the house, drawing Georgina, who was attempting a more civil leavetaking, along with her.

"I vow," she declared, as she stripped off her gloves and handed them, with her hat, to a footman, "there was never a more vexatious creature than that man! There is no doing anything for him—not that I should even wish to attempt it, for he has a shocking character, but I dislike seeing *any- one* set on as he has been. Giles! Giles! What do you think?" she went on, leading Georgina into a red saloon elaborately decorated in the Chinese taste, where three gentlemen sat together. "We were nearly overturned in the phaeton by the most shocking mischance, and Shannon felt obliged to drive us home—as if I could not manage my own horses! If I had been driving myself, of course, it need not have occurred, as Miss Power tells me that, in spite of her being such a notable horsewoman, she is quite an ama- teur at handling the ribbons."

Having flung all this information pellmell at the gentle- men, she demanded a glass of ratafia for Miss Power and herself and sank into an easy-chair, indicating to Georgina with a wave of her hand Major Rothe and Sir Manning Hartily. The latter, a florid, extremely stout gentleman in the palest of pantaloons, the most gleaming of Hessians, and a neckcloth arranged in all the intricacies of the Orien- tal style, at once demanded explanations of the ladies, creaking ponderously across the room to settle himself be- side them and raising his quizzing-glass to his eye to have a more appreciative stare at Georgina, while Colonel Malla- don occupied himself with seeing that she was comfortable and had what refreshment she desired—a task Lady Eliza seemed quite content to relegate to him.

Major Rothe, meanwhile—a sensible-looking man of

about eight-and-thirty, with none of the dandified airs of his fellow guest—also turned his attention to the less highly coloured account of the events Lady Eliza had sketched which Sir Manning was drawing from Georgina, and said with a faint smile, when she had done, "Yes, I am afraid that is quite in Mark's style. He has a horror of being beholden to anyone for the slightest favour."

Georgina looked at him in surprise. "Mark?" she said. "Oh—you mean Mr. Shannon? Are you acquainted with him, then?"

"Very well acquainted," Major Rothe answered. "I had an uncle who was a neighbour of Lord Cartan's in Scotland, and until his death a few years ago I was used to stay with him often. Mark is some years my junior, of course, but I have seen a good deal of him from the time we were both lads."

Lady Eliza broke in at this point to say, "Really? I did not know you had been so well acquainted with him. Now that I recollect, though, when we visited Nuala in Brussels, it seemed you were forever one of the company. Tell me—has he always been so disagreeable? Or is that merely something he has acquired over the years?"

Major Rothe answered her with a seriousness which he seemed conscious the flippancy of her question did not quite merit.

"Why, as to that, Lady Eliza," he said, "yes, he has always been a solitary person, with few social graces. But then you must remember that he has had scant opportunity to develop them."

He glanced at Georgina, as if unwilling to proceed further without knowledge of how much of Shannon's history was current in the neighbourhood. But Lady Eliza overrode his scruples by declaring at once, "Oh, you need not have the slightest concern about telling tales out of school, Major! Everyone knows that Shannon is a by-blow of Lord Cartan's; you cannot imagine that *that* would not have become common gossip here as soon as his marriage to Miss Power was found out."

Major Rothe, however, still appeared reluctant to discuss the matter, and turned the conversation to another topic, in spite of Lady Eliza's obvious desire to continue on the subject of Shannon. It occurred to Georgina, as she sat drink-

ing her ratafia, that Lady Eliza's interest in Shannon was so
patently displayed that her husband might well have reason
to feel jealousy; but apparently he was quite unconcerned.
Nor did he seem at all interested in the extravagant compliments that Sir Manning Hartily paid to his wife over the
next half hour.

Sir Manning, indeed, had at first seemed inclined to bend
the greater part of his attention on Georgina, whom he
pronounced in an audible undertone to Colonel Malladon
to be "a regular little beauty," adding, "Deuce take me if
I've seen a finer pair of eyes these two years in London!"
This, she later found, she was to take as a compliment indeed, for in the course of the conversation it developed that
Sir Manning was a member of that elegant and sophisticat-
ed group known as the Prince Regent's set, and that he was
considered, in all matters of taste and beauty, to be a con-
noisseur of the first rank. For her own part, however, she
could well have dispensed with his approval, since it involved a great deal of ogling and a number of compliments
so frank as to make her blush, and she was relieved when
Lady Eliza, who obviously was not fond of playing second
fiddle, imperiously demanded Sir Manning's attention for
herself, and she was able to turn to the conversation on the
subject of hunting that Colonel Malladon was carrying on
with Major Rothe. This eventually ended in Colonel Malladon's declaring that it would not do for such an accomplished horsewoman as Miss Power to depart from Stokings without seeing the two high-bred 'uns he had lately
added to his stables, and before Lady Eliza knew what was
afoot, he and Major Rothe were leading her young guest
outside through one of the long windows opening on the
terrace, and strolling with her across the lawn in the direction of the stables.

Georgina was not surprised that it did not suit Lady
Eliza to join their company, as she patently was not of a
disposition to enjoy tagging along as a belated partaker in a
scheme she had had no part in forming; but she was astonished that her pique at her guest's having purloined the attention of two of the gentlemen of her court would lead
her, within five minutes of their having reached the stables,
to send a footman after Colonel Malladon with the information that she must see him at once to decide on her

plan for the remainder of the day. This was a patent excuse, and Colonel Malladon showed, by the tempery manner in which he received it, that he was well aware of this fact.

His displeasure, though it did not extend to his ignoring his wife's summons, did rise to the point of his informing Georgina and Major Rothe that there was no need for *them* to return to the house, and of his requesting Major Rothe to act as his deputy in showing Georgina around until his return. He then strode off purposefully toward the house, leaving his two guests to discover, when they turned their eyes on the other's face, that a mutual smile was lurking behind a proper air of gravity on each. Georgina was the first to laugh, and Major Rothe then joined her in a quiet chuckle.

"Oh, no! There won't be wigs on the green," he assured her. "Malladon is really a very mild-tempered fellow, you know."

Georgina said a little tartly, "Perhaps it would be better for everyone if he were not," and then caught herself up, looking ruefully at her companion. "Oh, dear! My wretched tongue!" she said. "Grandmama has always warned me that a young lady should have *no* personal opinions to express except those that are of a complimentary nature."

"I am afraid we should have a dull world of it if *all* young ladies adhered strictly to that rule," Major Rothe said, with a slight, amused smile. He added, after a moment, "I take it that you are not well acquainted with the Malladons, Miss Power?"

"No. I have been in Kerry only a matter of a few weeks, and for the greater part of that time my cousin, Mrs. Quinlevan, has been out of frame, so that I have not gone about much until very recently. You know my cousins, the Quinlevans, I expect, if you have often visited here?"

"As a matter of fact, I have not; this is my first visit to Kerry, also," Major Rothe explained. "But I have heard Malladon and Lady Eliza mention them. They are the family Mark Shannon has dispossessed from The Place of the Oaks by marrying—your cousin, was it, Miss Power?"

"Yes." She looked at him curiously. "I was surprised to hear that you were Shannon's friend," she said then, frankly. "I had not supposed him to have any, as uninterested as he seems to be in making himself agreeable to other people. But perhaps you merely meant that you have been *acquainted* with him over a long period of time?"

"On the contrary, I consider him to be one of my closest friends," Major Rothe said.

"Oh! Do you?" She asked naïvely, "Then he is not always so—so disagreeable as he seems here?"

Major Rothe smiled. "Since I arrived only yesterday and haven't yet seen how he performs here, I can't speak for that," he said. "As I remarked to Lady Eliza, he has few social graces, yet I do not recall that his manner, when he is among people who are willing to accept him for what he is, is such that it would repel a man of sense."

Georgina nodded thoughtfully. "Well, I rather thought as much," she confessed. "I daresay he came here expecting to be set down, and that is why he has had his hackles up from the start. But it was the very worst thing that he could have done, you know. I am sure that people like Sir Humphrey and Lady Mott are not so high in the instep that they would not have been willing to accept him in the neighbourhood, once they had seen that he was not the odious sort of adventurer they had been led to expect. But he has done nothing to conciliate them or anyone else, and the result is that he is in a fair way to being quite ostracized."

"I am sorry to hear that," Major Rothe said, looking grave. "But it is early days for him here still. Perhaps when he is better known—"

"He will not be known at all if something is not done soon," Georgina said bluntly. She added, "Of course it is his own fault. I will own that I felt much the same about him, except then I saw his kindness to my cousin Brandon, who is lame and often slighted on that account, and that he has already won the good opinion of his tenants—"

"I am glad to hear that," Major Rothe said. "It could scarcely have been otherwise. He has more knowledge of the land than any man I have ever met; in the old earl's day it was always said that the Cartan land was in better heart than any other in the neighbourhood, and he had the full management of it then."

"I wonder Lord Cartan did not make some provision for

him when he died, since he had been so useful to him," Georgina said, her curiosity getting the better of her again. "I gather that he did not?"

"No," Major Rothe replied. "I must admit that has puzzled me, too, but then the relationship between them was an odd one, you know. They were very much alike, in many ways—both hard men, who neither gave nor received easily. Mark, when he was a lad, had to earn every privilege, every word of approbation, he ever had from the old earl. I suppose Cartan was probing to find if the resemblance to himself that was so marked physically was there within the boy, as well. And then," he added, drawn on to speak further, apparently, by the obvious interest with which she was attending to him, "Lady Cartan never liked him, you see. She was an excellent woman, and a very fair one, I believe, but she could not care to have Mark brought up in the house with her own children, almost on terms of equality, and she had great influence with her husband. They had a numerous family, and I daresay she might have persuaded Cartan that any provision he made for Mark must have been taken out of the pockets of their children."

Georgina, her underlip caught in her teeth, had been following this speech while absently stroking the mane of a beautiful little mare that had come inquisitively to look at the intruders. She remarked thoughtfully, when Major Rothe had concluded, "And I suppose, when the old earl died, the present Lord Cartan felt the same?"

"Yes. The two of them had never dealt together, you see. Mark was the older and stronger, so he escaped the petty persecution one boy can visit on another when he is in a position of superiority, but I daresay his bread was made bitter for him more than once by the taunts that he was obliged to bear." He added quickly, "I should not like you to think that he complained of this to me. Any knowledge I have of it comes from one of the younger boys, Edmund, who was rather well disposed toward Mark and used to tell me tales occasionally that might perhaps better have remained in the family."

"And so, when the old earl died, the present Lord Cartan gave Shannon his *congé?*" Georgina asked.

"No, not immediately. I must admit I was surprised that Mark did not make a move then himself, but he was much attached to the place, I believe, and perhaps thought he and the new earl might rub on tolerably well together if each would agree to keep out of the other's way. The fault in that arrangement was that Cartan had a fancy to take the reins into his own hands, and within a year matters had come to such a pass between them that Mark was on notice to find some new post for himself. I didn't learn of this until some time later, after his marriage, as a matter of fact, for he is stiff-necked enough not to wish to seek assistance from a friend, even though it would be gladly given. The first I knew of it, he had married your cousin and was travelling on the Continent."

Georgina, who was finding the conversation of considerable interest, was somewhat vexed at this point to see Colonel Malladon coming toward them, as his arrival must inevitably mean that the subject would be dropped. So, in fact, it was. Colonel Malladon, his good humour apparently restored by the explanation he had had with his wife, at once reverted to the good points of the mare Georgina had been stroking, suggesting that they must certainly get up an excursion on which she should be Georgina's mount, and in the conversation that followed the subject of Shannon was quite forgotten.

There was no opportunity for Georgina to speak further about him to Major Rothe before the carriage was ordered to take her back to Craythorne. But this did not at all mean that he did not occupy her thoughts almost to the exclusion of any other topic during her homeward journey. She had been made to feel more and more acutely, as her conversation with Major Rothe had progressed, how improbable it was that her first opinion of Shannon had been a just one. Major Rothe was a sensible, well-bred man, with agreeable manners and an intelligence that she had realised to be superior. If he, after an acquaintance with Shannon that had covered many years, was able to describe him as one of his closest friends, it seemed that the uneasiness she had been feeling over her own instant dislike of him must be only too well founded.

Then, too, the account that the Major had given of Shannon's early years had done much to explain to her the harshness of Shannon's manner. Brought up in a household in which the stigma of his illegitimacy was constantly held before him, able to form none of the ordinary attachments of youth except for his father, whose nature had apparently been as reserved as his own, it was small wonder, she thought, that he had failed to develop the social ease that would have smoothed his way in the situation in which he now found himself. He had come expecting to be rejected, and rejected he assuredly would be, unless something was soon done to set matters to rights. Major Rothe's presence at Stokings might help, she thought, but, as a guest there, he was in no position to instigate any positive action in his friend's favour.

An idea began to take shape in Georgina's mind, and she determined to discuss it with Brandon at the earliest opportunity.

CHAPTER 10

The opportunity offered itself that very evening, when Mrs. Quinlevan had gone upstairs for her after-dinner nap. Georgina followed Brandon into the yellow morning-room, whither he had retired with a book, and said directly, "Brandon, I want to speak to you. About Shannon."

"About Shannon? What about him?"

"I intend to make a push to have him accepted in the neighbourhood. Do you think your mother would be willing to give a small informal party here next week if I dropped a few hints to her?"

Brandon closed his book and looked at her suspiciously. "Now what the deuce are you up to?" he demanded. "You must be dicked in the nob if you think Mama would invite Shannon here, to an informal party or any other kind!"

"Yes, I know that," Georgina acknowledged. "But if *I* were to offer to send out the cards of invitation—"

She did not feel it necessary to conclude the sentence, looking at him with a serene expectation of his understanding her drift that drew a sudden shout of laughter from him.

"You mean *you* would invite him? Well, you are a Trojan! But what do you think Mama would have to say when he came walking in the front door?—that is, if she didn't take one of her spasms and collapse on the spot!"

"I should warn her beforehand, of course," Georgina assured him, seriously. "Not too *far* beforehand, for that wouldn't do, but enough so that the shock would be taken off. Do you think it a good idea, Brandon? Once he is here, she can hardly send him packing, and if it is seen that he is invited to *this* house—"

Brandon was still chuckling. "Of all the corkbrained schemes!" he said. "He won't come, in the first place, and

even if he did— Lord, I'd give a monkey to see the stir it
'ud make! But it won't fadge, Coz."

She sat down beside him. "Why won't it?" she asked, obstinately. "Brandon, I have been talking to Major Rothe at
Stokings. He says he has known Shannon since he was a
boy, and the account he gives of him makes me feel quite
certain that I have misjudged him dreadfully, and *must* do
something to make up for the shabby way I have treated
him. *You* will not care for it yourself, you must own, if he
is not to be received by anyone in the neighbourhood. But
if we can once show people that he is not the ramshackle
sort of man they believe him to be, there will be no difficulty in *your* continuing your friendship with him."

This argument, she perceived, had some effect on her
cousin. She knew how galling he felt it to be obliged to give
up an association in which he had taken the liveliest pleasure, and, in fact, in spite of the misgivings which he continued to voice, his eagerness to stand on easier terms with
Shannon finally led him to admit that there might be some
merit in her scheme, after all, and to consult with her
seriously on the subject of how they were to go about in-
ducing Mrs. Quinlevan to give a small party at Craythorne
within the coming week.

As it developed, the matter presented fewer difficulties
than either of them had anticipated. The initiation of the
idea had been left to Brandon, who—as it was well known
that he did not care for parties himself—broached it merely by saying in a joking way to his mother that it surprised
him, in view of the many invitations Georgina had received
since they had come to Craythorne, that she had not started any plans to return all this hospitality by some entertainment of her own. Georgina was then about to take up her
part in the conversation, but to her surprise and satisfaction
she found herself interrupted before she could well begin.

"It is odd that you should mention that," Mrs. Quinlevan
said seriously to Brandon, "because that is exactly what I
have been thinking myself. Of course it is out of the question for me to be considering anything elaborate in my
state of health, but I do believe I could manage a small evening party, with dancing for the young people. A formal
ball would not be expected, and indeed the house is quite
unsuited for such a thing, for it is not at all to be compared

to The Place, where we had some charming balls, you remember, when poor Nuala was alive."

Georgina, anxious to see that she did not lose the thread of her thought by wandering off into reminiscences of the past, here interrupted in her turn, and declared that of all things she would enjoy a party given at Craythorne.

"And, indeed, ma'am, it need be very little trouble to *you*, at all events," she said, "for I am sure I could relieve you of many of the tasks that go along with such an undertaking. If you will give me your list, for example, I shall be only too happy to send out the cards of invitation."

"Would you, my dear? That would be very kind of you!"

"And I might deal with Mrs. Hopkins about the refreshments as well, if you would permit me, and—oh, I am sure there are any number of details I might take off your hands, if you will only let me know what you would like me to do."

Mrs. Quinlevan found all this helpfulness greatly to her taste, and, as she was a gregarious soul, who liked nothing better than to be giving or attending entertainments of almost any sort, she soon found herself, under Georgina's guidance, making definite plans for an event that until a few minutes before had been only a vague notion in her head.

A list was soon being discussed, which included the names of all the more prominent families in the neighbourhood. The Motts, of course, were to be invited, as were the Hessions, and the Malladons and their house guests, Major Rothe and Sir Manning Hartily. The latter, Mrs. Quinlevan informed Georgina, must be a notable addition to the party, if only he would consent to honour it with his presence.

"For he is a man of the first stare of fashion, you know, my love," she said, "and for him to have consented to make a stay at Stokings is a high compliment to Lady Eliza, I do assure you. I daresay he felt a quiet week or two in the country before the Season begins would be quite the thing for him, for he is somewhat troubled with gout, I believe."

Georgina sat listening to her cousin's rambling monologue, as each new name was set down on the list, in the greatest of good humour, secure in the knowledge that she herself was to be entrusted with the supply of elegant gilt-edged cards on which the invitations were to be inscribed; and the very next day penned them carefully and sent them out, with, shuffled among the rest, one addressed to Mark Shannon, Esquire, at The Place of the Oaks.

She wondered, during the next few days, what his emotions would be on receiving it. Astonishment, certainly, he would feel, for he could never have anticipated that her cousin would so far overcome her antipathy for him as to invite him to her home on any occasion. He might, she hoped, take the idea that Brandon had prevailed on his mother to include him.

But no matter how great his puzzlement was, she did not believe that he would decline the invitation. Even a man as careless as he was of the world's opinion could scarcely fail to see the advantages that recognition by his dead wife's family would bring to him. To reject such an olive branch would be to cut himself off indeed from any hope of future acceptance by them, and she could not believe that he was either vengeful or stupid enough to wish to salve his pride by the paltry gesture of returning a refusal.

As it developed, she was quite correct in her assessment of the situation. Instructions had been given that all messages and correspondence should be in her domain during the week, so that when Shannon's reply came in she was the one who opened and perused it. "Mr. Shannon accepts with pleasure, etc. etc." —she read the formally correct missive through and, repressing a crow of triumph, bore it off to show to Brandon.

To her surprise, he did not appear to share her satisfaction. Instead, he viewed the sheet of paper with some appearance of misgiving, and said at last, "Well, I never thought he'd come up to scratch, and now that he has— dash it, Georgie, I don't like it at all!"

"Why?" she demanded. "Because your mother will fly up into the boughs? I wish you will not worry yourself over *that*, for you know that she never bears a grudge from one moment to the next, and I am quite sure I shall be able to turn her up sweet by the very next day."

Brandon shook his head. "It ain't my mother. It's Shannon," he said bluntly. "If he should find out she never meant to invite him—"

"How could he find out? You won't tell him, nor will I, and Cousin Bella wouldn't! Well, you *know* what a high stickler she is; she simply would not insult a guest so in her own house!"

"She'll let it out somehow," Brandon said gloomily. "You wait and see. You don't know how jingle-brained she can be when she's really in a pelter over something." He added, "I wish you hadn't done it," which made Georgina demand of him why he had not said this to her when she had first broached the subject to him.

"I did. The thing is, you wouldn't listen," he said, firing up in his turn.

"Well, we can't cry off now. That's certain," Georgina said, with decision. "We shall have to go through with it. But I am quite sure we shall be able to carry it off."

"Are you? I ain't!" Brandon said, unencouragingly. "I have half a mind to ride over to The Place tomorrow and tell him the truth."

"Brandon! You wouldn't!" The scarlet colour flew into Georgina's cheeks. "He'll think— I don't know *what* he would think of me! Promise me you will do no such thing!"

But, as it happened, the promise she exacted from him was quite unnecessary, because by the next day he was in no condition to ride to The Place or anywhere else. A wetting he had received that afternoon when out riding brought on a troublesome sore throat and a chill that evening, and Dr. Culreavy, summoned the next morning by Mrs. Quinlevan, gave it as his opinion that his young patient would do well to spend the next several days in bed.

The news, conveyed to Georgina, cast her into double gloom: not only was she sorry for Brandon, who must spend an uncomfortable and boring time confined to his bed, the recipient of the cosseting he detested from Nora Quill and his mother, but she was also cast into some perturbation by the knowledge that she would now be without his support on the evening of the party. Her cousin's indisposition was not so serious that this must be cancelled— though Mrs. Quinlevan, in the pucker she had been thrown into by the doctor's pronouncement, did consider it for a time—and she would thus find the burden of calming her cousin Bella's justifiable indignation on that occasion thrown entirely upon her own shoulders.

In addition, she had greatly counted on Brandon to see to it that Shannon was not neglected during the evening, for her hovering about him herself, she considered, was quite out of the question. But now this task, too, would be her responsibility, and she found her resolution tested to the utmost by the idea.

Her one consolation lay in the assurance that Major Rothe was to be present at the gathering. Certainly she would be able to rely upon *his* support, and, with it, she believed she might squeak through. Lady Mott and Sir Humphrey, too, though both were outspoken in the extreme, were fair-minded enough, she believed, to be able to meet Shannon without feeling the necessity of turning a cold shoulder to him before he showed he deserved it, while Miss Betsy Mott seemed so kindly disposed toward him, as a figure—in her mind, at least—of romance, that Georgina was sure Shannon would meet with no rebuff from that direction.

The evening of the party arrived. The Motts and the Malladons and their house guests had been asked for dinner at eight, and at seven-thirty Georgina, attired in the gown of rose-pink sarcenet with tiny puff sleeves and a narrow skirt trimmed with a double pleating of ribbon that she had chosen for the occasion, scratched with some trepidation on the door of Mrs. Quinlevan's dressing-room. Bidden to enter, she stepped inside to find her cousin already arrayed in a gown of puce satin, with her maid engaged in arranging on her coiffure a headdress of the same colour, supporting a plume of curled feathers.

"Oh, my love, I was just about to send Anson to you," Mrs. Quinlevan exclaimed, as Georgina came into the room. "You cannot have managed with only that silly creature Mrs. Hopkins engaged last week!"

"On the contrary, ma'am, I managed very well," Georgina said, smiling, but feeling her heart thudding uncomfortably under the knowledge of the announcement that she must soon make.

Mrs. Quinlevan was surveying her critically, and seemed satisfied at all points, from the expression of approval that gradually came over her plump face.

"Why, yes, my love, I must admit you *do* look quite the thing this evening!" she said. "But then with hair like yours, one need never fret oneself over the arrangement of it, for it falls naturally into the most enchanting ringlets!" She frowned at her own reflection in the glass before her, sighed, and told her maid that she might go. "Oh, but do send Mrs. Hopkins to me at once!" she said, adding to Georgina, as Anson left the room, "I have the most *lowering* presentiment that ices and wafer-biscuits are not at all the thing to be serving tonight, as the weather has turned so cool and damp."

Georgina, foreseeing a monologue on the deficiences of the dinner and the refreshments to be served later that would endure until Mrs. Hopkins made her appearance, hurriedly interposed, "Cousin Bella! Indeed I do not wish to interrupt, but there is something of most particular importance that I must say to you."

Mrs. Quinlevan checked in some surprise. "Why, very well," she said. "But what can it be?" A sudden look of alarm crossed her face. "The lobsters!" she said. "Oh, *do* not tell me it is about the lobsters!"

"No, no! Indeed, ma'am, it is nothing of the sort," Georgina said, her own trepidation subsiding momentarily in a smile of amusement at the instant apprehension of high tragedy that had crossed her cousin's face. "I assure you it is nothing so paltry."

"Paltry!" Mrs. Quinlevan gasped, in indignant amazement. "How can you speak so, when I have Sir Manning Hartily about to sit down to dinner in this house, and everyone knows he is used to the first style of elegance in everything, particularly in cookery—"

"I am sure it is so," Georgina agreed hastily, anxious to head off another monologue, this one on the subject of Sir Manning. "But, indeed, to my knowledge there is nothing amiss with the lobsters, and I beg you will listen to what I must tell you!" Seeing from her cousin's face that she was still obstinately intent on the inner contemplation of some culinary disaster of her own imagining, she plunged desperately into the subject. "The fact is, ma'am," she said, "that I have taken the liberty of inviting Mr. Shannon to your party this evening."

If she had informed Mrs. Quinlevan that an aroused peasantry was even now at the gates of Craythorne, bent on massacring all its inmates and exhibiting their heads

upon pikes, in reprehensible imitation of what had occurred in France in the days of her youth, it was impossible
that an expression of greater horror could have appeared
on that lady's face. However, the very next moment it had
disappeared under a look of slight annoyance—such a ludi-
crous come-down from the tragic to the commonplace that
Georgina, as nervous as she was, had difficulty in repressing a giggle.

"I wish you will not be funning now, of all times, my
love!" Mrs. Quinlevan said reprovingly. "It puts me in
mind of your poor father, who was somewhat addicted, I
fear, to practical joking."

"But I am not funning, Cousin Bella, I do assure you!"
Georgina protested. "It is true; I *have* invited him! I know
it was shockingly forward of me, but—"

She got no further, for Mrs. Quinlevan, closing her eyes,
with one hand clasping her ample puce satin bosom in the
general direction of her heart, had sunk down alarmingly
in her chair and was distractedly murmuring something
about her vinaigrette. Georgina flew to procure that useful
article for her, and was relieved in a few moments to see
her cousin rouse herself and look up at her with piteous
blue eyes.

"My dear love," Mrs. Quinlevan implored her, "tell me
that you did not mean it! That *man*—no, you *could* not—a
girl brought up so *very* carefully—"

"I am dreadfully sorry, Cousin Bella, but indeed I *do*
mean it," Georgina said remorsefully. "I had no idea it
would upset you so greatly! You see, I had been talking to
Major Rothe—and he has known Shannon forever, and is
quite persuaded he is undeserving of the treatment he has
received here—indeed, he considers him one of his closest
friends—"

She broke off, conscious that the explanation she was offering was a very lame and disjointed one, but she had the
satisfaction of seeing that it had at least produced the effect
of returning a slight look of hope to her cousin's face.

"Major Rothe?" Mrs. Quinlevan repeated feebly. "Do
you mean that *he*—? But, indeed, it was very wrong of him
to encourage you to do such a thing!"

"No, no, Major Rothe knows nothing about the matter,"
Georgina said hastily, aghast at the thought of drawing that

gentleman into the imbroglio. "It was my own idea entirely
—and Brandon's, a little—for you must know that Brandon has always liked Shannon—"

"Brandon," Mrs. Quinlevan said with severity, "is a child! Surely, Georgina, you have not allowed yourself to be persuaded by his most unsuitable partiality—"

"I have been persuaded by no one," Georgina said. "It was entirely my own idea—and I must say, ma'am, that I wonder that you will set yourself so against Mr. Shannon, for the very credit of the family! Surely it must be better to have it thought that my cousin Nuala married a man who, except for the misfortune of his birth, is quite respectable than to persist in making it appear that he is the sort of person no one can receive!"

Mrs. Quinlevan, with doubt of the wisdom of her own conduct now added to horror over her young cousin's, could only clasp her vinaigrette for comfort.

"But—but Jeremy *said* I was to have nothing to do with him!" she wailed. "And it is quite settled in the neighbourhood: even Lady Mott, who is the *soul* of good nature, says that Sir Humphrey will not call upon him, and that is quite right of him—"

"Lady Mott is following *your* lead, ma'am," Georgina said, pressing the momentary advantage that she saw herself to have obtained. "Of course she does not wish to put herself in your bad graces by making overtures to a man with whom you are determined not to be friendly. But I am persuaded that she would also follow your lead in recognising him, if you were to do so."

"Would she? I don't know," Mrs. Quinlevan said dubiously. "It *may* be true—but still I cannot help feeling that we should all be *far* more comfortable if only you had not asked him here tonight, and we could go on exactly as we have been doing. I cannot *think* what possessed you to do such a thing—though Louisa Middlethorpe warned me before I ever brought you here that you had had a very strange upbringing with Sir John, and that Lady Mercer was often at her wits' end— But I should not have said that!" she broke off, conscience-stricken. "I am sure you have always behaved very prettily under *my* roof, and if it were not for that *odious* man, who seems to take pleasure in setting us all in a bustle—"

"No, really, ma'am! You shall not lay this at Mr. Shannon's door," Georgina said, half-laughing at her cousin's peculiar logic. "Mr. Shannon knows nothing of what I have done; as far as he can tell, he has received an invitation from you to attend an evening party at Craythorne, and I am sure you are too well-bred to snub him when he presents himself at your door. If you are to be angry with anyone, it must be with me."

"Yes, but—to receive him *here,* my dear, as if there were nothing odd about his being asked, when everyone *knows* I have said a dozen times that no one in the family intended to recognise him—! Oh, dear! Oh, dear! I *wish* I knew what I must do!"

Mrs. Quinlevan's face puckered up. She appeared to be on the verge of tears, and Georgina could only be grateful when the housekeeper's appearance at the door put an end to this highly unsatisfactory colloquy. She fled to her own room, reflecting in some dismay on her inability to obtain a pledge of cooperation from Mrs. Quinlevan, and looking forward with increasing dread to the remainder of the evening.

Only a firm conviction that her cousin, as caper-witted as she might be, would not wish to make a scandal by turning a cold shoulder to a guest in her own home sustained her, and even that reflection was tempered by the fear that Mrs. Quinlevan's nerves would get the better of her sense of propriety, and that the company might consequently be treated to a display that would make both Georgina and Shannon excessively sorry that she had ever conceived her well-meant plan.

CHAPTER 11

When she went downstairs a few minutes later she found the Motts, who had arrived with unfashionable punctuality, already in the hall, divesting themselves of their wraps. Fortunately for both her and Mrs. Quinlevan, who Georgina perceived was still in a flutter of agitation, Lady Mott was in a talkative mood, and carried the conversation until the arrival of the Malladons some quarter of an hour later.

But Georgina was then cast into an even greater apprehension than that which was already enveloping her, for she saw that Colonel Malladon and Lady Eliza were accompanied only by Sir Manning Hartily: Major Rothe was nowhere to be seen. Lady Eliza explained this at once by saying to Mrs. Quinlevan, in a careless voice, "My dear Bella, positively you must not eat me, for I know it will upset your table shockingly, but we were unable to bring Rothe! He has had an urgent summons to England; it appears that his only brother is at death's door, and he was obliged to go scrambling off at once, with no regard whatever for the proprieties. I promised to convey his deepest regrets to you—but what good do regrets do, I should like to know, when one's table has been set awry?"

Georgina, looking at her cousin, saw from the expression on her face that she considered this latest blow of fate so minor, in comparison with the ordeal before her, that she could accept Lady Eliza's offhand apology without a blink of dismay; but, for her own part, she was cast into flat despair. If Major Rothe was not to appear that evening she had lost her last ally, and would be obliged to carry the situation off alone—a quelling prospect, even for one of her optimistic nature.

Casting about desperately for expedients, she saw Miss

Betsy Mott, who, in a demure, pale-blue muslin gown
trimmed with knots of white ribbon, appeared to be agreeably contemplating an evening spent in the company of Mr.
Robert Darlington. An idea suddenly occurred to
Georgina. Betsy was not the ideal person to whom she
would have chosen to confide the straits in which she stood,
but at least she was well disposed toward Shannon, and it
might be that she would be willing to aid her in her attempt
to see to it that his appearance at Craythorne did not lead
only to his receiving an unmerciful snubbing.

She sat through a dinner that seemed interminable—for
Mrs. Quinlevan, anxious to satisfy the culinary expectations of Sir Manning Hartily, had inspired her cook to set
before them two full courses, with half a dozen removes,
and side-dishes ranging from a matelot of eels to broiled
mushrooms and a Rhenish cream. It was not, in spite of its
pretensions, a particularly successful meal, for Sir Manning
was seen to look dubiously at some of the dishes, and sub-
sequently sought consolation in a spirited but somewhat
one-sided flirtation with Georgina, who was seated beside
him. This did not at all suit Lady Eliza, who wished it to be
well understood that Sir Manning was her own property,
but neither Mrs. Quinlevan nor Georgina was inclined to
be disturbed by the thinly veiled conversational barbs her
pique led her to direct toward them. Each was already too
much occupied by the far weightier difficulties on her
mind.

When the ladies rose from the table, Georgina, instead
of following her cousin and the older ladies into the Green
Saloon, caught Betsy's arm and drew her aside in the hall.

"I must speak to you in private for a few moments," she
said urgently. "Will you come upstairs with me? You can
tell your mama one of your ribbons came unfastened and
you were obliged to have it tacked on."

Betsy, her blue eyes opening wide with interest at this
hint of a mystery, obediently followed her up the broad
staircase to her bedchamber. Once they were inside,
Georgina closed the door carefully and, standing with her
back to it, said rapidly, "I scarcely know how to begin;
there is not time to explain it all to you, but I am persuaded
you will help me if you can. The truth is that I am in the
most abominable fix! Brandon and I invited Shannon here

this evening without Cousin Bella's knowledge, and now Brandon is ill and cannot appear, Cousin Bella is in a pelter, and even Major Rothe, who is an old friend of Shannon's and whom I was depending on to smooth matters over, will not be present. Will you stand by me and help me see to it that Shannon does not have a most disagreeable evening?"

She halted, waiting for an answer from Betsy, who was staring at her with a look of fascinated interest on her face.

"*You* invited Mr. Shannon?" she repeated. "But why—?"

"Because I am persuaded he does not deserve the shabby treatment he has been receiving," Georgina said impatiently, feeling her colour rising slightly under her companions's candid stare. "It is too long a matter to go into now, but, according to Major Rothe's account of him, he is quite— quite respectable, and—and worthy of our notice—"

"Oh, I *do* believe you," Miss Mott said, so fervently that Georgina began to feel some slight qualms at having confided her secret to her. "And I shall do my very best, only —what exactly am I to do?"

"Do?" Georgina had not had time to consider this herself, and said after a moment, rather lamely, "Well, you can dance with him, of course, if he asks you to stand up with him—"

"Oh, I should dearly love to waltz with him!" Betsy said earnestly. "Only I should be quite petrified with fright: he has such a shocking reputation, you know! However, as you say it is not deserved, I think I may venture it." Another thought struck her at this moment, and she said doubtfully, "But if he does not ask me—?"

"If he does not ask you, of course you cannot stand up with him!" Georgina said, despairingly characterising her new ally as a hubble-bubble creature, whose support seemed likely to be of little value to her. "But you can at least speak pleasantly to him, and say to anyone who is interested that you think it is unfair to condemn him before he has had an opportunity to show what he is."

"I shall say *that* to Robert," Miss Mott decided. "He said only the other day, after we had passed Shannon on the road driving a very neat pair of chestnuts" —she wrinkled her brow—"or were they greys?—that he could not imagine that anyone who owned such bang-up horses could be so ramshackle a fellow as he is said to be. So you see he is well disposed toward him, to begin with." She added, much less brightly, "But I do not think I should dare say such a thing to Mama or Papa. I quite wonder at you, dear Miss Power, being so brave as to invite Mr. Shannon without Mrs. Quinlevan's knowledge! I am sure I should never have had the courage to do such a thing!"

Georgina, in her present desperate mood, felt that fool-hardiness, rather than courage, would have been a more accurate word to describe her conduct; but there was no shabbing off now. She accordingly gave Betsy a few additional instructions, with little hope of their being efficacious, and led her downstairs again into the Green Saloon.

Within half an hour of this time most of the other guests had arrived and dancing had begun. When another half hour had passed without Shannon's appearance, Georgina for the first.time that evening permitted herself to nourish a faint glimmer of hope. Perhaps, she thought, he had changed his mind and drawn back at the last moment, either from pride or from embarrassment, and she could at last discard the worry that had been dogging her dismally all day.

Apparently a similar glimmer had penetrated Mrs. Quinlevan's agitated mind, for she took the occasion of an interval between country dances to draw Georgina aside and whisper to her in a hopeful voice, "My love, you *were* hoaxing me, weren't you, when you said you had asked that dreadful man here? If you were, it was not at all kind of you, you know, for I have been in such a state all evening that I do not know if I am on my head or my heels."

"But I was *not* funning!" Georgina replied. "I have already told you so! Only—only perhaps he will not come, after all—"

The words died on her lips. She was looking at a tall, broad-shouldered man, dressed quite in the most approved fashion for evening—long-tailed coat, frilled shirt, knee-breeches, and silk stockings—who was just being ushered into the room, and though there were several people between them and she had been accustomed to seeing him only in a shooting-jacket and buckskins, she could not be mistaken. It was Shannon.

Beside her, she heard Mrs. Quinlevan give a gasp of dismay. "Oh, my love! Here he comes! Oh, what in the *world* am I to do? Before all these people—! I feel ready to sink!"

Georgina put an end to these agitated exclamations by seizing her cousin's elbow and propelling her ruthlessly across the room in Shannon's direction. The music was about to begin again, and she knew she was engaged for this set to Peter Hession, but she cast Mr. Hession's claims to the winds and approached Shannon with a smile on her face that she hoped conveyed the impression that she was delighted to see him.

"Mr. Shannon! How good of you to come!" She gave Mrs. Quinlevan's elbow a little shake. "Cousin Bella, do say good evening to Mr. Shannon and tell him how sorry we are that Brandon isn't able to be of the party this evening."

From the comprehensive glance that Shannon's grey eyes cast over her and her totally discomposed cousin, Georgina, with a sinking heart, saw that he was aware that something was decidedly amiss. Chatter as she might, she could not hide the aghast, helpless expression on Mrs. Quinlevan's face, or the surprised glances that were being directed at him from every part of the room. As he bowed over Mrs. Quinlevan's hand, uttering a few brief civilities, she had an overwhelming impulse to confess the whole truth to him; but instead she heard herself talking chattily on, in a way she would have despised in any other girl, deploring the dampness of the night and the closeness of the crowded rooms. Her one excuse was that Mrs. Quinlevan had managed no more than the faintest "Good evening" in response to all her promptings, so that obviously someone had to cover the awkwardness of the moment.

Her hand was in his then, as she automatically offered it to him and he bowed over it, and for one wretched moment she thought, to her own astonishment, that she was about to burst into tears. She had made a mull of it; she knew that now, as Mrs. Quinlevan stood fluttering in distracted silence beside her. Cousin Bella was not going to be able to carry it off; already it must be apparent both to Shannon and to the other guests that the situation was not one of her own making, but one into which she had been thrust entirely against her will.

Georgina saw the expression on Shannon's face as his

eyes met hers—an expression which, in spite of the control that had often vexed her, held surprise in it, and some mortification. It was gone in a moment, as the mask of indifference descended once more, but she responded to it immediately, saying, with a slight laugh which, in her confusion, she could not save from artificiality, "I hope you will not think me too forward if I claim the honour of being the first young lady to dance with you this evening. I believe you are not very well acquainted here as yet, but I shall do my best to remedy that a little later."

He could not, she thought, fail to respond to this bold invitation, and she saw, in fact, that she had caught him by surprise. To her great annoyance, however, as he was about to lead her into the set, they were accosted by Peter Hession, who informed her directly that he believed she was engaged to him for this set.

"Thought you might have forgotten," he said blandly, looking straight through Shannon in a way that made her long to shake him. "Asked you three days ago, if you'll recollect."

"Indeed, I do not recollect!" Georgina said mendaciously. "I am sure you said the quadrille, Mr. Hession."

He put up his brows at her slightly. "Did I? I don't think I could have done that, Miss Power," he said, still ignoring Shannon's presence. "Fact of the matter is, I'd had the bad luck to be trapped into asking Lizzie Flournoy for the quadrille before I ever spoke to you. Her mother and mine are bosom-bows, you know."

At this point Shannon put an end to the matter by saying in a coolly civil voice that he had no desire to stand in the way of such a long-standing arrangement and at once moved off. Georgina, in great vexation, was obliged to surrender her hand to Mr. Hession, and had the additional vexation of being asked by him, as soon as Shannon was out of earshot, what had got into her cousin to have invited such a curst rum touch to Craythorne. She fired up at once, and told Mr. Hession that she could not see what possible affair it was of his.

"I daresay it ain't any," he agreed, with a maddening imperviousness to the set-down she had meant to convey. "All the same, it looks bad for the neighbourhood, you know—

that sort of thing. I mean to say—none of us has called on the fellow, nor means to."

"That," said Georgina emphatically, "is entirely *your* affair, Mr. Hession. Who is asked to this house, however, is, I believe, my cousin's."

"Well, that's true enough," he admitted. "But it ain't at all her style, you know. Devilish timid little woman, Mrs. Quinlevan. Not like her to set the neighbourhood by the ears." He continued reflectively, as Georgina maintained a somewhat guilty silence, "Still, you never know what dashed queer starts you'll find a woman taking. Look at my mother: there ain't a higher stickler in all of Ireland, but she has a dotty old cousin she'll trot out before the company at every blessed party she gives. Believe that fact of the matter is, some female she has on her black books once gave the old lady a snub. That would be enough for my mother. Never forgets a thing like that."

Georgina could not help smiling. In spite of his dandified ways, which had expressed themselves this evening in higher shirt-points and a more intricately arranged neckcloth than could be boasted by any other gentleman in the room, to say nothing of a stunning array of fobs, seals, and pins and an elaborately chased quizzing-glass hung on a ribbon about his neck, he was really very much of an ingenuous boy still, with a good humour that made even his toploftiness lack offence. She could guess that, removed from the supercilious coldness of Sir Landers and the formidable self-consequence of Lady Hession, he might develop into an agreeable and amusing companion, but such an event seemed little likely to occur. The only boy in a family of girls, he had been courted and petted from birth by both his parents and his sisters, and his situation at home was made so agreeable for him that Georgina believed it improbable that these ties would be relaxed even on his marriage.

She had little leisure at the present moment, however, to indulge in thoughts concerning the character and prospects of her companion; she was too much occupied in endeavouring to discover how Shannon was getting on. She saw that Mrs. Quinlevan, coming at last to some recollection of her duties as hostess, was making a feeble attempt to present him to a pair of impecunious middleaged ladies who had been invited only because they were distant connexions of her husband's family, but the conversation did not flourish, and when next she was able to find him in the crowded room he was making his way toward the alcove that led into the dining-room, which was now serving as a supper-room for the dancers.

Immediately the set was over, she rid herself of Mr. Hession by requesting him to bring her to her cousin, and then, before Mrs. Quinlevan had had time to utter more than two words of an almost tearful complaint to her, flew off into the supper-room herself. To her relief she found that Lady Eliza, at least, was not above entering into conversation with Shannon, for she was standing beside him, looking up at him with a wicked sparkle of laughter in her eyes as she spoke to him, and tapping his arm with her fan.

But her relief vanished in utter confusion as Lady Eliza, catching sight of her, called out to her, "Oh, my dear, you are exactly the person I was most wishing to see! You must come and settle a wager for me: I have staked a guinea against Shannon that Bella knew nothing of his having been asked here until the moment he walked into the house! Was this your doing, you naughty creature? I expect you know you have set the whole company by the ears!"

Georgina, feeling that she could quite willingly have strangled the impudently smiling Lady Eliza, did not know where to look. She managed, however, to say with a tolerable assumption of composure, "Of course you are funning, Lady Eliza. Have you tried the lobster patties? I wish you will; I am assured that they are particularly fine tonight."

But Lady Eliza was not so easily to be led from her subject. She said, with another little laugh, "Well, my dear, that is all very well, but you shall not hoax me; I know you are 'running a rig,' as the gentlemen say. But I must bid you adieu, Shannon: Miss Power's reputation may be good enough for her to be able to play games with you in public, but I am persuaded that mine is not!" She bestowed another tap of her fan on his arm and said to him, the sparkle very pronounced now in her prominent brown eyes, "Come and see me in private at Stokings, when you are tired of romping with the nursery set."

She then moved out of the room, flirting her fan on its

ivory sticks and leaving Georgina in a state of such fury that she had much ado to maintain an air of decorum.

"Oh! What an abominable woman!" she exclaimed. "Mr. Shannon, you *cannot* believe—"

She could not go on; as she saw his grey eyes fix themselves steadily on her face the consciousness of guilt overwhelmed her, and her words faltered into silence.

Fortunately, it was that moment that Betsy Mott chose to inaugurate the action to which she had pledged herself earlier in Georgina's bedchamber. She had come into the supper-room with Robert Darlington; seeing Shannon, she gave a visible start, coloured, and then, with an appearance of equal hesitation and resolution, approached him.

"Mr. Shannon," she said rather breathlessly, holding out her hand to him, "you may not remember me, perhaps, but we met at The Place—when Mrs. Quinlevan was ill? Mama and I had come to inquire for her—"

"I remember you very well, Miss Mott," Shannon said.

He spoke civilly, but there was a slight frown between his brows as he glanced from Betsy to young Darlington, who was looking none too pleased at the spectacle of the young lady he considered almost as his affianced bride publicly soliciting the notice of a man like Shannon. Georgina, stepping quickly into the breach, said at once, "Mr. Shannon, I believe you have not yet met Mr. Darlington?"

Bows were exchanged, a very stiff one on Mr. Darlington's part and a very slight one on Shannon's. Apparently Mr. Darlington's admiration of Shannon's horses, which Miss Mott had signified earlier that evening to Georgina, did not extend to the point of his wishing to make their owner's acquaintance, at least under a dozen pairs of censoriously watching eyes.

Miss Mott, however, with a total disregard for her escort's uneasiness, had embarked on a rather disjointed monologue, directed toward Shannon, in which, having first informed him that she considered the party a delightful one and the house charmingly decorated for the occasion, she went on to inquire into his taste in dancing.

"Mama, of course, thinks the waltz shockingly *fast*," she prattled on. "But they say it is being danced even at Almack's now, and though we *are* very much cut off from London here, in the very *depth* of the countryside, you might say, still one does not like to think one is *entirely* out of the mode. Do you waltz, Mr. Shannon?"

This transparent dangling for an invitation had the effect of deepening the look of uneasiness on young Darlington's face to one of positive alarm.

"Well, I'd like to say—coming it a bit too strong, ain't you, Betsy!" he protested. He said to Shannon rather defensively, by way of explanation, "She don't waltz, sir, I'd have you know—not except at morning-parties, with only a few couples. Lady Mott don't approve of it."

Betsy turned on him, her blue eyes indignant. "Why, what a thing to say!" she exclaimed. "Really, I do not know what affair it is of *yours*, Robert! If Mr. Shannon chooses to waltz with me, I can't think what *you* should have to say to it!"

Shannon, who had been observing the altercation with a rather sardonic expression on his face, put an end to it at this point by saying bluntly, "But I do *not* choose to waltz with you, Miss Mott." She gave a gasp, and turned from Darlington to him with a high flush mounting in her good-humoured face. He went on at once, "Don't put yourself about. I have no wish to be rude, but I seem to have caused such a scandal already merely by walking into this house that I think I should do ill indeed to add to it by dancing with a young lady of such high respectability as yourself." He then turned to Georgina, said, "My compliments to you, Miss Power, on having succeeded in enlivening what must otherwise have been a rather tame evening for one of your tastes," bowed slightly, and walked out of the room.

Miss Mott was the first to recover from the stunned silence into which the three remaining participants of this scene had been cast.

"Oh, I think it is too bad!" she said, casting a reproachful glance at young Mr. Darlington. "Need you have been so *very* rude to him, Robert? Of course you have offended him."

"Well, deuce take it, I wouldn't have done if you hadn't put yourself forward like a brass-faced monkey!" Mr. Darlington defended himself. "Making a dashed cake of yourself before everybody! What's come over you, Bet? Just because Mrs. Quinlevan chose to ask the fellow here—" He broke off, looking uncomfortably at Georgina. "I beg your pardon, Miss Power. Of course it is none of my affair," he said.

"I should think it was not!" Georgina replied.

She was looking flushed and angry, trying to make up her mind whether to go after Shannon at once and have it out with him, or to forbear for the sake of causing no more public to-do than she had already created. She decided on the latter course, and as a result young Darlington received the benefit of the pent-up emotions she was unsuccessfully attempting to bridle. She told him in no uncertain terms that she considered his behaviour toward Shannon unpardonable, and compared it bitterly to that of the Hessions.

"I thought you had both more good nature and more good sense than they have, but it seems I was mistaken," she said. "Anything to puff up your own consequence at the expense of someone you do not know and have no reason to dislike!"

She then walked out of the room into the Green Saloon, where she was at once seized on by her cousin Bella.

"Oh, my love, he has gone!" Mrs. Quinlevan said, in a tone of devout thankfulness. "You cannot think how relieved I am! I shall say it was all a misunderstanding, and that as soon as he saw that he wasn't expected—"

"Cousin Bella, if you say such a thing, I shall never speak to you again!" Georgina said fiercely.

Mrs. Quinlevan fell back before her in slight alarm. "But, really, my dear," she expostulated, "you cannot wish people to go on saying that *you* asked him to Craythorne only for a lark, which is what they are all thinking now!"

"I am quite sure it is what they are thinking, with Lady Eliza to put the idea into their minds!" Georgina said, with no signs of mitigating her opposition. "She is *bent* on making mischief, and I will not have it! If you will not say you invited him yourself, I shall tell anyone who mentions the matter to me that I did indeed ask him here without your knowledge, but *not* as a lark—that I believe the neighbourhood is using him abominably, for no good reason—"

"No, no, my love, you must not say *that!*" Mrs. Quinlevan protested, quite horrified by the thought. "They will think you are setting your cap at him, or some such vulgar thing, and indeed it will not do, not after poor Nuala— Oh, dear! Oh, dear! I do wish Lady Mercer were here, or your mama! I am sure I do not know at all what to do. Nuala was such a pretty-behaved girl, though she *did* flirt a little I must admit, but no one can take exception to *that* in a girl as beautiful and as lively as she was, and then she kept the greatest sense of propriety with it all—"

Georgina said ruthlessly, "It is no use your holding Nuala up to me, ma'am. If you find my conduct offensive you must send me away, but I will *not* have people saying I was unfeeling enough to ask Mr. Shannon here so that he could be humiliated for my amusement. Either I tell them the truth or you will say you invited him yourself; there is no other course I will agree to."

Faced with this ultimatum, Mrs. Quinlevan could do nothing but capitulate. She said weakly that perhaps no one would mention the matter, after all—a piece of optimism that was immediately laid low by Lady Hession's sailing up to her, looking more Roman than ever in imperial purple, to commiserate with her on Shannon's having had the effrontery to show his face in her house.

"I *have* heard it said that Miss Power was playing a May-game with us," she said, in a tone that showed how majestic her disapproval of such conduct would be, "but I cannot believe—"

"No, indeed!" Mrs. Quinlevan interrupted hastily, with a helpless glance at Georgina. "That is *quite* untrue—and, in fact, if you will but consider, my dear Lady Hession," she floundered on, "that we are all Christians—and that it was only last Sunday that the Vicar was speaking of our duty— though, indeed, I cannot but think that it is sometimes very difficult to know just *what* one's duty is—"

"My dear Mrs. Quinlevan, this is all very well," Lady Hession said. "But still I cannot believe that *you*, of all persons, who have already suffered so much at this man's hands, should feel it incumbent on you—"

"No, no, indeed I do not feel it so!" Mrs. Quinlevan said earnestly, and then, seeing Georgina's stern eyes on her, faltered, checked, and went on in a rush. "That is—of course I *do* feel—but you must believe—I mean, you cannot believe— Oh, dear! There is poor Lizzie Flournoy without a partner, and I daresay Mr. Cartwright might— If you will excuse me, *dear* Lady Hession!"

She hurried off in an ample flutter of draperies, leaving

Lady Hession confronting Georgina with an expression of some surprise, which gradually melted into one of majestic approval as she surveyed Georgina's gown of rose-pink sarcenet and her golden curls.

"You are in quite exceptional looks tonight, my dear Miss Power," she said complimentarily, evoking a rather startled acknowledgement from Georgina, who had not thought to find herself at that moment in the good graces of the formidable matron before her. "Pink becomes you very well—though I must tell you that I am not myself in favour, on the whole, of seeing young girls dressed in colours for an evening party until they have had their first Season in London. I gather, from what my son tells me, that you have not yet made your come-out, Miss Power?"

"No. You see—my grandfather's death—" Georgina began.

But she discovered at once—as persons with whom Lady Hession conversed customarily did—that that lady's questions were usually meant merely as rhetorical ones, requiring the briefest of responses or none at all, for she went on at once, "It is a great pity that you are not to spend at least a fortnight in London this spring, my dear child, for my own Amelia, you must know, is making her come-out this year, and I should have been only too happy to have presented you as well. Perhaps you are not aware that my late mother, Lady Larkin, was one of your grandmama's dearest friends? Their parents' estates marched together in Lincolnshire. I had almost forgotten the matter until Peter chanced to mention to me that you were Lady Mercer's granddaughter, and that, of course, immediately brought it back to me."

Georgina had a puzzled feeling, as she murmured some appropriate response, that she was being summed up and her good and bad points catalogued for future reference, with the balance, it seemed, coming out in her favour. Was it possible, she was obliged to ask herself, that Lady Hession was considering her in the light of a future daughter-in-law? It was true that she had been seeing Peter Hession almost daily, at one or another of the rides or excursions or impromptu parties that seemed to abound among the young people of the neighbourhood, and that he always appeared to find the opportunity to spend much of his time at her side. But it had never crossed her mind that he was already entertaining serious thoughts concerning her.

Perhaps, she told herself, Lady Hession was the sort of woman who could not see her son stand up twice with the same young lady at a ball without making it her business to meddle in the matter by encouraging or discouraging his attentions to her. The rejected Mr. Smallwoods' mama had been just such a managing female, and, whatever Mr. Hession's personal advantages might be over that unprepossessing young man, Georgina could not but feel that they must be dimmed by his close relationship with such a gorgon.

Her perturbation was not decreased when Peter himself, encouraged by finding her attended only by his mother while a set of country-dances was forming, came up to request her hand. She could not refuse him, and, indeed, she was given no opportunity by Lady Hession to do so.

"I am sure," that fond mama said, bestowing a tap of her fan on her son's arm, "you will be quite the handsomest couple in the room! You must forgive a mother's partiality, Miss Power—though I daresay, when you consider the matter, you may wish to tell me that it is not partiality in the least, but a mere recognition of an indubitable fact."

Georgina, catching the wicked light of amusement in Peter's eyes, said demurely that modesty prevented her from making any such remark, as she herself had been involved in the compliment, and was thereupon led off to the set, carrying in her ears Lady Hession's parting remark that she really must induce Mrs. Quinlevan to bring her to Hauld Hall very soon, so that they might become better acquainted with each other.

"She's right, you know," Peter said, grinning as he walked down the room with her. "You really should know my mother better, Miss Power. Dooced efficient woman. Nothing you can think of she can't accomplish if once she sets her mind to it."

She could only guess that he was making oblique reference to the stamp of her approval that Lady Hession had just given his attentions to her, and she felt a sudden blush mounting to her cheeks. She was determined, however, not to let him see her discomposure, and only said with a smile, "Oh, I am afraid we should not deal at all. I am persuaded she is inclined toward young ladies of irreproachable conduct, and I have often been given to understand that I do not fit that description in the least."

"Well, I daresay you may not," Mr. Hession agreed imperturbably, "especially if you are generally fond of such kick-ups as inviting that fellow Shannon here tonight to see what a dust you could raise."

He was about to go on, but she cut him short, demanding, *"Who* says I did such a thing?"

He looked surprised. "Why, everyone is saying it. Ain't it true?"

"Of course it is not!" she said angrily. "This is Lady Eliza's doing. I cannot think why she has such malice against Mr. Shannon."

"I expect it's because she knows him better than the rest of us do," Mr. Hession remarked frankly, drawing an exasperated look from his partner that only made him grin at her again. "Don't try to tell me you ain't cutting some sort of wheedle," he said. "I ain't exactly a flat, you know!"

Nothing that she could say could move him from this opinion, and it was almost a relief to her when, at the end of the set, her hand was claimed by Sir Manning Hartily, who was of no mind to concern himself with anything so unrelated to his own interests as speculation on the reasons why Shannon had been invited to Craythorne.

Relief, however, soon gave way to discomposure when it became evident that she was to be obliged to endure a ponderous flirtation as long as the set lasted. Sir Manning even took the opportunity of remarking soulfully to her that he was devilish close to letting London go hang, Season or no Season, so that he could bask a while longer in the light of her blue eyes.

"I beg you will do nothing of the sort, Sir Manning," she said, in some slight alarm that he really meant what he said. "I am quite sure your friends would be sadly disappointed."

His corpulent frame shook in a satisfied chuckle. "Mind you, I don't say they wouldn't be," he acknowledged. "If I must say it myself, Manning Hartily is generally considered to be the life and soul of any gathering to which he lends his presence. But one word from you, my dear little puss, and they shall be obliged to do without me."

She gave him an immediate assurance that word would

not be spoken by her, to the blighting of the expectations of so many of his noble friends, and presently succeeded in making her escape from him, only to fall into the hands of another partner bent on eliciting from her the whole tale of Shannon's presence there that night. She was obliged to improvise explanations for the remainder of the evening, and then, when the last guest had gone, to bear with her cousin Bella's lamentations and reproaches for a good half hour before she was permitted to go upstairs to her bedchamber.

All in all, she decided bitterly, it had been a dreadfully unsuccessful evening. The only thing she had accomplished was to make Shannon—and probably at least half the guests whom her cousin had assembled—believe that she was an unfeeling romp, who would go to any lengths to perpetrate a hoax. Decidedly, this would not do, and before she went to sleep that night she had made up her mind that the first thing she must do in the morning was to go about setting matters straight.

CHAPTER 12

How this was to be accomplished, however, presented her with something of a problem. Obviously, she could not simply request Mrs. Quinlevan to order out the carriage to take her to The Place, so that she might see Shannon and explain matters to him; her cousin would be horrified at the very thought.

She carried her dilemma to Brandon's room that morning and found him sitting up in bed, feeling a good deal better and eager to hear all that had happened the night before. His disgusted—"I told you so!"—at the conclusion of her recital did nothing to raise her spirits, which were so low by this time that she did not even resent his censure, but only asked him despairingly, "But what am I to *do?*"

"I should think you had done enough already," Brandon said, unhelpfully. "You've made a mull of it, and as far as I can see there's nothing you *can* do now that will set matters straight."

"But I *can't* have him thinking that I asked him here only to make game of him!" Georgina expostulated. "I must put him right on that score, at least. Only I haven't the least idea how to go about it."

"Write him a note," Brandon suggested, adding pessimistically, "I daresay he won't believe you, at any rate. It was a dashed harebrained thing to do, you know, and after the way you've always behaved toward him, you can hardly expect him to think you were only trying to help him."

As such was the conclusion that Georgina had already arrived at in her own mind, she could not controvert it with any real conviction. She accordingly left her cousin's room in even lower spirits than she had been in when she had entered it, and somewhat hopelessly went downstairs to the morning-room to try to compose a letter to Shannon that would, however inadequately, convey an explanation and an apology to him.

After several fruitless attempts she was about to throw her pen down in despair when Miss Mott was announced. Georgina was scarcely in a mood to welcome being obliged to rehearse once more with Betsy the disagreeable events of the previous evening, but she asked resignedly that the visitor be shown into the Green Saloon, where she herself presently joined her.

She found Betsy, becomingly attired in a simple high-necked gown of jaconet muslin and a *bergère* hat, in a state of the dismals that quite equalled her own. She embarked at once on a tearful account of the quarrel with Mr. Darlington that her imprudent championing of Shannon had provoked, looking at Georgina, at its conclusion, as if she felt she must be the one to advise her on how to mend it, since it had been her plea for aid that had landed her in the suds in the first place.

Georgina's response to this was a rather impatient suggestion that, since Mr. Darlington was obviously head over ears in love with her, she had only to wait a few days and his pique would wear itself out.

"But if it does not—?" Betsy protested.

"Don't be a pea-goose!" Georgina replied. "Of course it will." she added darkly. "If you think *that* is a problem, I could wish you had mine. I am quite certain that Shannon thinks I asked him here only to roast him, and he will go on thinking it unless I can somehow manage to see him and explain—" A sudden inspiration flashed into her mind; she broke off and said rapidly to Miss Mott, "I cannot go to The Place alone, you see, but if you were to go with me— Yes, I am persuaded that would be quite the thing to do!"

"If I were to go with you?" Betsy faltered. She looked at Georgina with a wariness born of the unhappy results that had followed on her earlier attempt to be of assistance to her. "But I couldn't possibly—" she protested. "I mean, Mama would never permit me—"

"Your mama need know nothing at all about it," Georgina said. "We shall simply make an engagement to go for a ride tomorrow morning. I suppose you have a groom you can trust? Or we might make some excuse to rid ourselves of him for half an hour—" She checked, seeing

Betsy staring at her in dismay, and said, "Good God, what harm would you be doing? I cannot visit Shannon alone, and how I am to contrive to tell him I meant only to help him by asking him here last night is something that has had me at my wits' end all the morning."

It did no good for Betsy to suggest, as Brandon had done, that Georgina set her explanation down in a letter; Georgina demolished that argument at once by stating that that was exactly what she had been attempting to do for the past hour, with absolutely no success.

"One can always *say* things so much better than one can write them," she said incontrovertibly. "And then the person one is talking to is obliged to answer, and one gets into a discussion or even a quarrel, when one can say all kinds of things one would feel exceedingly silly trying to write in a letter."

Miss Mott obviously did not see how quarrelling with Mr. Shannon would mend matters, but she was a biddable girl, with a strong romantic tendency that made her look on a visit to The Place as a desirable, though perilous, adventure. In the end she agreed to go with Georgina, and forthwith engaged herself to ride over to Craythorne the following morning, bringing Sir Humphrey's roan hack as a mount for her friend.

As no objections were entered either by Lady Mott or by Mrs. Quinlevan to the unexceptionable plan of two young ladies to take a morning ride together, accompanied by one of Sir Humphrey's grooms, Georgina and Miss Mott set out at an early hour on the following day. It was Georgina's plan to attempt to forestall Shannon before he rode out over the estate; they need not then even go into the house, she assured Betsy, for she could say all she desired to while she remained on her horse and Shannon on his.

"You had best ride out of the way a little with Hussey while I talk to him," she said, "for I shall have to tell him, of course, that it was I, and not Cousin Bella, who sent him the invitation, and if *that* is spread about the neighbourhood I had as well spare all my trouble."

Instead of engaging to do this, however, Betsy unexpectedly spent the following half hour in urging Georgina to abandon her scheme entirely. It appeared that she had made up her quarrel with Mr. Darlington the previous evening, and that he had lectured her so strongly on the inadvisability of having anything to do with so ramshackle a fellow as Shannon that she had ended by meekly promising to heed his advice.

Her conscience was therefore troubling her severely this morning, and she did her utmost to convince Georgina that her plan of seeing Shannon in secret was not only reprehensibly unbecoming, but must, in addition, very probably become known in the neighbourhood, leading to dire consequences not only for Georgina but for herself.

"For Robert will be so dreadfully angry if he hears of it," she pleaded, "and indeed I cannot blame him, for I promised him faithfully—"

"Well, *I* have promised nothing at all," Georgina said mulishly, "and it makes no difference to me what your precious Robert says— *I* am going to see Shannon!" She added, "If you don't care to go with me, of course you need not. I shall go alone, and bring your father's horse back to Mott House when I have finished my errand."

But to this Betsy, knowing full well what her mother would say if she allowed Georgina to go jauntering about the countryside alone, could not agree. After a good deal of rather heated discussion a compromise was finally reached: Betsy would ride with her friend toward The Place until it could be seen if Georgina's plan of meeting Shannon outside the house could be carried out, but at the first sight of the master of The Place she and Hussey would make off, leaving Georgina to have her conversation with Shannon alone and then rejoin them later at a prearranged spot.

What would happen if they were not fortunate enough to meet Shannon was not decided, Betsy no doubt hoping that in that case she would be able to persuade her friend to abandon her plan, and Georgina quite determined to do nothing of the sort.

Luckily for both, the first thing they saw when they came in sight of The Place was Shannon just leaving the stable area on his mare Juno. He did not immediately perceive them, and was turning the mare's head in another direction when Georgina called to him, spurring the roan toward him while Betsy ordered Hussey in an agitated tone to follow her and rode off in the way they had come. Shannon, raising his eyes at Georgina's hail, checked the mare and brought her around. In another few moments Georgina was beside him and, reining her horse in, said to him eagerly, "Mr. Shannon! How fortunate that I have met you! I have something of particular importance to say to you—"

She had progressed so far when it occurred to her that the cool grey eyes she was looking into were regarding her with something less than cordiality, and she faltered, breaking off.

"Yes?" Shannon prompted her, ironically. "Something of particular importance, Miss Power? May I be permitted to guess that it has to do with the prank you played the other evening? An apology, perhaps? I assure you it is quite unnecessary. I was no doubt somewhat credulous to have been gulled into thinking that such an action was quite beneath a young lady of your breeding, but in these cases the butt of the joke has only his own lack of wit to blame, I believe."

For a moment, finding the ground cut from under her feet in this way, she could only regard him in dumbfounded protest. Then the colour flew into her face and she said with dignity, "I was *not* about to apologise to you! I have nothing to apologise for! I merely wished to offer you an explanation."

"I imagine that it makes very little difference whether we call it an explanation or an apology," he said indifferently. "Consider it made, Miss Power. And now, if there is nothing else to detain you here—"

"But there *is* something! You do not understand in the least, and now you will not even listen to me! Oh," she continued, her fury rising as she looked into his unmoved face, "you make me sorry that I even *tried* to help you!"

"To help me?" He gave her a swift glance; then the sardonic expression returned again to his face. "No, that won't fadge, Miss Power," he said dryly. "You must think of some better tale than that."

"But it's true! I thought I should be doing you a good turn, and that if people saw you were invited to Craythorne they would stop behaving toward you in such an abominable manner—which I am *quite* sure now that you thoroughly deserve!"

To her surprise, she saw a rather ironical smile suddenly light his face.

"Good God, I believe you are telling the truth!" he said. "You addlebrained child, did you really think you could play such a May-game as that off on people and bring it to any good end?"

"Yes, I did!" she said. "And I might have carried it off, too, if Brandon had not become ill and Major Rothe been obliged to go to England."

He looked at her incredulously. "Did Rothe know of this, then?"

"No, of course not! I met him only once, at Stokings; it is not very likely that I should make any plans with *him*. But he let fall a few words about you—that he considered you one of his closest friends, and—and certain other things that made me even more sure that an injustice was being done you—"

"Which you thereupon took it upon yourself to right," he said.

She saw that he was looking amused again, and her anger returned.

"I see nothing to smile about!" she said crossly. "You will be excessively uncomfortable, living here, if no one will recognise you."

"Oh, I believe not," he said carelessly. "I am not a very sociable creature, Miss Power—as you have probably discovered for yourself. But I suppose I must thank you for your good intentions, at any rate."

"Pray don't put yourself to the trouble," she said stiffly. "Sir John—my grandfather—was used to say that pretended gratitude is worse than none at all."

He knit his brows, surveying her oddly. "Was it your grandfather, I wonder, who gave you your peculiar notions of propriety and your severe sense of justice, Miss Power?" he asked. "As I recall, young Quinlevan told me you were in the care of two female relatives who were the highest of sticklers, which has given me something to puzzle over from the start."

She blushed, interrupting him. "Grandmama and Mama," she said. "But that is only since Sir John died. Before that, I was almost entirely in *his* care. And I am sure his ideas were all very good ones," she added, firing up again, "except that I am not a boy, which is what he would have liked, Grandmama always said. Only I cannot see that that signifies, for if it is just and honourable for a boy to do certain things, it cannot be less so for a girl."

He smiled again, this time, it appeared to her, without irony. "Now you are putting *me* to the blush, Miss Power," he said. "I am beginning to believe that, if apologies are in order, it is I who owe you one, instead of the other way around. But how was I to guess that you were not like other well-looking girls of your age?—thinking only of your own amusement, and the devil take anyone who is burned in the process—"

He broke off, seeing the rather startled look on her face. The remembrance had suddenly entered her head that Nuala had been much of her own years when he had married her, and certainly one might have thought that, with her memory so fresh in his mind, he would scarcely have voiced such a sweeping stricture.

He seemed to read what was passing through her head, for after a moment he said, rather shortly, "Are you thinking of Nuala? You should know as well as I whether that description fits *her*."

She shook her head; the renewed harshness of his tone, which seemed to her to have softened somewhat in the course of their conversation, made her uncomfortable.

"No, I *don't* know," she said. "You see, I never met her." She ventured tentatively, "She was very beautiful, I'm told."

"She was," he said, so briefly and coldly that she was made quite aware that he did not wish to continue the subject. She was left to wonder whether the sudden alteration in his manner was due to the fact that his loss was still too painfully recent for him to be able to discuss it, or to indifference toward—or, indeed, positive dislike of—his dead wife. He did not give her the leisure to resolve the question in her mind, but went on almost at once, in much the same tone, "Speaking of the proprieties—you are not left to wander about the countryside alone by that pair I saw shabbing off just now, are you?"

"Oh, no," she assured him. "I am to meet them later: that

was part of the plan. You see, Betsy was afraid to come this far with me because she had promised Mr. Darlington—"

She broke off in vexation at having almost been betrayed into uttering what could only sound to him like another slight.

But he finished it for her quite coolly: "—Because she had promised Mr. Darlington that she would have nothing to do with me. Do you imagine that surprises me? I assure you it does not. The only thing that *does* surprise me is how you prevailed on her to come this far with you—and to be so obliging to me the other evening at Craythorne, for I am sure that must have been your doing as well."

"Well—yes," she admitted, adding demurely, with just the hint of an upturn of the corners of her lips, "but I must confess that it wasn't difficult. You see, she considers you a romantic figure."

He stared at her wrathfully for a moment. "Getting your own back, Miss Power?" he demanded.

"No, no! I assure you, it's quite true."

His rather harsh smile erased the frown. "You'll not deny that you're roasting me now," he said, "whatever you may have intended the other evening." Somewhat more grimly, he added, "I only hope you do not share Miss Mott's bird-witted delusion. There is not a grain of truth in it, as you may discover some day to your cost."

"Oh, I am quite aware of *that!*" she said at once. "Sir John always told me that men who were long on length and brawn, like yourself, were hardly ever poetically inclined and usually turned out to be much more prosaic than some little dyspeptic creature a girl reared on lending-library novels would never trouble to turn her head after. But I am not romantically inclined, you see, like Betsy—Miss Mott. Indeed, Grandmama often says that I have a *loweringly* practical mind, which she considers quite unsuitable in a well-bred young female."

She looked hopefully at him and saw that, in spite of his continued dourness, there was the glint of a smile in his grey eyes.

"If your ideas of practicality include inviting unwanted guests to your unsuspecting relatives' homes, I can see that your grandmother's opinion may be justified," he said.

"Do you? I do not at all! I still think it would have been a splendid idea, if only I had had a little help in carrying it off. Even as it is, no one knows for certain that Cousin Bella did not ask you to Craythorne herself, for I persuaded her not to give me away."

"Persuaded her or coerced her?"

"Oh, very well—if you wish to cavil!" she said. "But she really is a very good-hearted creature, you know; it is only that she is frightened half to death of you, and of what people will think—" A thoughtful expression came over her face. "As a matter of fact," she went on. "I wonder if it would not be a good idea for you to call at Craythorne to apologise for having come in upon her without her knowledge? If you did, I am quite persuaded she would take it in good part, and if you were civil to her she might even begin to like you a little, and to see that there really can be no objection to your being friendly with Brandon—"

"How is Brandon keeping these days?" he cut in, ignoring this hopeful suggestion.

"Well, he is not in very good frame just now," she admitted. "He came down with a putrid sore throat the other day, and Dr. Culreavy has insisted on his keeping his bed —which he finds excessively boring, poor boy. I am sure *he* would be very grateful for a visit from you," she added perseveringly.

She saw his lips twitch, the coldness again gone from his face. "I see that you are still determined to rehabilitate me," he said. "Do you never admit defeat, Miss Power?"

"Hardly ever. Sir John always said—"

He flung up a hand, halting her. "Thank you, I can guess what Sir John's sentiments were on the subject. I doubt, though, that he would have considered your present project an entirely admirable one."

"Well, I do not know that, either," she disagreed, "but we will not argue over it. The main thing is—you *will* come, will you not?"

"I shall do nothing of the kind. Mrs. Quinlevan was shockingly upset by my arrival the other evening, and I have no intention of repeating my blunder." He added, after a moment, "You may tell Brandon that I am sorry he is laid up, and that if he cares to ride over some morning, when he is feeling more the thing, I shall be happy to see him."

"Thank you!" she said. "He will be pleased, you know, for he *does* consider it hard that he is not to be allowed to see you merely because of people's stupid prejudices." She gathered up her reins, saying, with a look of mischief on her face, "Will you drop your ban against the rest of us at Craythorne as well if I prevail on Cousin Bella to ask you to tea some afternoon?"

"I should take such an invitation for exactly what it is worth, Miss Power—as another of your well-meant hoaxes."

"Oh, no—that is too bad! Depend on it, I shall send no more invitations without Cousin Bella's knowledge; I have been burnt too badly already at that game! But it really *would* be much better if the two of you cried friends, you know. Family quarrels are always a cause for gossip, and if she wishes whatever scandal there may have been in your marrying Nuala to be forgotten, she would do far better to go on terms of ordinary civility with you than to keep up this stupid quarrel." She saw that he was regarding her oddly, and asked involuntarily, *"Now* what have I said to make you look so—so queer?"

"I was only wondering—has it never occurred to *you* to resent my having carried off your cousin's fortune, when you might have been mistress of The Place now yourself? You told me once that you did not, but—"

"But you were out of patience with me at the time and did not believe me," she finished it for him. "Well, I *don't* resent it. I daresay I might if I were to have nothing, but Grandmama is very well to pass, you see, and unless she becomes out of reason angry with me, she is certain to provide very well for me." She gave him a straight look and added, "So you see, not having my cousin's fortune merely means that *I* shall run less risk of having people say when I marry that the offer was made only because I was an heiress."

The expression in his eyes as she concluded this speech disconcerted her: under that direct, penetrating gaze she felt all the artificialities of their relationship suddenly stripped away, leaving her defenceless, almost breathless, in the presence of an emotion she had scarcely dreamed of only instants before.

But he merely said to her curtly, after a moment, "I hardly think they will be able to say such a thing of *you*, in any event," and then turned his horse's head in the direction in which Betsy had disappeared, remarking, "I'll ride with you until you are in sight of your friend. Come along!"

He set his mare into a brisk trot, taking it for granted, apparently, that she would follow him. Nothing was said until they came in view of Betsy, who had halted her horse at the top of a slight rise and seemed to be anxiously awaiting her friend's reappearance. Shannon then checked his mare and, turning in the saddle, said to Georgina in a harsh tone that seemed quite altered from any he had used to her previously, "I'll leave you now. May I give you one piece of advice? I am a poor subject for altruism, Miss Power. You had best lay no more plans concerning me."

Their eyes met; hers were the first to fall, as she felt perturbed colour flooding her face. The next instant he had wheeled his horse and galloped away, leaving her to pursue her way more slowly up the rise toward Betsy.

Miss Mott's face, as Georgina approached her, wore an expression of mingled relief and curiosity.

"What did he say to you? Was he very angry?" she whispered, as they turned their horses' heads toward Mott House.

The groom was at a discreet distance behind, out of hearing of a low-voiced conversation, but Georgina was not communicative.

"No," she said briefly. "Not—angry."

"He *looked* angry—or at least very odd," Miss Mott persisted. "I should think—"

"Well, it is of no use for you to think anything at all! You didn't have the spirit to come along with me, so you have no right to ask questions now," Georgina said, in a voice which, in spite of herself, was not quite steady.

She saw Betsy's startled gaze on her, and took herself sharply in hand. It would be quite like Miss Mott to whisper the tale of her discomposure to everyone who would listen, if she were to allow her to see it, but the task of appearing her ordinary self was a severe strain on her powers of dissimulation. She did not feel at all like her ordinary self; she had become aware of something, in those few moments when her eyes had met Shannon's, that had set her brain in a whirl and her pulses racing.

She wished now, fervently, that she had never been so unwary as to involve herself with him. At one time she had thought, with some incredulity, that she might be conceiving an interest in him; it occurred to her now, to her shaken amazement, that she was already far gone in love for him, and that—unless she had quite mistaken the look in his eyes that had so perturbed her on their parting—it was highly probable that her feelings were returned.

CHAPTER 13

She gave only a brief report of her encounter with Shannon to Brandon—merely enough to convey to him the message about Shannon's willingness to see him at The Place—and none at all to Mrs. Quinlevan. She had thought it would be as well if her cousin knew nothing of the purpose of the expedition on which she had set out that morning, and had accordingly pledged Betsy to secrecy, without a great deal of hope, however, that Miss Mott would abide by her promise.

Her mistrust was not unjustified. Two days later Mrs. Quinlevan came home from a gossip with Lady Mott to inquire of her, in the utmost dismay, whether she had indeed gone off to meet Shannon at The Place.

"Lucinda said Betsy could not be perfectly sure it was an *assignation*," she said agitatedly, "or, rather, the fact is that she could not manage to get a straight story out of her after Betsy had let slip a word about the matter. But she was certain you had seen Shannon—"

"It was *not* an assignation!" Georgina said warmly. "Betsy Mott is a goose-cap! If she *must* let her tongue fly about matters that are no concern of hers, she might at least see that she tells the truth! Shannon knew nothing about my intending to see him. I wanted to apologise to him for the bumblebath I led him into here the other night, and I did, and that is the whole of the affair!"

Mrs. Quinlevan plumped down in the nearest chair, turning a distracted countenance on her young cousin.

"But, surely, my love, you *must* know how improper it is for you to be putting yourself in a position where such things can be said of you!" she protested faintly. "I vow I was ready to sink when Lucinda confided the matter to me—not that I believe she is ill-natured enough to repeat it to anyone else, but you know yourself how Betsy allows her tongue to run away with her. I have no doubt it is all over the neighbourhood by this time."

"I hope it is!" Georgina said unrepentantly, bringing a moan of horror from Mrs. Quinlevan, who was vainly attempting, with fluttering fingers, to untie her bonnet-strings. "Yes, I do!" she repeated. "I should like them to know that there is one person, at least, who feels properly about the disgraceful rudeness to which he was treated here the other evening. And if they wish to gossip about me because I have done what I am sure Sir John would have considered the right thing for me to do, I don't care! In fact I am glad of it!" she declared, throwing caution to the winds.

"Yes, but Sir John is dead, my dear," her cousin reminded her piteously, finally succeeding in disentangling the strings of her bonnet and flinging that elegant article of *gros de Naples* and purple ribbon down with a disregard that betrayed her perturbation. "We must think of your grandmama now, and I am *sure* Lady Mercer would never approve— Not but what I *will* admit that he acted very properly here the other evening, for I will give the devil his due, and I am sure he was got up as elegantly as any gentleman present, which was a compliment to me, I have no doubt, as Lucinda says no one ever sees him except in a shooting-jacket and muddy boots, with one of those horrid Belcher neckerchiefs instead of a proper cravat—" She broke off, waving a plump hand distractedly. "Oh, where was I? That is not at all what I meant to say!"

"I know exactly what you mean to say, ma'am, so I beg you will give yourself no more trouble over it," Georgina said, smiling in spite of herself. "You will put yourself quite out of frame if you allow yourself to be so upset by a word of gossip. And, at any rate, I can assure you that I plan no further meetings with Mr. Shannon."

"Yes, but, my love, you *will* meet him, you know," Mrs. Quinlevan objected, "for Lady Eliza has sent him a card for her ball and he has accepted." Georgina looked startled, but her cousin nodded her head in agitated confirmation of her words. "Yes, indeed she has," she said, "for she told Lucinda so herself, and though she vows it was out of consideration for Major Rothe, who is a great friend of his,

Lucinda says *she* is persuaded that what she really wishes is to set us all in a bustle."

"Is Major Rothe at Stokings again, then?" Georgina interrupted, wrinkling her brows in an attempt to unravel all the significance of her cousin's disjointed account. "I thought he had not meant to return."

"Yes, so did we all, but it seems his brother is much recovered, and Lucinda says Lady Eliza tells her he came back on Mr. Shannon's account, because he had scarcely had an opportunity to see him when he was here previously. But if that is true I do not see why he does not stay at The Place, so that Lady Eliza will not be obliged to invite Mr. Shannon to Stokings."

"She is not obliged in the least to invite him," Georgina said, in a cool little voice. "She did it, I am sure, only because she wished to."

Mrs. Quinlevan stared at her. "My dear child, you do not know what you are saying!" she protested. "I know she flirts with every man she takes a fancy to, in that shocking London fashion of hers, but Mr. Shannon is quite beneath her touch!"

"Oh, yes!" Georgina agreed. "I am sure she thinks so, too. But she is determined to bring him round her thumb, all the same." She became aware that she was speaking with a bitter emphasis that was causing Mrs. Quinlevan to regard her in astonishment, and hastily added, "Not that it is any concern of mine, of course. Lady Eliza may do as she pleases, but I should think that Colonel Malladon——"

"Oh no, my dear, Colonel Malladon will have nothing to say to it," Mrs. Quinlevan assured her. "He has never been able to control her, and, indeed, I believe he has ceased to try to do so. But one would think, after what happened to poor Nuala while she was under her protection, that she, of all people, would take care not to put herself into a position where she will be open to scandalous gossip on Mr. Shannon's account! I am *persuaded* that she must be asking him only from good nature."

Georgina had little opinion of Lady Eliza's good nature, but she did not choose to debate the matter further with her cousin, and therefore made some excuse to break off the conversation and leave the room.

But the news that Shannon would be at Lady Eliza's ball had furnished her with a great deal of food for thought. She believed she knew very well what Lady Eliza's motives had been in sending him a card of invitation, but what his had been in accepting it, after the embarrassing situation into which he had stepped at Craythorne, she could only conjecture. Her imagination suggested that it might be because he knew he would see her there, and then fell before the practical consideration that he might merely be taking advantage of another opportunity to better his position in the neighbourhood.

But in spite of her lack of assurance in this head, she certainly felt called upon to make every attempt to look her best on the evening of the ball at Stokings a week later. She had accepted Mrs. Quinlevan's offer to have Anson dress her hair, and had gone to considerable pains to procure the exact shade of ribbon that would most becomingly trim her three-quarter dress of white spider gauze, worn over a slip of jonquil satin. Even Mrs. Quinlevan, who was accustomed to speaking of her as a very well-looking girl, though not, of course, to be compared to her poor Nuala, admitted, when she appeared before her in her *delicate,* high-waisted gown, her golden curls dressed *à la Tite,* and with a shawl of silver net drapery, Denmark satin slippers, and long French kid gloves completing her costume, that even Nuala would not have been able to cast her in the shade that evening.

But the exceptional looks in which her young cousin appeared merely served to deepen Mrs. Quinlevan's apprehensions over the ball. She had noted with misgiving Peter Hession's attentions to Georgina on the evening of the party at Craythorne and the fact that he seemed to be impelled to call at her house very frequently of late; and the disagreeable idea now occurred to her that perhaps, dazzled by Georgina's appearance that evening, he might be led on to make an outright offer, which it would be her duty to convey in form to Lady Mercer and Mrs. Power. She had little doubt of what the outcome of such a situation must be. The two ladies in Bath, known to be anxious to see Georgina settled in a suitable marriage, would certainly find nothing to object to in young Mr. Hession's fortune, person, or position in life, and their approval of the match must therefore be taken for granted.

Nor had Lady Hession's complaisant manner toward Georgina on the evening of the Craythorne party been lost on Mrs. Quinlevan, and if Lady Hession were to be found forwarding the match, she knew that Sir Landers' consent to it must be assured, for that gentleman seldom moved contrary to his wife's wishes.

Of Georgina's feelings she was less certain, but even in this direction the outlook seemed gloomy. She and Mr. Hession appeared to be on the best of terms, in spite of an occasional disagreement arising from the young man's adherence to the overconsequential ideas of his parents, and, although Georgina had shown no signs of a definite partiality, Mrs. Quinlevan did not doubt that the united influence of Lady Mercer and Mrs. Power would soon overcome any hesitation she might feel over accepting an offer from him.

All in all, it seemed to her that her plans to marry Brandon to his cousin were in a fair way to be completely overset—an apprehension that quite drove her fears regarding Shannon from her head. As a result, during the drive to Stokings she bestowed scarcely a thought on the probability of his appearing there that evening, occupying herself instead with a series of schemes for seeing to it that Mr. Hession had no opportunity to do more than stand up once with Georgina during the evening.

When they arrived at Stokings they found the house lit from attic to cellar, and a steady succession of carriages drawing up at the front door. Alighting from her own landaulet, Mrs. Quinlevan passed with Georgina up the broad steps to the door and entered the house. Like The Place of the Oaks, Stokings had been built in Tudor times, but, unlike it, it had received extensive alterations, and Lady Eliza, since becoming its mistress, had instituted a plan of campaign in regard to its interior decoration that had made it the talk of the neighbourhood. On her previous visit Georgina had seen little beyond the hall and the Red Saloon, which had impressed her, even in daylight, as being somewhat startling apartments, with dragons writhing on crimson silk draperies and Buhl tables bearing porcelain tigers and pagodas.

Now, in the blaze of the hundreds of candles that illumined it, with all its rooms thrown open for the entertainment of the guests, she positively blinked on entering the great hall. Lady Eliza, obviously influenced by her visits to the monstrously ornate Pavilion which the Prince Regent had had constructed in Brighton, had done her best to emulate its Oriental splendour in the unlikely Tudor surroundings of Stokings, and the result was a phantasmagoria of blue and crimson and yellow, blazing with lustres of rubies and brilliants and assaulting the eye with the golden suns, stars, pagodas, water-lilies, and dragons that decorated its walls and sprang from each sofa back and pillar head.

Passing up the stairs to the ballroom, Georgina and her cousin found Lady Eliza receiving in a gown of crimson silk quite in keeping with her surroundings, with a fantastic creation of gleaming brilliants, lace, and ostrich plumes nodding from her head. She greeted them with her usual vivacity, but Georgina felt that there was a certain malice in the glance she cast over her.

"I see you have already learned that I am taking a leaf from *your* book this evening, my dear," she said. "Positively, I have seen you in such looks! But you must not expect too much, you know. It is possible that Shannon will not dare to show his face, after the snubbing he received at Craythorne. You had best content yourself with dazzling young Peter Hession."

Georgina, who had begun to colour vividly as soon as she had caught the intent of Lady Eliza's remarks, was spared the necessity of making any rejoinder by Mrs. Quinlevan, who turned from the civilities she was uttering to Colonel Malladon to say, in a perfect quiver of indignation, "Lady Eliza, I do *beg* you will not make such nonsensical insinuations! What has Mr. Shannon to say to my cousin? He is none of *her* concern, I assure you!"

Lady Eliza laughed. "No?" she asked. "I devoutly hope you are right, Bella dear! But I have been hearing the oddest stories, you see—about excursions on horseback leading to strange meetings, and— But of course I never repeat gossip, you know!"

She turned to the next guest, leaving Georgina and Mrs. Quinlevan to pass on into the ballroom. Here they were at once accosted by Sir Manning Hartily, who begged the honour of standing up with Miss Power for the quadrille.

"Consider myself fortunate to have snatched you up the minute you stepped inside the door!" he beamed. "Daresay you'll have a shocking crowd of young fellows around you all evening. No time then for an old fogey like me!"

"Oh, Sir Manning, how can you say so!" Mrs. Quinlevan cried, making up with her own eager cordiality for a marked lack of enthusiasm in her cousin's demeanour. "I am sure Georgina is always honoured to stand up with you —such an elegant master of the art as you are!"

"Well, I fancy I *am* up to all the latest rigs," Sir Manning said complacently. "Can still keep up with the young fellows, you know, ma'am—dance all night, waltz, quadrille, along with the best of 'em. Do you waltz, Miss Power?"

"No, sir," Georgina was thankfully able to answer, leaving Mrs. Quinlevan to go into voluble explanations of her own feelings concerning such "fast" modern dances, feelings that she was sure even the approval of the august patronesses of Almack's could not alter.

"For what," she inquired of Sir Manning, "can be more distasteful to a well-bred young female than to be twirling about a ballroom floor in the *public* embrace of a young man?"

Here, however, she soon perceived that she had taken the wrong tack, for Sir Manning was very fond of waltzing, to the extent to which his girth permitted him to indulge in it, and considered such old-fashioned notions as Mrs. Quinlevan had expressed to be quite beneath his reputation as a gentleman of the first stare of fashion. Fortunately for her, her brother, Mr. Jeremy Barnwall, who was an old friend of Sir Manning's, walked into the room at that moment, and in the flurry of greetings and demands for the latest London *on-dits* that ensued, Mrs. Quinlevan's solecism was forgotten.

Georgina had not previously met her cousin Jeremy, as he had not returned to Ireland since his precipitous departure from it on the day following her arrival. She greeted him with suitable cordiality, which was somewhat diminished, however, when, after he had surveyed her with the utmost attention for several moments, he remarked frankly to his sister, "You must be touched in your upper works, Bella, to think she'll do for Brandon. Damme, she must have the young fellows buzzing about her like flies!"

"What's this? Brandon? Who is Brandon?" Sir Manning demanded jovially, and, finding himself suddenly jostled by a young gentleman who had been hovering on the edge of the group, waiting for an opportunity to enter the conversation, looked around wrathfully into the perturbed face of Mr. Peter Hession.

"Beg pardon, Sir Manning! Servant, Mrs. Quinlevan—Miss Power—Mr. Barnwall!" Peter gasped, apparently as overcome by his own rudeness as was Sir Manning.

All the same, the expression of indignant reproach that had leaped into his eyes at the moment when he had so far gotten himself as to intrude into the circle around Georgina failed to disappear, and it was not difficult to guess that it had been put there by his overhearing Mr. Barnwall's blunt reference to his sister's scheme of marrying Georgina to her son.

It had evidently been Mr. Hession's intention to solicit Georgina's hand for the set of country-dances that was just then forming, but in his embarrassment over having intruded into the conversation in such a peculiar manner he did not immediately speak, and as a result had the mortification of seeing her led off a few moments later by another young gentleman. This circumstance, though displeasing to him, was highly gratifying to Mrs. Quinlevan, who confided forebodingly to her brother, as soon as Peter was out of hearing, that she greatly feared that that young man was on the point of making an offer for Georgina.

Mr. Barnwall, raising his brows, pursed his lips and kindly observed, "No need to fly into a pucker, Bella. Told you so when you first mentioned the scheme to me. If it wasn't him, it 'ud be another young sprig. Pretty as a picture, that girl, you know."

Mrs. Quinlevan uttered an aggrieved and indignant exclamation. "One would think you cared nothing at all for poor Brandon!" she accused him. "If you would have made the smallest push to assist me, instead of running off to London in that inconsiderate manner, I daresay we should have the matter settled by this time. And I must say I take it very ill that you did not so much as notify me that you were returning to Kerry, and that I am obliged to run

across you here as though we were the merest acquaintances!"

"Dash it all, Bella, you know I'm a bird of passage," Mr.
Barnwall objected. "Never know where I'll be from one
minute to the next. Popped over only to buy a horse for a
friend of mine. Thought while I was here I might just look
in on Lady Eliza's ball—"

"Well, I hope, now that you *are* here, you will not object
to obliging me by doing your possible to see to it that
Georgina does not stand up above once with Peter Hession,
and that she has no opportunity to speak privately with
him." She added, with awful civility, "After all Brandon *is*
your only nephew, and as I, a widowed mother, am left
alone in the world to look after my son's interests—"

"Not at a ball, Bella!" Mr. Barnwall said, with a look of
injury equalling her own appearing on his face. "Damme if
I ever saw such a woman for choosing the wrong time and
place to enact a Cheltenham tragedy! No!" he added hastily, seeing her open her lips to speak. "Don't come down on
me here! I'll do what I can for you, I promise you, but
you're fighting a losing battle—may as well make up your
mind to *that!*"

He moved away, greeting Sir Humphrey and Lady Mott,
who had just entered the room with their daughter Betsy,
with an eagerness that Mrs. Quinlevan darkly considered
was due more to his desire to escape from her than to any
interest in conversing with them.

A short time later she had established herself on one of
the rout chairs that had been set out along the walls of the
ballroom for those guests who preferred to watch the dancing rather than to engage in it, joining a group of which
Lady Hession was a member. Lady Hession, evidently considering that a country ball which she had postponed her
departure to London to attend was worthy of her most elegant finery, was wearing a gown of purple-blue taffeta lav-
ishly ornamented with rouleaux of blue satin, and a turban from which several ostrich plumes rose. Being satisfied
that she was putting her companions quite in the shade, she
was in an affable mood, and took the first opportunity to
congratulate Mrs. Quinlevan on Georgina's being in such
high bloom that evening.

"I am sure she and my Peter will be a picture to behold when they stand up together," she said, "as I am persuaded they will, for Peter has confided in me that he will be certain to make every effort to engage her hand not only for a set of country-dances, but for the quadrille as well."

Mrs. Quinlevan tossed her head. "Well, *there* I believe he must be disappointed," she said complacently, noting with approval that Georgina was now safely partnered with Major Rothe, "for we had scarcely set foot inside the door before Sir Manning Hartily was soliciting her hand for the quadrille."

"Indeed!" Lady Hession said, rising her brows. "I am sorry to hear that, for I am persuaded she would have enjoyed herself a great deal more if she had had the pleasure of standing up with Peter. He is accounted an excellent dancer, you know; indeed, I have heard him praised for his skill even at Almack's, where so many gentlemen of the highest dexterity in the art are to be seen. However," she went on, with a majestic attempt at archness, "I daresay if Miss Power is to bestow her hand only on such—shall we say, mature?—gentlemen as Sir Manning and Major Rothe, my Peter will have little to fear in the way of a rival."

Mrs. Quinlevan, rising to the challenge, felt it incumbent on her to plunge in here with a remark which she was well aware Mr. Barnwall would have strongly deprecated her making, had he been present.

"I wonder that you should speak so, Lady Hession," she said, "for I am persuaded you must be aware that, while dear Georgina behaves with perfect civility toward *all* the young gentlemen who count themselves among her admirers, she keeps her deepest regard for her cousin Brandon. Indeed, she is not at all one of these light-minded modern young girls who enjoy racketing about constantly to balls and parties, but is perfectly content to spend a quiet day with her cousin as often as may be."

Lady Hession seemed much struck by this speech. "Brandon!" she said, in considerable surprise, which seemed to be strongly intermingled with disapproval as well. "But, my dear Mrs. Quinlevan, this cannot be! I wish to say nothing against the boy, but surely you cannot believe that he is of an age to think of settling himself in life! He cannot be nineteen!"

"He is past nineteen," Mrs. Quinlevan said, her feathers ruffling at this outspoken opposition, "and, indeed, he is very mature for his years—much more mature, I might say, than young men who have their minds fixed on nothing but curricle-racing and dandyism and, for what I know, gaming as well."

Lady Hession turned a repressive stare on her. "Surely," she said, "you do not think to accuse my Peter of being such a young man!" Before her formidable gaze, Mrs. Quinlevan quickly lost her courage and uttered a hasty disclaimer, which drew a satisfied nod from Lady Hession and the amiable concession, "Well, well, we will not talk of it *here*. I have always felt that, out of regard for one's hostess, one ought at least to *attempt* to enjoy oneself at a ball, and I am sure Lady Eliza has been at such pains to make this an agreeable occasion that we should be ungrateful indeed if we did not show her pleasant faces." She let her gaze travel around the room and said with satisfaction, observing the steadily increasing throng of guests, "She has done very well for herself this evening, I believe. As I told Sir Landers, since *we* were postponing our journey to London in order to attend, I made no doubt that there would be many others who would do the same. Even Manning Hartily, as you have observed, is here, and it is most unusual for *him* not to be in London by this date."

One of the younger matrons ventured to repeat a piece of gossip which had lately begun to be discreetly whispered in circles more knowing concerning events across Saint George's Channel, to the effect that Sir Manning was said to be rolled-up, and, finding himself *de trop* amongst his erstwhile noble companions, was hanging out for a rich wife as the only method by which to make some recover for his fortunes.

"At his age! Nonsense! Who would have him?" Lady Hession said loftily, but Mrs. Quinlevan jumped, and looked around anxiously to see if Sir Manning were anywhere in the vicinity of Georgina. It had never entered her head to place *him* on the list of gentlemen to be discouraged from being allowed too free an access to her young cousin, but it occurred to her now that he was always extremely attentive to Georgina when he was in her company, and that, while her cousin's expectations could not be considered brilliant, they were certainly comfortable, perhaps as comfortable as a gentleman of Sir Manning's years and lack of fortune could hope to aspire to.

Her nervousness increased when another piece of gossip—this one referring to the rumour that Lady Eliza had invited Shannon to her ball—was brought into the conversation. She believed she could be certain, from Lady Eliza's words to her and Georgina on their arrival, that their hostess did indeed expect Shannon to be present that evening, and the very thought of what Georgina might feel called upon to do if that abominable man were to walk into the room made her ply her fan distractedly. Looking about for her young cousin, she saw with dismay that she was now standing up with Peter Hession for the boulanger. She endeavoured to compose herself with the thought that it was to be expected that she must dance with him once during the evening, but she could not prevent herself from keeping an anxious watch on them, and several times during the ensuing minutes answered quite at random when a remark was addressed to her.

Had she but been aware of it, her anxiety, at this particular moment at least, was quite misplaced. Far from taking advantage of their proximity in the dance to utter sweet nothings in his partner's ear, Mr. Hession had embarked on a bitter quarrel with her.

"Brandon Quinlevan!" had been his opening gun, uttered in a tone of outraged disbelief. "Do you mean to tell me that you—or anyone else—has taken it seriously in mind that he should marry you! Dashed near floored me to hear your cousin say such a thing, I can tell you! A girl like you, and that—that limping halfling!"

Georgina's colour rose dangerously, and had Mr. Hession been observant—which, unfortunately, even in his calmer moods, he was not—he might have swallowed his disapproval and beat a hasty retreat to a safer subject. As it was, he failed even to catch the menace in the cool tone in which she stated to him, "I cannot see what interest *my* affairs can possibly have for *you*, Mr. Hession!"

"Well, they *do* interest me," he said aggrievedly, "and I should dashed well think you'd know it by this time! I can tell you, too, that I don't like it above half, thinking of your living under the same roof with that young chub day in, day out, and your cousin crying him up in your ears all the while. He may be a bright 'un—I don't say he ain't. But, Lord, he ain't for *you!*"

"I prefer—I *much* prefer not to discuss the subject, Mr. Hession!" Georgina interrupted, this time on a rising note of displeasure that did penetrate into her partner's mind. "You are taking a great deal too much on yourself!"

"Well, I beg your pardon if I have offended you," Peter said, still too perturbed to make more than a perfunctory gesture in the direction of civility. "But there's no bearing such a thing, you know—to hear your name bandied about publicly with young Quinlevan's, as if it was quite an understood thing. I wonder that Mr. Barnwall should show such a want of conduct!"

"Mr. Barnwall," Georgina said, herself incensed beyond civility by this time, "is not the only person I could name who shows a want of conduct! If you do not leave this subject immediately, Mr. Hession, I assure you I shall walk off the floor! *You* may believe it proper to discuss such matters in public, but *I* do not!"

To tell the thruth, she was more indignant at his slighting references to Brandon than at his lack of propriety in speaking to her in such a manner in a public place, and there was still a third cause for her perturbation at that moment: she had just seen Shannon enter the room. The evening was by that time so far advanced that Lady Eliza and her husband were no longer stationed at the head of the grand staircase to receive their guests, but had themselves come into the ballroom, and Georgina saw that Lady Eliza, who had apparently perceived Shannon at the very moment that she herself had, was already moving quickly across the room toward him.

Shannon, attired in the same correct evening dress that he had worn on the night of the party at Craythorne, stood for a moment in the doorway with an expression on his face that Georgina could only characterise as saturnine. He seemed, she thought, to have no idea of having come to make himself agreeable. Knowing that he had certainly not put in an appearance to oblige Lady Eliza, she could not help reverting to the disquieting notion which had previously entered her mind—that if he accepted Lady Eliza's invitation it would be for the sake of seeing *her.*

She found herself paying so little heed to the steps of the dance in which she was engaged that Peter, in astonishment, was compelled to recall her to what she was doing. When the set ended a few minutes later, she saw that Shannon was still engaged in conversation with Lady Eliza, who was looking even bolder than was her wont, laughing and behaving as if it were quite the thing for her to have asked Shannon into her house. However, the matrons ranged along the walls of the ballroom all had their heads together in scandalised comment, and even among the younger set there seemed to be no one willing to brave the disapproval of his elders by coming up to speak to the newcomer. Georgina looked around for Major Rothe, but he was nowhere to be seen, and she guessed that he might have sat down to a game of whist in one of the other rooms.

She made up her mind abruptly, and when Mr. Hession offered her his arm to lead her back to Mrs. Quinlevan said to him decisively, "I wish you will take me to Lady Eliza instead."

"Lady Eliza?" Peter looked around, saw their hostess in conversation with Shannon, and immediately entered a protest. "Oh, no! I think not, Miss Power!" he said. "She's talking with Shannon just now. Dashed rum thing to do, asking him here, in my opinion, but, at any rate, *you* don't want to have anything to do with him. Take you back to your cousin."

"No, indeed, you will not!" Georgina said. "If you will not take me to Lady Eliza, I shall go alone." She looked at him challengingly and inquired, "Are you afraid to meet Mr. Shannon? I can assure you that he does not bite."

Peter reddened slightly. "Not afraid in the least," he said. "But I don't see the sense in having anything to do with the fellow. He ain't received, you know."

"He is received here," Georgina pointed out, incontrovertibly. She put her chin up. "*And* I will remind you that he was received at Craythorne. *I* am going to speak to him!"

Mr. Hession, confronted with this ultimatum, could do nothing but accompany her reluctantly across the room. He noted with disapproval the smile she had for Shannon as she greeted him, and for his own part, when she waved a hand at him and said airily, "You don't know Mr. Hession,

I believe? Mr. Shannon!" he scowled and muttered a minimal acknowledgement of the introduction.

Shannon's reply was equally cool, and it was Lady Eliza who, with her tinkling laugh, moved in to cover over the somewhat awkward pause that ensued.

"Oh, dear! I can't have the pair of you glowering at each other like sulky schoolboys!" she said. "Shannon, really—you have already had your innings, you know; you ran off with *one* Miss Power and you shan't be so rag-mannered as to do it again! This time it is Mr. Hession's turn—and, if I am to believe his mama, the matter is already all but settled, at any rate, so you had best take your defeat with a good grace." She turned about, seeing someone come up beside her, and, while Georgina stood staring at her in thunderstruck silence, exclaimed brightly, "Good gracious, Sir Manning! What are you about, stealing upon one like a shadow! May I present Mr. Shannon? Sir Manning Hartily—"

Sir Manning acknowledged the introduction briefly, disclaimed any resemblance to a shadow, and said purposefully that he had come to claim the promised favor of Miss Power's hand for the quadrille. Not being a sensitive man, he did not perceive that he had blundered into a situation so pregnant with ill feeling that, under more propitious circumstances, it might have seemed likely that murder might have been committed. Indeed, Georgina, furious at Lady Eliza's calculated misrepresentation of the relationship between herself and Peter, could cheerfully have strangled her, while Shannon surveyed Mr. Hession's rather startled approval of what had been said in his behalf from narrowed grey eyes that had suddenly taken on an extremely hard, almost implacable expression.

Even Lady Eliza seemed affected by a degree of nervousness under that grim gaze, and her laughter faltered. But Sir Manning, in happy unconsciousness, saw none of this, and merely said to his partner that they had best bestir themselves, as the set was already forming. Georgina mechanically allowed herself to be led off, repressing a strong desire to wrest her hand from Sir Manning's and return to correct the piece of misinformation that Lady Eliza had uttered. But there was no way for her to do so without creating a stir on the ballroom floor, and her sense of propriety, faulty as she had often been assured it was, forbade her to make such a to-do.

Instead, she took her place miserably in the set, looking back over her shoulder as she did so to see that Shannon had disappeared from the place where she had left him and that Lady Eliza, with a high colour in her face and a rather too ready laugh, was now talking to Sir Humphrey Mott.

For the first several minutes of the dance Georgina did not attend to a word that her partner uttered. She was reflecting bitterly that there was not the slightest doubt now that Lady Eliza intended to do everything in her power to prevent the development of any closer relationship between her and Shannon. She was equally certain that Lady Eliza's efforts in this direction were likely to be approximately as efficacious as a straw barrier against a hurricane if Shannon were of a mind to run contrary to them.

That he might very well determine to do so, she could no longer doubt. It had been impossible to mistake the expression that had leapt into his grey eyes when Lady Eliza had given her entirely unjustified interpretation of the situation between Georgina and Peter Hession. Georgina herself had had a strange sensation of being scorched by that sudden blaze, and certainly even Lady Eliza had been taken aback.

An odd, foreboding feeling that the evening was going to turn out to be one of those occasions that one remembers, for good or for ill, all one's life began to take possession of her. She was brought back to her present situation with a start, however, by Sir Manning's aggrieved statement that he had already inquired of her three times when she would be returning to Bath, and gave him a hurried apology for her absent-mindedness.

"Balls are such—such *distracting* occasions!" she said, as she made a rapid attempt to gather her wits. "Don't you find them so, Sir Manning? But I daresay you don't; you are so accustomed to them."

Sir Manning regarded her suspiciously, as if he rather imagined that he was being fobbed off. "Well, if you don't care to tell me—" he said.

"Tell you what? Oh! When I am returning to Bath? Why, I am not at all certain, you see. As long as Mama and Grandmama do not require me there—"

"Thought I might pop down there myself one of these

days," Sir Manning said, regarding her with what she could only describe to herself, with a sinking feeling, as a hopeful eye. "Just as you said—deuced bore London can be during the Season, when you've seen as many of 'em as I have. Might look in on you if I do. Great Pulteney Street, is it? Lady Mercer? Don't believe I've had the pleasure of meeting her, but I'll do myself the honour of calling on her. Many mutual friends, I'm sure—including yourself, my dear little girl!" he said, giving her hand a significant squeeze.

The unhappy thought crossed Georgina's mind—as it had her cousin Bella's earlier in the evening—that Sir Manning's attentions might have some more serious purpose than mere flirtation. No doubt it might seem to him that she must be dazzled by the prestige of his long and successful social career, by his intimate knowledge of the world of fashion into which she had scarcely entered even by the impeccable taste in dress that had earned him the reputation of being a veritable Tulip of the Ton. Certainly, matches were made every day in which the partners were of more disparate years; but she had no desire to be a party to one of them, and told herself in some alarm that the sooner she succeeded in setting down Sir Manning's pretensions—if pretensions they were—the better it would be for everyone concerned.

She accordingly took pains to behave toward him with the coolest civility for the remainder of the dance, and when it came to an end was pleased to be able to walk off at once with Betsy Mott, who had had the misfortune to tear one of the lace flounces of her gown the moment before, and now applied to her to accompany her into an anteroom and help her pin it up.

"I daren't take the time to run upstairs and ask Lady Eliza's maid to do it," she confided breathlessly, "for I am to stand up with Robert for the next set, and I would not disappoint him for the world." As she and Georgina walked into a small room at the back of the house which, like the others, was furnished in the Oriental style and was lit by a single lamp in the shape of a water-lily that shed a rather murky light over the assembled dragons and mandarins, she chattered on: "Mr. Shannon is here! Have you seen him? Of course I shall not dare to speak to him; I could not, after the dreadful quarrel I had with Robert over him! I do hope he does not ask me to stand up with him! Do you think he will?"

Georgina said curtly that she was very sure he would not, attempting to discourage the subject as she knelt beside Betsy, repairing the damage to the flounce with the pins which her friend provided from her reticule. She had almost finished her task when she heard the sound of hasty footsteps approaching, and the next moment Mr. Hession burst into the room.

"Miss Power! I must speak to you!" he exclaimed at once, disregarding Betsy, who gave him a startled stare and asked him frankly, "Good gracious, Peter, whatever is the matter with you? One would think the house was on fire!"

Mr. Hession looked at her imperatively. "Go away, Betsy!" he commanded. "I want to speak to Miss Power."

Betsy's stare widened. "Indeed, I shall do nothing of the sort!" she said downrightly. "It would be *quite* improper to leave you here alone with Georgina. Mama would make me very sorry indeed if I were to do such a thing."

"You will be even sorrier in a brace of seconds if you do not go away at once!" Mr. Hession declared, advancing a few steps threateningly toward her. "Don't make a nuisance of yourself now, Bet. Be off! What I have to say to Miss Power," he added more grandly, "is not for your ears."

Georgina, who had by this time risen from her knees, had a moment's apprehension that pink champagne was responsible for Mr. Hession's peculiar behaviour. But a second glance at him made it necessary for her to discard this theory in favour of one involving the mingled effects of ardour and jealousy working together in a young man's impetuous brain. She was not alarmed—indeed, she was rather amused by her young friend's lofty manner—but Miss Mott seemed inclined to take her old playmate's words at their face value. Before Georgina could detain her she had scurried out of the room, uttering some obscure threat as she did so about informing his mother of what he was up to.

Georgina, who could not help smiling at this warning, attempted to follow her, but she was astonished to find her way barred by Mr. Hession, who informed her in no uncertain terms that he had come to have it out with her then and there.

"Can't go around all evening thinking you're angry with me!" he said. "I know I shouldn't have said that about Brandon—very fond of Brandon—always was! But dooce take it, you can't marry him! Your cousin must have windmills in her head even to think of such a thing."

Georgina's colour rose. "I have told you before, Mr. Hession, I won't discuss the matter with you," she said. "Now if you will please to stand aside—"

"But I don't please!" Mr. Hession said desperately. "Dash it, Miss Power—Georgina—can't you see I'm all to pieces over you? There's no bearing it—first this talk about you and Brandon, and then that fellow Shannon— I should think, after the way he behaved toward Nuala, you wouldn't care even to be in the same room with him, yet there you were—"

"I *cannot* see that Mr. Shannon is any more your affair than my cousin Brandon is!" Georgina said. "You are being extremely tiresome, Mr. Hession!"

She again attempted to move past him, but this time he seized her arm and the next moment, before she could realise what he was about, he had thrown prudence to the winds and was attempting rather wildly to sweep her into his embrace. She was a tall, well-built girl, but her struggles were somewhat hampered by the knowledge that if she tore her gown or ruined her coiffure it must be observed by the other guests at the ball, and she might have ended by being kissed had not aid abruptly reached her in the shape of a heavy hand laid on Mr. Hession's shoulder, which flung him reeling across the room. Georgina, regaining her own balance, looked up, startled, to see Shannon standing before her, sardonically regarding Mr. Hession, who was picking himself up from the sofa on which he had landed and was showing every evidence of rushing to attack the intruder.

His martial instincts were quickly dampened, however, by Shannon's voice advising him rather brutally, "I don't recommend it. I know a little about that game, and can give you four inches and two stone, besides."

Peter, halting, regarded him doubtfully, as the justice of these words was borne in on him. He was no coward, but the sight of Shannon's formidable figure looming before him was enough to give any young man of his moderate inches pause, and he was conscious, as well, of a certain weakness in his own moral position. Certainly it would be easier for Shannon to defend his action in rescuing a young lady from attentions that must have appeared forced upon her than it would be for him to uphold his own in doing the forcing.

He swallowed down his wrath and said stiffly, "If you think I am such a shagrag as to start a mill here, you are mistaken, sir! All the same, it was no business of *yours* to come barging in on a private conversation."

"I suppose that might be one term for it, but it is not the one that *I* would choose," said Shannon, with a cool expression of scorn on his face. "And if you have any ideas of continuing such behaviour on another occasion, I shall warn you that you had best forget them, for nothing would give me greater pleasure than to toss you into the nearest horse-pond, my lad!" He turned then to Georgina, the harsh expression on his face not altering. "I might add, Miss Power," he said, "that you might not find yourself in hot water quite so frequently if you would not agree to remain alone with young men in dimly lit apartments—"

"I didn't!" she interrupted, indignantly. "That is—it was not in the least my fault! Betsy *would* leave, and when I tried to follow her—" She felt her cheeks flaming scarlet and broke off, exclaiming, "I might have known you would try to put me in the wrong! But if you had not been spying after me, you would not have known I was here, and *that*, let me tell you, I do not consider to be at all gentlemanly behaviour!"

Mr. Hession, plucking up his courage as he heard her launch into this spirited attack on her rescuer, intervened here to say vehemently, "She's right, you know. What the devil business was it of *yours?*"

"Oh, Peter, *do* be quiet!" Georgina interrupted, rounding on him heatedly. "I wish you will go away and leave me in peace; you have caused quite enough botheration for one evening!"

"And leave you here alone with *him?*" Mr. Hession exclaimed, outraged. "I most certainly will not! If *that* wouldn't be the outside of enough!"

Georgina paid no heed to him; she was looking at Shannon, who met her gaze with an ironical glint in his own eyes that did not long remain there. She had the oddest feeling, as those hard grey eyes, strangely softening now, met hers, that her heart was trying to jump into her throat, and for a moment she quite forgot her surroundings—the Oriental splendour of the room in which she stood, Lady Eliza's ball, even the indignant Mr. Hession—and might have answered, rather dazedly, if she had been questioned on the matter, that she was standing in a wide empty space of some sort, far removed from any place she knew, and quite alone with Shannon.

CHAPTER 14

Only a moment elapsed, however, before she was abruptly recalled to her true circumstances. The matter that brought this about was Lady Eliza's brisk entrance into the room. She checked just over the threshold, and, looking from Mr. Hession's thunderstruck face to Georgina's bemused one, turned her own maliciously sparkling eyes on Shannon, who was favouring her with no very friendly regard.

"Oh, it's true, then!" she said. "I thought the Mott child was quite out of her reckoning, but it seems she really was speaking the truth. And you, Shannon—no, let me guess!— *you*, of all men, have taken up the unlikely role of knight-errant, galloping in to rescue the maiden in distress! Oh, dear! I shall fall into whoops, and that won't do in the least, for I can see you are all three of you determined to play your scene out in deadly earnest."

She broke off suddenly, even *her* assurance failing before the contempt she read in Shannon's eyes. Georgina, quite confounded by this new turn of events, could for the moment think of nothing at all to say, and it was Mr. Hession who came to Lady Eliza's aid by beginning a very stiff and sheepish exculpation of his conduct, which allowed his hostess to regain her own composure by playfully attacking him.

"Oh, you need say no more to me, you odious boy!" she said. "I quite know how it is with you young men when you have taken it into your head to become nutty upon someone—but, indeed, you must not play your little games under *my* roof. If you have the slightest regard for my reputation as a respectable hostess, you will go back instantly into the ballroom—and you as well, Shannon," she said, turning to him. "And I beg that when the two of you have arrived there you will behave properly, and give the lie to the story Miss Betsy seems only too anxious to spread about. Peter, you are the younger—do you go first."

Mr. Hession, pokering up at the suggestion that he leave the field to his rival, looked obdurate, but he was not, in the end, obliged to put his valour to the test, for Shannon suddenly and without a word turned and walked out of the room. Mr. Hession, who by this time was beginning to feel the full embarrassment of the wide publicity his ill-timed amorousness was receiving, was only too glad to stammer an excuse and follow Shannon's example, and in a matter of moments Georgina and Lady Eliza were left alone.

Georgina was still too disturbed by the events of the past few minutes, and in particular by the implications of what she had read in Shannon's eyes, to speak. She would have given a great deal, in fact, to be able to be alone for a few minutes, and had to struggle for sufficient control to face Lady Eliza without betraying her emotions.

That she was not entirely successful in her efforts was evident from the shrewd expression on Lady Eliza's own face as she stood regarding her, slowly tapping her ivory-handled fan against the palm of her left hand.

"My dear," she said abruptly, in a smooth voice, "you will not mind if I speak frankly to you? I am some few years older than you are, and have had a great deal more experience in the world, and I should feel the shabbiest creature alive if I did not put at least a word of warning in your ear. Will you sit down for a moment?"

She gestured toward a sofa covered in yellow-and-white satin, with tigers' heads carved on the ends of the arms, moving toward it as she spoke, but Georgina did not follow her lead. Instead, she gathered her disordered thoughts and said, with as much civility as she could muster, "Indeed, I had rather not, Lady Eliza. I am engaged for this set—"

"My dear child, if you are afraid to hear what I have to say to you, you must be in a worse case than I had imagined," Lady Eliza said. She sat down and patted the sofa beside her. "I promise that I shan't keep you more than a pair of minutes." she went on, "and that I have no intention of scolding you. Indeed, I am quite sure, from Betsy's tale, that you are not in the least at fault in what has happened. Young men who fancy themselves in love are quite unaccountable creatures—as I know only too well! Now *do* sit down here beside me and listen to what I have to say!"

Georgina had an uneasy feeling, as she looked into Lady Eliza's smiling face, that she would do much better *not* to sit down beside her. But she could not walk out of the room at this point without being guilty of the grossest incivility, so she reluctantly moved to the sofa and took the place that Lady Eliza had indicated to her.

"That is much better," Lady Eliza said approvingly. "Of course I have put you in a flurry by being so grave about all this—but, really, it is a very serious affair when one sees a young girl about to jeopardise her whole future happiness by her imprudence! In your cousin Nuala's case, I did not know what I now know concerning Shannon, nor did I believe that she would be so foolish as to be cozened into an elopement—"

Georgina, who had stiffened at the mention of Shannon's name, broke in here to say, as coolly as she could manage it, "Indeed, I cannot imagine why you should take it into your head that this can have anything to do with me, ma'am. I am sure you know that what Mr. Shannon did these few minutes past was only what any other gentleman would have done who found me in the same predicament."

Lady Eliza shook her head disbelievingly. "My dear, I am not a pea-goose!" she said. "Anyone with eyes must have seen that there was something more to it than that, from the very expression on your face, and on Shannon's, when I walked in here. Now you may flirt with young Peter Hession as much as you choose, and nothing worse will come of it than a stolen kiss—and, if I am not sadly mistaken, an abject apology accompanied by a formal offer the next time he manages to come into your presence. But *do* believe me when I tell you that the same behaviour directed toward a man like Shannon is not only dangerous, but absolutely foolhardy. You do not know him—"

"I do not know him well, but I believe I may say that I know him better than you do if you think I stand in any danger from him," Georgina said, her anger mounting, though she strove to preserve a calm demeanour.

She would have gone on, but Lady Eliza interrupted her, her sparkling eyes for once excessively grave.

"My dear child, I am sure that is precisely what your cousin Nuala thought," she said. "She could have had no idea, when she agreed to marry him, of his true character; indeed, she told me herself that she had not, in Brussels, shortly before her death. She was a most unhappy creature at that time, you must know—sadly changed from the bright, happy girl her friends had been acquainted with."

"That may well be, ma'am," Georgina said, still endeavouring to keep her indignation under rein. "But I am not so green—and certainly *you* are not—as to be unaware that there are many couples who find, after marriage, that they do not suit, through neither's fault."

Lady Eliza again shook her head, and shrugged up her shoulders slightly with a fatalistic air. "Oh, if you are of a mind to make yourself his champion, I see that there is nothing for it but for me to speak plainly," she said. She laid one hand on Georgina's, which were clasped tightly together in her lap, and went on, in a lowered voice, "You must believe me when I say that it is excessively painful for me to spread such a story as this, but I feel, under the circumstances, that it is my duty to tell it to you. It was said quite openly in Brussels at the time, my dear, that Shannon was not guiltless in the matter of his wife's death."

For a moment Georgina could scarcely credit her ears. She said in a stunned voice, "Not guiltless! But what are you trying to say, ma'am? That he—"

"Murdered her?" Lady Eliza supplied the words Georgina had not been able to bring herself to utter. "No, I do not say that in so many words. I only say that the suspicion is there. She died very oddly, you see—of an internal disorder associated with a fever, it was given out, yet no medical man ever professed to have found the cause of that fever. I must tell you that the rumour of poison was rife in Brussels after Shannon buried her so quickly and then disappeared from the city that same night—to go to Greece, it was said, or some such out-of-the-world place. If Brussels had not been in such an uproar at the time—it was just before the battle at Waterloo, you know—I am quite certain that inquiries must have been set on foot." She looked into Georgina's dazed face and patted her hand sympathetically. "Of course this must come as a dreadful shock to you," she said. "Shannon's manners are harsh, but there is nothing in them to suggest that he might be capable of such a horrid crime. But when one considers what he stood to gain—"

Georgina wrenched her hands from Lady Eliza's grasp and jumped up. "I don't believe you!" she said hotly. "It could not be! Pray, ma'am, do you mean to warn me, by repeating such a piece of gossip to me, that Shannon has it in mind to murder *me?*"

"Not at all," Lady Eliza said. She looked up at Georgina with the pitying expression still on her face. "It may be that he is genuinely attached to you, as he never was to Nuala —for I am bound to say that, as often as I saw them together, I never saw him look at her as he was looking at you when I walked into the room just now. But, my poor child, what has that to say to anything? It cannot be that, no matter how strong an attachment he may feel for you, *you* would be able to think of uniting yourself with a man who is capable of murder—and murder of the vilest sort, of a young girl whom he had sworn to cherish as his wife—"

Georgina stood staring blindly at a lacquer screen on which a bowing mandarin in a flaming crimson robe was portrayed. She felt physically sick; in spite of her resolution to place no credence in Lady Eliza's words, she could not help recalling that Shannon had never mentioned his wife to her in a manner that had implied the least affection, and that, in fact, it had more than once occurred to her that he was anxious to avoid the subject of Nuala, not out of grief, but—she broke off an anguished thought that suggested to her that the emotion he had felt might well have been guilt. Clinging to straws, she rounded on Lady Eliza accusingly.

"This is all very fine, ma'am," she said, "and yet you would have me believe that, even though you are convinced that this wicked gossip is true, you have invited such a man into your own home—"

Lady Eliza shrugged again, a more familiar expression of malicious recklessness appearing in her eyes. "Oh, as to that," she said, "I own to being sadly wicked, my dear, but I did think it might be amusing to tame such a brute of a man! Have I shocked you very much? You do not know London ways, my love; there are too many of us who will do anything to stave off boredom, and you must confess that such an adventure might keep one entertained for months. But *I* should be risking very little, you see—only my reputation, which I shall take care is not damaged beyond repair—but you— My dear child, it is your whole future that is at stake! I should blame myself bitterly if I had not spoken out to warn you, and, believe me, I shall speak to your cousin Bella, too, if need be, repugnant as it would be to me to add to the burden of her grief over Nuala's loss by repeating such an unsavoury tale to her."

Georgina felt that she could listen to no more. She managed to say, in a far firmer tone than she would have believed herself capable of, "Indeed, there is no reason for you to do that, Lady Eliza. I have no interest in Mr. Shannon, and I beg you will not repeat this story to my cousin on any account."

She then turned and walked out of the room, hurrying back at once to the ballroom for fear Lady Eliza would persist in continuing the conversation if she were able to be alone with her.

The last thing in the world she desired to do at that moment was to engage in inconsequential chitchat, but there was no escaping it. Before half a dozen moments had passed she had been seized on by the eager young gentleman—one of the London Tulips Lady Eliza had boasted she would bring to Stokings for her ball—with whom she had promised to stand up for this dance, and for the next half hour she had to endure the misery of smiling and responding to her partner's polite gallantry when every thought in her mind was still agonizingly on the conversation she had just had with Lady Eliza. At one moment she was inclined to put her hostess's revelations down to sheer malice; at another, she felt obliged to acknowledge that it seemed improbable that even so reckless a woman as Lady Eliza would have invented such a story out of the whole cloth.

That there was some unsavouriness about Shannon's marriage she had always sensed, yet everything she knew and felt about him gave the lie to the idea that he might have done away with his wife. Harsh-mannered and uncompromisingly abrupt he assuredly was, and that a young girl who had been petted all her life by her adoring family and admirers might have found him an uncomfortable sort of husband she could well imagine. But that he could cunningly and cold-bloodedly have contrived her death she could not believe.

When the set was over, she was seized on at once by her cousin Bella, who demanded in the greatest agitation to be told the truth of the story that was being whispered about, she informed her, on all sides.

"That silly little Mott girl has been saying that Peter Hession insisted on making you an offer here, this very evening!" she said, almost tearfully. "Oh, my love, *do* tell me that it is not true! I was quite of the opinion, when I saw you leave the room with the chit—who I am persuaded was in a plot with the Hession boy to lure you off alone—that I ought to hurry after you, but that prosy Lady Kilmarnan seized on me and I *could* not manage to escape!"

Georgina said dampingly, "I wish you will not put yourself in a taking, ma'am. You are making a great piece of work about nothing. No offer has been made to me——"

She was looking around the ballroom as she spoke, observing that, though Shannon was nowhere in sight, Mr. Hession was standing across the room regarding her uncertainly, as if he were endeavouring to make up his mind whether or not to approach her. She felt at that moment, with the knowledge of what Lady Eliza had told her still fresh in her mind, that she could not possibly face another scene with Peter, and turned impulsively to her agitated cousin.

"The thing is, ma'am," she admitted, "that I did have a somewhat disagreeable time persuading Mr. Hession that this was *not* the place to speak of such matters, and I find that it has brought on a shocking headache. Would you object very much if we were to leave now? I believe I am too much discomposed to dance any more this evening."

Mrs. Quinlevan's face brightened visibly at these words. Evidently she had noticed Mr. Hession's brooding gaze turned in her young cousin's direction, and she was only too happy to be given the opportunity of sweeping her away from the young man's obviously ill-restrained ardour.

"Of course we shall not stay if you are not feeling the thing," she said, with eager sympathy. "It is the most disagreeable thing in the world to be obliged to stand up in a hot room and smile and make insipid conversation, when one wants nothing so much as to be laid down on one's bed. I am sure Lady Eliza will understand."

Georgina felt that Lady Eliza would understand a great

deal more than Mrs. Quinlevan had any notion of, but at that moment she was too overset to care. She felt for the first time in her life that if she could not manage to be alone soon she might burst into tears in spite of everything she might do to attempt to restrain them.

As it was, she had to endure the slow journey back to Craythorne behind her cousin's fat, lazy horses, and Mrs. Quinlevan's lengthy animadversions concerning young men who showed such a shocking want of conduct as to indulge in making scenes at a ball. It seemed an eternity to her before she could close the door of her bedchamber at Craythorne and indulge in a hearty cry.

She then felt better, told herself stoutly that she did not believe a word of what Lady Eliza had disclosed to her, and fell asleep at last in the rather frightening happiness of her remembrance of the expression in Shannon's eyes as he had looked at her that evening, just before Lady Eliza had come into the room.

Why that expression should give her so much satisfaction she was at a loss to understand, for it was obvious that, even if Lady Eliza's words had been wholly false, the fact that Shannon might be in love with her could not rationally be supposed to bring about any results that might be counted on to lead to her future tranquillity. In a state between waking and sleeping, however, reason has little command over the mind, and for that brief space of time, at any rate, she was free to indulge in delicious fantasy, in which the hard facts of her present circumstances need play only the smallest part.

CHAPTER 15

She was brought back to a drear daylight review of those facts, however, when, at a rather late hour the next morning, she descended the stairs to the breakfast-parlour to find a letter directed to her in her grandmother's hand lying beside her plate. If she had had any idea that morning must bring some solution to the problems that had beset her the previous evening, it was demolished at once by the first line of Lady Mercer's brief and exceedingly trenchant missive.

Her grandmother wrote that it had been brought to her attention, by a person who had her granddaughter's interests at heart, that Georgina had succeeded, during her stay in Kerry, in embroiling herself to a most unseemly degree with the *gentleman* (the word was heavily underscored, as if for sarcastic emphasis) who had married her unfortunate cousin, Nuala. Lady Mercer felt that she need not point out to her granddaughter that she had anticipated no such shocking want of conduct in her when she had agreed to her visiting her cousins, and she was now of the opinion that it was imperative that Georgina return to Bath at once.

"I have been informed," the letter went on, "that Sir Landers and Lady Hession—the latter of whom I find is the daughter of one of my dearest friends, now unhappily long deceased—are about to make their annual visit to London. I am sure that Lady Hession, to whom I am writing at the same time that I send this off to you, will be agreeable to your accompanying her party, and I shall make all the necessary arrangements for your conveyance to Bath once you have arrived in England under her protection. Be so good as to hold yourself in readiness to attend her convenience.

"Naturally I shall write to inform Mrs. Quinlevan of the termination of your visit. I may add that I have been *most sadly disappointed* (again the heavy underscoring) in the quality of the chaperonage she has given you."

It required only a single glance, when Georgina raised her eyes from her perusal of this missive to look across the breakfast table at her cousin, for her to gather that the letter Mrs. Quinlevan was at that moment engaged in reading also came from Lady Mercer's pen. Her cousin's plump face had grown quite pale under its lilac-beribboned lace cap, and expostulations began to pour from her lips even before she had looked up and found Georgina's eyes upon her.

"Oh, no! What a shocking thing to say! As if I would— As if *you* would— Oh, my love, I have had the most *dreadful* letter from your grandmama!" she cried. "She writes that you must return to Bath at once, and that I— Oh, dear! Where *did* I put my vinaigrette? I am quite sure I feel one of my spasms coming on!"

The fact that Georgina was required to spend the next few minutes in ministering to her cousin's agitation gave her a welcome opportunity to master her own, and she was thus able to discuss the matter with tolerable composure when Mrs. Quinlevan had become sufficiently calm to pour out a great many tearful questions.

"Who could have been so spiteful as to write such nasty gossip to Lady Mercer?" she demanded. "I cannot believe it was Lucinda Mott, for though she *did* tell me that story of Betsy's about your having ridden over to The Place to see Mr. Shannon, she swore to me most solemnly that she would not repeat it to anyone else, and I have always found her to be the most trustworthy creature alive. And it cannot be that Betsy would have dared address your grandmother, who is *totally* unknown to her, with such a tale—"

"No, indeed. I am sure it was not Betsy," Georgina agreed. After the first shock of reading Lady Mercer's letter, her mind had begun to work with an odd, cool clarity, and she went on to say to her cousin, with a calmness that surprised even herself, "It must have been Lady Eliza, of course. No one else of our acquaintance could have thought of doing such a thing."

"Lady Eliza!" Mrs. Quinlevan turned an astonished face on her. "But why should *she*—? Oh, my dear, I hesitate to say such a thing to you, but I assure you that she is entirely lacking in the feminine delicacy that would lead her to be so nice as to censure you for your imprudent behaviour in regard to Mr. Shannon!"

"Yes," Georgina admitted, "with that I must agree, ma'am. But her reasons for addressing Grandmama with such a tale, I am persuaded, had nothing to do with a tender regard for my reputation." She saw that her cousin was regarding her with an expression of doubtful inquiry on her face, and, unwilling to enter into explanations that would necessarily involve a revelation of the scene that had taken place between her and Lady Eliza on the previous evening, said quickly, "But it does not matter a great deal *who* the talebearer was, I am afraid. The question is—what am I to do?"

Mrs. Quinlevan had found her handkerchief and was applying it to overflowing eyes.

"Oh, my love, you must return to Bath, of course!" she said. "You cannot disregard your grandmama's wishes— though perhaps if I were to write to tell her that she is *quite* mistaken—" The momentary ray of hope that had kindled in her face faded. "But there will never be time for that," she said dejectedly. "Lady Hession remarked to me last evening that she and Sir Landers are intending to set out no later than Thursday, which is but two days from now."

Georgina's own mind, while her cousin spoke, was rapidly surveying the alternatives that were open to her, and it appeared to her that Mrs. Quinlevan's gloomy evaluation of the situation must be set down as the correct one. Even if her cousin were willing to abet her in flouting Lady Mercer's wishes by continuing to make her welcome at Craythorne, there was nothing that she could hope to gain by such an act of defiance. She certainly did not wish to be pushed into a marriage with Brandon, and as for Shannon—

She broke off the thought abruptly. Try as she might, she could not put the words that Lady Eliza had spoken to her the night before out of her mind: *It was said quite openly in Brussels at the time that Shannon was not guiltless in the matter of his wife's death.* She did not for a moment believe that Lady Eliza had spoken from anything but the same selfish malice that had prompted her to send Lady Mercer such a highly coloured account of Georgina's relations with Shannon, but still she felt an imperative need to hear from his own lips a retraction of her monstrous insinuation.

And if she received it? This was a question that she could not answer. That he loved her she could scarcely doubt, after the look she had surprised in his eyes the evening before. But that he would offer marriage to her if she were to remain in Kerry was another matter altogether. She could not believe that he would. Nothing that he had ever said to her had given her the least impression that he intended again to disregard the universal disapproval that must attach to his marrying a well-brought-up young girl against the wishes of her family. He had been burnt once— or, if one chose to accept the vulgar view, he had already obtained the fortune that he had desired—and it seemed unlikely that he would venture into such a marriage a second time.

Tormented by these doubts, she was obliged at the same time to bear with Mrs. Quinlevan's agitated attempts to discover if there were any hopes to be placed on her arriving at an understanding with Brandon before she returned to England, and the afternoon brought still further complications with the arrival of Lady Hession at Craythorne.

That formidable matron, ushered into the saloon where Mrs. Quinlevan and Georgina were sitting, presented herself to them in a pomona-green carriage dress and a hat of the same colour with a full-poke front, trimmed with drapings of thread-net and puffs of ribbon, and disclosed at once that she, too, had been the recipient of a letter from Lady Mercer.

"I need not tell you, dear child," she said to Georgina, with what she evidently felt must be the most gratifying condescension, "that Sir Landers and I will be only too happy to have the pleasure of your company on our journey. Indeed, I discussed the matter with Sir Landers this morning, after I had received Lady Mercer's letter, and he agreed with me that it would be quite the thing for us to convey you to Bath ourselves. It will not signify if we arrive in London a little later than we had planned, and both Sir Landers and I are most anxious to make the acquaintance of Lady Mercer and your dear mama. I fancy you can guess why!" she said, casting a glance of majestic archness in Georgina's direction.

Georgina, with a sinking heart, felt that she could indeed make such a guess, but she schooled herself to return the visitor's glance calmly and to say quietly that she would be very sorry to put Lady Hession to so much trouble.

Lady Hession gave her affected laugh. "Oh, my love, we will not talk of trouble, if you please!" she said. "I have become quite attached to you, you know! But, really, I see what it is—you are still somewhat put out over last evening, and so I told Peter it would be. 'Depend upon it,' I said to him, 'Miss Power has very pretty notions of propriety, and you have done yourself no service with her by allowing your feeling for her to display itself before you have addressed her guardians in form.' But so it will be with these ardent young men, my dear!"

Georgina, trapped by civility into listening to these broad hints of what lay in store for her, could only cast a glance of mute appeal to her cousin. But she was rewarded merely by having now to attend while Mrs. Quinlevan pertinaciously brought Brandon's name into the conversation, the two matrons renewing their contest of the evening before over the relative merits of their respective sons, while Georgina sat by in miserable embarrassment. She had never in her life been more relieved than when Lady Hession at last rose to bring her visit to a close, stating that she would have the carriage sent round to Craythorne at nine o'clock on Thursday morning to pick Georgina up for the journey.

When she had gone, Mrs. Quinlevan seemed disposed to continue her arguments on Brandon's behalf, and Georgina, in despair, fled to Brandon himself, who was enjoying the spring sunshine and his release from his sick room in an easy-chair in the yellow morning-room. By this time she was so full of the various problems that were besetting her that she could not help pouring the whole of them into his ears, reserving only any mention of her feelings concerning Shannon or his for her.

She was rewarded by seeing an indignant frown gather on her cousin's brow as she told him of Lady Eliza's insinuations, and by his quick, angry remark, when she had concluded, of: "Gammon! She must be touched in her upper works to put such stuff as that about! Why, it would mean he must have poisoned her— Shannon! Of all men in the world, I would not believe it of *him*. He may be rough, but a scheming scoundrel he is *not!*"

"That is exactly what *I* thought," she agreed, her spirits rising a little at this confirmation of her own opinion. "It is completely out of his character to do such a thing."

She checked, seeing the suddenly suspicious look that had appeared in Brandon's eyes.

"But why should she have told such a tale to *you,* of all people—and at a ball—after she had kept mum about it all this time?" he demanded. "Is she caper-witted enough to have taken it into her head that you and Shannon—?" The vivid flush that he saw instantly appear on his cousin's face as he uttered this question brought him to a blank halt. "Good God, Georgie," he burst out, when he had recovered his powers of speech, "you can't mean to tell me you've fallen in love with him!"

She attempted a confused denial, but was so unsuccessful that he flung up a hand almost at once to halt her.

"No, stop trying to bam me!" he said. "It won't fadge; why, it's written all over you, girl!"

She put up her chin. "Very well, then, perhaps I do— care for him—somewhat," she conceded. "And what affair, pray, is that of yours?"

"Now don't get up on your high ropes," he recommended, with cousinly frankness. "It *ain't* my affair, naturally— except that I like him, and I like you, and so if I see you about to stick your head in a hornets' nest I ought to try to stop you, hadn't I? Lord, a rare dust my mother'd kick up if she heard what you just said! To say nothing of your own mother, and Lady Mercer—"

"They are not likely to hear it," Georgina said bitterly, torn between confusion at having betrayed herself and the strong impulse, once she had done so, to confide her difficulties to a sympathetic listener. "The Hessions are to leave on Thursday, and I am to go with them, so the whole matter is at an end—or," she added, as a new thought struck her, "it will be unless I can contrive to see Shannon before that time. Brandon, I *must* hear from his own lips whether there is any truth or not in that dreadful story Lady Eliza told me last evening."

"What good will that do?" Brandon objected. "He ain't likely to give himself away to you if it *is* true—not that I think for a moment that it *is*."

"Nor do I," Georgina averred. "But at least he will know then what is being said of him, and *I* will know—"

She broke off under her cousin's understanding and censorious gaze. "You will know whether he has tumbled as head-over-ears in love with you as you have with him, is that it?" he asked. "Well, if you want *my* opinion, he hasn't —because, though you are a well-enough-looking girl, you've been coming to cuffs with him ever since you first laid eyes on him, and, from as much as *I* know about it, that is *not* the way to fix a fellow's interest. Here, what are you about?" he demanded in some surprise, as Georgina, sitting down abruptly in the nearest chair, suddenly appeared to him to show an alarming tendency to burst into tears. "You ain't going to cry, are you?"

"No, I am not," Georgina said, incensed, blinking the suspicious moisture from her eyes. "But it doesn't matter what you think, Brandon—I *must* see Shannon before I go! May I borrow your cob tomorrow morning, early? I can ride over to The Place then and perhaps catch him before he goes out."

"Alone?" Brandon demanded. "*I* can't go with you, you know; Culreavy has me chained to this curst house for at least a few more days. And to tell the truth, even if he hadn't, I doubt that I'd be able to make such a jaunt. You'd best give *that* idea over."

"No, I won't," Georgina said obstinately. "There is no reason why I shouldn't go alone. I shan't stay above ten minutes, and you may tell Cousin Bella, if she asks for me, that I have gone out for a last ride about the countryside."

Nothing that Brandon could allege against this plan had the least effect upon her determination; and the next morning, long before Mrs. Quinlevan had left her bedchamber, found her at the stables, where she discovered to her satisfaction that Brandon had indeed given instructions for the cob to be made ready for her use. She gave a decided negative to Grady's plans to accompany her, to his considerable disapproval, and in a few minutes was trotting sedately off in the direction of The Place through the early morning mist.

It would be a fine day, and even the cob's mild disposition seemed to be enlivened by the fresh May morning, with the skylarks singing over his head and the blooms of the whitethorn bushes shining like stars through the thin lifting mist. Georgina felt her own spirits rising, and hopefully envisioned any number of improbable scenes with Shannon, all of which ended in her being assured that he returned her feelings and that the tale Lady Eliza had confided to her on the night of the ball had not an iota of truth in it.

As she neared The Place, however, these optimistic imaginings began to fade before the necessity of considering what she was actually to say to him. The closer she came to the house, the more forcibly it was borne in upon her that what she was doing was quite beyond the acceptable pattern of behaviour for any properly reared young female. Certain bluntly descriptive phrases Shannon had used in the past in reference to her conduct began to recur blightingly to her mind, and she had all but reached the point of turning her horse's head and riding cravenly back to Craythorne when the sight of Shannon himself, cantering toward her on his chestnut hack, made her draw rein abruptly. He was beside her in a few moments, and accosted her with a greeting that she could scarcely regard as a cordial one.

"What are you doing here?" he demanded.

"I came to see you," she replied, feeling again that strange racing of the blood, almost like anger, that his presence invariably provoked in her.

"Then you had better turn round and go back to Craythorne again." he retorted as uncompromisingly as before, "for I have no wish to see *you*, my girl!"

She flushed up slightly, this time in genuine indignation. "You might have the civility to wait until I have told you why I have come before you send me to the devil!" she exclaimed.

A faint, twisted smile touched his lips, but it faded at once before a harsher expression, one more bitter than any she remembered ever having seen there before.

"I am not sending you to the devil, Miss Power," he said. "On the contrary, I am doing my best to keep you out of those regions—with very little cooperation from yourself, I might add."

She said decidedly, "Well, if you are speaking of avoiding gossip, that is a very stuffy way to look at it, *I* think. I am sure you have not ruled your whole life by consideration of what people may say of you, and I have no intention of doing so, either." The chestnut, who was taking exception to standing tamely at a halt after having had every expectation, on being taken out of the stables, of stretching his legs in a satisfactory gallop, required Shannon's attention at that moment, and Georgina said impulsively, "Oh, *do* let us dismount and walk a little way! We can't talk properly like this."

He looked at her directly for a moment, and then gave rather odd, sardonic agreement to her request.

"Very well!" he said. "I see you still have that rather dramatic little scene that took place at Stokings tickling your brain. It may be as well to put an end to *that* business at once."

He swung himself from his saddle and, tethering the impatient chestnut to the great crooked sally tree beside which they had halted, assisted Georgina to dismount. For a moment, as she felt his hands grasping her in their strong clasp, she had a very odd impression that she was about to be swept into his arms, but the next instant he had released her and was busying himself with the cob.

When he had tethered it securely, he said to her in the same curt voice in which he had spoken before, "We will walk for five minutes, and then you will return to Craythorne, Miss Power. Are you under the impression that there was any significance in that singularly foolish little scene I enacted for you at Stokings the other night? I assure you that there was not. I am not usually accounted a chivalrous man, to be sure, but it has become a habit with me, it seems, to happen along to pull you out of your more embarrassing difficulties. It was no more than that—believe me."

She had caught up the tail of her dark-blue riding-habit over one arm, and was endeavouring to match her own steps to his long strides. A little out of breath, she said, "You are in a great hurry, are you not?" He halted and looked down at her, and as she saw the look of compunction in his eyes her spirits rose and she went on rather mischievously, "Oh, I was really not speaking of your stride, though I must confess that in another few moments, if we kept on at that pace, I should be too much out of breath to say anything at all—which I daresay is exactly what you would wish! But what I actually meant by it was that you are in a great hurry to explain away something for which I have asked no explanations. How do you know that I came to talk to you of what happened the other evening at Stokings?"

His brows snapped together in a frown. "Did you not?"

"Not at all—though if *you* would like to discuss the matter," she added obligingly, "I might tell you that I think you have just taken some shocking liberties with the truth. For example, you did not *happen* to find me with Peter Hession, I believe. Would it not be more accurate to say that you followed him when you saw him following *me?*"

She looked up into his face suddenly, surprising a look there that made the dawning smile fade quickly from her own. He did not wear his heart upon his sleeve, and she had never thought to see a look of such bleak unhappiness in those grey eyes. It was gone in an instant, and he said in an almost jeering voice, "You may believe so if it pleases you. Are you thinking to add me to the list of your conquests, Miss Power?"

A frown touched her own clear eyes. "I wish you will stop calling me 'Miss Power,' " she said. "I always have the strangest feeling when you do so, that you are reminding yourself of Nuala."

"I have no need to remind myself of her."

She regarded him puzzledly, her heart sinking as she saw the grimness of his expression and remembered the hideous insinuation that Lady Eliza had dropped into her ears on the night of the ball.

"You did not—love her?" she found herself asking, in a very gruff little voice that she could scarcely recognise as her own.

"No, I did not."

She felt a shiver creep down her spine as she heard the uncompromising coldness of the words. After a moment she raised her eyes rather blindly to his face.

"Lady Eliza says—" she whispered, rather than said.

The bitter, mocking expression was there again in his eyes. "Oh, I can well conceive what Lady Eliza says!" he said. "You may spare yourself the recounting of it!"

"Is it—true, then?"

She felt that her heart had stopped, waiting for his answer, and when it came she took it like a blow.

"Yes."

"All of it?"

"Oh, yes! The worst of what she can find to say! By God, you *are* an innocent if you did not believe her! What sort of schoolgirl nonsense have you been fool enough to nourish in that green head of yours, not to see at a glance what I am capable of?"

She walked on mechanically. There were blue Kerry skies above her, with wisps of fleecy cloud making patterns on the grass, and violets springing in the shadow of the fresh green ferns that grew among the rough stones of the old wall beside which they walked, but she saw none of this. She felt only that a numbing hand had been laid on her hopes for future happiness, pressing the life from them with its cold weight. If what Lady Eliza had told her was true—and that it was, she had just heard confirmed from Shannon's own lips—she must forget him, forget every feeling she had ever had for him except one of revulsion.

She could no longer bear to walk there beside him in the blue Kerry morning. Abruptly she came to a halt and said to him in a voice that sounded queer and strained even to her own ears, "I must go now."

"Yes," he said, his own voice grim. "I have been telling you that. Come along!"

He took her arm and turned her about. As she came face to face with him suddenly she raised her eyes to his and before she knew what she was about the wretched words came tumbling out: "But you should not lie to me, at all events! It wasn't chance the other evening; I couldn't have been mistaken! I saw it in your eyes—"

He gave his bitter laugh again. "Oh, yes—if that is any comfort to you! You may add me to your list, my love—though I know you too well to believe that that will afford you any satisfaction." He seized her wrists for a moment, as if in spite of everything he would have drawn her to him —but then, flinging them away, said almost roughly, "It is

too late for that, however! If things had been different—
But they were not!"

He strode back to where the horses were tethered; when
she came up beside him he had loosed the cob and was
waiting to toss her up into the saddle. Mounted again, she
gathered her reins and looked down at him standing there
beside her.

"I am going away tomorrow morning," she said, in a
voice that she was obliged to struggle to keep from shaking.
"Back to England—to Bath—"

His own face grew stony as he heard the words. "Good-
bye, then, and Godspeed. I doubt we'll meet again."

She tried to smile. "Oh, yes! I shall come back again to
visit some day—and you will have The Place running just
as you like, and everything will be—"

Everything will be different! her heart cried. *He will be
married, or you will have grown tired of living with Grandmama's reproaches and will be the wife of some acceptable
young man, like Mr. Smallwoods or Peter Hession—*

She choked back a sob and, turning her horse's head,
gave him the office to start back to Craythorne. Only once
she looked back: Shannon had already swung himself into
the saddle and was riding off—slowly, under rigid control,
it seemed—in the opposite direction.

She did not return immediately to Craythorne. Some
time must elapse, she felt, before she could face her cousin
Bella's questions. So she turned into side lanes, dallying beside sleepy little streams or walking the cob slowly through
lonely glens. It was long past the luncheon hour when she
left her horse at the stables and walked up to the house,
and the first person she met as she stepped through the
doorway was Brandon, who came limping out of the yellow
morning-room to warn her that his mother was in the
deuce of a pucker over her long absence.

"What's more, she has Peter Hession on her hands now
as well," he said. "Came to see *you*, he says, and ain't about
to leave until he does." He glanced keenly into her white face
and asked abruptly, "Did you see Shannon?"

"Yes."

She bit her lip. Watching her, he ejaculated suddenly,
"Good God, you don't mean to tell me that that story is
true!"

She nodded numbly, turning toward the stairs to forestall any further conversation. But at that moment Mrs. Quinlevan sailed out of the Green Saloon, exclaiming, "Georgina! My love! Where have you *been?* Oh, what a dreadful pelter we have been in over you! Brandon assured me you had only gone for a ride, but at such a time, and quite alone! And here is that odious Hession boy absolutely *rooted* in my house, and refusing to leave except I give him my permission to go searching for you—for we were *both* persuaded, as you can well conceive, that some accident had befallen you!" She waved a distracted hand, which was clutching, Georgina saw, her vinaigrette. "Do come in with me at once and let him speak to you, so that he will agree to leave us in peace," she implored. "He wishes to apologise to you, he says—but why he must do so in *my* house, when I am sure Lady Hession will give him every opportunity he desires to converse with you while you are travelling to Bath with them, I *cannot* conceive!"

Georgina, whose first sensation was one of relief that Mrs. Quinlevan's preoccupation with young Mr. Hession prevented her from inquiring more closely into her own activities that morning, took the opportunity of a pause in her cousin's breathless recital to indicate her willingness to see the visitor, and walked into the Green Saloon, with Mrs. Quinlevan at her heels. Here she found Peter, alerted by the conversation in the hall, standing in expectation of her entrance. He had got himself up for what he had apparently conceived of as an important, if somewhat embarrassing, situation in an impeccably fitting coat of corbeau-coloured superfine, pantaloons of a dashing yellow, and a neckcloth arranged in the elaborate folds of the Osbaldestone, but the face that emerged from between his extremely high shirt-points bore the expression more of a guilty and rather sulky stripling than that of the supercilious Pink of the Ton he aspired to be.

"Miss Power!" he exclaimed, starting forward on Georgina's entrance. "Dooced glad you've come! Began to fear all manner of accidents had happened to you!" He sent a rather glowering glance at Mrs. Quinlevan's direction. "Your cousin didn't like it above half, my staying here," he went on, "but what could I do when no one could tell what had become of you? Dash it all, I might have been *needed!*"

Georgina did not sit down, nor did either she or Mrs. Quinlevan invite Mr. Hession to do so.

"I am much obliged to you for your concern, but indeed it was quite unnecessary," she said, surprised to find how commonplace a tone she could give to her words as she spoke. "I merely went for a last ride about the countryside and forgot the time." Casting a glance at Mrs. Quinlevan, who was standing beside her, she saw, with the rigid erectness of one who perceived her duty to remain in the room and would in no wise be fobbed off from doing it, she added, "I am excessively sorry to have kept you waiting, but, as you see, I am hardly dressed to receive callers just now."

Mr. Hession, however, was not disposed to take the broad hint that was conveyed to him in these words.

"Yes, but—dooce take it, I came to offer you my apologies!" he expostulated. "Can't go away until I've done that! Would have come yesterday, but m'mother persuaded me I ought to let her see you first and smooth you down—not that I think she *did,*" he added, eyeing her set face doubtfully. "I *told* her I'd best come myself!"

"If you mean to imply that I am angry with you, I am not," Georgina said, her civility strained to the utmost by the necessity of dealing with Mr. Hession's volatile feelings when her own were crying out for solitude in which to recover from the shock they had received. "It is only that we are in a bit of a scramble here, you see, over my sudden departure, and—and, do believe me, I should much prefer simply to forget the whole incident!"

To this Mrs. Quinlevan, judging it to be time to take a hand in the proceedings herself, added in a severely virtuous tone that if Mr. Hession believed for a moment that she did not know her duty better than to allow him the opportunity of discussing any *particular* matters in private with her cousin before he had received the permission of her mama and Lady Mercer to do so, he had *quite* mistaken her.

"Not," she said, with bitterness that betrayed the extremity of her agitation at the unfair advantage over her own son that Mr. Hession was being allowed in making the journey to Bath in Georgina's company, "that I daresay they won't jump to give it, but while you are in *my* house, the proprieties will be observed!"

Mr. Hession, somewhat abashed, remarked that it was not at all his intention to flout anyone's notions of propriety, and, finding himself confronted by a pair of entirely unencouraging faces, appeared to judge that the time had come to beat a strategic retreat. He accordingly took his leave, promising to ride over beside the travelling-chaise when it came to take Miss Power up the following morning.

As soon as he had departed, Georgina, cutting short Mrs. Quinlevan's agitated attempts to bring her to a sense of the extreme unwisdom of accepting an offer from a young man of Mr. Hession's known Corinthian tendencies —"as ridiculous as he makes himself, my love, in trying to ape such gentlemen, who care for nothing but curricle-racing and pugilism and such vulgar sports, and I am sure make the worst husbands in the world"—excused herself and went to her bedchamber, where she had rather expected to unburden herself with a hearty cry.

But no tears came. She could only pace the room, revolving again and again in her mind Shannon's bitterly jeering words: "By God, you *are* an innocent if you did not believe her! What sort of schoolgirl nonsense have you been fool enough to nourish in that green head of yours, not to see at a glance what I am capable of?" She had heard it from his own lips, that he was guilty of the dreadful deed of which Lady Eliza had accused him, and the fact that he had, almost in the same breath, admitted his love for her only added to her anguish over the revelation.

She might have borne it better, she told herself, if she could have believed that he was indifferent to her. Then pride might have come to her rescue; but now there was only the aching sense of what might have been, if only—

"If only he were not a scoundrel!" she told herself fiercely. "A man utterly without principle or heart, a man I should despise—and I do despise him—I do!"

With this determined asseveration she turned her attention to the many matters requiring her attention that her projected departure had brought up, resolving to banish

Shannon from that moment from her mind. This was accomplished the more easily for her having presently to deal once again with her cousin Bella, and with the maids who were engaged in packing her portmanteaux for her journey. But it was long before she slept that night, and she awoke with the first birdsong, remembering how lightheartedly she had come to Kerry so short a while before, never dreaming of the misery that lay in store for her there.

What she would do when she returned to Bath she could not imagine, nor did she wish to speculate on the future now. She must live from day to day for a time, it seemed; and as she viewed the dreary succession of them that stretched before her, her spirits dulled and her heart dropped like lead.

CHAPTER 16

The Hessions' travelling-chaise arrived to take her up promptly at nine o'clock. She said her farewells to Brandon and to Mrs. Quinlevan, the latter assuring her tearfully that she would write immediately to Lady Mercer, informing her of the gross misrepresentation of Georgina's conduct that had been made to her, in the hope that Georgina might soon be permitted to return to Craythorne.

Georgina herself had no such hope, or even desire. It seemed to her that, no matter how disagreeable her situation might be in Bath, anything was preferable to remaining in Kerry, where she might chance to meet Shannon at any time and everything must remind her of him. Better to make a clean break, she thought. Whatever her problems might be in Bath, they would, she told herself, most certainly not include her falling in love with a man who was wholly unworthy of her regard.

She had not been looking forward with any pleasure to the journey that must precede her return to Bath, and, in the event, her premonitions turned out to have been quite correct. Nothing could have exceeded the discomfort of the situation in which she found herself, bound to the company of a family with whom she had nothing in common and who seemed to follow Lady Hession's lead in taking it for granted that she would soon be one of them. Sir Landers, though a singularly undemonstrative man, put himself out to give her this impression, and even Miss Amelia several times forgot her absorption in the subject of her approaching come-out sufficiently to drop a giggling hint of her approval of having Georgina as a sister.

As for young Mr. Hession, it was perfectly clear, from the restrained ardour of his manner, that he was waiting only until he was afforded the opportunity of requesting the permission of Lady Mercer and Mrs. Power to make her an offer in form. She could not dislike him—he was in every way so anxious to please her, and so ingenuous in his belief that she must accept his offer, when it was made—and at times, in despondency, she almost felt that she *would* accept it. At least, she thought, if she were married she would be mistress of her own household, instead of an unwanted dependent in her grandmother's. And certainly it was not to be expected that she would ever fall in love again.

A very rough crossing, somewhat delayed by a spring storm, did nothing to add to her pleasure in this vexatious journey, and by the time the post-chaise in which she arrived in Bath had turned into Great Pulteney Street her dread of facing her grandmother's wrath had quite succumbed to her relief at finding herself at the end of her enforced intimacy with the Hessions. Her travelling companions had engaged rooms at the York House, and, as it was quite late when they arrived in Bath, went on to their hotel at once as soon as they had deposited her at Lady Mercer's door, promising themselves, as Lady Hession majestically put it, the pleasure of calling there in the morning.

Lady Mercer had already retired to her bedchamber by the time Georgina entered the house, but she found her mother in the Long Drawing-room when she had greeted Finch and run upstairs, and from her face she read at once the fact that she was in deep disgrace. It was not that Mrs. Power was not happy to see her, or that she was at all inclined to give her a quelling scold; but she had lived for so many years in dread of Lady Mercer that she was entirely unable to set herself against her mother's opinion, and what that opinion now was Georgina could very well see in the tearful eyes that greeted her.

"Your grandmother is *extremely* vexed," Mrs. Power confided to her, dismally. "Indeed, I am persuaded that she retired to her bedchamber so early only because she could not bear to see you this evening, my love! Of course I do not wish to reproach you, for I am *sure* those odious stories about you must be grossly exaggerated, but—oh, dear! — I *do* wish you might have conducted yourself with a *little* more circumspection, so that your grandmama would not have been cast into such a taking!" She looked anxiously into

Georgina's set face and went on, "My dear, it is *not* true, is it? You have not conceived a—a *tendre* for that dreadful man?"

"No, I have not," Georgina said roundly. "In fact, I should much prefer never to set eyes on him again!"

Mrs. Power's face brightened. "Oh, my dearest love, indeed you do not know how happy I am to hear you say that!" she exclaimed. "I *told* your grandmama that I was sure the whole story was nothing but a Canterbury tale—not that I would wish to say anything against Lady Eliza Malladon, for I am persuaded that she must have believed it her duty to write to your grandmama, or she would never have addressed herself to a lady who was quite unknown to her—"

Such a dangerous sparkle appeared in Georgina's eyes at this confirmation of her suspicions concerning Lady Eliza's meddling that Mrs. Power, seeing it, paused doubtfully. But Georgina, who had no desire to become embroiled in a discussion of the reasons for Lady Eliza's interference in her affairs, said nothing, merely letting her mother's expressions of relief over the news that she had, after all, no interest whatever in Mr. Shannon run their course and then, admitting her weariness after her journey, allowing herself to be led off to her bedchamber.

By the time she made her appearance the next morning she was happy to see that her mother had already informed Lady Mercer of the main points of their conversation of the previous evening. Lady Mercer, however, was not quite so complaisant toward her as might have been anticipated from this fact, for she had had the wind taken out of her sails, and that was an experience that she did not at all relish.

It was fortunate for her that the occurrences of that very day gave her a new stock of ammunition against her granddaughter. She had been obliged, at breakfast, to fall back upon Georgina's rejection of Mr. Smallwoods' suit to justify her general dissatisfaction with her; but the arrival of Lady Hession and Mr. Peter Hession in Great Pulteney Street, and the events that followed it, immediately drove that rankling occurrence out of her mind.

As chance had it, Georgina was in her bedchamber when the guests were announced, and Mr. Hession, with his mother's strong support, at once seized the opportunity of laying his hopes of obtaining their permission to address Georgina before the two elder ladies of the household.

It could not be said that Lady Mercer was favourably impressed by a young gentleman who, as she afterwards expressed it to Mrs. Power, seemed to her to be somewhat addicted to dandyism and who made use, in her presence, of several cant phrases which she felt were quite unsuitable for a lady's drawing-room. But any personal objections that she had to Mr. Hession were quite outweighed in her mind by the fact that he was a highly eligible *parti*, the only son of a baronet whose estate was respectable and whose affairs stood in excellent order, and that he was the grandson of one of her oldest friends. Lady Hession's mother, as Lady Hession had informed Georgina in Kerry, had been an intimate of Lady Mercer's in earlier days, and though Amelia Court had now been dead for many years and the connexion between the families had been allowed to lapse, Lady Mercer was much inclined to believe that any young man who bore the blood of Amelia Court in his veins could not, in the long run, turn out to be a disappointment to her.

To add to her inclination to approve the match, she and Lady Hession almost immediately discovered in each other a kindred spirit, who, on every topic that was broached between them, could be counted upon to take the proper attitude. Mrs. Power, indeed, who found herself reduced to the merest cipher in the presence of the two older ladies, had an unhappy presentiment that it might not be very comfortable for Georgina to have such a woman as Lady Hession as her mother-in-law, but, when she was applied to for her own consent to Peter's addressing her daughter, she did not venture to utter a word of disagreement.

So Georgina was sent for to come downstairs, and Lady Hession, secure in the belief that she and Lady Mercer had arrived at a most satisfactory agreement, took her leave.

Georgina, when she was informed that she was to come down to the Long Drawing-room, had a fairly accurate notion of what was in store for her there. As a matter of fact, she had lain awake for several hours during the night, trying to decide what answer she would return to Mr. Hession. Every point in his favour—his excellent birth, his respectable fortune, his personable appearance, his easy temper, his manifest partiality for her—was brought up and reviewed, and she came several times to the conclusion that she would be perfectly henwitted not to accept his offer, only to have all her certainty whirled away in an instant by the memory of a harsh-featured face and a pair of cool grey eyes that she had seen grow so unexpectedly warm when they had fallen upon her.

This weakness on her own part infuriated and distressed her, and as she descended the stairs to the Long Drawing-room she adjured herself sternly not to be gooseish, and to accept with suitable gratitude the answer to all her difficulties that was to be offered to her.

But no sooner had her eyes alighted on young Mr. Hession's resplendent form as he started up to greet her than doubts began to mount in her mind. How, she asked herself, was she to marry a man whose taste in waistcoats would come near to sending her into whoops each time she looked at him, and whose shirt-points were of such a monstrous height that it would be impossible for him to turn his head to attend to what she was saying? It was in vain that she hurried through a hasty mental catalogue of all the points in his favour as they exchanged civilities; all she could feel was a mounting vexation at the assurance with which he plunged into his declaration to her.

"Wouldn't have held off this long," he confided, "except m'mother said you'd prefer it if I did it all in form. But I must say *your* mother and Lady Mercer have both been dooced kind, so I shouldn't think there need be any rub now."

He looked into her face and, apparently somewhat surprised at the suddenly mulish expression he saw there, added hastily, "You *know* how I feel about you, don't you? Made a dashed cake of myself that night at the Malladons' ball—should think you couldn't help realising I'm nutty on you."

Georgina, obliged to say something at this juncture, agreed reluctantly, "Yes—yes, I *do* know, but—"

"No point in going all over it again, then," Mr. Hession said, relieved to find himself so well understood. "I should think we might have the wedding in a couple of months—

give you time to get your bride-clothes and all that flummery—"

"Mr. Hession, you are taking a great deal for granted!" Georgina said, an astonished and not too cordial light appearing in her eyes. "I have not said that I will marry you!"

Astonishment made its way into Mr. Hession's face as well. "Well, you ain't said you won't," he reminded her, reasonably. "Matter of fact, what have we been talking about all this time?"

"*You* have been talking about your feelings for me. I don't believe you have yet inquired about *mine* for *you!*"

The astonishment on Mr. Hession's face turned to something like dismay. "But—but, dash it all, you oughtn't to have any— I mean to say, not like mine for you!" he objected. "Young females don't, m'mother says—at least if they've been brought up properly! It ain't at all the thing—not until you've received an offer, you know. I daresay you'll grow fond enough of me after we're married."

Georgina, struggling with a strong desire to laugh at this extremely proper concept of how her emotions were expected to bloom, once they had received official authorisation to do so, managed to smile instead, and to remark in a somewhat unsteady voice, "That might very well be true, if I were to wish to put the matter to the test. As I do not, I expect we shall never know whether it is or not."

He stared at her. " 'As I do not—' " he repeated, in amazement. "But—what do you mean by that—?"

She shrugged her shoulders, the smile fading into a contrite expression. "Oh, Peter, believe me, I do not wish to offend you!" she said, with a frankness that took the sting from her words. "But we are *quite* unsuited; you *must* see that, if you will only consider the matter coolly."

"Coolly!" Mr. Hession interrupted, with a violently aggrieved air. "How can I consider it coolly? I'm in love with you—head over ears—told you that at the start, didn't I? And your mother's agreeable—Lady Mercer, too—"

"Unfortunately, you do not wish to marry either my grandmama or my mama," Georgina pointed out, suppressing an unsuitable impulse to smile at the picture of outrage Mr. Hession was presenting.

"Of course I don't!" he sputtered. "What a cork-brained

thing to say! Years and years older than I am—both of 'em! I shouldn't think of making such a cake of myself!"

"No, of course you wouldn't," she said soothingly. "But, really, you must see—if they objected to you, I should be obliged to take their objections very seriously, but I cannot —I really *cannot* be expected to marry simply to please them!"

The aggrieved expression did not leave Mr. Hession's face. "Never thought you would," he said. "Dash it, I ain't *that* gothic—but when you say we shouldn't suit, you're bamming me! You know as well as I do that we've always got on famously. Never stood up with a girl in my life I enjoyed dancing with more, and you've the best seat and hands of any female I ever saw—be a pleasure to hunt with you!"

"Thank you," Georgina said. "But I *do* think—don't you?—that there is more to marriage than dancing and hunting. Indeed, I am *very* sorry to disoblige you, but I can't believe, really, that we should suit."

To her surprise and considerable discomposure, Mr. Hession, instead of showing dejection at this rebuff, which was uttered in as decided a voice as she could command, seemed cast down by it only for a moment. He then brightened and said, "Oh, well—no need to tie it down fast and firm today, of course. M'mother warned me—girls like to flutter about a bit before they settle down to give you a tight answer. I'll be popping down from London any time this month, and we can settle it then. Know how you feel! Took me the better part of a fortnight last year to make up my mind to buy Jack Worthing's chestnuts. Knew I'd do it in the end, of course. Never saw such a well-matched pair in my life!"

Nothing that Georgina could say could bring him to the realisation that she was not, in fact, merely coquetting with him, and he went off at last in quite an amiable mood, leaving her to explain to her mother and Lady Mercer what the situation was between them.

This she was entirely unable to do to those ladies' satisfaction. Lady Mercer said acidly that she was a pea-goose, and demanded to know what sort of paragon she was expecting to snare that she had refused two such eligible offers as Mr. Smallwoods' and Mr. Hession's. Mrs. Power, as usual on the occasion of any disagreement between her daughter and her mother, burst into tears and declared herself in sinking tones to be the most unhappy creature in the world.

"Depend upon it," Lady Mercer said to Mrs. Power severely, when Georgina had fled to the sanctuary of her own bedchamber, "she is thinking of that abominable man who cozened your niece into marrying him. She may pull the wool over *your* eyes, Maria, but she cannot flummery me! What else would lead her to refuse such an offer?"

As Mrs. Power had no answer to this question, she returned none. Her own view of the matter was that her incomprehensible daughter was determined, for her own reasons, to end up on the shelf—a matter of considerable concern to her, as she had frequently thought that, when Georgina was married and presiding over a home of her own, she might contrive to visit her rather frequently and so escape, at least for a time, from her mother's domineering ways. The years of her widowhood had not been easy for the poor lady, and it was hard for her to give up such a dream as this for the harsh realities of the sort of household in which it seemed she was henceforth doomed to live, with brangling and disagreement around her all through the day. She wondered naïvely how Georgina could bring herself to reject an offer—and so eligible a one, too!—that would remove her permanently from such a situation.

"I am sure I should jump at the chance, if it were presented to *me!*" she told herself, in the privacy of her own bedchamber that night—and then, looking at her face in the mirror (she was not yet forty, but the beauty that had led Owen Power to run off with her had long since faded, and there were threads of grey in her fair hair), admonished herself mentally, in Lady Mercer's own forbidding tones, not to be such a widgeon as to imagine any such chance would ever again be offered to *her*.

CHAPTER 17

As it happened, the brangling that Mrs. Power had foreseen over Georgina's rejection of Mr. Hession's offer did
not rise quite to the heights that she had dreaded.

The fortunate circumstance that brought this about was
the appearance in Bath, only a few days after Georgina
herself had arrived there, of Sir Manning Hartily. Sir Manning lost no time in calling on the ladies in Great Pulteney
Street, as he had promised Georgina that he would do, and
it was obvious from the start that his purpose in doing
so—and, indeed, in coming to Bath at all at this season of
the year—was to seek her hand in marriage.

This fact, in Lady Mercer's eyes, at once put a new complexion on the whole affair of her granddaughter's future.
As it happened, Lady Mercer, though herself in no way addicted to fashionable frivolities, had long been an avid fol-
lower of the activities of the Court, and in particular those
of the Prince Regent, who in his youth—roughly coincid-
ing with her own—had epitomised for her the glamour and
courtly romance which her own life had sadly lacked.

Marriage with a blunt-mannered country squire and her
subsequent years of retirement in Herefordshire had afforded little opportunity for this veneer of romantic-imag-
ining to be rubbed off by reality. The Prince—now an extremely stout, florid-faced libertine to those who were well
acquainted with him—was to her still the handsome Flori-
zel of her youth, and the appearance in her drawing room
of Sir Manning Hartily, who, she was well aware, had long
been privileged to be one of the Regent's "set," cast her
into a highly agreeable flutter.

Her perception of the fact that that gentleman's purpose
in presenting himself was to attempt to fix his interest with

her granddaughter at once drove Mr. Hession's pretensions out of her mind. It did not signify to her in the least that Sir Manning was more than twenty years older than Georgina. She was even impervious to the insinuations cast out by envious Bath acquaintances to the effect that Sir Manning, finding himself, after years of improvident living in Dun territory, was now hanging out for an heiress. Georgina's expectations, to Lady Mercer's mind, were far from brilliant enough to attract such a man as Sir Manning, for she never doubted—quite overlooking his years, his rather scandalous reputation, and his imposing bulk, which he made manful efforts to confine in a Cumberland corset—that he might marry any number of young ladies with far greater fortunes than Georgina's any time he chose to throw his handkerchief.

Sir Manning himself could have disillusioned her on this point, for he had made several attempts during the twelve months just past to "snabble a warm 'un," as he frankly put it to his friends, without encountering the least success. The ladies he met in his usual haunts were either too well acquainted with his situation or too well guarded by equally knowledgeable parents to succumb to the lures he had cast out to them, and not until he had gone to Ireland had he found, in Georgina, what he believed might be a modestly satisfactory solution to his problems.

To be sure, it might be some years before she would come into possession of Lady Mercer's considerable fortune, but his expectations, on marrying her, would be sufficiently improved to quiet the most importunate of his creditors. He also rather fancied that, in dealing with females of the age of Lady Mercer, he was adept enough to make certain that she came down handsomely in the marriage settlements.

Sacrificing the amusements of the London Season, therefore—for, in truth, in his impecunious state, it had become more than a little embarrassing to him to remain in town—he had driven himself to Bath in his curricle and installed himself at the York House. Introducing himself at once to the ladies in Great Pulteney Street, he became, within a week, an indispensable member of their little circle, squiring them to the Pump Room or to such concerts and other amusements as this unfashionable season of the year provided. He had little fear of meeting any of his own particular set in Bath at this time, who might throw a spoke in his wheel by giving Lady Mercer an uncomfortably accurate picture of his current financial situation, and, as he was of a sanguine disposition, he did not at all despair, with Lady Mercer's good will, of soon obtaining her granddaughter's hand in marriage.

Georgina herself made every effort in her power to discourage these pretensions, but found herself sadly at a disadvantage in her attempts because of the decided partiality of both Lady Mercer and Mrs. Power for her admirer. She was finally reduced to the stratagem of pleading a headache or a similar indisposition whenever she was invited to accompany her mother and Lady Mercer on an excursion in Sir Manning's company—a fact that was responsible for her being alone in the Long Drawing-room on a fine morning, some two weeks after his departure for London, when Mr. Peter Hession called in Great Pulteney Street.

So plagued had she been by Sir Manning's ebullient courtship that she almost welcomed the arrival of her younger suitor, and she greeted him with a cordiality that caused him to exclaim, "Well, that proves it! Knew you only wanted a little time to come about! How have you been keeping yourself? Looking a little down pin, ain't you?"

"I should think I might!" Georgina said, trying not to blink at the splendour of Mr. Hession's elegant attire, which included a coat of blue superfine with very long tails and very large buttons, a pair of exquisitely fitting pantaloons of the palest primrose colour, and a number of fobs and seals depending from a rather startlingly striped waistcoat. "Do sit down, Peter," she invited him, "and *try,* if you can, not to plague me into marrying you, at least for today! I have had *quite* enough of that this past week."

"Why, what the dooce do you mean?" Mr. Hession demanded, in some surprise. "I ain't been near you, or even sent you a letter— Oh! You mean some other fellow's been at you!" he suddenly took her meaning, his hackles rising, "Who is it?"

"Sir Manning Hartily," she said, between despair and

amusement. Peter gave a shout of laughter and she said, in some asperity, "Yes, you may well laugh, but it is very disagreeable for *me*, I can tell you. Mama and Grandmama have been completely taken in by him."

"What! That old court-card!" he said incredulously. "You're bamming me! They can't think that a girl like you— I mean to say, it would be different, of course, if you were some fubsy-faced old maid at her last prayers! But what would a regular out-and-outer like you want with that bag-pudding? Why, he's as fat as a flawn, and more than twice your age, into the bargain."

"Yes, I know," Georgina said, sighing. "But I assure you, Grandmama thinks him an elegant figure."

"Rats in her upper works!" Mr. Hession said, decidedly. "I don't say, mind you, that he ain't of the first stare when it comes to *what* he wears, but, good God, even Weston can't do anything about *how* he looks in the coats he makes for him. Enough to send any first-rate tailor into the dismals, having to cut a coat for that tub of lard!"

He cast an approving glance over his own figure as he uttered this stricture, an action that drew a slight gurgle of mirth from Georgina. Mr. Hession reddened slightly, and demanded to know if she found anything amiss with the way he looked.

"Nothing at all!" she assured him. "You are *bang up to the nines,* as Sir Manning would say. You must forgive me. I have been used to live in the country, you know, where gentlemen are not quite so—so *particular* in their dress."

"Now *there* you are mistaken," Mr. Hession said seriously, and went on to describe to her in full detail the boots he had just ordered from Hoby for country wear—"white hunting-tops, you know, with very long tops, the latest crack"—a description that was presently interrupted by the entrance of Lady Mercer and Mrs. Power. They had just returned from Meyler's Library, where they had had the pleasure of a conversation with Sir Manning, and the sight of Georgina entertaining Mr. Hession alone in the drawing-room, when she was presumed to be laid down on her bed with the headache, sent Lady Mercer's lips to pursing in instant disapproval.

Mr. Hession, who had left Bath a fortnight before in the

happy belief that the two elder ladies of the household favoured his suit, heart and soul, was then treated to a
quarter of an hour of coolly civil conversation, containing
several hints of his want of conduct in encouraging
Georgina's ramshackle behavior in receiving him alone. It
ended in Georgina's feeling obliged to come to his defence,
which she did so warmly that, when he had taken his departure, Mrs. Power was moved to say to her mother that
she believed Georgina would accept him after all, if only
she were left to herself for a time.

"And Sir Manning, you know, Mama," she ventured to
remark, *"is* rather old for her."

To this speech Lady Mercer merely replied that she was
a fool, and recommended her to stop casting sheep's eyes at
Sir Manning herself.

"You made yourself quite conspicuous this morning,"
she said blightly, "hanging on his words with that *gooseish* look on your face. Do try for a little conduct, Maria!"

She added darkly that she was persuaded Georgina was
certainly not likely to oblige them by doing anything so
proper as accepting Mr. Hession's offer, and gave it as her
opinion that she was playing him and Sir Manning off
against each other, while still mooning over that odious
wretch in Ireland.

For Lady Mercer to accuse Georgina of "mooning" over
Shannon was undoubtedly unjust, but still the truth of the
matter was that she was far from happy, and the passing
days seemed to make it no easier for her to dismiss him
from her mind. She had resolved a hundred times that she
would forget him, and a hundred times had found herself
breaking this resolution when some memory of him intruded without warning into her consciousness. That he had
been guilty of the vilest conduct she could not deny, with
his own words of admission still ringing in her ears, yet she
found herself persisting in believing that there must be
some extenuating circumstances. A manifestly absurd belief, she told herself bitterly, and took herself roundly to
task for indulging in it.

But, no matter how she scolded herself, she could not
dispel the cloud of misery and anxiety that seemed to have
been hanging over her since her return from Kerry.

Of her friends in Ireland she heard little news. She had, indeed, had a long letter from Mrs. Quinlevan, but, as it consisted chiefly of lamentations over Lady Eliza's perfidy in having caused Georgina to be spirited away from Craythorne and assurances of Brandon's continued devotion to her, she learned scarcely anything from it that she had not already known. A missive from Betsy Mott was equally unenlightening, for its chief—and, indeed, only—topic was the fact that Sir Humphrey had at last given his consent to her dear Robert's making her an offer in form. She had, of course, accepted it, and the announcement of the engagement, she informed her friend, in a spate of exclamation points, would soon appear in the *Gazette*.

Brandon, who detested writing letters, had not favored her with a line.

One morning in early June, however, when she had been unable to think of an acceptable excuse for not accompanying her mother and Lady Mercer to the Pump Room, an unexpected reminder of her visit to Ireland came upon her notice. The three ladies had scarcely entered the room when Georgina's eyes lit on a large, middle-aged gentleman in a well-cut blue coat and Angola pantaloons, standing in conversation with a retired general well known in the quiet Bath circles frequented by Lady Mercer. Recognising Mr. Jeremy Barnwall, Georgina gave a jump and a gasp, which brought down on her a look of disapproval from Lady Mercer.

"It is Cousin Jeremy," Georgina explained. "Cousin Bella's brother, you know, Grandmama—Mr. Barnwall. I had no notion that he was in Bath!"

Lady Mercer favoured Mr. Barnwall's ample figure with a disapproving stare, and gave it as her opinion that if he were indeed the gentleman whom Georgina had named, it was highly remiss of him not to have called in Great Pulteney Street to present his compliments. As she had never met Mr. Barnwall and had evinced no desire to do so over the years since her daughter had become connected with his family, Georgina could not feel that the omission was one that should cause her any great concern. At any rate, she was determined, for her own part, to speak to her cousin, and therefore made a persevering attempt to catch his eye, once General Tufts had left his company.

She was successful: Mr. Barnwall, perceiving her, came across the room—rather reluctantly, it seemed to her—and greeted her politely. She presented him to her mother and to Lady Mercer, and, these civilities having been accomplished, applied to him at once for news from Ireland.

Mr. Barnwall shook his head. "Haven't any, I'm afraid," he said apologetically. "Never was one to write letters, you know. Had a scrawl from Bella a sennight since, but you know what a curst bad hand she writes—couldn't make out the half of it. The usual story, I expect—Brandon's health, and troubles with the servants. Nothing much ever happens in that corner of the world."

He did not seem inclined to explain his presence in Bath, and made only the vaguest of promises to call in Great Pulteney Street, saying that he was on the point of departing for Kerry, where business demanded his attention. Sir Manning, however, who joined the ladies just as Mr. Barnwall was taking his departure from the Pump Room, was able to enlighten them on the reasons for his reluctance to speak more plainly to them concerning his presence in Bath.

"Rolled up," he said succinctly. "Heard it from Larraby. Ought to have stuck to faro or whist. Always said deep basset would be his ruin. Came here to Bath on a repairing lease—stopping at the Pelican or some such deuced unfashionable place. Attached himself to old Tufts, I hear—travelled down from London in that antiquated chaise of his only to save posting charges. But Tufts ain't going to stand the nonsense here. Poor Jerry'll be obliged to go back to Ireland soon."

"Yes, he said as much," Lady Mercer agreed.

She eyed Mr. Barnwall's departing form in disapprobation, and delivered it as her opinion that gaming was the curse of modern society—an animadversion with which Sir Manning, hoping devoutly that his own losses did not reach her ears before he had succeeded in coming to the point of a public announcement of his betrothal to her granddaughter, promptly agreed.

No more was said concerning Mr. Barnwall, but Georgina, returning to Great Pulteney Street, was for the rest of the day in as low spirits as she ever fell into, for her cousin's unexpected appearance in Bath had vividly recalled to her mind the last occasion on which she had met him—at Lady Eliza's ball at Stokings. She slept but little that night, and at the breakfast table in the morning, when Lady Mercer proposed that she accompany her and Mrs. Power to do some shopping in Milsom Street, she was truthfully able to plead that she felt not at all disposed to leave the house.

She was inclined to consider this circumstance a fortunate one when, just as the meal was coming to an end, Finch brought the post into the room. Among the letters there was one, which appeared to be of several sheets, for her from Brandon, and when she broke the wafer with which it was sealed the first thing that met her eye was Shannon's name. Knowing full well that she could not hope to read such a letter without betraying herself by a change in colour that would bring inquires down on her from Lady Mercer, she hastily refolded it and said, with an assumed air of lightness, that it appeared Brandon had written such a volume that she would put it by and read it later.

Lady Mercer remarked that she could not conceive what her cousin could find to write of to her at such length—a sentiment with which Georgina, for once, heartily agreed. She was on tenterhooks to know the meaning of Brandon's sudden epistolary enthusiasm, and scarcely waited until the front door had closed behind Lady Mercer and her mother before she fled into the Long Drawing-room with her letter.

It began without the least attempt at the usual civilities.

"Dear Cousin," Brandon had written, "I thought I must write to tell you what I have found out concerning Shannon. There is likely to be the devil of a dust kicked up when it all comes out, which it is bound to do as soon as he begins to take the necessary legal steps, though at present no one knows of it but Rothe and me. You see, he intends to give up The Place to you and go to America. It is the most dashed addlebrained thing in the world for him to do, I am persuaded, for you will not know in the least how to go on there, besides having expectations of your own from Lady Mercer, while *he* has not a farthing besides; but I had as lief talk to a brick wall as try to argue with him about it. He says that The Place would have been yours if he had not married Nuala, and that he does not wish to benefit by that step."

Georgina, by the time she had read so far, had been cast into such perturbation that her hands shook as she held the paper, and she could scarcely comprehend the meaning of what she read. At one moment it seemed to her that this determination of Shannon's must have its root in his regard for her; at another, she thought with sick apprehension that his resolution not to benefit by his marriage to her cousin could only be a confirmation of his guilt in regard to her death.

She read on, hastily: "I am making a great muddle of this, I expect, for I should have told you first that it is as I suspected, and that that maggot you have taken into your head about Shannon and Nuala is nothing but moonshine. You have met Rothe, so you will know that his word can be depended on. He is staying at present at The Place with Shannon, and, as I ride over there almost every day now, I have had several opportunities to talk with him alone, while Shannon is engaged on estate matters.

"The other day I put it to him direct about that bouncer Lady Eliza told you when you were at Stokings. I have never seen a man more shocked in my life. He said he was in Brussels himself at the time of Nuala's death, and that nothing could have been farther from the truth than that Shannon had any hand in causing it. On the contrary, he said, he was excessively disturbed, called in no less than three physicians to attend her, and these the very first in their profession. Rothe says, furthermore, that if there was any gossip it must have been set about by Lady E. herself, for he never heard it, and indeed there was no reason for it. Lady E.—how I am to put this delicately enough for your ears I don't know—but the fact of the matter is that she took a great fancy to Shannon from the start, and, as he has always set her down in that cool way of his, I daresay she was bound to have her revenge—especially when she saw in what quarter the wind sat as far as you and he were concerned. It is like a woman to cut a man up behind his back!

"As for your saying he told you himself that the story is true—I fancy that, ten to one, if you will look back on what was said, you will find that you jumped to conclusions in your usual harebrained way. I must say it seemed dashed unlikely to me from the start that any man who had committed murder would admit it to the first person who put a question to him about it. I expect he *does* feel it wasn't the thing for him to have married Nuala, for Rothe is persuaded that it wasn't a love match on his side. But he was in a curst bad situation at the time, with Cartan throwing him on the world without a groat to his name, and I daresay thought he could do worse than to marry Nuala, who had set her heart on marrying *him*. You never knew her, of course, but she was a devilish good-looking girl, and up to all the rigs when it came to getting her own way. I should think a man would have to have been a saint to resist the chance to have her *and* The Place without lifting a finger, and Shannon ain't a saint, as you well know.

"I asked Rothe what should be done about Lady Eliza's spreading that story, and he was at *Point Non-Plus* about it, just as I was. Said he thought the best thing to be done was to say nothing at all to Shannon, but to put a flea in Colonel Malladon's ear when the opportunity arose. I expect he thinks it may all have been done for your benefit and that she won't repeat it, now you are gone, for I imagine he knows how the land lies as far as you and Shannon are concerned. He could scarcely fail to, with this scheme of Shannon's of giving The Place up to you—besides which, Shannon has been going about looking as blue-devilled as if he had lost his last friend ever since you left Kerry. I'm dashed if I ever saw him in this mood—or Rothe, either, so he says.

"It's my opinion that you had best come back here and have the whole thing out with him, one way or the other. I daresay there would be a rare dust kicked up if you decided to marry him, and of course I am only guessing that that is what *he* wants, for he's never so much as mentioned your name to me, except for this business about The Place, and wouldn't have then if Rothe hadn't brought the matter up. I must say it don't seem to me that the two of you would suit in the least, but that is your affair, and I should be devilish glad to see the thing settled, for I can tell you that I shan't like it above half if he holds to his word and goes to America . . ."

Georgina could read no further. She started up, crumpling the letter in her hand, tears of frustration springing into her eyes. How like Brandon it was, she thought bitterly, to advise her calmly to return to Ireland! There was not the least possibility that her mother and Lady Mercer would consent to such a scheme, and without that consent she could not move.

In a fever of agitation she began to walk up and down the room, pausing now and again to unfold the crumpled letter in her hand and hastily reread one of Brandon's blunt sentences. *Ten to one, if you will look back on what was said, you will find that you jumped to conclusions in your usual harebrained way,* he had written. She searched her memory. Could it be true indeed, as Brandon had surmised, that she had misinterpreted Shannon's words, and that the guilt which he had affirmed to her had had reference only to Lady Eliza's frequently voiced insinuations that he had married Nuala for her fortune? She remembered now that he had cut her short before she had succeeded in telling him the whole of what Lady Eliza had said to her, that, in fact, she had done no more than utter the barest hint that that lady had made her the recipient of confidences concerning him before he had curtly informed her that those confidences had been based on fact.

She cast the letter down upon a table, pressing both hands to her burning cheeks.

"Oh, what a *fool* I have been! He thought I was speaking of Lady Eliza's hints that he had run off with Nuala only because she was an heiress; there was not a word he spoke that indicated anything other than that! If only I had been plainer—!"

She picked the letter up again and began to pace the room in wretched agitation, trying to think what she must do. Write to him—yes!—and tell him that she would not accept The Place, but how would that help to clear up the worse matter of the misunderstanding between them? Even if she were able to make it plain to him that she had been labouring under a misapprehension on the day of their last meeting, it was more than probable that he would persist in his belief that he had no right to ask her to marry him. She would never be able, she thought despairingly, to convince him by a mere letter that she did not care a fig for the accident of his birth, or for his having been human enough to succumb to the temptation of her cousin's beauty, fortune, and importunity. And the end of it would be that he would go to America and she would never set eyes on him again.

CHAPTER 18

She was still turning the matter over hopelessly in her mind when she was disturbed by the sound of carriage wheels in the street, and a few moments later Finch announced the arrival of Sir Manning Hartily and ushered that gentleman into the room. Sir Manning looked gratified to find her alone, and, after complimenting her on being in high good looks, began at once, with a complete insensitivity to her obvious agitation, on a speech of formal gallantry, which she saw to her dismay was very likely to end in an offer for her hand.

"You must not believe, my dear Miss Power," he said, inclining himself toward her in his chair with an alarming creak of corsets, "that the assiduity of my attentions to your worthy mama and Lady Mercer has been due to my pleasure in their company alone. No, indeed! I have had an eye," he proclaimed, allowing himself a ponderously roguish smile, "on—if I may so express myself—younger game. In other words, my dear—your own fair person! From the moment that I was first privileged, at Stokings, to gaze upon the perfection of face and form embodied in your—"

"Oh, do stop!" Georgina broke in, forgetting her manners completely under the stress of this new vexation. Sir Manning rolled his eyes at her in astonishment, and she attempted to cover over her lapse by saying hurriedly, "I am very sorry to seem rude, but indeed, *indeed,* I am in no mood to listen to pretty speeches this morning, Sir Manning! I have had" —she glanced down at the letter, which she still held crumpled in her hand—"some very distressing news—"

"No, by God, have you?" Sir Manning exclaimed, staring. "From Ireland, perhaps—is it? Your cousins? But I ran into Jerry Barnwall only last evening—never said a word of anything amiss there to me."

He checked, looking uneasily at Georgina, on whose face a startled and quite radiant expression had suddenly appeared.

"Cousin Jeremy!" she gasped. "Of course! Why didn't *I* think of that! It is the very thing!" She sprang to her feet. "Sir Manning, will you do me a very great favour?" she demanded.

Sir Manning stared harder. "Happy to, of course!" he stammered. "Anything in my power! But I must say I don't quite understand—"

"It is a very long and very complicated story," Georgina assured him recklessly, "and I have no time to go into it at present. You know, I presume, where my cousin Barnwall is putting up? The Pelican, I believe you said yesterday? Will you drive me there—at once, please? That is, as soon as I have had time to run upstairs and put on my bonnet and gloves?"

Sir Manning, who was by this time completely at sea, assured her once more that he would be happy to serve her, but added that it seemed deuced queer to him that she couldn't wait until her mother or Lady Mercer returned to accompany her to the Pelican.

"Not quite the thing for a young female to go calling alone on gentlemen in hotels," he reminded her. "Cousin or no cousin. Lady Mercer wouldn't like it."

"Of course she wouldn't," Georgina agreed cordially. "Which is exactly why I know that I can rely on you, dear Sir Manning, not to breathe a word to her about it. But we really must hurry, or I shan't be back by the time she and Mama return. Will you excuse me, only for a moment? I presume you have kept your curricle waiting?"

Without pausing for a reply she dashed out the door, returning a few minutes later to find Sir Manning standing in the middle of the room with a bemused expression on his face.

"Don't understand this at all!" he proclaimed. "Dashed peculiar business! What do you want with Barnwall? And why should your cousins have written to you instead of to him?"

"I expect they were not sure of his direction in Bath,"

Georgina said, improvising rapidly. "Dear Sir Manning, I *cannot* explain the matter to you, but I am assured that I can trust you! Can I not?"

She gave him a coaxing glance, which had the effect of melting his opposition to the point that he followed her to the front door, where he received his hat, gloves, and cane from Finch with the air of a man who had not yet succeeded in deciding whether to be flattered or alarmed. Finch, for his own part, betrayed some slight surprise at seeing Miss Georgina leaving the house alone with Sir Manning—a circumstance which reminded Georgina that he might well mention the matters to Lady Mercer if the latter did not find her granddaughter at home when she returned. It also occurred to her that, even if she were fortunate enough to arrive back in Great Pulteney Street before her grandmother and her mother, she could not be sure of escaping the observation of one of her grandmother's bosom-bows while riding about the town in an open carriage with Sir Manning, so that she must certainly concoct some explanation to satisfy her as to the reason for her action.

At the present moment, however, she was far too involved in pulling together the threads of the scheme that had flashed into her mind when Sir Manning had mentioned Mr. Barnwall to have room for anything else in her head. She had only a few minutes, she was well aware, in which to manufacture a story that would induce Mr. Barnwall to take the extraordinary step of escorting her to Ireland without the knowledge of either her mother or Lady Mercer, and, completely occupied with this task, she cast out answers quite at random to Sir Manning's attempts at conversation.

Not until Sir Manning's match-greys were drawing up before the Pelican, in fact, did she realise that she had given absent-minded assent to his inquiry as to whether it was her young cousin Brandon who had met with some mischance.

"Well, if that is so," he objected, "I still can't make out why you are in such a deuced rush to see Barnwall. Nothing *he* can do about it, is there? And he's on the point of leaving for Ireland, at any rate."

"Yes, I know that. I *can't* explain, Sir Manning, because —because, you see, there are family matters involved which

I can't properly discuss with you— No! You mustn't go inside with me!" she added hastily, as he seemed inclined to entrust the horses to an ostler and descend from the curricle. "If you will only be so good as to wait for me here for a quarter of an hour—"

She jumped down from the curricle without staying for his expostulations and hurried inside, where she sent up her visiting-card to Mr. Barnwall in the fervent hope that that gentleman would not be found to be already gone out. Luck was with her, however, and in a very short time she was being ushered into a parlour on the first floor, where she found Mr. Barnwall regarding her card with a rather distrustful expression on his plump face. He was wearing an elegant, much-befrogged brocade dressing-gown, for which he apologised, adding immediately, as he looked at the card in his hand, "Thought there must be some mistake. You didn't come here alone?"

"Yes, I did," she said. "I—I was obliged to! I mean to say— Sir Manning Hartily drove me here in his curricle, but he has no idea why I wished to see you, and I am quite sure that if he had he would never have brought me!"

The uneasiness which her arrival at the Pelican had aroused in Mr. Barnwall did not appear to be allayed by this cryptic confession, but he recollected himself sufficiently to set a chair for her and to sit down himself.

"He wouldn't, eh?" he asked then, regarding her fixedly out of his round blue eyes. "I expect you'd best let me have the whole story, my dear. What is it? Come to cuffs with the old griffin?—your grandmother, I mean, Lady Mercer. Daunting sort of woman, but I can't for the life of me see how running off to tell *me* about it can save your groats."

Georgina reached into her reticule for her handkerchief, and was relieved to find that the tears necessary for the scene she would have to enact were quite ready to flow after the agitations she had suffered that morning.

"Oh, indeed, sir, you must believe that if there were anyone else to whom I could turn I would do so!" she said feelingly. "But there is no one! Grandmama has *quite* made up her mind that I am to marry Sir Manning, and Mama will have nothing to say against it—"

"Manning? Manning Hartily? Mr. Barnwall looked thunderstruck. "Nonsense!" he said decisively. "Old enough to be your father! Matter of fact, he's older than I am. And hasn't a feather to fly with, into the bargain. Your grandmother must be dicked in the nob if she's even considering such a thing."

"Yes, that is what *I* think," Georgina agreed fervently. "But he has *quite* taken her in, you see—and Mama too. They will not *hear* of my marrying Brandon!"

Mr. Barnwall, who up to this time had displayed the somewhat uncomfortable mien of a man being dragged against his will into a matter that is not at all his concern, suddenly lost his air of reluctance and sat up straighter.

"Brandon, eh?" he said. "Then Bella wasn't talking moonshine when she said it might come to a match between the two of you!" He looked at Georgina with a more benevolent air. "Do you *wish* to marry Brandon, my dear?" he inquired.

"Oh, yes!" she sighed, with a feeling of inward shock at her own mendacity. "You see, we had quite come to an agreement with each other on that head when I was in Ireland, only Grandmama would not hear of it, and packed me off home to Bath instead. And now she wishes me to marry Sir Manning, and I am so *very* unhappy!"

Mr. Barnwall was looking thoughtful. "Well, you needn't marry Manning if you don't like the idea, you know, my dear," he advised her, in a fatherly tone. "I daresay, if you stick to your guns, your grandmama will grow tired of urging you, sooner or later."

"Oh, no, I am quite certain that she will not!" Georgina assured him tragically. "And even if she were to do so, there is *still* Mr. Hession."

"Mr. Hession?" Mr. Barnwall looked blank for a moment. "Oh! You mean Sir Landers' young chub? What the deuce has *he* to say to anything?"

Georgina cast her eyes down in maidenly confusion. "He —wishes to marry me, too," she confessed. "And Grandmama says that the title is a very respectable one, and the estate as well, while poor Brandon will have nothing at all but Craythorne—"

"I see, I see."

Mr. Barnwall rose and took a turn or two about the room. It was obvious to Georgina, regarding him from under lowered lashes, that he was considering the advantages that must accrue to an impecunious gentleman from having his nephew marry a young lady of considerable expectations. She felt a strong qualm of guilt about deceiving him so grossly, but resolutely put it aside, feeling that the time was now ripe to come forward with the proposal that was the reason for her visit.

"If you would only take me with you to Ireland when you return there—" she suggested cautiously. "I am sure, if Mama and Grandmama were to see how much in earnest I am about not marrying Sir Manning—"

Mr. Barnwall's first response to the feeler she had cast out was not encouraging.

"Help you to run off?" he ejaculated. "No, no! You are a naughty puss to think of such a thing! Deuce take it, my dear, reason—persuasion—always carry the day in the end!"

Georgina cast her eyes down at her hands, which she had folded tightly in her lap. "I fear you do not know my grandmama, sir," she said sadly. "When she takes a scheme into her head, *nothing* will move her from it—and I am quite dependent upon her, you know."

Mr. Barnwall took another turn about the room. "Yes, yes, I see!" he said. "Dashed awkward situation for you, of course—but still I can't think what you hope to gain by running off to Ireland. You ain't of age, are you? Couldn't marry Brandon at all events without the old lady's consent."

"No, I couldn't," Georgina admitted. "But I am quite persuaded that if Grandmama is brought to see how *unalterably* opposed I am to marrying anyone but Brandon, she must come round. Only how I am to accomplish this merely by reason I cannot see! She quite bears me down, and there is no one to take my part. But if I were to go to Ireland she *must* realise that I am truly in earnest—and besides," she added ingeniously, "she is in the greatest dread of scandal, you know. So I daresay, if I *were* to succeed in running off, she would make the best of it and allow me to marry Brandon, rather than being obliged to come and fetch me back, and have everyone know of what I had done."

She paused, fixing her blue eyes rather anxiously on her cousin's face. Mr. Barnwall was frowning, but he had been struck, she could see, by her arguments. Certainly it stood entirely within the bounds of probability that a young girl, left alone to face the pressures of her family, might eventually find herself obliged to succumb to them. Mr. Barnwall, also—though Georgina could not know this—was thinking of the tearful recriminations and frequent applications to him for aid which he would be forced to endure from his sister if she were to discover that Brandon had missed his chance at landing a fortune merely because of his uncle's timidity.

He sat down abruptly, slapping his hand against his thigh. "Tell you what," he said, "I'll do it! Curst rum business if a pretty gal like you is to be forced into Manning Hartily's arms! Nothing to say against Manning—devilish obliging fellow—but *not* the husband for you, my dear. Troubled with gout, you know. Wouldn't do for you at all."

Georgina could scarcely restrain herself from jumping up and throwing her arms about his neck. She controlled herself, however, and managed to express her gratitude in somewhat less exuberant terms. Mr. Barnwall, who found himself rather enjoying playing St. George to Sir Manning's dragon, with Georgina's blue eyes rewarding him for his labours by bestowing the sweetest of glances on him, was inclined to prolong the moment, but her more practical mind had flown quickly to the arrangements still to be made, and she brought him back at once to more mundane considerations. The possibility of adding to the propriety of her flight by taking her abigail with her was quickly raised and as soon abandoned, for, though she believed she might rely on that damsel's loyalty, she was not at all certain of her discretion, and any premature betrayal of her scheme to Lady Mercer must, she was well aware, result in its instantly being interdicted. Mr. Barnwall, whose own notions of propriety were not of the strictest, and whose straitened circumstances made the idea of any additional financial burden unwelcome, readily agreed to this, possibly considering that the reprehensibility of his action in abetting her granddaughter to run off from her home would scarcely be alleviated in Lady Mercer's eyes by his bringing along the young lady's maid.

"But we must really decide on our plans quickly, you

know," Georgina reminded him, unwilling to dwell on a subject that she was aware might raise scruples in her cousin's breast, "for Mama and Grandmama may return at any moment, and there is Sir Manning waiting outside—"

Mr. Barnwall, who had not previously considered the oddity of a gentleman's having been obliging enough to escort his inamorata to visit a second gentleman who was to assist her to run away from him, interrupted her here to inquire with interest how she had managed to accomplish this feat.

"Oh, I told him the most shocking story!" she acknowledged. "He thinks that Cousin Bella has written me bad news from Ireland on a very *delicate* family matter!"

Mr. Barnwall laughed indulgently. "Well, well," he said, "I suppose we must grant that a little deception is warranted in a good cause."

Georgina, endeavouring to quell a blush, agreed, and hastily turned the conversation once more to the arrangements to be made for her departure. It was her idea that Mr. Barnwall should await her in a hired post-chaise at the corner of the street before sun-up the next morning. It would be some hours after that, in the normal course of events, before her absence would be discovered, and, when it was, she believed that the household would be thrown into such turmoil that it would be at least several more before anything would be done, or even decided upon.

"That," she said, "should give us a clear enough start so that we shan't be overtaken before we are safe on board the packet for Ireland." She considered. "If I write a note now, will you have one of the servants here deliver it to Great Pulteney Street no earlier than three o'clock tomorrow afternoon? I don't wish to worry poor Mama more than is absolutely necessary, you see, but I dare not leave a note in my room at home for fear it may be found, by some mischance, before we have had time to get well away."

He agreed to this plan, and she accordingly sat down and dashed off a hasty missive to her mother, in which she assured her that she was perfectly safe, and on her way to Craythorne under Mr. Barnwall's escort. She said nothing at all about what she intended to do when she reached there, merely informing Mrs. Power that she was excessively sorry to cause her so much worry, but that she could not bring herself to accept either Sir Manning's or Mr. Hession's suit.

Having sealed her letter with a wafer, she left it in Mr. Barnwall's keeping and took her leave to rejoin Sir Manning. She found him waiting impatiently, an uneasy expression clouding his brow.

"Not at all the thing, this business, you know, my dear Miss Power!" he said reprovingly, as she mounted up beside him. "No matter how urgent it was for you to see Barnwall, should have waited! Sent him a message! Would have been glad to pop round to Great Pulteney Street, if I know Jerry. Very obliging sort of fellow!"

"Exactly what he remarked of you," Georgina said approvingly. "And I am sure he was quite right, Sir Manning, for I cannot find words to express how very grateful I am to you for your kindness to me this morning! I do not know what I should have done without you."

She had been racking her brains to discover an excuse for asking him not to speak of their little excursion to her mother or to Lady Mercer, but to her relief he solved the matter for her himself by remarking a little doubtfully, as they left the Pelican behind, "By the bye, no need to mention to Lady Mercer that *I* drove you here this morning, Miss Power—that is, if some tabby on the high gab don't get to her with the tale. A devil of a high stickler, your grandmother, you know. Wouldn't do to cast her into high fidgets over nothing."

"Well, I *do* think it might be better if I were merely to tell her that you had called, and had taken me for a short drive when you saw I was not quite in spirits this morning," Georgina agreed. "There is no need to trouble her over the affair, for I find, on talking with my cousin Barnwall, that the matter is not at all as bad as I had believed, so that there is no need for her to concern herself in the least."

She was glad, as she uttered this exceedingly vague explanation of her activities that morning, that Sir Manning's understanding was far from being acute, for no man of sense, she thought, would have accepted such a Banbury story. Sir Manning, however, appeared much more preoccupied with the possible repercussions that might occur if Lady Mercer discovered he had been unwise enough to abet her granddaughter in visiting a gentleman alone at a hotel, and fell in at once, with an air of considerable relief, with her mildly deceptive scheme.

Mildly deceptive, she thought, she might call that portion of her morning's work, but what words, she asked herself in dismay, as she untied her bonnet-strings in her own bedchamber after Sir Manning had set her down in Great Pulteney Street, was she to use to describe the rest of her behaviour? She had perpetrated a shocking hoax on her unsuspecting cousin; she had involved Brandon, who, as she well knew, had not the slightest wish to marry her, in a romance which was likely to prove highly embarrassing to him, if nothing more; and she had devised a scheme for running off from her home for the sole purpose of meeting a man of whom her relations strongly disapproved and who, as far as she knew, had no desire whatever to meet her. And she had done all this without an instant's hesitation, as if such reprehensible conduct were second nature to her. When she sat down to think calmly of what she had done, she was so horrified that she could find relief only in a hearty burst of tears.

A few minutes' reflection, however, and a reperusal of Brandon's letter, had the effect of convincing her that, blameworthy as her actions had been, there had actually been no other course open to her if she wished to forestall Shannon's plan of giving over The Place to her and going to America. Lady Mercer, she knew, would never consent to her returning to Ireland, and she could not go alone— for financial reasons, if for no other. She had very little money, certainly not nearly enough for such a journey, and if she had confided to Mr. Barnwall the real reason for her wishing to go to Kerry, she was quite sure that he would not have agreed to take her.

Having come to this somewhat comforting point in her mental arguments, she made up her mind to put the topic of her distressing lack of principle out of her head, and to bend her thoughts instead to the more immediate problem of how she was to succeed in smuggling herself and a proper supply of luggage for the journey out of the house in the small hours of the following morning.

The first of these matters presented few difficulties. Both Lady Mercer and Mrs. Power were sound sleepers and late risers, and she had had sufficient forethought to appoint an hour for her rendezvous with Mr. Barnwall early enough that none of the servants would be stirring.

The problem of her luggage, however, was a more vexing one. It would be impossible for her to have a portmanteau brought to her bedchamber, or even for her to fetch one there herself, without its being observed, and she was at last obliged to content herself with the plan of packing a pair of bandboxes with the bare essentials she would require, after the rest of the household should have retired for the night. Of course she would find herself horridly at a stand as to her wardrobe when she arrived in Ireland, but as she had not the slightest idea what she would do when she reached there, or how long she would remain, she decided to trust to luck and to Mrs. Quinlevan to see to it that she might appear at least respectably attired during her stay.

With these decisions arrived at, she had now nothing further to do but to concoct a version of her morning's excursion with Sir Manning that would be suitable for Lady Mercer's ears, and to await with what composure she could the arrival of the hour when she would begin her journey.

CHAPTER 19

At first light on the following morning she crept down the stairs, carrying her bandboxes, let herself out the front door, and walked rapidly down the street to the appointed rendezvous. She had a horrid moment of doubt, when she reached the corner and saw no waiting chaise, that Mr. Barnwall had reconsidered his pledge to her; but the instant appearance of the vehicle she had been hoping to see allayed her fears, and in a few moments she had the satisfaction of being handed up into it by her cousin, and of leaving Great Pulteney Street safely behind her.

She had been in the chaise for only a very few minutes, however, when she began to realise that she was not yet out of the woods. Mr. Barnwall, having had almost four-and-twenty hours in which to consider the rashness of assisting a young female to run away from her lawful guardians, was in a nervous mood, and spent the better part of the first hour of the journey in an earnest endeavour to induce his companion to reconsider her decision.

"Thing to be done," he put it to her, "is for Brandon to come over *here*, not t'other way about. Two of you, hand in hand, make a push to change the old lady's mind. Much better that way, I assure you. Chances are the two of you together could bring her about. Devilish engaging young chub, Brandon, you know. Shouldn't wonder in the least if the old Tartar were to take to him amazingly."

He went on in this way for quite some time, in spite of Georgina's obstinate objections, and when he finally gathered that she was not to be moved in her determination lapsed into discontented mutterings. She began to fear that the journey might turn out to be a far from agreeable one—a foreboding that was strengthened when the skies shortly afterward clouded over and a steady rain began to fall. Mr. Barnwall, sitting back in his own corner of the chaise, relapsed into a sulky silence, and Georgina now had the leisure she had hitherto lacked to consider what course she had best pursue when she arrived at Craythorne.

Her one purpose in making the journey, of course, was to obtain an interview with Shannon, but she could scarcely imagine that she would have the hardihood to confess this to Mrs. Quinlevan. It was equally impossible, though, for her to conceive of carrying on with her cousins the deception by which she had lured Mr. Barnwall into taking her to Ireland. Rack her brains as she might over the matter, she could not but come to the dismaying conclusion that, once she had arrived at Craythorne, she would be in a situation so embarrassing that she might well wish she had never set out on this journey.

Even her full conviction of this fact, however, was not sufficient to make her agree to Mr. Barnwall's obvious desire to return her to her grandmother's house before her flight from it had been discovered. A telling mental vision of Shannon, penniless and thousands of miles removed from her in America, made her grit her teeth and determine to go on with her scheme. Her resolution supported her through Mr. Barnwall's sulks, through the dismal weather, through posting-houses that seemed to be in a conspiracy to render their journey inconvenient and disagreeable, through a miserably rough crossing, during the course of which both she and Mr. Barnwall became intolerably sick, and through the final discomfort of being obliged to put up for the night, on the road to Kerry, in what Mr. Barnwall scathingly characterised as a hedge-tavern, owing to the accident of a broken perch on the chaise which he had hired to take them to Craythorne.

Added to the inconvenience of this final stroke of the malignant fate that had pursued her was her fear that the comfortable start she had had on any pursuit that might have been begun behind her had been so greatly diminished by these delays that she could no longer be certain that she would not be overtaken before she had reached her goal. This anxiety cast her into a fit of the dismals such as all the discomforts of the journey had been unable to produce, and as a result she quarrelled so roundly with Mr. Barnwall, who was also in a snappish mood, during the final miles of the journey that they were scarcely on speaking terms when the chaise at last drew up before the door at Craythorne.

It was by that time late in the day, since the problem of having repairs made to the chaise in an out-of-the-way spot had obliged them to make a very late start. Georgina, mounting the steps to the door beside Mr. Barnwall, found that her apprehension over the scene before her had risen to such a pitch that her knees were trembling under her. Her fears were not at all allayed when Murtaugh, the butler whose services had replaced, but scarcely improved upon, those of the unlamented Higgins, opened the front door in response to Mr. Barnwall's vigorous summons, and gazed upon the pair of them with such palpable astonishment that Mr. Barnwall was moved to say peevishly, "Well, don't stand there gaping, man! We've had a deuced bad trip, and I want my dinner! Where's your mistress?"

Murtaugh closed his mouth, but opened it again to stutter, as Georgina and Mr. Barnwall walked past him into the hall, "G-gone out, sir! Dining at Mott House. Excuse me, sir! Was she expecting you? And—*and* the young lady, sir?"

"No, she wasn't," Mr. Barnwall said. "Exactly like that woman to be out when she's wanted! And I daresay there's not a curst thing fit to eat in the house on the head of it; I'll do better to go straight on to my own place and see what Mrs. Banting can do for me. A nice dish of ham and eggs, if nothing more! Here, you!" he addressed a bemused footman, who had appeared at the back of the hall and was regarding the visitors out of a stolid country face. "Fetch in Miss Power's luggage, and tell the post-boy I shall want him to take me on to my own house."

The footman, receiving a corroborative nod from Murtaugh, hastened to carry out this order. At the same moment the door of the yellow morning-room opened and Brandon appeared, one finger marking his place in the book he held in his hand and an abstracted frown upon his face.

"What's this infernal racket, Murtaugh?" he demanded. "Who's doing all the shouting?" His eyes fell upon Georgina and his uncle and flew wide. "Uncle Jerry! And Georgie! What the *devil*—?"

"Well, you needn't look at us as if we'd fallen from the moon," Mr. Barnwall said crossly. "The pair of you have cost me the deuce of a worry, I can tell you, but I warn you, now that I've brought the gal here, I wash my hands of the whole affair." He satisfied himself that Murtaugh was engaged in superintending the bringing in of Georgina's luggage, and said in a somewhat lower voice to Brandon, with a glance of marked disfavour in Georgina's direction, "Curst obstinate piece, if you want my opinion! Glad *I'm* not the one has to marry her. Lead you a dog's life, my boy! Take my advice and think twice before you do it!"

"Before I do what?" Brandon asked, looking puzzledly from his uncle to Georgina, who seemed to be trying to signal him, with a slight, agitated motion of one hand, to let the matter rest.

Mr. Barnwall put up his heavy brows over his baby-blue eyes. "Now *don't* try to gammon me that you haven't a notion what I'm talking about," he said, with asperity. "*I* know what kind of rig the two of you are running."

"Do you?" Brandon asked. "Well, that's more than *I* do! What the devil is this all about, Georgie? Did you travel here in my uncle's company?"

"Dragooned me into it," Mr. Barnwall corroborated gloomily, as Georgina merely stood looking at her cousin in imploring embarrassment. "Said that fellow Hartily would be sure to have her if I wouldn't stand buff . . . And no budging her, either, once she'd made up her mind. Wild horses wouldn't have done it! I'll tell you what, my boy, nobody would like better than me to see you snugly settled, but when it comes to leg-shackling yourself for life to an obstinate female—well, I wouldn't do it, and that's a fact! The money ain't worth it; a man can always contrive in another direction."

He broke off, eyeing his nephew with misgiving, for Brandon's face had suddenly become alarmingly red. He appeared to be doing his utmost to restrain some violent emotion, but his efforts were of no avail, and the next moment he had broken into a shout of helpless laughter.

"Oh, Georgie! You *Trojan!*" he cried, wiping his streaming eyes with his handkerchief when he could speak again. "You *didn't* gammon him into bringing you over here by pitching him a Banbury story about wanting to marry *me!*"

The answer must have been clear to him without Georgina's uttering a word: the guilty colour that had overspread her face told its own tale. Mr. Barnwall as well —though his mental processes were not noted for their rapidity—had begun to grasp the fact that something was sadly amiss in the Romeo-and-Juliet tale in which he had been induced to play a part, and stared belligerently from his nephew to Georgina and back again.

"What's this? What's this?" he demanded. "Do you mean to tell me she *don't* want to marry you, after all?"

"Brandon, *do* be quiet!" Georgina begged him, herself torn between a reprehensible desire to giggle and a lowering conviction of her own complete depravity. "I'll explain everything to you later. But now you must see that Cousin Jeremy is fagged to death and wants his dinner—"

She broke off as a new voice introduced itself into the controversy. It was Murtaugh, standing beside the young footman who had borne her two wholly inadequate bandboxes into the hall.

"Begging your pardon, miss," he said deprecatingly, "but there appears to be a slight misunderstanding on the subject of your luggage. The post-boy persists in stating that you have brought no more than these—these—"

"He is quite right," Georgina said hastily, not daring to catch Brandon's eye. "I—I was obliged to leave very—very unexpectedly, you see!"

"Yes, I'll warrant you were!" Brandon said, showing a marked tendency to give way to mirth again. He said to Murtaugh, "Have them taken up to the Blue Bedchamber, Murtaugh, and you'd best warn Mrs. Hopkins that Miss Power is come. And tell her as well that my uncle is here, and that both of our guests would appreciate sustenance at the earliest possible moment—"

"No, no! Not for me!" Mr. Barnwall said, raising a restraining hand. "I'm on my way! You may tell Bella I'll drive over to call on her tomorrow." He added severely, to Brandon, "I don't know what sort of wheedle you and your cousin are trying to cut, my boy, and, what's more, I don't want to know! It will be bellows to mend with me as it is, when Lady Mercer finds out my part in this affair. I'll give you one word of advice, and then I'm off. If you *ain't* going to marry this young woman, pack her back home by the very next boat. That is," he concluded, again bestowing a glance of concentrated disfavour on Georgina, "if she'll oblige you by going—which I very much doubt!"

He turned toward the door, leaving Georgina to stammer her belated thanks for his assistance behind him. Brandon laughed again, and took her arm.

"Come along," he said. "I want to hear the whole story of this adventure. Murtaugh, tell Mrs. Hopkins my cousin and I will be in the morning-room; she may have a tray brought to Miss Power there. Are you hungry?" he asked Georgina, as he led her into the room and assisted her to remove her bonnet and pelisse.

"Famished!" she confessed. "But, oh, Brandon, I am so overset that I don't think I shall be able to eat a morsel! What an odious wretch you were to laugh at me! And so slow to take my meaning! You *might* have pretended, only for this evening, at any rate, that you really did want to marry me! We could have made up some story later—a falling-out, or some such thing—instead of which you landed me in a dreadful hobble!"

"I should think you had landed yourself in it," Brandon said unrepentantly, still frankly enjoying the situation. "How was *I* to guess what brummish tricks you were up to? Good God, did you *have* to involve such a bobbing-block as my uncle in this? And what have you been doing to him, to make him regard you with such loathing?"

"Well, I could not help it!" Georgina said, sitting down and putting up her chin defiantly. "He wanted me to go back to Grandmama and Mama as soon as he had had time to turn the whole matter over in his mind, and of course I would not do it. I couldn't possibly have done, for how else was I to manage to get over here?" She looked at him a trifle resentfully. "It's all very well for you to ask why I needed to involve Cousin Jeremy," she said, "but you will admit that *you* were of no help to me, merely throwing it out to me that I ought to come here. How in heaven's name did you suppose I was to manage it, with my own pockets to let and Grandmama and Mama both certain to oppose any such scheme if I had even dared to broach it to them?"

"They don't know where you are, then?" Brandon inquired. "Good Lord, what a kick-up there must have been when they discovered you were gone!" Mirth overcame him again, and he lay back in his chair and laughed until he cried. "I c-can't help it!" he gasped at last, as he saw Georgina regarding him in high dudgeon. "It's too m-much —the picture of you and Uncle Jerry p-posting away together in secret like a p-pair of lovesick—"

"Turtledoves," Georgina finished it for him obligingly, her own lips curving into a smile in spite of herself. "Only we weren't," she confided. "He was as cross as crabs all the way. I *did* think he might become reconciled to the idea once we were fairly on our way, but he didn't—and then the weather was dreadful, and the chaise broke down—"

"Don't!" said Brandon, threatening to relapse once more. "Dash it, we had better be serious for a while, Georgie. We shall have to concoct some sort of story before Mama comes home to account for your coming here, and we haven't much time."

"Well, I do not see how we are to say anything other than that I came to marry you, because that is what Cousin Jeremy will tell her," Georgina said doubtfully. "I shall tell her, too, of course, about Sir Manning's wanting to marry me—"

Brandon grinned again. "Not seriously! You're bamming me!"

"No, indeed I am not! And Grandmama is *quite* persuaded that I ought to accept his offer, for she likes him much better than she does Peter Hession. So I shall tell Cousin Bella that all I could think of was to come over here and marry *you* instead—only now that I have arrived I have changed my mind—" She broke off suddenly and started out of her chair. "Oh!" she exclaimed. "I must be a perfect moonling to sit here talking of such things, when there is no doubt that Grandmama has already sent someone posthaste after me to fetch me back to Bath! Brandon, I *must* see Shannon at once! Will you drive me to The Place?"

"Now?" Brandon asked. "I should think not! Besides, he ain't there."

"Not—?" She stared at him, her eyes wide with fright. "He hasn't gone to America?"

"No, no! Nothing of the sort. Not that I expect Rothe will be able to hold him here much longer—but he's only gone to Kenmare just now, he and Rothe. They ain't expected back until late, so there's no use your getting into high fidgets about going there tonight." He looked at her curiously as she reluctantly sat down again. "What are you going to say to him when you do see him?" he asked bluntly. "I expect you still feel the same way about him that you did when you left here?"

She nodded, colour suffusing her cheeks. He saw that she was looking at him imploringly, and shook his head.

"No, you needn't expect me to tell you how *he* feels," he said. "You know he wouldn't confide in me—and from what Rothe says, he's buttoned up against him as well." A more sober expression appeared on his face. "I know I've seemed to be taking this as a great jest, Georgie," he said, "but to tell you the truth, it's nothing of the sort. Shannon is determined on this crazy start of his, and to my mind it won't answer at all. Oh, I know it might suit you to be independently wealthy, but, dash it, Lady Mercer will leave you very well to pass, whereas Shannon would be without a feather to fly with."

"There is no need to argue with me on *that* score," Georgina said decisively. "I have no intention of allowing him to give up The Place to me."

"Yes, but how will you stop him? It's no use your saying that you can solve the whole affair by marrying him because ten to one he's got it in his head that he ain't going to ruin your prospects and create another scandal by offering for you. That is, if he even wants to do so—though I'm dashed if I see why he'd go about to do a crackbrained piece of work like giving over The Place to you unless he was nutty upon you. Rothe says there is *something* the matter with him—says he never saw him so resty as he is these days."

They were interrupted at this point by the entrance of Nora Quill, who came in bearing a tray on which a pot of tea, a mutton pie, and a dish of fruit held prominent places. As she was highly disposed to linger in the room with the stated purpose of expressing her pleasure at Georgina's unexpected return to Craythorne, and the unstated one of satisfying her curiosity as to the reason for it, the two cousins found, when she had finally been prevailed on to leave them, that they had very little time remaining before

Mrs. Quinlevan might be expected to return from Mott House, and put their heads together in earnest as to their future course of action.

It was decided between them that Brandon would drive Georgina over to The Place on the following morning, on the pretext of taking her for a jaunt about the countryside. Shannon, he assured her, was likely to be found at home at that time, for he had disclosed to Brandon that he was expecting a visit from a Cork attorney that morning.

"To draw up the papers turning The Place over to you, I should think," he remarked, "though of course he didn't tell *me* so. At any rate, he won't be out and about the estate, as he usually is. It won't look so odd, your going over there, if *I* go with you—and then I'll sheer off, if you like, and leave you to have it out with him alone." He looked at her rather curiously. "*I* should think it 'ud be deuced awkward for you, bearding him in his den like that," he said frankly. "No other girl I can call to mind who'd do such a thing. But I expect you didn't come all this way to turn craven now."

"No, I didn't!" Georgina said, wishing her heart would not mount so uncomfortably into her throat every time she thought of that unnerving interview before her. "I *must* go! How else can I stop him from giving me The Place?"

"*Or* give him a chance to say whether he wishes to offer for you or not," Brandon said cheerfully. "You'll be in a deuce of a hobble if he don't, won't you? Your grandmother will be mad as fire about your running off like this. But then I expect she will be in just as great a pelter if you wish to marry Shannon. Lord! I wouldn't be in your shoes, in either case!"

"Well, you are not in my shoes, and you are not being very helpful, either, talking of such things," Georgina said, with some asperity. She had been recruiting her spirits with tea and mutton pie, and, while these did nothing to untangle the apparently inextricable confusion in which her affairs stood, they at least made her feel somewhat more fit to face the difficulties that lay before her. "The thing is," she said, "we must decide at once exactly what I am to say to Cousin Bella when she comes in. I have been thinking it over, and I believe it will not do at all to tell her that shocking rapper about my coming over here to marry you.

She has been too kind to me; I cannot deceive her so grossly! I shall simply say that I ran away to escape being forced into marrying Sir Manning Hartily." She looked ruefully at her cousin. "O, dear! I feel such a complete wretch!" she said. "Grandmama is sure to give her a dreadful rakedown if she does not send me directly back to Bath, and I am persuaded that she is far too kind-hearted to do that!"

She was quite correct in her estimation of her cousin's probable behaviour. Mrs. Quinlevan, arriving home shortly afterward from an evening spent in the atmosphere of pleasurable anticipation, with romantic overtones, produced by the recent betrothal of Miss Betsy Mott to Mr. Robert Darlington, was exactly in the proper frame of mind to appreciate the difficulties in which her young cousin found herself in being forced into a loveless marriage with a man old enough, as she declared, to be her father.

"It is the most shocking thing I ever heard of," she exclaimed, when she had got over her first amazement at finding Georgina once more at Craythorne, and had been given the expurgated account of the reasons for her flight from Bath on which she and Brandon had decided. "Indeed, I am quite surprised that your grandmama should do such a thing, my love, for she is a woman of strong good sense, and must know that such matches *never* answer. I recall poor Caroline Mullingar, who could never bear to be called by that odious name, which she disliked before she had so much as laid eyes on the man—she swooned dead away in the church just as she was called upon to pronounce her vows, and not six months after the ceremony ran off with a half-pay officer. Not that *you*, I am sure, would ever do such a ramshackle thing as that, my love!"

She rambled on for some time in this fashion, happily losing sight of the difficulties of her own situation when Lady Mercer and her daughter should demand an accounting from her, and gazing fondly at the picture the two young people made sitting together on the sofa, until Georgina was obliged to believe that she had herself conceived the very idea she had so scrupulously omitted to put into her head—that her young cousin had come to *this* house for refuge because she had marriage with Brandon in her mind.

Mrs. Quinlevan put an end to the conversation at last by

saying that she was sure Georgina was fagged to death and would like to go upstairs to her bedchamber—a suggestion with which Georgina very thankfully fell in. She was, indeed, grateful to be allowed to retire early, but she had little anticipation of enjoying a restful night, and in the event she was not mistaken. The clock had chimed midnight before she at last fell into a restless sleep, and long prior to the first cockcrow in the morning she was lying full awake again, nervously awaiting the hour when she and Brandon would set out for The Place.

CHAPTER 20

They had a fine summer morning for the excursion, but the drive was accomplished in almost total silence, Georgina apparently being completely occupied with the task of plaiting and unplaiting the handkerchief she held in her hands, and Brandon falling prey to a very young man's natural embarrassment at finding himself in the position of interfering in a much-admired older friend's affairs.

But as he and Georgina did not allow themselves to voice their misgivings to each other, the gig proceeded steadily onward and at a still early hour bowled up the sweep to the door of The Place. A stable-boy, coming around at the sound of carriage wheels on the drive and going to the horse's head, looked on without surprise as Brandon dismounted from the driver's seat, but stared with some astonishment when he saw him hand a young lady down. The same startled expression appeared on the face of the sturdy individual who opened the front door to the youthful pair.

"Good morning, Sturgess," Brandon said, trying to carry the situation off and managing only to look as uncomfortable as he felt. "Is Mr. Shannon in?"

"Yes, sir, he is," Sturgess said, looking doubtfully at Georgina, whose efforts to appear unself-conscious were, she knew, quite as unsuccessful as Brandon's. "But—is he expecting you, sir? I rather fancy he is engaged. I shall have to inquire—"

"You needn't. I'm not," said a voice that made Georgina's heart turn over and then begin to beat most uncomfortably fast. She looked up and saw Shannon, who had apparently just emerged from the estate-room, regarding her with a quite unfathomable expression on his face.

For a single joyous moment it had seemed to her that there had been glad, incredulous welcome in those grey eyes— but the moment had passed at once, and the expression she saw now seemed to be compounded of indifference and a rather sardonic coolness. "What brings you here at this hour, Brandon?" Shannon went on, dismissing Sturgess with a curt nod and ushering his visitors into the book-room. "And you, Miss Power? I was not aware that you had returned to Ireland."

"Yes, I arrived last evening," she said, in a voice which, in spite of her efforts at composure, was most lamentably tremorous. "I—had to see you."

"To see *me?*"

She received the full force of a glance of harsh surprise, and, quailing visibly, turned to Brandon for support. He came to her rescue manfully, if somewhat confusedly, saying, "Yes, sir. You see, I had written to her—well, deuce take, it, I felt I had to!—about your intending to make over The Place to her—"

This time it was Brandon who received that direct, harsh glance, and he, too, fell into instant discomposure.

"Well, I *know* I had no right to interfere, of course—" he began, defensively.

"You are quite correct! You had none," Shannon said grimly. "In fact, it was a piece of damned unconscionable meddling on your part, my lad!"

"*I* do not think so!" Georgina said, instantly rallying her own forces against this attack on her cousin and finding, to her relief, that quarrelling with Shannon restored her to her natural spirits much more rapidly than civility had done. "After all," she continued, "the matter concerns me quite as much as it does you, and it appears to me that I had a perfect right to know of it." She glanced around for a chair. "Are you not going to ask us to sit down?" she inquired. "Or do you mean to keep us standing here the whole while?"

A reluctant grin forced itself on Shannon's face. "No, you little gypsy, I do not," he said, "though you would be properly served if I did!" he added, as Georgina and Brandon sat down side by side on the sofa, "What is it that you wish to say to me? If it has anything to do with The Place you may save your breath, for my mind is made up on that point."

"Is it?" Georgina asked, looking speculatively at the determined lines of his face and deciding that an indirect attack might be the better policy. "Well, as a matter of fact," she said, "perhaps that is not what I came to speak to you about, after all." She saw Brandon, beside her, give a start of surprise, but she went on quite serenely, "The truth of the matter is that I came to apologise to you."

Shannon's brows snapped together. "To apologise? To *me*? For what?"

"For misjudging you so dreadfully the last time we met. But, really, it was quite your own fault, you know, for cutting me off before I had had time to tell you what it was that Lady Eliza had said of you."

Brandon, turning slightly pale as he gathered what subject it was that his unpredictable cousin now meant to introduce into the conversation, at this point rose abruptly and muttered something rather inarticulate about going to see if he could find Major Rothe.

"You won't find him. He's gone fishing," Shannon said. His brows drew together again. "What is the matter with you, Brandon? Sit down!"

"No—really—not my affair!" Brandon managed to say. "I never believed it from the start, sir! Told my cousin so!"

"Believed what?" Shannon demanded. "Either you've gone as mad as Bedlam, Brandon, or I have! And what has Lady Eliza to say to this?"

"She—made some dashed ugly insinuations to my cousin," Brandon said, in a placative voice. He frowned down meaningfully at Georgina. "No need to repeat them, Georgie!"

"Oh yes, there is every need!" Georgina said. "Otherwise Mr. Shannon will go on believing that I was so shocked by the idea that he had married my cousin Nuala without being head-over-ears in love with her that I was quite overcome!" She turned to Shannon. "It is not at all so," she said kindly. "I know I have had very little experience in the world, but I *am* aware that gentlemen, even of the first respectability, frequently marry ladies for whom they do not care a great deal, merely to possess themselves of a handsome fortune. In fact, I am quite assured that that is Sir Manning Hartily's chief reason for offering for *me*, and Grandmama, who is the soul of propriety, is extremely anxious for me to accept him—"

This time she had the satisfaction of seeing a positive explosion of wrath appear on the strong-featured face before her.

"Manning Hartily! You are not serious! That bag-pudding offer for you!"

"But indeed he has," Georgina assured him. "What is more, nothing would please both Grandmama and Mama more than for me to become Lady Hartily."

Shannon, who had recovered himself by this time, said sardonically, "Coming it a little too strong, my girl! No one in his right mind can seriously contemplate such a marriage."

"Oh, but they can!" she retorted. "In fact, that is one of the reasons that I ran away—"

"Ran away!" Shannon sprang up and stood looking at her in unmixed disapproval. "Good God! Do you mean to tell me your grandmother does not know where you are— that you travelled here alone—?"

"Oh, no! I came with Cousin Jeremy," she reassured him. "And Grandmama knows where I am *now*—or, at least, she knows I have gone to Craythorne. I left a note for her, you see."

Shannon, who had taken up his position before the fireplace, driving his hands into his breeches pockets as if rejecting a pressing impulse to shake her as she deserved to be shaken, received this statement with something less than satisfaction and demanded, "And all this for the sake of apologising to *me?* In what way did you misjudge me so grossly, Miss Power, that you felt it necessary to take such an extraordinary step?"

She wrinkled her brow in distaste. "I wish you will not call me 'Miss Power' in that odious way," she said. "You *know* I do not like it. And it is quite unnecessary to remind yourself any longer about Nuala, because she is dead, and as you did not kill her, there is really nothing for you to tease yourself about."

"As I did not—!" She looked into his thunderstruck

countenance as he uttered the words. "Of course I did not kill her!" he ejaculated. "But what—who—?" His eyes narrowed suddenly. "Eliza Malladon!" he exclaimed. "So that is what it was! And, my God, you believed—you actually believed—!"

"What else was I to do, when you assured me yourself that it was true?" she pointed out, reasonably.

"But I had no idea—! By the Lord, if Malladon doesn't wring that harpy's neck, I shall do it myself one of these days! Is this story going around the neighbourhood, then?"

"Oh, no, I shouldn't think so," Georgina said placidly. "I am quite sure now that she only told it to me because she believed you were becoming far too interested in me—though I daresay," she observed, with a well-paraded innocence, "she was quite mistaken about that, too?"

He did not answer her. She saw his lips twitch slightly and, somewhat encouraged, was about to go on when she was interrupted by the appearance of Sturgess in the doorway. He wore a rather shaken air, which became quite explicable to all three persons in the room when he announced woodenly, "Lady Mercer!"

Brandon was the first to recover himself. "Good God!" he exclaimed, and made a dash for the open window, only to be restrained by Shannon's iron grip on his arm.

"Oh, no, you don't, my lad!" Shannon said grimly. "You came here to play chaperon and you shall do it!" He went on, to Sturgess, "Show Lady Mercer in"—a quite unnecessary command, as it developed, for the next instant Lady Mercer herself, in an olive-brown pelisse and flat-crowned bonnet, both of which still bore the dust of the roads, appeared in the doorway. Her eyes fastened themselves at once on Georgina, and an outraged exclamation overbore the curt civilities with which Shannon was welcoming her to his house.

"So, you wicked girl! You are indeed here!" She plumped herself down on the sofa from which Georgina had risen in dismay. "I am *quite* overcome! Quite overset! You must forgive me, Mr. Shannon—if you *are*, as I presume, Mr. Shannon—if I do not wait for an invitation to be seated! The shock of finding my granddaughter *here*!"

"Quite understandable, ma'am," Shannon said dryly.

"May I offer you some refreshment—a glass of sherry, perhaps?"

"Nothing," declared Lady Mercer with a shudder, sitting bolt upright on the sofa, "would induce me to swallow a mouthful of refreshment in this house, sir! If I may represent to you the infamy of your conduct in luring a delicately bred young female to leave the protection of her home—"

"But he didn't *lure* me, Grandmama!" Georgina protested, her blue eyes kindling as her dismay passed into anger at this unfounded accusation. "In fact, he had not the least notion that I meant to come here! Had you, Shannon?"

"I had not," Shannon agreed. "I am afraid, though, that my word will carry very little weight in this matter with Lady Mercer."

"You are quite right, sir! It will not!" she snapped. "I flatter myself that my granddaughter—as faulty as her education may have been—would not have flouted the proprieties in this shameless manner, and refused two highly advantageous offers of marriage as well, if she had not been encouraged to do so by—if I may put the matter without roundaboutation—an experienced libertine."

"No, really, Lady Mercer!" Brandon protested, finding his tongue in his indignation at this attack on his friend. "There you are fair and far out, you know! Mark had nothing to do with the matter. It was I who wrote the letter to Georgie that made her come here."

Lady Mercer favoured him with a comprehensive glance, which seemed to take in and record for uncompromising judgment every item of his appearance, from the Belcher handkerchief he wore in place of a neckcloth to the lack of a proper polish on his boots.

"You, I presume," she stated, "are young Quinlevan. In what way you are involved in this most distressing affair I do not care to learn. I have already had a most disagreeable interview with your mama on the subject, and, from the lack of principle she herself has shown in receiving and countenancing my granddaughter, I can only say that I shall not be surprised to find you involved to any extent in these proceedings."

Georgina looked perturbed. "Oh, dear!" she exclaimed. "I do hope you have not upset Cousin Bella, Grandmama!

Indeed, she is not in the least to blame, for what else could she do when I appeared on her doorstep but take me in? Is she *very* much disturbed?"

"I left her," Lady Mercer said austerely, "indulging in a fit of the vapours in the drawing-room. I may say that if *I*, who have at my age endured the discomforts of a lengthy journey, am able to retain *my* spirits and composure under the agitations I have had to bear, it might not be too much to expect that Arabella Quinlevan should do the same. That, however, is neither here nor there. I have your cousin's landaulet waiting outside the door, Georgina. You will oblige me by stepping outside and waiting for me in it while I exchange a few words with Mr. Shannon."

Georgina cast a despairing glance at Shannon, saw that he was regarding her grandmother with a quite impassive expression on his face, and said, "No, Grandmama! Indeed, I cannot leave here yet! I came to Ireland because I had something of particular importance to discuss with Mr. Shannon—"

"I can well imagine *that!*" Lady Mercer said, her lips curving in a thin, contemptuous smile. "However, I fancy *he* will be something less than eager to discuss this important matter with *you* when I inform him that he can no longer hope to gain any pecuniary advantage from it. In point of fact, I intend to alter my will in favour of your mama, who at least has a proper sense of what is due to her name and breeding." She concluded majestically, with a full appreciation of the bombshell she was dropping on the company, *"She* is soon to become the wife of Sir Manning Hartily!"

If she had hoped that this disclosure would have a discomposing effect upon Shannon, she was doomed to disappointment. He received the news with the utmost equanimity. It was Georgina who ejaculated faintly, *"Mama!* But he wants to marry *me!"*

Lady Mercer turned a quelling gaze on her. "I find such a statement *quite* lacking in delicacy, my dear Georgina," she said. "I am sure that Sir Manning has always distinguished *both* of you by his attentions—and how you can imagine, at any rate, that a gentleman of his impeccable manners would care to ally himself with a young female who has had the shocking effrontery to run away from her home in the company of a gentleman—even though distantly connected with her—is entirely beyond my comprehension. I may tell you as well that Lady Hession and young Mr. Hession had the misfortune to arrive on my doorstep just as your mama and I were perusing the note which you left behind you. It was naturally impossible to conceal our distress from them, and Lady Hession, whom I consider to be a woman of excellent principles, at once gave it as her opinion that a young woman who had compromised herself as recklessly as you have done could no longer hope to contract a marriage with any gentleman of birth or fortune. Mr. Peter Hession seemed somewhat less thoroughly convinced of this fact, but I make no doubt that his mama will soon succeed in bringing him to a proper realisation of the justness of her observations."

Brandon, who had been listening to this speech with an increasingly wrathful expression on his face, at this point appeared to be incapable of keeping silent any longer, and burst out angrily, "Well, by Jupiter, it *ain't* so, ma'am! I mean about no gentleman's being willing to offer for Georgie! I'll do it myself if she'll have me! No wish to be rude to a lady of your years, but, dash it, she can't go back and live under *your* roof now, if that's the way you think of her!"

Georgina, quite startled, and blushing at this totally unexpected offer, looked rather confusedly at her cousin, but she was spared the necessity of making him any reply by Shannon's calm voice, addressing him.

"No need to go to such lengths of sacrifice, you young cawker!" he said. "I fancy Miss Power will not lack for offers, in spite of anything her grandmother may believe to the contrary." He glanced at that lady with an expression almost of lazy amusement on his face. "What would you say, ma'am," he inquired, "of the matrimonial prospects of a young lady who is able to call herself the mistress of this estate? Would not such a fortune cause even so strict a female as Lady Hession to have second thoughts about discouraging her son's pursuit of her?"

Lady Mercer looked at him, dumbfounded. "Mistress of *this* estate!" she ejaculated. "But how is that possible? This property, I understand, sir, belongs to *you!*"

"At the present moment, you are correct," Shannon said coolly. "Tomorrow the matter will be altered, however. It is my intention to give it over at that time to Miss Power. Then, ma'am, you may spite her to the top of your bent and she may feel herself quite independent of you. I realise that she is not of age, and so must be subject for some time still to her guardians' wishes, but her fortune will be in the hands of trustees who are entirely beyond either your reach or her mother's."

Georgina could remain silent no longer. She jumped to her feet and said with all the emphasis she could command, "I won't accept it! Do you understand me, Shannon? I *won't!* If you can give it over to me, I am sure it is just as possible for me to give it back to you—and I shall do it! You may go to America or anywhere you please—"

She checked, regarding him suspiciously. There was a glint in those grey eyes that she was quite sure did not betoken submission to her wishes, yet there seemed no hint of obstinacy in them, either.

"Very well," he said, equably. "If that is how you feel, there appears to be only one solution to the problem, for it seems to me that we cannot spend the rest of our lives enriching the legal profession by passing this estate back and forth between us. If you were to agree to marry me, however, I believe the difficulty might be overcome."

Georgina choked. "What an abominable way to make me an offer!" she said indignantly. "Is *that* your only reason for doing it?"

"Oh, no!" he said immediately. "I have several others. One is the dislike I have of seeing you obliged to return to live under either your grandmother's roof or Sir Manning Hartily's. I have been used to consider that you could not possibly do worse with your life than to marry me, but I see now that I was sadly mistaken, for you would no doubt run away with the first plausible scoundrel who offered for you, merely for the sake of escaping from either of those ménages. And I flatter myself that I have one advantage, at least, over any man of that sort."

"And that is—?" Georgina asked shyly.

But before he could reply, or Lady Mercer give vent to the emotions which this new turn of events had aroused in *her* breast, the conversation was once more interrupted by Sturgess.

"Mrs. Quinlevan—Mr. Barnwall!" he announced.

CHAPTER 21

The lady and the gentleman in question entered the room hard on the heels of this announcement, for apparently, as had Lady Mercer, they considered the urgency of their errand to be such as to preclude any attention to conventional niceties of conduct. Mrs. Quinlevan, in fact, with her bonnet on quite askew and a pelerine hastily draped over her half-dress of lilac cambric, appeared to be in a state of such agitation that she could scarcely speak, and it was Mr. Barnwall who said to Shannon, surveying the group before him with an appearance of the greatest uneasiness, "Must offer you a thousand pardons, sir! Uncalled-for intrusion—unseasonable hour—but, dash it all, you know what females are! Insisted I drive her here instantly—nothing else to be done—threatening strong hysterics—"

"There's no need to put yourself about," Shannon said, taking pity on him and interrupting this somewhat incoherent apology. "You are perfectly welcome, I assure you." He turned to Mrs. Quinlevan. "Will you sit down, ma'am? Perhaps a glass of wine—"

"No! No, I thank you, I will *not* sit down!" Mrs. Quinlevan said, her bosom swelling with an animosity which seemed, however, to be directed at Lady Mercer rather than at her host. "Not in the same room with That Woman!" She stretched out one hand—in which, unfortunately for the dramatic effect, she was clutching her vinaigrette—in Lady Mercer's direction, and ejaculated with the greatest indignation, "How dare you—how *dare* you madam, take advantage of my indisposition to order out *my* carriage and *my* horses to bring you to this house! If you had had a spark of humanity, you would have remained to look after me when you saw how greatly your quite unfounded accusations had affected me—yes, unfounded, I say!—for I had no more idea that that poor child intended to fly to me for protection than—than—"

"A babe unborn," Mr. Barnwall supplied helpfully. He, too, turned to Lady Mercer. "She's quite right, you know, ma'am," he assured her. "Perfectly innocent, my sister. If anyone is to blame, I'm your man. But deuce take it, if you've been behaving to the girl as you have done to Bella, I can't say I wonder at her rubbing off! Devilish uncivil sort of thing to do—leaving a lady in strong hysterics, while you order out her carriage to come jauntering over here!"

"If I had known, sir," Lady Mercer said, favouring him with a freezing glance, "that your sister would allow herself to be cast in such a taking over a few home truths plainly put to her, I should of course have remained. However, as she seems to be recovered now, and as it was quite imperative for me to extricate my granddaughter *at once* from the compromising situation in which I was persuaded she had placed herself, I cannot regret my decision. My one miscalculation, it seems," she concluded, with bitter emphasis, "was in dismissing the post-chaise in which I arrived at Craythorne, in the belief that hospitality and assistance would be offered me there."

Georgina, who had been a distressed spectator to this acrimonious dispute, now moved toward Mrs. Quinlevan, crying warmly to Lady Mercer, "But you are mistaken, ma'am; indeed, my cousin does not look at all recovered." She put her arm around Mrs. Quinlevan. "Dear Cousin Bella, let me make you comfortable in this chair," she urged. "And perhaps a glass of wine, as Mr. Shannon has suggested—"

She glanced at Shannon. He moved at once to the bellrope, and ordered Sturgess—who appeared on this summons with a promptitude suggesting that he had not removed to any great distance from the interesting scene going forward in the book-room—to fetch a bottle of sherry.

Georgina, meanwhile, had prevailed on Mrs. Quinlevan to sit down, but, as the chair in which she found herself seated was directly opposite the sofa on which Lady Mercer sat, hostilities between the two ladies were continued in an exchange of highly unfriendly glances. Mr. Barnwall who had also accepted his host's invitation to be seated, broke the pregnant silence that had fallen by saying puzzledly, "Thing is, I don't know at all why we've come here in the first place. Couldn't make head or tail of what Bella was trying to get at as we were driving over here. *She* says the gal don't want to marry Brandon. Well, I can understand that. Rather thought from the start she was cutting a sham of some sort; sure of it when we arrived at Craythorne yesterday and my young nevvy didn't seem to know what the deuce I was talking about when I mentioned the idea to him. But what has Shannon to do with the affair?"

"Mr. Shannon, sir," Lady Mercer informed him icily, "has had the brazen effrontery to offer marriage to my granddaughter in this room, under my very eyes—which I can scarcely say surprised me, in view of the fact that she has flung herself at his head by coming to him here with a complete disregard for all propriety!"

At this point Georgina, her eyes kindling dangerously, cut in to say, "Oh, no, Grandmama, how can you say you were not surprised, when you were so perfectly certain that, once you had informed him that you intend to cut me off without a penny, he would have no further interest in me?"

She would have gone on, but Shannon, effectually silencing her by a firm hand laid on her shoulder, said coolly, "It seems to me that we have had quite enough of this brangling. Lady Mercer, you are right; I have indeed made an offer for your granddaughter's hand. I shall of course apply to her mother for her consent. If it is necessary for me to obtain yours as well, I shall hope to receive it, but I must tell you that, in any event, unless your granddaughter herself does not desire it, our marriage will eventually take place. You may, I believe, save yourself a good deal of unnecessary trouble if you do not require us to wait until she has attained her majority, for, from my own rather limited experience with her character, I have been led to believe that it is one of remarkable firmness—not to say tiresome pertinacity—"

"Wretch!" Georgina interjected, blushing.

"No, indeed!" Mr. Barnwall said earnestly. "Couldn't have put it more neatly myself, sir! Devilish obstinate gal; no doing a thing with her once she has taken an idea in her head!" He turned to Lady Mercer. "Not my affair, ma'am, of course," he advised her, "but if I were you I wouldn't throw a rub in the way. Look at the trouble she's cost you already, having to jaunter all this way after her when I daresay you would much prefer to be sitting snug at your own fireside. Point is, though she's a fine-looking gal, ten to one, with no fortune and the devil's own obstinacy, you won't find another fellow willing to become a tenant-for-life who'd be able to settle her as handsomely. A fine property this, you know. First in the neighbourhood, even though there ain't a title to go with it."

The arrival of Sturgess with the sherry caused a temporary suspension of the conversation. When he had left the room again Mrs. Quinlevan, somewhat fortified by the excellent wine, showed an alarming tendency to resume her altercation with Lady Mercer, stating with some belligerence that even though, as she gathered, that lady intended to cast her granddaughter on the world without a fortune, she herself would not see the girl sacrificed to marry merely for the sake of an establishment, but would give her a home at Craythorne and do her possible to bring about a suitable marriage for her.

"But you do not understand, Mama!" Brandon said impatiently. "There is not the slightest need for Georgie to marry anyone she don't like. Shannon is prepared to hand over The Place to her tomorrow, if she will only agree to receive it from him. But I think she had much better marry him, myself. Then Mark will be able to stay here, too—"

His mother interrupted him, her eyes widening in disbelief. "Hand over The Place to her! Oh, no, what are you saying, Brandon? That cannot be! No one could be so generous!"

"Generous! Besotted!" Lady Mercer said, rising abruptly and gathering her pelisse about her with the air of a woman who has finally reached the end of her patience. "No one but a madman would do such a thing! I shall wash *my* hands of the whole affair. You, sir"—she looked bitterly at Shannon— "will live, I expect, to regret this day!"

"Oh, I think not," Shannon said, the glint of amusement still in his eyes. "Whether the property is my wife's or my own, I believe I shall contrive to keep her tolerably in hand. But I daresay it will be a great deal more comfortable for *you*, ma'am, when you no longer need to worry yourself over her getting into such scrapes as you have just been attempting to extricate her from." He perceived that Lady Mercer, who apparently had been about to follow her last speech to him with a majestic exit from the room and his house, had been brought to a stand by the sudden realisation that she had now no means of transportation from it, and inquired civilly, "May I order out a carriage to take you—er—wherever it is that you wish to go, ma'am?"

"I thank you—no!" Lady Mercer snapped, regarding him with loathing. She turned to Mr. Barnwall. "If *you* would consent, sir, to drive me to the nearest respectable inn in whatever conveyance you used to bring your sister to this house, I should be highly obliged to you," she said. "Mrs. Quinlevan may then make use of her own carriage—a matter which seems of such *paramount* importance to her—"

Mrs. Quinlevan began ruffling up again. "I am sure," she said stiffly, "you might have taken the carriage and welcome, ma'am, except for the manner of it—" She caught Shannon's unencouraging eye and said hastily, "Oh, very well! It does not signify, I am sure! After all, there has no harm been done—and I daresay everything will turn out very well in the end, for it will not do at all for Brandon to think of marrying his cousin if she is to have no fortune—which she will *not* have, of course, if you intend to behave so shabbily toward her, ma'am. And if she *is* to have The Place, I expect Mr. Shannon would much rather marry her himself than not, which seems only fair, and I give you warning, Lady Mercer, that if *you* will not give her a proper wedding, she will be married from Craythorne in the *first* style—which will give me great pleasure, I am sure, if only to spite that *odious* Lady Hession, who was so certain that *her* Peter could cut *my* Brandon out with dear Georgina."

She was still rambling on in this vein when Shannon, having seen Lady Mercer and Mr. Barnwall off in that gentleman's phaeton, ushered her firmly outside to her waiting carriage.

"You are not at all so bad as you have been painted, I daresay," she said, smiling confidentially at him as they parted, "for Major Rothe has already brought Sir Humphrey Mott, in whose judgment I have the *greatest* confidence, to believe so. And I am sure I shall be so very happy to have dear Georgina settle near me that it will not matter a button to me *who* her husband is!"

Her host was still smiling over this last remark as he re-entered the book-room, where he found Brandon and Georgina in animated discussion.

"*She* wants to stay here. *I* say she shall come back to Craythorne with me at once!" Brandon said, frowning. "Ain't I right, sir? If my mother weren't so jingle-brained, she'd have taken her with her—but though *she* hasn't sense enough to see to it that people ain't set in any more of a bustle about the two of you than they already will be when the news that you are to be married gets about, *I* have!"

"You are quite right," Shannon said. "I fancy if you were to go around to the stables now and tell Hanger you wish to have your gig, your cousin will be ready to leave by the time you reach the front door." Georgina began to protest, but Brandon only grinned and limped out of the room, and Shannon then effectually put an end to any further remonstrances on her part by taking her quite ruthlessly into his arms and kissing her in a manner that left her breathless.

"Oh!" she said, burying her face against his coat as he released her. "I am sure I should not say this, but I believe I have been wanting you to do that ever since the first day you walked into this room!" She raised her eyes to his. "Am I very shameless to say such a thing? You have not even told me that you love me, you know!"

"The fact that I do," Shannon assured her, kissing her once more in a manner that left her with no reasonable doubts as to his feelings, "is the advantage I spoke of, which I have over any other of the unsuitable husbands you might choose if I were to allow you to go back to your grandmother's house."

She made some slight demur, however, at his expressing himself in this oversimplified way, and remarked thoughtfully that Sir Manning had made a very pretty speech about "perfection of face and form" when *he* had been on the point of making her an offer.

"But you did not, I collect, wish to accept Sir Manning's offer," he reminded her.

She shook her head. "No, for I could not possibly have fallen in love with *him!*" she said, finding occupation for herself in twisting one of the buttons of his coat. "Still, it would be nice to be *quite* certain that you did not offer for me merely because, once you had determined you must give The Place over to me, you found, on consideration, that you really could not give it up."

His arms tightened about her. "Is that what you think?"

"N-no! But—why *do* you wish to marry me?" she asked naïvely. "You said I was tiresome—you've often told me that—"

She saw his face twist slightly. "Nay, I'm no hand at speeches!" he said, in a rough voice she had never heard before. "I knew you were *my girl* when I first laid eyes on you—only I had no right, I never had the right, to tell you so. Well, I've taken it now, let the world say what it may, and I'll not let you go again, no matter what a stir it makes!"

She looked into his face, a little awed and wholly satisfied by what she saw there. Even the sound of Brandon's footsteps in the hall scarcely brought her to herself, and she was still standing in the circle of Shannon's arms when her cousin came into the room.

"Oh!" he said, regarding the two of them with some disapproval. "I thought you might have got through with all that by this time. Are you ready to leave, Georgie?"

"She is not," Shannon said, releasing her, "but leave she certainly shall. No, my little love," he said, with mock severity, as she would have uttered a remonstrance, "you are going to become a pattern of propriety from this day out. *I* do not mind being ostracised by society, but I shall mind it very much if my wife is, and so—for the time being, at least—we shall contrive to be a model couple. Go back to Craythorne with Brandon, and when I have returned from Bath, where I shall see the future Lady Hartily and request her permission to pay my addresses to you, I shall lose no time in calling upon you there."

"It sounds very respectable and unsatisfactory," Georgina said, with a sigh. "I had much rather you did not go—at least just yet."

"Well, of course he must go!" Brandon said, with asperity. "Don't be such a gudgeon, Georgie!" He looked at Shannon, sudden doubt in his eyes. "You're *quite* sure you want to go on with this, sir?"

"Quite sure."

"Well, I can't think why! You'll have a deuced amount of trouble with her, you know!"

"No doubt," Shannon said. "But I believe I shall be able to fortify myself to endure it. If you will wait only a moment in the hall outside, Brandon—I find I am in need of a slight additional degree of fortification before I allow your cousin to leave."

"A slight additional—Oh!" Brandon grinned. "Oh, very well, sir! I daresay a minute or two more won't signify."

He left the room. As the door closed behind him Georgina said approvingly, "That was very clever of you!"

"I thought so," Shannon admitted. "And now, my love, shall we endeavour to convince me that you are really *not* going to be too much trouble for me to cope with during the long and—I have no doubt—turbulent years of our married life?"

"Oh, yes!" Georgina agreed, with a satisfied sigh, allowing herself very willingly to be taken into his arms.

Brian Moore's newest triumph is . . .

"The purest, most passionate love story in years!" —*The National Observer*

"Skillfully paced . . . Powerfully erotic . . . Stunning in impact!" —*Newsweek*

The Doctor's Wife

"Powerful . . . His portrayal of a woman in crisis is unusually adept." —*The Milwaukee Journal*

"The most alluringly complex adulteress to come along in some time!" —*Time Magazine*

The Doctor's Wife

"Brian Moore has never written with more authority, greater conviction or a truer grasp of a woman's nature!" —*John Barkham Reviews*

"Brian Moore's novels are so readable . . . intelligent, lyrical, ironic—civilized in the most agreeable way." —*Boston Globe*

"There is no better living novelist than Brian Moore; and he is at his peak in this novel of adultery." —*Buffalo Evening News*

The Doctor's Wife
A Dell Book by Brian Moore $2.25

Dell Bestsellers

- [ ] **MAGIC** by William Goldman $1.95 (15141-4)
- [ ] **THE USERS** by Joyce Haber $2.25 (19264-1)
- [ ] **THE OTHER SIDE OF MIDNIGHT**
      by Sidney Sheldon $1.95 (16067-7)
- [ ] **THE HITE REPORT** by Shere Hite $2.75 (13690-3)
- [ ] **THE BOYS FROM BRAZIL** by Ira Levin $2.25 (10760-1)
- [ ] **GRAHAM: A DAY IN BILLY'S LIFE**
      by Gerald S. Strober $1.95 (12870-6)
- [ ] **THE GEMINI CONTENDERS** by Robert Ludlum $2.25 (12859-5)
- [ ] **SURGEON UNDER THE KNIFE**
      by William A. Nolen, M.D. $1.95 (18388-X)
- [ ] **LOVE'S WILDEST FIRES** by Christina Savage . $1.95 (12895-1)
- [ ] **SUFFER THE CHILDREN** by John Saul $1.95 (18293-X)
- [ ] **THE RHINEMANN EXCHANGE**
      by Robert Ludlum $1.95 (15079-5)
- [ ] **SLIDE** by Gerald A. Browne $1.95 (17701-4)
- [ ] **RICH FRIENDS** by Jacqueline Briskin $1.95 (17380-9)
- [ ] **MARATHON MAN** by William Goldman ... $1.95 (15502-9)
- [ ] **THRILL** by Barbara Petty $1.95 (15295-X)
- [ ] **THE LONG DARK NIGHT** by Joseph Hayes . $1.95 (14824-3)
- [ ] **IT CHANGED MY LIFE** by Betty Friedan ... $2.25 (13936-8)
- [ ] **THE NINTH MAN** by John Lee $1.95 (16425-7)
- [ ] **THE CHOIRBOYS** by Joseph Wambaugh .. $2.25 (11188-9)
- [ ] **SHOGUN** by James Clavell $2.75 (17800-2)
- [ ] **NAKOA'S WOMAN** by Gayle Rogers $1.95 (17568-2)
- [ ] **FOR US THE LIVING** by Antonia Van Loon . $1.95 (12673-8)

At your local bookstore or use this handy coupon for ordering:

Dell | **DELL BOOKS**
P.O. BOX 1000, PINEBROOK, N.J. 07058

Please send me the books I have checked above. I am enclosing $_____
(please add 35¢ per copy to cover postage and handling). Send check or money
order—no cash or C.O.D.'s. Please allow up to 8 weeks for shipment.

Mr/Mrs/Miss_____

Address_____

City_____State/Zip_____